T H

A Romance of the Fifteen

There are few writers of historical romance who can match Jeffery Farnol's power of plot and counter-plot; his adroit dramatic effects, and, above all, the enduring charm of his characters. It is a tribute to his art as a storyteller that his novels are as popular today as they have ever been. These magnificent stories appear for the first time in PAN in response to countless requests from our readers.

'Jeffery Farnol bears his readers buoyantly through packed pages' – *Evening Standard*

Although born in Birmingham, Jeffery Farnol spent much of his youth in Kent, which county formed the background to many of his novels. At the age of twenty, he left the Westminster Art School and went to America. While a scene painter at the Astor Theatre, New York, he wrote *The Broad Highway*. Rejected by American publishers as 'too English' it was eventually published in England in 1910. So began the chain of delightful historical romances which have made Farnol a bestseller for over sixty years.

By the same author in Pan Books
THE BROAD HIGHWAY

OVER
THE HILLS

A Romance of the Fifteen

Being the Narrative of Adam (Called Thursday)
with Particulars of his Adventures, his Joys and
Sorrows, his Friends and Right-beloved Enemy

JEFFERY FARNOL

UNABRIDGED

PAN BOOKS LTD : LONDON

First published 1930 by
Sampson Low, Marston and Co Ltd.
This edition published 1971 by Pan Books Ltd,
33 Tothill Street, London, S.W.1.

ISBN 0 330 02786 7

PRINTED AND BOUND IN ENGLAND BY
HAZELL WATSON AND VINEY LTD
AYLESBURY, BUCKS

To
WALTER
BENYON-TYNKER
who was Hector MacFarlane's
First Friend
I Dedicate this Narrative of
His Griefs and Triumphs

Jeffery Farnol
September, 1930

CONTENTS

1	IN WHICH THIS NARRATIVE BEGINS	9
2	IN WHICH I BECOME MY OWN AMAZEMENT	16
3	TELLS HOW I RECEIVED A STRANGE PRESENT	24
4	IN WHICH I AMAZE MYSELF YET MORE	28
5	WHICH TELLS OF A PROPHECY	31
6	TELLETH OF NAKED STEEL	34
7	DESCRIBETH HOW AND IN WHAT STRANGE FASHION THE PROPHECY BEGAN TO BE FULFILLED	39
8	WHICH RECORDS A PORTENTOUS MEETING	43
9	TELLETH HOW AND IN WHAT MANNER I LOOKED UPON DEATH	46
10	GIVETH SOME DESCRIPTION OF A MACGREGOR	53
11	DESCRIBETH OUR ESCAPE FROM THE SOLDIERS	61
12	GIVETH SOME DESCRIPTION OF A WEDDING	67
13	TELLETH HOW WE PUT TO SEA	74
14	TELLS OF DIVERS HAPPENINGS ON BOARD THE LUGGER 'SUSSEX LASS' AND HOW WE TOOK UP A MAN FROM THE SEA	76
15	TELLETH OF RECRIMINATIONS AND ALARMS	89
16	TELLETH SOMETHING OF THIS FRENCHMAN	94
17	CONCERNING, AMONG OTHER MATTERS, ONE JAPHET, A MARINER	100
18	TOUCHES SOMETHING ON THE ART OF SWORDSMANSHIP	104
19	TELLETH OF A WARNING	110
20	TELLETH HOW OUR FRENCHMAN QUELLED MUTINY	112
21	TELLETH HOW, IN THE MIDST OF DEATH, WE TALKED TOGETHER	117
22	GIVETH SOME DESCRIPTION OF HOW I CAME ASHORE	124

23	HOW MISTRESS BARBARA AND I, BEING ALIVE, AGREED TO PART	128
24	TELLETH HOW WE SET OUT FOR THE NORTH COUNTRY	136
25	THE WHICH IS CHAPTER OF WEARINESS	140
26	WHICH TELLETH OF AN ALARM BY NIGHT	142
27	TELLETH HOW I HAD WORD WITH SIR HECTOR	145
28	SHOWETH HOW WE LEFT AUCHTERLOCHIE	154
29	GIVETH SOME DESCRIPTION OF VISCOUNT SCARSDALE, A FUGITIVE	160
30	TELLETH VERY LITTLE	168
31	TELLETH WHAT BEFELL AT DRUMLOSSIE TOWER	170
32	TELLS HOW I FOUND HAPPINESS, AND A WARNING CAME TRUE	178
33	GIVETH SOME DESCRIPTION OF MY WANDERING BY NIGHT AND BLACK DESPAIR	184
34	TELLETH HOW SIR HECTOR WAS BALKED OF HIS VENGEANCE	186
35	IN WHICH I STRIVE TO COMFORT MY ENEMY	193
36	TELLETH OF A MAN'S AGONY AND THE REASONS WHEREOF	200
37	GIVETH PARTICULARS OF A MOMENTOUS CONVERSATION	205
38	TELLS OF A SUDDEN ONFALL	209
39	HOW WE WERE TAKEN BY THE MCLEODS	221
40	HOW I MET A FRIEND AND PLEADED FOR AN ENEMY	223
41	TELLETH HOW I FOUND AGAIN SIR HECTOR AND HIM QUARRELSOME	229
42	OF HOW WE WRANGLED BY THE WAY	236
43	TELLETH HOW IN THE DARK WE JOINED HANDS	239
44	OF MY GOOD COMRADE	244
45	GIVETH SOME DESCRIPTION OF A MAN OF PEACE AND HIS METHODS	246
46	TELLETH OF JOYFUL REUNION	253
47	WHICH IS CHAPTER OF FAREWELL	261

CHAPTER 1

IN WHICH THIS NARRATIVE BEGINS

I HEARD it first of a bright midsummer night in the dark coppice beyond the Ten-acre meadow; a sound of faerie, marvellous wild yet very sweetly mournful; a sound that seemed to echo the sighing of wind amid desolate trees, the gurgling sob of misty waters; a sound, indeed, that seemed to hold for me a magic and mystery, like stars and moon and the deep wonder of this brooding night – and yet this sound no more than a man's whistling.

Presently, as I stood thralled by these tender, silvery notes, the plaintive melody changed to a happy, lilting measure that ended in a merry, flute-like trill; and so came silence, save for the rustle of leaves astir in the soft night wind. And then the whistle rose again, a run of bubbling, liquid notes oft-repeated until, guessing this a summons to myself, I whistled them back as well as I might, whereupon was more leafy rustling, and forth of the underbrush stepped a tall man.

I remember that despite his wild aspect and great size I felt nothing fearful of him, by reason of the merry glance of his eyes and good-humoured curve of his lips. A comely-faced man he was, young, and of a grace and pride of bearing, for all his draggled garments, as he stepped lightly forth of the shadows into the full radiance of the moon.

'What, ma wee mannie,' says he in voice methought vastly pleasing, 'ye'll no hae aboot ye the noo aught a man may stay his hunger on whateffer?'

'No, sir,' I answered, pulling off my cap with due respect.

'A'weel, 'tis the waefu' luck o't!' he sighed. 'But tell me hae ye by chance spied a man hereaboots the day, a slim, quick, dark-eyed gentleman in a Ramillie wig and braw, green riding-coat?'

9

'No, sir,' I answered again. 'No indeed!'

'Hum!' quoth he, glancing furtively round about. 'Then will ye hae heard mention o' sic a name as Keith, or, say – Weaver or Weir?'

'No, sir, but there were soldiers—'

'Ay, ay!' says he, with another keen glance up and around, 'I ken that right weel.'

'Are you very hungry, sir?' I questioned, staring up into his haggard face.

'Laddie, I am that!' says he with whimsical look, 'I'm sae empty that ma puir wame plays flip-flappit wi' my back-bane whilk is no juist a canny feeling – I'm sae clammed I'd gie a gowden guinea for twa-three bannocks an' a dish o' brose ... I'll be meaning,' he explained in very exact and careful English, 'I would expend a whole guinea for a loaf of bread, crusty forbye, and a whang of cheese.'

'A guinea is a lot of money, sir,' says I, glancing towards the far distant, twinkling lights of the village.

'Ay, it is so!' he agreed, very readily. 'Dod, 'tis wise y'are, ma wee mannie – mebbe I was ower hasty wi' my guinea! And yet, when a man's clammed wi' hunger he's apt to be gey reckless.'

'I might contrive to steal you my supper, sir—'

'Could ye so, laddie, could ye so?' cries he, clapping hand upon my shoulder, a gentle hand for all its size.

'I will, sir!' said I, the solitary, unhappy soul of me thrilling responsive to that so friendly touch. 'There's only old Betty in the house tonight, this is why I was able to away to this moonlight and the wonder of it all.'

'The wonder, ay!' he repeated. 'There's aye the wonder o' moon and stars and silent woods as few hae eyes for – had I ma pipes I'd play 'em tae ye, but I left 'em ower the Border – ay, ower the Hills and Far Away, and mysel' here famishing so – fetch me your supper and we'll ca' it a guinea, though 'tis a wheen o' money – aweel rin, laddie, rin – awa' wi' ye!'

Staying for no more, away I sped, nor stayed until I had reached the village and could descry the loom of that particular house, its dark gables frowning austerely upon its humbler brethren, which had ever proved for me a place of misery, humiliation and suffering. Climbing the fence which enclosed its precise garden, I stole cautiously until I might peep into the kitchen, clean and comfortless, where burned a small fire beside which old Betty slumbered in the elbow-chair, as was her custom at this hour. Hardby upon the table lay my supper, a flake of cheese, a stale crust and tankard of small beer; beholding the which miserable viands, and minding the wonderful man for whom they were destined, I felt myself glowing with shame and humiliation.

Silently I drew the latch and crept across the floor, then paused trembling in sudden joyous trepidation to see a certain door stood ajar – it seemed for once old Betty had forgotten to lock the pantry. Next moment I was inside breathing an air redolent of such delectable cates as never came my way; here also hung divers baskets very proper to my purpose. Stealthily, and with feverish haste, I began to fill one of these with such things as came to hand, objects hard to distinguish in the dimness, thus whatsoever my hand chanced upon, that clutched I, and thrust into my basket; bottles there were and meat, with other shapeless things – in they went pell-mell until the basket was full – and then I stood suddenly rigid, for old Betty, choking upon a snore, groaned, sighed and I heard the creak of her chair as she rose, mumbling to herself ... in another moment I should be caught, and bethinking me of my master's crab-tree staff, I shivered in a panic while ever old Betty's shambling step drew nearer. Here then, in sheer desperation I snatched an empty basket, clapped it over my head and, thus masked, caught up my burden and burst from the cupboard howling very horridly.

Through the meshes of my enveloping basket I saw old Betty stagger backward to the elbow-chair wherein she fell heavily, goggling at me and gasping ... then I leapt across the kitchen and was out and away, pursued by the old woman's wailing outcries.

I found my wonderful man where I had left him.

'Aha!' cries he, perceiving my burden. 'Wha' hae ye gotten

there, ma mannie?' For answer I thrust the basket upon him and sank panting upon the grass.

'Bottles!' quoth he. 'Oho, a bonnie lad!' and, drawing one from the basket, whipped out a short, heavy knife, and, striking off the neck very neatly, raised the bottle to eager lips. What then was my horrified amaze to hear him choke suddenly, to see him cast away the bottle and spit wildly.

'Vinegar!' he gasped. 'Vinegar, ye devil's imp!' At this I trembled, and nothing to say whiles he, having spit forth such as he had not swallowed, cautiously essayed another bottle, looked at it, shook it and having tasted, sighed, nodded and drank deep. He now proceeded to unload the basket, and seemed overwhelmed by the amount of its contents – as indeed so was I. First came a bone miserably scant of meat, whereat he scowled; next the better part of a ham, whereat he smiled; followed three or four sausages (raw), a capon (the same though trussed for the oven); a jar of pickled onions; a loaf; a good-sized piece of cheese and a small pasty.

'Losh!' exclaimed my companion, staring at these many and varied edibles. 'Save us a' – d'ye always eat siccan vasty supper, ma bonnie wee lad?'

'No, sir!' I answered bitterly, and recounted the manner of my theft, to his no small joy, the which manifested itself in fits of strange, silent laughter, though his keen eyes were continually glancing hither and thither. And now, his merriment subsiding, he insisted I must eat with him, the which I did, something timidly, yet gladly enough. So thus, side by side upon the grass, we supped together, and the moon very bright above us. At last, his hunger appeased, he dived hand into pocket and, fetching out a net-purse (woefully light, by its looks), took thence a guinea which, having looked at and sighed over, he tendered to me on his broad, open palm.

' 'Tis an unco' deal o' money!' says he.

'Yes, sir!' I answered.

'And ye're but a wee bit laddie!' he nodded and back into purse went the guinea but, in the act of pocketing it, he paused to rub smooth-shaven chin and eye me askance:

'A'weel,' sighed he at last, 'a ham's a ham, a bargain's a

bargain, and McLeod o' McLeod is the McLeod!' and, seizing my arm in powerful gripe, he placed the coin in my unwilling fingers and fell to his supper again.

'Sir,' said I, 'pray take back your money, I – I don't want it.'

'Hoots, laddie,' he exclaimed, 'there's nought wrang wi' it, 'tis honest gold.'

'Yes, sir, but . . . please . . . I won't have it.'

'And why for no?'

'Because I fear 'tis your last and—'

'Ye leein' gomeril!' cried he, frowning. 'D'ye tak' the McLeod for a beggar body wi' but ae guinea in's breeks?'

'No, sir, but pray take your money,' said I, and laid the coin beside his knee.

'Eh?' quoth he, staring at me. 'The laddie'll no tak' it! Losh, it's no canny!' Here, taking up the guinea, he fobbed it, and went on eating, eyeing me the while.

'Laddie,' he questioned suddenly, 'what might your name be?'

'They call me Adam, sir, because, like Adam, I had no father or mother.'

'Dooms me!' he exclaimed, staring at me with a piece of ham on his knife-point. 'But we all hae parents—'

'No, sir,' says I, miserably. 'I was found on a Thursday under the hedge of this very field by old Zachary Trent, the sexton, so they call me Adam Thursday. And they've bound me to Master Bragg, the attorney . . . pens and ink . . . and I would be out in the world doing great things . . . teaching myself to be brave and bold to adventure. . . . Ah, sir, do you laugh at me like all the rest?'

'Na, na, laddie!' cried he, his features comically twisted, however. 'I'm no juist what ye'd ca' laughing, no, no!'

' 'Tis true I'm not big or strong, sir,' says I, clenching my fists and scowling down through bitter tears at my puny person, 'oh, I know that indeed—'

'Why, ye're no exactly a Goliath o' Gath,' he nodded. 'But – whisht, laddie, never greet! Nay, what's thy grief, friend?' says he in his careful English, and set his long arm about me, very kindly.

13

'I'm so ... miserable!' I gasped, striving not to sob out-right. 'My master beats me, the village lads mock me ... I've never a friend in the world save Zachary and old Penelope. And ... I'm so small and can do nothing well save run and swim ... and ... my hateful red hair!'

'Red hair – hoot toot, never let that fash ye, ma mannie – red hair's a fighting colour, 'tis ware o' the lad wi' the red poll, ay, and lassie, too. Whatever o't, I've seen a man wi' red hair, ay, a littlish man nae higher than ma shoulder, set three muckle great loons rinning for their dear lives, the fourth man couldna rin whateffer, him being dead as mut-ton! Sae if ye hair be red tak' joy therefore. And as for size, 'tis no a muckle body as maketh the man, 'tis the great heart o' him. Think o' this little man wi' the red hair, forbye he covers it wi' modish wig – him as bested four men wi' his single blade nane sae langsyne, and be joco.'

'He must have been a wonderful man, sir!' cried I.

'Ou, ay, he is that – black be his fa'!'

'What was his name, sir, not Adam, for sure?'

''Tis Keith, laddie, Hector Keith o' Inverkeith; 'tis also Weir and Weaver, and sometimes MacFarlane, for he goeth by many names 'twixt here, France and bonnie Scotland. And now,' says my companion, leaping nimbly afoot, 'I'll awa' – guid nicht t'ye—'

'Must you go, sir?' cried I, rising also. 'Ah, pray where?'

'Hither and yon, laddie, wheres the wind blaws, ower the hills and awa'.'

'Oh, sir,' cried I, passionately, 'pray take me with you?'

'Losh!' quoth he, staring down on me as I supplicated thus upon my knees amid the wrack of our supper.

'Sir – sir,' I pleaded, reaching up my arms to him, 'I am so friendless ... solitary. Suffer me to follow you, serve you—' my voice broke and I covered my face.

'Now, by the Good Being,' says he, touching my bowed head, 'I'd tak' ye, lad, but there's reasons, scores of 'em in red coats, do forbid. No, faith, I must gang my lane – forbye death's on the heels o' me.'

And very heroical I thought him as he crowned himself

with belaced hat and stood smiling down on me, very gallant
and a little swaggering. .... Then, even as I looked, his handsome face was suddenly transfigured, his eyes glared, his
shapely mouth grew hard and fierce, his whole aspect became
strangely terrible; and all this for no reason unless it were a
faint, far sound that throbbed intermittently upon the stilly
night, yet a sound that, presently, even my inexperienced
ears knew for the roll of a drum. All at once he had me by
the collar and his broad knife glittered at my throat.

'Ha, was it you?' he demanded in harsh whisper. 'Was it
ye'sel' brought the soldiers on me?' And then, as I shrank
trembling from the steel, he loosed me.

'Forgi'e me, lad,' quoth he with his kindly smile, 'you've
honest eyes, and are too young to hae learned sic dupleecity.'
Then, stooping, he whipped up a great sword whence it had
lain hidden in a bush, and with it in his hand stood hearkening to that distant throb of sound that now seemed nearer
and dreadfully ominous.

'They are coming!' I whispered, clutching his arm in
trembling hands.

'Ay!' he nodded. 'The county will be thick wi' red-coats
ere dawn, I doubt. A'weel, a'weel, 'tis long sword and short
heels. And hey, laddie, yon was a bonnie supper!' So saying,
he thrust the purse into my unready hand and turned away.
'Tak' it, laddie, tak' it,' he cried cheerily, seeing I hesitated,
''tis like to be more use tae you than me by the look o'
things.'

'Ah – you mean because of the soldiers, sir!'

'I mean the hempen cravat, ma wee man, axe, block and
jibbet – one or all. Howandever, should they question ye, lee
your best for me. And so Guid keep ye, lad Adam, dinna
forget the pibroch o' the McLeod and – live up tae your red
hair, your bonnie red hair!' And so, with a merry smile and
flourish of his hand, he strode into the wood and vanished
amid the shadows.

CHAPTER 2

IN WHICH I BECOME MY OWN AMAZEMENT

HARDLY was he gone than I cast myself down amid the underbrush, crushed with such extravagant and overwhelming sense of loneliness as I had never felt, no not in all the years of my miserable and desolate boyhood, for this man (and he so grand and heroical!) had looked and spoken as a friend, had even uttered comfortable things of my so hateful red hair and lack of size; and, because kindness and friendship were blessings all unknown in my experience, I fell to a passion of tears, bitterly weeping and lamenting my miserable estate, like the poor, solitary creature I was.

Thus forlornly sobbing lay I, bedewing the grass with my tears, until roused suddenly by a hoarse, warning shout, followed, almost immediately, by the loud report of a musket and then the wood was full of tumultuous stir, a snapping of twigs, shouts, cries and a fury of trampling feet. Sick with apprehension, and scarce knowing what I did, I cowered amid the leaves, listening fearfully to the sound of desperate fight in those leafy glooms beyond.

... They dragged him out into the moonlight, four great soldiers, and, having bound his arms, marched him off, laughing and cursing together, their white cross-belts agleam and bayonets twinkling to the moon.

When they were gone some distance I got me afoot but, being much shaken by the brutality and suddenness of it all, was fain to lean against a tree, peering about me in a marvellous perturbation of spirit; thus I chanced to espy something that winked at me from the grass within the wood, and, coming thither, saw this for my gentleman's basket-hilt sword. Glancing fearfully about, I took up the weapon, finding it play very light in my grasp for all its size; and having wielded it, I held it that the moonbeams made a glitter on the

16

long, broad blade. Now as I stared watching this deadly sparkle, I trembled no longer, my sick fears were forgotten, a new strength nerved me, and I raised my head, teeth clenched in sudden purpose so desperate bold indeed as filled me with marvellous astonishment at myself; and all this (as I do think) by the mere feel of this glittering sword.

Then, stripping off my threadbare jacket, I lapped it about the bright steel lest its gleam betray me, and set off in pursuit of the red-coats. Very stealthily ran I, yet at speed, until I had gained the friendly shelter of a hedge whence I might watch the soldiers; six of them now I counted, marching with the prisoner in their midst.

Thus came they into the village at last, and I heard their heavy tread echoing loud in the cobbled street until, reaching the inn, they halted with ring and clatter of grounded muskets. And now was the roll of a drum, loud voices in sharp question, and instant answer, and the prisoner was marched to the yard behind the inn.

By this, the drowsy village was astir, lights gleamed, doors and casements opened, voices called, and the street began to fill with newly-waked folk.

As for me, I turned aside down a narrow lane or twitten, whence I might reach the inn yard and here, espying a great country wain in remote corner, I crept beneath this and crouched there, peering betwixt the wheel-spokes at a certain lighted window of the inn through which I espied much coming and going of scarlet coats, and where, as I suppose, they examined their prisoner.

After some lapse of time a door opened and forth stepped Master Fry, the landlord, bearing a lanthorn, and after him the prisoner, guarded, and though he walked with head bravely aloft, his face showed ghastly pale in the bright moonlight.

'This way, sirs!' quoth Master Fry. 'The villain shall lie safe enough I'll warrant me; my barn be stout and strong, sirs.'

Now at this my heart leapt, for what reason you shall presently see.

They trooped past my hiding place, and so near that I could see the very epaulettes on the officers' shoulders, and catch all they said :

'The poor devil made a good run for it !' said one.

'And will make a delicate corpse !' said another.

And so they passed : and I, bethinking me of this 'delicate corpse', shivered again and clutched the sword closer to me. Presently, having locked up their captive and set a guard upon him, back tramped soldiers and officers to their quarters, the street became again deserted, doors and windows were shut, the whole village grew dark and silent and sank once more to slumber.

But there lay I beneath the market wagon, hearkening to the heavy tramp and occasional mutter of voices where the sentinels kept their watch about the great barn that stood in Master Fry's rick-yard and backing upon the narrow twitten I have mentioned.

Now it so fortuned that this very barn had long been a favourite haunt and hiding place of mine, on high-days and holidays, since, having no friends, I had been wont to steal hither with some book for company, and here, safe hid among the hay, to read until the light failed : for the which purpose, and that I might come and go unseen, I had contrived a secret entrance, in that dark corner which abutted on the twitten, and this a fissure in the worn masonry screened from sight by a great pile of rotting hop-poles. Thus, despite the prisoner's situation, I had some hope I might succeed in my desperate purpose.

The moon, riding high, made the world wellnigh bright as day, and much I yearned for some beneficent cloud to veil her too-radiant splendour, but she swam serene in a clear immensity, while I crouched listening to the monotonous tramp of the sentinels, until I was pretty sure there were three of them. This put me at my wits' end, for, what with these three soldiers and the moon so bright, how was I to come at my secret entrance into the barn ?

I was debating this question and hearkening to the tramp of these three sentinels when I sat up suddenly, wondering fearfully why now I could hear but one. At last, with infinite caution, I ventured from beneath the wagon and crept where I might peep into the twitten, and recoiled panic-struck, for within a yard of me stood a soldier who leaned upon his musket, puffed at his pipe and stared up at the moon.

'Ain't married are ye, comrade?' he inquired. I started – for a moment I had some wild notion he was addressing me; then :

'Not me. Gimme a suck o' your pipe!' answered a growling voice, and peering, I saw a second man, whose broad back was planted against that pile of hop-poles which (as I have written) masked my secret entrance to the barn.

'I never,' quoth soldier Number One, 'I never see that there horb so bright afore, and—'

'You never see what afore?'

'Horb, comrade, above there!'

'Horb, d'ye call it?'

'Ah, horb – poetic for—'

'Oh, gimme a suck o' your pipe!' growled Soldier Number Two.

'Why then tak' it, comrade, but draw gentle! I never see that there bright horb but I don't wish I was a farmer.'

'O! Why?'

'Because I should be asleep in bed 'stead o' looking at it now.'

Thus they talked while I, utterly dismayed, cowered in the shadow, miserably afraid and pretty well hopeless; and then my gaze lighted upon a broken pitchfork, and, moved by swift impulse, I took it up and, whirling it with all my strength, sent it hurling aloft, to fall clattering loudly upon the roof of the barn, whence it thudded to the paved yard beyond.

'Did ye hear that, comrade?' inquired a voice in the twitten, and I distinguished the sharp click of cocked musket.

'Ay for sure, Tom, I ain't deaf!' And a second musket clicked.

'Well, wot was it, comrade?'

'Burn me! 'Ow should I know? Ask Will. Come on and be ready!' And then I heard the jingle of their accoutrements as they ran to join their comrade in the rick-yard. Staying for no more, I scurried into the twitten, wriggled in behind the hop-poles and, diving into the hole, like rabbit into burrow, crawled in among the hay, and so lay, trembling and breathless, in the fragrant gloom of the barn, and all so still and silent that I could hear the murmur and muttering of the soldiers in the yard outside. And then:

'Wha's yon? Who is it?' whispered a voice at no great distance.

'Hush, sir! 'Tis only me.'

'Eh, is it Adam? Ma bonnie, braw wee man!'

'Listen!' I whispered and instantly buried myself in the hay, for hands were fumbling at the door, I heard the key turn and, making a spy-hole in the hay, saw the three soldiers enter, one bearing a lanthorn, by whose light they examined the prisoner very narrowly.

'Ah, my good fellows,' says he, cheerily, in his careful English, 'if ye'll hae the kindness to but loosen these cords a trifle I shall sleep the better—'

''E be fast enough!' said the foremost soldier. 'Whoever throwed that there brooms-tail, it weren't him, that's sure!'

And away they went, locking the door behind them.

'Whisht, Adam ... are ye there, lad?'

'Here, sir!' I answered creeping to him. 'And I've brought your sword—'

'Eh, eh – hae ye gotten Andrew? Oho, bonnie lad! Cut me these cursed bonds and tak' heed ye don't slice me, for Andrew's unco' sharp!' And so, fumbling in the darkness, I contrived to cut away the ropes that bound him, and next moment was fast in his arms, kindly arms that yet crushed me in painful embrace while his big hands patted me wondrous tenderly for all their size, but all he said (and this in whisper) was:

'Red hair for ever!' And when we had lain hearkening a while and all very silent about us: 'Now then, young Adam,' says he, 'show me how ye got in.'

'Nay, sir, 'tis how you shall get out, for 'tis very strait and narrow.'

'Losh, man,' he exclaimed, cheerily, 'I'd thank ye for chance at a knot-hole! And faith,' says he, when I had brought him thither, ''tis no sae much larger, I'm thinking! Howandever, gang first and watch, I'll contrive somehow wi' Andrew to aid me.'

So, wriggling forth into the moonlight, screened behind the hop-poles, I peeped and listened and sweated in a very agony of fear for the moon seemed brighter than ever now, and the soldiers' tramp the louder; once, indeed, one of them came marching up the twitten and paused so near our hiding place that I could smell the reek of the pipe he was smoking ere he wheeled and went marching back again.

'Now!' I whispered; ensued a desperate scuffling, a hoarse panting and the fugitive lay grovelling beside me; and next moment we were afoot and running for our lives. Turning into the street we sped on, silently as possible, and keeping in the shadows as much as we might until we were clear of the village and the dusty high road stretched before us white beneath the moon. But the King's highway was not for us poor fugitives, so, turning in full career, I leapt a stile and took to the fields, running my best, nor did I pause until I had reached the friendly shelter of the woods; here my companion halted to fetch his breath:

'Oh, lad,' says he, clapping me on the shoulder, 'Oh, young Adam, ye're an unco' bonnie runner!' Now at this I bowed my head lest he see how my eyes had filled, for praise was new to me and such words from him (and he man so heroical) were very precious:

'Where now, sir?' I enquired.

'Tae the coast – the seashore. Whisht d'ye ken a sma' fushin'-village they ca' East Bourne?'

'Very well, sir,' I answered eagerly. 'This way!'

Across country I led him, avoiding highway and bye-roads, along desolate ways and field-paths and through lonely woods, until at last we climbed the steep ascent of Firle Beacon, and from that eminence saw the countryside stretch below us wide and dim and mysterious beneath the moon, away to the dark forest of Battle, Pevensey Level and a vague, distant sheen that was the sea.

And now, as we trudged high above sleeping hamlet and village, my companion questioned kindly of myself :

'So art a foundling, young Adam?'

'Yes, sir, 'neath a hedge – they took me from the arms of my dead mother.'

'My puir, wee man! 'Tis dooms bad hearin', yon!' says he, patting me gently on my weather-beaten cap, 'whatever o't ye bear yerself wi' an air, Adam, and talk like ane o' the quality.'

'I have been schooled, sir, thanks to Squire Masterton's lady, but, alas, she is dead, God bless her! And now I am bound to Master Bragg, a hard man, sir, and merciless in especial to such as do lie in his power or be poor and friendless.'

'Humph – hum!' quoth my companion, a sound this betwixt a snort, sigh and groan, the which I thought very strange, whereafter we went a great while in silence, my gentleman seeming lost in thought and I not daring to interrupt.

'Adam,' says he, halting suddenly, 'in twa-three hours 'twill be dawn, and here's you and me maun twine, yet first—'

'Twine, sir?' I questioned, chilled by sudden fear.

'Part, lad, gang our several ways.'

'Part, sir?' I repeated, and, forgetting all but my bitter disappointment, I caught his arm and shook it in a very passion of entreaty. 'Oh, Mr McLeod,' I gasped, 'pray ... take me with you ... don't leave me again. ... Let me be your servant ... only take me,' and here my voice was choked by sobs that shook me with their violence.

Now hereupon he glanced at me askance 'neath puckered brows, then stared up at the moon and round about him in lost sort of fashion.

'Lookee, Adam,' says he, clapping an arm about me, 'I'm a man running for his life, in jeopardy o' the noose, the axe and dismembering-block, y' ken.' Here he related, and very particularly, the obscene horrors of a traitor's doom, until my very soul grew sick, and I appalled, to learn how much more of evil was in the world and cruelty in man than I, in my ignorance, had ever dreamed.

'So, Adam, it maun be goodbye. But dinna greet, laddie, dinna greet, 'tis a world o' partings, specially o' late. I hae parted wi' divers guid friends, braw gentlemen all, and mony on 'em too young for death, but some lie over the Border at Preston and Sherriffmuir and others, wae's me, their bonny heids will be falling 'neath the bluidy axe and stuck atop o' Temple Bar back yon in London town – ay, as mine would, like as not, but for thee, young Adam. So now dry your een, laddie, cock your bonnet and—'

'Will you take me, sir – oh will you – pray?'

'Nay, 'tis impossible!'

'Then – goodbye!' And, sobbing, I turned and sped upon my desolate way. But presently I heard him call, and, turning eagerly, saw him hurrying after me with great strides.

'Bide a wee, young Adam!' says he, gripping my arm. ''Tis mighty service ye did me the night, and words be puir things ... and so ... so ye'll juist tak' this!' And into my hand he thrust the guinea.

'No, sir, no!' cries I, thrusting it back at him. 'Ah, indeed and indeed I want no payment for what I did.'

'Nay, but, Adam ... laddie ... what for will ye no—'

'Will you take me with you, sir?'

'Alack, young Adam, 'tis impossible!'

'Then neither will I take your money!' cried I and tossed it at his feet.

'Save 's a'!' he gasped, and stood staring from the coin to me and back again, rubbing his touzled head the while, as very much put out. 'Adam,' quoth he, at last, ''tis in my mind there's unco' guid blood in ye. I like your pride, fine – ay I do – though 'tis sinfu' shame tae spurn sae muckle guid money, 'tis wanton, 'tis waefu', and I'm fair amazed at ye.'

'If you would but suffer me to go with you—' I began; then, seeing how he frowned and shook his head, I turned

23

and ran from him, choking with grief. But even so, I must needs presently turn for a last look, and thus beheld him stooped in the act of picking up the fallen guinea.

So, in the chill of dawn, came I to my master's house and, clambering up the ivy-stems to my gloomy little chamber, got me to my wretched bed.

CHAPTER 3

TELLS HOW I RECEIVED A STRANGE PRESENT

It was next morning as I sat crouched above my desk copying a deed, that I heard a familiar sniff, and, glancing round towards the open casement, beheld old Zachary, the village sexton, nodding and beckoning.

'Be Master Bragg safe out o' t'road?' he questioned in hoarse whisper.

'Yes,' I answered, laying down my quill.

'Then dang 'im!' quoth Zachary aloud. 'And now, lad, I got a bit o' wonnerful noos : they soldiers was back again las' night.'

'Ay, I know this, Zachary.'

'Aha, but they cotched a pris'ner – one o' they rebels!'

'I know this, also.'

'Ah, but wait, lad, wait! I ain't told ee my wonnerful bit yet – and no more I bean't agoin' to nohow unless thee hold thy dratted tongue.'

'I'll be silent, Zachary.'

'Well, then, this yer rebel-prisoner, spite them soldiers, wi' arl their guns, an' swords, an' bagnets, an' locks, an' chains, an' sich loik, goes and vanishes away afore their very eyes in a cloud o' brimstone fire! An' wot d'ye say to that now, Adam?'

'Wonderful! But who told you all this, Zachary?'

''Tis no matter oo, but I heered it. Some says it be the Devil's doin's, an' some says witchcraft, and do blame it onto old Pen, 'er being a witch—'

'No, no, 'twas never poor Penelope!' said I. 'Why should the fools blame her?'

'Why, ye see they soldiers says as someone throwed a broomstick at 'em – an' oo should be going about wi' broomsticks but a witch – ah, an' wot be more, old Pen do ha' vanished away, too! And wot d'ye think o' that now?'

'Poor old Pen! I wonder she hasn't vanished before now seeing the way folk treat her – the fools!'

'You be a strange b'y, Adam, to hold wi' sich a brimstone witch as old Pen.'

'She's been good to me, and I love her.'

'Well, so 'ave I been good to ee, ain't I? Wasn't it me as—'

'Yes, yes!' said I, grasping the old man's gnarled hand, 'you have been kind and good to me also, Zachary.'

'Well then, Adam, I'm a goin' to be good to ee again, for 'ere be I come to give ee j'y, lad, for today be's thy birthday.'

'Birthday?' I repeated bitterly. 'Ah, Zachary, you know very well I can't have 'em, not knowing when I came into this pestilent, cruel world.'

'Pest'lent? Nay, but it be's thy birthday sure'ly, Adam, for 'twere nineteen year agone this very day as I found ee a'layin' 'neath the stoile in the dead arm's o' your pore—'

'Ah, would to God you'd left me there!'

'Nay, 'twould ha' been the death o' thee.'

'So much the better!' said I, scowling at the sunshine.

'Weren't much of ee, I moind – a poor, little scrimp of anatomy you was, lad; so small an' weak – though you bean't no giant, today, Adam, no – you ain't growd overmuch, seein' as you be nointeen year old.'

'Well, I'm – what I am!' said I, miserably.

'Ay, you be a scholard, for sure, an' 'tis a gert thing to be a scholard, so they say – though, to be sure, ye can't do much but read an' cypher—'

'I can swim, Zachary; there's no one in the village can swim so far or stay so long!'

'Ay, ay, lad, 'tis wonnerful, an' you s'small an' arl!'

'I'm as big as you!' said I, frowning at the little, old man;

but, seeing his stricken look, I reached out and clapped his bowed shoulder. 'But, indeed, for your age you're a wonder, Zachary.'

'So I be, so I be, sure-ly! I can eat an' drink wi' the best – specially drink, ah, that I can! And as for thee, Adam, tidn't thy fault thour't such a weevily scrimp – no! 'Tis the Lard be to blame for mekkin' thee such a whipper-snapper! No offence, lad!' said he, for I had turned away lest he see how the word stung. 'Blame it on the Lard, lad! – And I do loik thee moighty well, whipper-snapper or no. So never turn thy back on old Zachary.'

'No, no,' said I, with rueful laugh, 'for thour't right – whipper-snapper am I, indeed, and a spiritless slave to sit and drudge here all my days for a rogue-rascal.'

'Do ee mean thy master, lawyer Bragg, dang 'im?'

'Ay, him.'

'A man wi' no bowels, an' empty o' all compassion! They do say as 'e 'ave turned old Pen out of her bit o' cottage.'

'Ah, has he, Zachary?'

'Ay, and 'er so old, tu – to be sure she be a witch but—'

'But I love her!' said I. 'She was always kind and good to me!'

'Well, I be full o' kindness for ee likewise, Adam.'

'Ay, I know, I know – you and old Pen and Squire's lady, God rest her, you three are the only folk ever showed kindness to me since I came into this hard world.'

'And today be thy birthday, so I've brought a present for ee – leastways 'tis summat as I found in the churchyard – layin' ahint Gaffer Brewster's tombstone, it were, and a foine praper pistol it be, Adam, leastways to look at!'

'A pistol?' I repeated. 'Show it me, Zachary.'

Sniffing loudly, the old man delved into capacious pocket and slowly drew thence a small, beautifully finished weapon, ornate as to mountings and slender stock enriched with silver-work.

'It bean't able to go off, lad, seein' as th' trigger-spring be broke-loike,' explained Zachary, holding the pistol up for my inspection. 'So it can't nowise do ee nor nobody never no

manner o' harm, but it du be a right praper pistol t'look at —
eh, lad?'

'Indeed,' said I, turning the weapon in my hand, ''tis
mighty fine!'

'So it be, Adam, so it be sure-ly! 'Twere lucky me findin'
of it, seein' 'tis your birthday, an' the buryin' trade bein' s'bad
'count o' me not never 'avin' nobody needin' no graves!
Nobody don't never die 'ereabouts, lad, more's the pity!'

''Tis a fine piece, 'spite of its broken lock,' said I examin-
ing my new possession, 'and I thank you right heartily,
Zachary.'

'Why you an' me is friends, lad, ever an' allus — eh, Adam?'

'Ever and always, Zachary. Friendship is a rare, good
thing in this world.'

'Ay, lad, it du be a bad world sure-ly for them as be poor
an' friendless, or weak and small — not as 'tis any shame to
nobody bein' small, mind — no! Small 'uns be generally allus
quiet 'uns, not bein' made for no fightin' an' deviltry — so
weak 'uns be generally scholards seein' as they be's generally
stay-at-homes, an' like 'andlin' books and pens better nor
swords and pistols. So you be dooly thankful, Adam, as the
good Lard ain't made ee gert an' strong, for gert, big men
gen'rally turns out bad 'uns — cut-throats, pirates or 'ighway-
men and gets theirselves 'ung for bloody rogues — an' a good
job tu! So be j'yful as the A'mighty made ee little an' not
over strong, Adam — an' theer be passon a-beckin' me! I'll
lay it be Joel Jordan's 'ogs a'wallerin' among my graves
again, dang 'em! Many 'appy returns, Adam lad, and O be
j'yful!' So saying, the old man smiled, nodded, sniffed
violently and hobbled away, leaving me to stare down at the
weapon in my fist, and scowling blacker than ever.

27

CHAPTER 4

IN WHICH I AMAZE MYSELF YET MORE

MASTER Hosea Bragg was a large man of plethoric habit, a ponderous man in every sense, so that it was ever a marvel to me how one so cumbersome should move so noiselessly, creeping on his large feet so stealthily, drawing latches and opening doors with his great hands so softly that he (as it were) dawned upon one's senses unheralded by any sound – even as now.

'Aha!' he murmured in his gentle, hateful voice as, hiding the pistol in my bosom, I sprang about and faced him, 'So I catch my petty rogue idling again, do I – a-wasting of my precious time, eh? 'Tis a lad shall suffer, I fear! A lad shall to the gallows anon, I nothing doubt! Also 'tis a lad shall feel my staff this day, 'tis a rogue lad, shall carry sore bones awhile. Ha – go to!' he roared, 'is it thus ye rob me o' time and money? Off wi' that jacket and doublet – strip thou small, paltry rogue and snivel not!'

Trembling and mute stood I, staring up at the great red face, the heavy lips, the broad thick nostrils that snuffed and quivered, the baleful glare of these small, close-set eyes that had ever filled me with such loathing and sickening dread; thus fell I to sickening tremors that I might nowise hide, and licked and licked at lips grown suddenly dry, beholding which, he smiled and flourished heavy staff.

'Come, strip!' he commanded. 'Ha, must I wait? Strip I say!' But instead of obeying, I backed away towards the open casement whereat he sprang after me, striking viciously with his staff, but I eluded the blow, and in that same moment, whipped forth my pistol and levelled it full in his astonished face. So, for breathless moment, we stood, I trembling but desperately determined, he staring, stricken suddenly aghast.

'Why – why, lad – why, Adam—' he mumbled.

'Give me your staff!' said I, reaching out my hand.

'But – but, Adam—'

'Give it me!' says I, and thrust the pistol nearer, whereat he blenched but obeyed, and I tossed the staff out through the window.

'Now – lock the door!' I commanded.

'Nay, lad, nay,' he faltered, 'what would—'

'Lock the door and bring me the key!'

With his wide gaze fixed upon the pistol, he backed to the door, locked it and handed me the key, which I put in my pocket.

'Master Bragg,' said I, forcing the words between quivering lips, though my pistol-hand was steady enough, 'Master Bragg, you have treated me like a dog since I was a child. – You have beaten me – starved me – forced me to slavery – so now am I minded to kill you—'

'No, no – for God's sake!' he cried.

'Master Bragg, speak softly – whisper or I shoot.'

'Don't shoot me, Adam – for God's sake, don't!' he gasped in hoarse whisper, 'I'll never whip thee more, lad – shalt eat what thou wilt – shalt be free o' work Saturdays and Sundays, Adam, only don't shoot!'

Strange was it to hear this great creature whispering so passionately the while he dabbed at sweating face and neck with clumsy, shaking hands.

'Today, Master Bragg, I am done with you, but ere I leave ye to the Devil I will have the fifty guineas bequeathed me by my lady Masterton.'

Answered Master Bragg, staring into the pistol-muzzle.

'So you shall, Adam, ay, ay, but 'twill be robbery, lad!'

''Tis my money!'

'Ay, but not till art of age, Adam. Come now, put by that murderous thing ere it go off, put it by now like a good, kind, sensible lad and I promise, nay, I'll swear to thee—'

'Where is my money?'

'In my desk yonder.'

'Get it!'

'But, Adam – but, lad, you . . . never—'

'Get it!'

''Twill be robbery, Adam, robbery with violence—'

'It will unless you obey!'

'Wouldst murder thy master, lad?'

'With joy unless he give me my money this moment!'

'Ha – villaineous rogue!' he cried in sudden ferocity and, as suddenly, quailed: 'Nay, now, nay,' he whimpered, 'never look so bloodily at me, boy. Shalt have thy money – yes, yes. So – there! Take it, Adam, take what ye will, only—'

'Master Bragg, hold your tongue! And I will have gold, count it into the money bag yonder!'

So, while I stood over him, he counted the fifty guineas into the bag which he tied.

'And now, get up!' said I, dropping the bag into my pocket, 'Up with ye and open the cupboard yonder!'

'The cupboard, lad? But why? There be nought there worth your taking – nought there but odds and ends, as you well know.'

'Open it! And when you speak remember to whisper!' Fumbling awkwardly he unlocked and drew wide the massy door of the cupboard.

'Lookee, Adam,' he whispered, 'there's nought here but—'

'Get in! Get you inside!' I commanded.

For a moment he hesitated, and I saw a devil glare at me from his eyes, and feared he would leap at me, and therefore, trembling in my fear, I crept a slow pace nearer to him – nearer yet. All at once he cowered, uttered a strange, inarticulate cry and shrank into the cupboard; then, clapping to the heavy door I locked it secure and leaned against it overcome with sudden weakness. And as I stood there shivering yet wiping sweat from me, I spoke to him through the panel.

'Master Bragg,' said I, breathlessly, 'if such as you ever pray, thank God now this pistol o' mine is unloaded and hath a broken lock, otherwise, remembering my cruel childhood, I might ha' been tempted to shoot you indeed for the evil man and pestilent brute you are!'

Then, while Master Bragg kicked and uttered muffled roars, I covered my red hair with weather-beaten hat and,

climbing through the window, was halfway down the village
street ere I found that I yet grasped my broken pistol.

CHAPTER 5

WHICH TELLS OF A PROPHECY

HAVING got me out of the village I turned aside into the
fields and, so soon as I had lost sight of the highroad, began
to run my hardest, nor bated my speed until I had reached
the woods. And where now should I bend my course but
towards the village of East Bourne with some fond hope that
I might, perchance, meet again with my wonderful young
gentleman. Fired with this purpose then, I kept to the woods
whose leafy boskages were pretty familiar to me (as hath
been said) with intent to come out opposite Firle village
which lies nestling under the Beacon.

Hidden thus amid the green solitudes my fears of immediate pursuit abated, and I went at my ease, pausing ever
and anon to look about me glad-eyed, rejoicing in my new-
won freedom. It was as I went beside a little brook a-wind
between ferny banks that I was arrested by sound of a voice
at no great distance.

'Who creepeth yonder? If ye be evil go your ways and
strive to do good. If ye be good come that an old one may
bless ye.'

'Pen,' cried I, and, pushing through the dense underbrush,
came forth into a little clearing and beheld the speaker – this
tall, strange, solitary old woman whom all seemed to fear,
save only me. She was crouched before the crumbling ruin
of a little cottage, hands crossed upon her staff, bony chin
on bony knuckles, and what with her great black eyes,
wrinkled face and snow-white hair a very witch-like figure
she made, and yet to me the dearest in all the world; so ran
I to clasp that bowed form, to kiss her wrinkled cheek while
she, setting her long arms about me, held me close.

'My lamb!' sighed she, 'My babe – my bonny boy! And is it running away ye are at last?'

'Yes, yes!' I answered, and sinking before her on my knees I told her all that had befallen since my first meeting with the fugitive in the wood, while she sat watching me with her wise, old eyes and no word spoken until I'd done.

'So 'twas you – aha, 'twas you tricked they red-coats? 'Twas bravely done! And you've run off at last, my Adam? And locked up the man Bragg – why this was likewise brave.'

'Nay, but 'twas fear made me do it, Pen, quaking fear. See how I tremble yet when I do think on him!' and I held out my shaking hands. 'O, I'm a very coward Pen!' said I, miserably.

'Ay, wi' red hair!' says she, laying gentle hand upon my bowed head, 'and Master Bragg a-roaring in his own cupboard!' Here she laughed suddenly, 'Aha, there be some cowards dangerous to meddle wi', Adam! The coward as overcomes his own fear may overcome all else – so comfort ye, lad!'

'But, indeed, Pen, my fear is so great it choketh me at times, and makes me weaker even than Nature hath already, and moreover – O, Pen, am I indeed nought but a whippersnapper?' At this she chuckled, then taking my hand she kissed it, and opening the clenched fingers, peered down at the deep-lined palm.

'Hearkee, dear boy,' she murmured, 'these old eyes may see, sometimes, that which is not yet; many a hand have I read and many destinies foretold, yet none like to thine. Mark now! Here is a hand shall grasp much and what it graspeth, hold. Here be journeyings by land and sea. Here be dangers and perils a-many! Here is love and hate and bloodshed! Here shame and grief and great joy! Fear shall go with thee belike, yet in thee is that shall be mightier than fear—'

'Ah, Pen, Pen,' cried I, 'would all this might be so! But I am no hero – alas, shameful outcast, rather – a nameless creature that none regard and all despise – so puny and small that I never stood up to any village lad but to be knocked down – a pitiful, friendless soul, a poor lad in threadbare homespun, and yet you would make me a very paladin, like King Arthur's knights – O, Pen, would thy spells might so transform me!'

'Content ye, sweet lad,' said she, setting her two hands upon my head, much as if she would have blessed me, 'O content ye, lad o' my love, for now will I give thee a sign for truth o' what I foretell. Now, heed me! Ere long thy homespun shall be changed for laces and velvets, and thy young eyes behold hate and grief, love and death, ay – ere the moon change!'

Now, as I hearkened to her solemn voice and looked up into her strange, bright eyes, she seemed no more the gentle, kindly creature I had loved and pitied, but rather as one remote and all unknown, transfigured far above my poor understanding so that there grew within me an awe of her akin to fear. And then she sighed and, smiling, bent to kiss my brow, and in this moment became again as she had ever been, the patient consoler of my childish ills and boyish sorrows.

'But, Pen,' said I, after some while, 'what do you here? 'Tis an evil place, and this old cottage haunted, they say.'

'Haunted,' she nodded, 'it well may be, or it will be, like enough, for here must I bide since 'tis all I have to shelter my old bones – mayhap none shall dare trouble me by reason o' the ghosts.'

'Why, Zachary told me how Master Bragg had made thee homeless, and so I – I brought thee this!' And, drawing the money bag from my pocket I loosed the string and poured the guineas into her lap.

'O Lordy – Lord!' she whispered, clasping her hands and staring down at the money in an ecstasy, 'O lad – sweet lad, here be a fortune sure-ly!'

'No, 'tis fifty guineas, Pen.'

'O, Adam,' says she, touching the coins with one bony forefinger almost fearfully, 'I never see such vasty sum in all my days! Fifty golden—' she gasped suddenly, and looked up at me with eyes greatly troubled, 'Adam,' she whispered, 'O, child, as I love – ye didn't – ye didn't—'

33

'Steal it, Pen? No, no, my dear. I took it from Master Bragg, 'tis the legacy left me by my lady Masterson and now 'tis thine.'

'Mine?' she whispered, and now I saw her eyes full of tears.

'Every guinea!' said I. 'Shalt never starve whiles I live, my dear old Pen.'

'Ah no – ah no!' she cried. 'I couldna' take it, Adam.'

'Ay, but you must and shall,' said I rising.

'But – O, my dearie lad, I cannot tak' all ye have – nay, I will not!'

'And so, goodbye, dear Penelope! Someday, if my fortune prove true, I will bring thee more.'

'But Adam – O, my dear, my loved boy—'

'Dear Pen, thou wert always so good to me, so tender and kind all my lonely days – and I haven't known much o' kindness hitherto. So would I thank thee if I could, old Pen. But in good fortune or ill, I shall never forget thee – no, never!'

Then, stooping suddenly, I kissed her silver hair, her wrinkled brow, and hastened away, while she stared after me through her falling tears.

CHAPTER 6

TELLETH OF NAKED STEEL

A VIVID flash of scarlet, the glint of gold lace, and down I cowered amid the bracken at the edge of a broad glade, beyond which the road made a sharp bend for Firle village; so there lay I upon my face wellnigh aswoon with the sudden shock, while they (for it seemed there were two of them) drew slowly nearer my hiding place – nearer, until I could hear the jingle of their spurs – nearer yet, until I could catch the air one of them hummed, and then they stopped and my poor heart so thumping I trembled lest they hear it. Thus stood they for some moments, as if listening, for both were now silent, and then at last one of them spoke in a singularly pleasing voice I was destined never to forget, so rich was it, so soft yet sweetly clear; and this voice, being so beautiful, made the words it uttered only the more horrible :

'His head should look uncommonly well adorning Temple Bar. His right arm and leg should go, I think, to Carlisle, his left to Newcastle, his trunk to Perth or Inverness, but his head must to London for – family reasons.'

'Family reasons,' repeated another voice very languid and sleepy. 'Gad's life, sir, what should they be?'

'His father's London house chances within an easy walk of Temple Bar, my dear Captain.'

'His father, sir? You mean?'

''Twould be an easy pilgrimage for the doating sire, 'twould not fatigue the old gentleman—'

'By heavens, sir, 'tis vile suggestion!' quoth the Captain, his voice sleepy no longer, ''Tis devilish! Also, Sir Hector, before we may so exhibit his poor remains to a grieving father, we have first to capture him, I would remind you of this, sir.'

'Capture him, ay, true, my dear Dallas, and very joyous duty 'twill be, to you as a zealous soldier of his thrice blessed Majesty King George whom God defend, and to me as – hum!'

'As what, may I ask?'

'As one equally zealous, sir.'

'O faith, Sir Hector Keith MacFarlane's loyal zeal is notorious!'

'Sir, you overwhelm me!' answered the soft voice gently and yet a little mocking, I thought; and then they walked on but only to halt again well within earshot. And now, venturing to lift my head, I saw one for a tall gentleman in the dreaded gold and scarlet of a King's officer, who stood arms folded, booted legs apart, frowning a little, but it was his companion that drew and held my gaze.

A smallish, slender gentleman, who lolled against a tree, holding a snuff-box in fingers white as his long lace ruffles; a graceful gentleman of uncertain age, his full-skirted riding-coat of green velvet brave with rich embroidery, his long, brown riding-boots adorned with gilt spurs; all this finery I was instant to heed, but beholding his face I looked no other where.

A thin, dark face half hid in the flowing curls of his great periwig, a face in whose haggard, pale oval two restless, dark eyes glittered beneath a languor of drooping lids, a high, thin nose, and a mouth faint-smiling and disdainful above pointed chin; a face whose cold and mocking serenity I feared and hated at my first glance.

'You would seem strangely anxious for this particular gentleman's capture, sir!' said the Captain, chin aloft, 'I might say even passionately anxious.'

'Admitted, Captain, admitted full and freely.'

'You have a – personal motive, perhaps, Sir Hector?'

'This, my dear Dallas, is as may be,' he answered, and, as he spoke, there rushed upon me a strange sense of familiarity, and therewith something deadly in his languid pose, his look, his smile – some nameless evil in the man appalled me, and made him ever the more hateful. And now, too, I recognized him for that same man whose name was MacFarlane or Keith, Weaver or Weir of whom my fugitive young gentleman had spoken.

'Howbeit, Captain,' said he, 'the King's enemies are mine.'

'His Majesty should rejoice to know it, sir!' retorted the Captain scornfully, whereupon the other, always smiling, saluted him with profound obeisance.

'Referring to this – ah – highly elusive fugitive of ours, he was a one-time friend of yours, I understand, my dear Dallas?'

The Captain stood up very straight, and squared his shoulders.

'In happier days, sir,' he answered, very red in the face, 'we were at school together.'

'So – indeed, Captain – he was your friend? And now, alas, he is an enemy of your King, to be hunted down or killed by his Majesty's loyal subjects! Touching, sir, and very sad, considering his youth and his aged father. None the less, as a faithful subject of King George, whom God bless, I would humbly suggest your men beating the adjacent woods; 'tis beyond doubt our rebel hath gone to earth hereabouts.'

'Sir,' answered the soldier stiffly, 'I lament to disoblige so loyal a subject as yourself, but 'tis out o' the question.'

'Indeed, my very dear Dallas?'

'Indeed, sir! Seeing I have but scant twenty men, and that they have beaten the coverts beyond Firle since dawn and are hard at it still, I submit 'tis out o' the question.'

'Hum!' says Sir Hector, stroking his chin, 'Major West reports he had sight of him 'twixt here and East Bourne early this morning and turned him back in this direction – now, if you would spare me a few of your men—'

'Impossible, sir!'

'Aha!' sighed Sir Hector tapping his box delicately and extracting a pinch of snuff, 'friendship, it seems, may have its – saving virtues.'

'Sir!' exclaimed the Captain in choking voice, 'I object to the insinuation and demand you retract it or—'

'Or?' questioned the other, gently. For answer the Captain flashed out his sword :

'This, sir!' said he, looking very fierce.

Sir Hector glanced at the Captain's suffused face, glanced at his sword and motioned it aside with languid hand.

'Put up, sir!' said he. 'Pray put up! Had I the misfortune to kill you 'twould grieve me sensibly to do such disservice to the King, God bless him!'

'I cast the insinuation in your teeth, sir!' cried the Captain. 'And what now?'

Sir Hector inhaled his pinch of snuff with apparent enjoyment.

'Talking of friendship, sir—' he began.

'Well?'

Sir Hector dusted his fingers and fobbed his box.

'Had I the happy capacity for winning friends, my dear Dallas, which, alas, seems denied me, I should count myself extreme fortunate in such friendship as – yours.'

'MacFarlane,' says the Captain in a fume, 'you put a slur

upon my honour as a soldier which, by Heaven, you must and shall retract – this instant !'

'But, my dear Dallas, I never retract—'

'Then so be it, sir. Draw – draw, I say !'

'Nay, nay !' laughed Sir Hector, shaking his head, 'what folly ! Yon mountain's but a molehill. And, sir, I draw but upon the King's enemies – or my own.'

'What – what?' stuttered the Captain, 'must I strike you?'

'Indeed, I think you must, sir.'

Hereupon the Captain rapped him lightly upon the crown; next moment Sir Hector's sword was out and they were at it, thrusting and parrying, stepping lightly to and fro; now though the Captain was taller and longer in the arm, I sweated to see his antagonist so much quicker and (as it seemed even to my inexperienced eye) infinitely the more dangerous. The narrow blades glittered in the sun as they circled and darted viciously, and then all at once was a whirl of rasping steel, a quick stamp of feet and the Captain (to my horror) stood empty-handed, his sword tucked securely beneath Sir Hector's arm, and all in less time than I write it.

For a moment they eyed each other, the Captain a little breathless and very red in the face.

'A – a devil's trick !' he panted.

'Though useful !' smiled Sir Hector.

'Well, – damn you – strike !'

'Tush, sir !' said Sir Hector, lowering his point, 'I strike only to kill, and your death could advantage me no whit. So pray accept your sword and with it all the good wishes in the world, my dear Dallas.'

The Captain hesitated, frowning and biting his lip, but he took his weapon at last and rammed it back into the scabbard.

'What now, sir?' he inquired.

'With your leave I'll inflict myself upon you as far as the inn – my horse is there.'

'As you will, sir,' answered the other gloomily, and they moved off together side by side, the soldier very stiff in the back, his companion seemingly more languid than ever, and

I heard him once more humming to himself in his strangely pleasant voice.

CHAPTER 7

DESCRIBETH HOW AND IN WHAT STRANGE FASHION THE PROPHECY BEGAN TO BE FULFILLED

AND after I had waited some while, I rose and hurried away in the opposite direction, whither I cared not so long as the woods sheltered me; before my mind's eye rose a vision of Master Bragg kicking half-stifled in the dusty cupboard; I could picture all the passionate rage and murderous ferocity of this man who had ever been the boding terror of my boyish days and who now, helpless though he was, would be planning pursuit and dire vengeance upon me, nay, might at this very moment have won free of his prison and be in the act of raising against me the terror of the hue and cry.

Thus on I pressed at speed, now running, now walking, plunging ever deeper in these mazy woods until at last, faint with the heat, spent and breathless, I stumbled and sank beneath a great tree, to lie there, panting yet heedful, often holding my breath painfully that I might listen for the first dreadful sounds of pursuit. But all was hushed save for the stir of leaves about me, and the faint carolling of a happy lark high in the blue. So by degrees my panic subsided, but only to make place for a bitter self-scorn, that old contempt for my lack of courage and general unheroical attitude of mind the which haunted me so persistently, since I knew myself for no better than a poor, despised, spiritless drudge. And now, sitting beneath this tree, I viewed my puny shanks, my meagre person and small, nervous hands, always so ready to shake and tremble, and, despising myself thus body and soul, sank to a black despond. At last, in my despair, I got to my knees and, raising clasped hands towards Heaven, most passionately besought God to change the very nature of me; and yet even as I prayed I doubted (God forgive me) that such stupendous miracle might be.

'O Father ! O God, let me be strong – give me a courageous heart – teach me to be unfearing.'

Now as I called thus upon the Lord, behold – through the leaves above me shot a sudden beam of sunlight dazzling me with its glory, and I knew wonder and an awful joy for, to me in my despairful wretchedness, it seemed as it were a sign that God had indeed heard my supplication; and I sprang to my feet filled with a marvellous new confidence, feeling myself to be, in very truth, a child of God.

So on I strode, my spirit wonderfully uplifted, looking about me with eyes that found new beauties in sun-dappled sward, in tree and leafy thicket, since these were all works of God, even as I myself.

Now presently there reached me a sound very pleasant to hear on such hot day, the soft, murmurous ripple of running water. So turned I thither and came beside a stream that flowed singing by leafy ways, a stream that led me on until I reached a deep and shady pool.

The place was sequestered and deeply remote, and this pellucid water looked deliciously cool and refreshing, insomuch that I began to loose points and buttons and, stripping my heated body, I came to the grassy verge and plunged down – down to pebbly bed, swimming deep with effortless ease, anon rising to the sun-kissed surface and, buoyant and tingling, I swam on and on so far as the deep water allowed. Gone now my depression, forgotten my bitter self-disparagement – above, below and around me was an element that seemed to acknowledge me master; thus swam I exulting, athrill with joyous vigour and heedless of woes past, present or to come.

Howbeit, all joys must end, and, turning reluctantly at last, I made for the bank, clambered from the water and stood a moment to enjoy the sun's warm glow; and thus I fell to wondering regard of the strange talisman I bore about my neck on stout length of cord, turning it this way and that (as I had done many and many a time ere now) and this, a small, oval, gold piece or medallion with, upon the one side, a cross and upon the other a cabalistic sign or hieroglyphic done in coloured enamels, which strange thing was my only heritage from my unknown mother. I stood looking on this some while, being lost in thoughts of that young and most unhappy mother, until becoming aware of my nakedness, I crossed to my clothes, stooped for my shirt – and so remained, hand outstretched, mouth agape and eyes wide, staring in stupified amazement, for these garments (though lying where I had tossed my own) were none of mine.

Utterly confounded I rubbed my eyes and looked again. Here, in place of coarse linen was delicate lawn and costly lace, coat of velvet brave with silver embroidery, spurred riding boots, belaced hat, periwig, silver-hilted small-sword.

Hastily I turned and (naked as I was) began to seek desperately among the adjacent underbrush but, search how I would, my own familiar, threadbare garments had vanished as if, indeed, they had been transformed into these rich habiliments. Hereupon I started as there rushed on me the memory of old Pen's prophecy; much reading had shaken my faith in witchcraft, black magic and the like, but now my mind groped.

As one in a dream I took up the shirt, handling the dainty thing reverently, cast a fearful glance left and right, and furtively slipped it on. So progressed I from one garment to another, viewing, feeling and finally getting into it, hastily, half fearing to be caught in the act, until I was completely dressed even to hat and wig. And, O marvel of marvels, I found these handsome garments none so much too large.

And now, very conscious of my new splendour, I became seized of burning desire to behold myself and stepped riverwards, but halted, startled (yet thrilling) to hear the musical jingle of my spurs. Then, left hand poised on sword-hilt, I came to the stilly pool, and, bracing myself by serviceable branch, leaned over, looked down and, uttering a gasp, peered over my shoulder expecting to see there a pale, haggard face with eyes a-glitter and lips faint smiling and disdainful as when they had uttered those dreadful words:

'His head should look well adorning Temple Bar—'

But, peer where I would, I saw nobody; except for myself the place was deserted; so I turned and once again surveyed myself in the placid water. And now (to my wonder and dismay) I saw that my be-wigged head and face had about them something hatefully akin to this evil man, Sir Hector MacFarlane; and this vague similitude troubled me greatly.

But, O Angels of Light! How marvellously changed was I, how gloriously transfigured! In place of the ill-dressed, shambling country lad, went a dignified gentleman, who bore himself with an easy grace, a gallant cavalier, his cheek of modish pallor beneath the glossy curls of his long, black peruke; and beholding the mighty difference these same curls wrought in me, I touched and fondled them, ordering them this way and that.

Very like I should have stayed admiring my watery image longer but the posture was trying so, uttering a sigh tremulous with pleasure, I drew reluctantly away.

Now as I went I stumbled over something in the grass and picked up my broken pistol, but was minded to throw it away as useless encumbrance, fearing to pocket it lest its weight spoil the hang of my fine coat; then, slipping it into the band of my breeches, I went on, keeping now to the more open ways, lest obtrusive twig or thorn do outrage to my finery. Moreover, instead of undignified trot, I paced sedately by reason of the high heels of my riding-boots and enchanting jingle of my spurs.

Going leisurely thus, I made divers and several discoveries as:

In the right hand pocket of my small-clothes a solitary guinea; in the left, a small compendium containing a mirror, a comb, a pair of tweezers and an eye-brow brush. In my coat pockets – nothing.

So absorbed was I by these my new possessions, that I blundered into a gate which opened upon a grassy lane; and here I paused awhile to survey my garments more particularly. The silver-spurred riding-boots (of soft and very pliant leather) were furnished with extreme high heels, and thus lent me height and dignity (to my vast satisfaction!); the coat, though something the worse for wear, was of dark blue velvet, very handsome, turned up at cuff, pocket and button-hole with silver lace, very rich; the long, narrow-bladed sword was adorned with hilt of silver wondrously chiselled, and altogether I looked and (poor youth that I was!) felt a very fine gentleman indeed.

My head was twisted in painful endeavour to observe the hang of coat-skirt over silver-chaped scabbard, when I heard a voice singing; starting erect, I beheld a country maid coming up the lane; she bore a yoke on her buxom shoulders, and, perceiving she had not yet espied me, I made an instinctive movement to hide, but my scabbard caught the gate-post, and remembering my so altered appearance, I restrained myself and, posed against the gate with as much of gracious ease as I could achieve, I waited her approach in a twitter of apprehension.

Beholding me, the girl ceased her singing and, meeting my glance, tittered shyly, blushed and, as she passed this splendid-seeming gentleman, dropped him a timid curtsey – and left me staring after her, tingling from head to foot, for no woman had ever so made me her reverence or blushed beneath my eye ere now.

Hardly was she out of sight than again I had recourse to my small looking-glass, studying myself therein with wondering eyes and oblivious of all else.

CHAPTER 8

WHICH RECORDS A PORTENTOUS MEETING

I WAS roused by the quick muffled tramp of galloping hoofs, and, glancing up, saw a horseman close upon me and turned to run; but, reining his horse violently, he sprang to earth and had me by the throat and a pistol beneath my ear all in a moment.

'Ha – Ancaster!' he exclaimed, 'at last, by God! 'Tis London for you – 'tis the block and bloody axe, ay, by—'

'No!' I gasped and stared up into the evil face of Sir Hector MacFarlane; then, sobbing with fear, I staggered free as he fell back to eye me over while I blenched from the pale fury of him.

'What – what fool's game is here?' he demanded, eyes wide and fierce, white teeth snapping, 'what accursed mummery is this? Whence had ye these clothes?'

'Sir, I – I went a-bathing,' I stammered, 'a-bathing, sir, and when I came to dress me I – I found my own clothes were not and – these were—'

'What manner o' clothes were yours? Quick, fool, quick – in a word!'

'Old!' I answered, whereupon he took me by the throat again.

'Ha, will ye palter with me?' he cried, shaking me passionately. 'Describe them, rogue, their sort – their colour, quick, I say!'

Forthwith I contrived to gasp forth some description of my vanished garments, whereupon he cuffed me for my trouble, bidding me begone for a pitiful knave. Now at this (and minding the beam of sun in the wood), my affright left me and I fronted him, never heeding his pistol.

'Hearkee, sir!' I began, 'I tell you—' here, meeting his fierce look, I stopped, a little breathlessly.

'What, oaf, what?'

'Sir, you called me "rogue" – so now—' again my voice failed; Sir Hector stamped impatient foot:

'Well, clod?' he demanded.

'Well, sir, you – are a damned rogue – and villainous knave also!'

His delicate nostrils expanded suddenly, the pistol quivered in his clutching, white fingers and for a moment his eyes glared into mine, then all at once he laughed softly.

'My poor boy,' said he in his strangely sweet voice, 'some

day you may be worth a man's powder and shot – unless you are taken and die by the axe like so many o' your betters—'

'The axe!' cried I.

'Ay, or gibbet, my poor innocent. There are red-coats hereabout!'

'Sir – sir, what do you mean?'

'Those garments, fool! You are become a scapegoat for a rebel, to be taken or shot down!'

So saying, he turned to his horse that cropped the grass hard by and sprang lightly to saddle. Now as I stared up at him, horror-stricken and dismayed beyond words, he looked down at me and laughed.

'Poor innocent!' said he. 'D'ye blink the axe already then, or is't the noose? Hearkee, fool, should the red-coats take you – ask for John Weir – Weir, mind – 'tis a good plain, honest name easily remembered – John Weir. So may you live to die some other time and less quickly.'

So saying, he laughed again, rammed pistol into holster, and spurring his mettled animal, galloped rapidly away, and left me propped against the gate, sick and faint with a new terror.

For these fine garments (that in my blind folly I had thought so becoming) I now loathed extremely, since their very splendour was a menace to my life and bitterly yearned I to be safe again in my own poor clothes; while Master Bragg's crab-tree staff, nay, prison itself, seemed of none account beside the chance of capture by the soldiers or the searing shock of a musket-ball.

Thus, terrified by my so conspicuous grandeur, and quaking to the musical jingle of my spurs, back crept I miserably into the woods, and there loosing off the spurs, lest they betray me to unseen ears, I buried them beneath a pile of leaves. Then I wandered on again (and very wretched) heedless of direction, since I knew not whither to go, often pausing breathless to listen for the tramp of feet while my eyes stared hither and thither for the gleam of musket-barrel or flash of scarlet cloth; and now all my prayer was:

'O God, keep me from the red-coats!'

CHAPTER 9

TELLETH HOW AND IN WHAT MANNER I
LOOKED UPON DEATH

I T W A S (as I judge) late afternoon, for the sun was trending westwards, when wearied with my aimless rambling I sat, very disconsolate, wondering what was to become of me. And the more I pondered, the more hopeless seemed my situation, with no haven of refuge beyond these desolate woods, and they full of soldiers in quest of me (or rather the clothes that covered me), with no friend to aid or comfort me, even supposing I won free of the red-coats, and but one guinea betwixt myself and destitution.

The longer I thought, the more hopeless I grew, so that at last I came to the following desperate resolution, viz, that since I might not lurk for ever in these solitudes, since I must eat, I would therefore no longer seek to hide, but would quit the woods forthwith, letting chance direct me, and either make my way Londonwards (a weary journey) or deliver myself up to the soldiers, trusting to prove my true identity even though I must fall into the eager, merciless clutches of Master Bragg.

With this purpose in mind then, I rose and set forth easterly, but had gone scarce a dozen paces when I leapt to the sharp report of two shots fired in rapid succession, and stood as it were thunderstruck, scarce breathing, and head twisted to stare in the direction whence these ominous sounds had come.

At last, minding my so recent resolution, I set my teeth and began to walk thither, determined to cry out and yield myself at the first glint of scarlet coat. And thus, all at once, I came upon a narrow glade or ride and stopped aghast, as well I might.

Within a few yards of me lay a man all asprawl and half

46

buried in the bracken, with arms wide-tossed, above whom stood another man in the act of writing, and though the face of this second man was averted, I knew him instantly for Sir Hector and turned to fly; but a stick snapped beneath my unwary foot, and in that moment he spun round and saw me.

'What, my oaf,' he exclaimed in queer, high voice, 'd'ye haunt me yet? There's a fate in't, methinks. Tell me, what did you see?'

'Nothing!' I answered, staring into his compelling eyes, though very conscious of the dreadful still shape in the bracken.

'What did you hear?'

'Two shots!' I answered, my lips suddenly dry.

'Ha – two? So shall you witness here was fair duello. Come you hither – nearer – nearer, fool! Ha what now? What ails you?' For I had seen at last the face of this sprawler in the bracken and, even as I looked, there brake from me a gasping cry, my knees gave and I sank down, shaken by violent tremors, for this dead face, that gazed heavenwards with eyes so untroubled and serene, was young well-nigh as my own.

'What, d'ye know him, my clod? Speak, bumpkin speak!' For answer I pointed with shaking finger.

'Well, fool, well?'

'He – he is – wearing my clothes!' I gasped.

'Ay, and you his, so you may cry quits. He made you his scapegoat, as I warned you. Now you may go – and remember you heard two shots! Off with ye – stay!' exclaimed Sir Hector, and stared from me to the paper in his hand, then laughed softly, and folding this missive, thrust it into his bosom and grasped me by the collar. 'Come!' said he, and dragging me to unsteady legs, hurried me away, with never so much as one backward glance at his handiwork, that pitiful thing lying there so dreadfully silent and still.

'Come, hold up!' exclaimed my companion, for I shuddered so violently I might scarce go. 'Pah, what ails ye, boy?'

'He – he was so – young!' said I, 'twixt chattering teeth.

'Why, then, he has had the less time for sinning.'

And after some while he brought me where was his horse, the which he mounted and, bidding me to his stirrup, on we went together though whither, or for what end, I cared not.

'Oaf,' says he after some while, glancing down at me with his keen eyes, 'who are ye?'

'Nobody, sir.'

'Tush!' he exclaimed peevishly. 'What's your name, fool?'

'Adam, sir.'

'Adam what, fool?'

'Thursday they named me, sir.'

'An odd name, boy.'

'I am a foundling, sir, and 'twas on a Thursday I was taken up from the arms of my dead mother.'

'Ah – dead was she? Dead, say you, boy?'

'In a ditch beside a stile, sir.'

'Poor lass! Poor, sorrowful creature!' said he in voice so marvellous sweet and gentle that I glanced up in amazement, to see that his look matched his tone.

'God comfort her, boy!' says he, meeting my look.

'Amen, sir!'

'Any man that should bring a woman to such miserable end – such suffering and death, should himself suffer and die – eh, boy, eh?'

'Yes!' cried I, clenching my fists, 'Yes!'

'Being a devil fit only for the deepest hell – eh, boy? Aha!' he exclaimed, and, raising gauntleted hand, he clenched and shook it so fiercely and with laugh so wild and savagely triumphant that I ventured a question, whereon he cuffed my hat over my eyes calling me 'cursed lout'.

And now we reached a narrow lane which, as I judged, should soon bring me to the high road.

'Hast ever seen a devil, boy?' enquired my companion suddenly.

'No, sir,' I answered, wondering.

'Then, if we're in luck, I'll show ye one, an aged devil, a very pompous, very arrogant devil, and prouder than the arch-fiend!'

After this we went in silence some while, my companion

48

seemingly lost in gloomy thought; at last, reaching a little eminence, he checked his horse and pointed towards a goodly mansion that peeped mid bowery trees within a noble park.

'D'ye ken yon house?' he enquired, scowling at it.

'No, sir.'

'Well, 'tis there we're going, 'tis there, if fortune prove kind, we shall find our devil – come!' So saying, he wheeled his horse aside into a narrow, leafy track, hard to be discovered save by eyes familiar, which presently brought us to a mossy wall. Here he dismounted and, having tethered his horse, led me where bushes grew and a rising ground made the wall easy to be scaled.

'Up!' said he; and next moment we were in a fair garden, where flowers bloomed backed by hedges wonderfully shaped and trimmed. And now, clapping hand on my shoulder, he guided me along mazy, winding paths, like one very familiar with the place, never faltering, though once he turned aside where stood an ancient sundial and paused awhile his head bowed, his two hands resting on the weathered stone; then he led me on again till, reaching an arch cut in the thickness of the great yew hedge, he halted, and I saw we stood close upon a certain wing of the house. Before us rose a flight of stone steps leading up to a noble terrace, where was a door with a row of windows beyond.

'Bide ye here!' says my companion softly, 'Keep out o' sight and stir at your peril!' Then he was gone, and I no sooner alone than, despite his warning, I began to look about me, wondering where I might hide; but then back he comes, his eyes aglow, his lips faint-curving in their disdainful smile.

'Fortune is with us, boy!' says he in my ear. 'Our devil comes, watch now – the door on the terrace yonder!' Even as he spoke this door opened wide and a full-toned, masterful voice reached us :

'My cane, Thomas, my cane! Ha, must I wait, rogue?' And then forth into the sunset glory stepped the most splendid old gentleman I had ever seen. Very tall he seemed and of portly habit, haughtily erect despite his years, a disdainful, arrogant figure, cold pride in every line of him, from glossy periwig that curled below his shoulders to the diamond shoe-buckles that flamed and glittered with his every stately stride. He was attended by two liveried footmen, who followed close on his heels; reaching the terrace steps he paused to glance about him in slow, dignified fashion, and thus I saw his face very lined, as with more than years, and his deep-set eyes very bright and piercing.

'Thomas, my snuff-box! John, my hat! You may go!'

Mutely the two servants bowed and departed, and slowly, step by step, this grand gentleman began to descend the stair.

'Boy,' said Sir Hector, in my ear, 'behold our devil! Faith he might be Satan himself!' Now, glancing up, I saw the speaker's face convulsed with such hate as appalled me; and yet his voice was mild and gentle when next he spoke, 'A pompous devil – eh, boy? A very proud, ancient devil! He will go to the arbour on the lawn yonder – you will follow – now, mark me! So soon as he sees you – bow and give him – this!' And into my unwilling hand Sir Hector thrust a small, folded paper. With this in my fingers and Sir Hector's clutch upon my arm, I stood wondering what it all might mean, then:

'Go, boy! After him, Adam, lad, and remember – you bow and offer this paper. Should he refuse it, say "Eustace". Off with you!'

The grand gentleman had nearly reached the arbour when, hearing me behind him (as I suppose), he halted and turned about, staring down at me beneath thick, black eyebrows.

'How now?' he demanded in manner so peremptory that I cowered instinctively, quite forgetting to bow, 'How came you here, sir? I protest 'tis an outrage! Ha, the devil, sir! Begone, I say, begone instantly!'

Here, and very humbly, I ventured to proffer him the folded paper.

'No, sir!' said he, waving me off with imperious gesture, 'I will transact no business here, I say begone, sir, ere I summon my grooms – away, sir!'

'"Eustace"!' said I and recoiled, for the change in him was so instant and amazing, his stately form seemed to shrink, his fiercely arrogant eyes blenched to glance furtively this way and that, his haughty face, quite chapfallen, took on a strange mottled hue :

'Eustace?' he gasped in broken whisper, 'My boy – my Eustace? Give – give me—' And, speaking, he snatched the paper and unfolding it began to read – A horrible gasping— The paper fluttered to the grass; and then, beholding the awful face above me, I shrank appalled.

'God – O merciful God – O Christ-Jesus!' cried he in dreadful voice, and, casting up his arms, clutched frantically at the air and fell headlong so that his great wig flew off and there, within a yard of my dusty boot, lay his aged head and pitifully bald save for a few straggling, grey hairs.

Now as I stared down at this splendid, stately gentleman thus shamefully abased, I beheld the paper lying within reach and (scarce knowing what I did) caught it up and read these words scrawled in great, bold characters

'My Lord and right accursed father-in-law,
'This to inform you that your son, and my brother-in-law, Eustace, is this day most happily dead by the hand of
'Your son-in-law very devoted,
'MACFARLANE.
'There is left now only Richard and yourself.'

Dropping this dreadful missive I glanced towards the aged and stricken father, then, overcome with sudden horror, turned and ran, nor did I stop until I had reached the wall and clambered over into the lane. Here the first thing my eyes lighted on was Sir Hector's horse and himself seated beside it, snuff-box in hand.

'Well, Adam,' says he, beckoning me to approach, 'we have contrived to thrust our devil deep into hell, betwixt us. Now long may he bide there, until his own turn be come.'

"'Tis – 'tis you,' I stammered, 'surely – surely 'tis you are the devil and no man!'

'Hum!' quoth Sir Hector, taking his pinch of snuff, 'Art a strange, something – audacious lad, I'm thinking, Adam, for now might I shoot ye for rebel and earn twenty guineas for the doing of't. And yet canst keep bold tongue in shivering, coward body, so I'll leave the money to be earned by the first red-coat that spies ye.'

'I mean to yield myself up as soon as maybe,' said I.

'A happy thought, boy, unless, being soldiers, they shoot ye first and inquire after.'

Thus in a moment Sir Hector renewed all my fears, so that I stood drooping before him, the very picture (I nothing doubt) of abject despair.

'You – you think they'll – kill me, sir, on sight?'

''Tis most likely!' he nodded, tapping his snuff-box and surveying me thoughtfully. 'And you are afraid to die, boy?'

'Yes, sir,' I answered, 'O yes, indeed—'

'Ay, to be sure, you are young – and yet – not too young!' says he, still eyeing me with the same musing expression. ''Twould be an admirable stroke – and you might serve! A nameless foundling! Ay, you might serve to a marvel—'

'Not to die, sir?'

'Why, no,' he answered, 'no, not yet awhile – if you will be guided by me, boy.'

'Sir – sir, what do you mean?'

'I'll bring ye where you may lie safe. Come!' So saying, he fobbed his snuff-box and rose.

'But how if the soldiers meet us?'

'None shall dare touch my prisoner.'

Then he mounted and rode slowly down the lane; and, because I hated and feared him less than death, I followed whither he led.

CHAPTER 10

GIVETH SOME DESCRIPTION OF A MACGREGOR

EVENING was upon us as we came in sight of a small, desolate inn standing upon that lonely coast road which shall bring the traveller to the little hamlet of Seaford. A remote house this, perched hard beside the pebbly foreshore that stretched, bleak and deserted, away to the vague white cliffs beyond the Cuckmere, and nothing of life to be seen or heard save the gulls, that wheeled against darkening sky, uttering their harsh and dismal cries. As we approached I saw this inn was very solid-built, with narrow casements and stout, deep-set door above whose lowering arch swung a battered sign-board whereon I made out :

THE MARINER'S JOY.
B. VENUS.

Reaching this door, Sir Hector dismounted and knocked, whistling, as he did so, a merry, lilting air I instantly recognized, and drew back from him, wondering, and very shocked that he should thus whistle the air of that fugitive gentleman, Mr McLeod.

All at once the door opened, and a square, sailorly man appeared, who instantly made a leg and butted his head at Sir Hector in salutation.

'Why, be this yourself, Mr Weir?' said he hoarsely, 'Step in, sir, step in an' welcome – though, to be sure Cap'n Sharkey be gone, sir—'

'Ha, gone?' exclaimed Sir Hector, frowning. 'D'ye tell me Sharkey Nye is gone?'

'Ay, sir, 'e be, arl along o' they Preventives, dang 'em ! Slipped 'is cable hours agone, sir, being so obleeged d'ye see – Ay, Sharkey's away, sir, but – she ain't !'

'Why, very well, Ben. You may lay supper above for this gentleman at once.'

'But soap and water first, sir,' I pleaded, whereupon they brought me where I might wash and brush me, the which I did as thoroughly as I might, and to my great refreshment. Then, bidding me follow, Sir Hector led the way up an exceeding narrow pair of stairs (like one well used to the place) and brought me into a small yet cosy chamber with the picture of a grim-faced lady upon one panelled wall, and a prodigious wide chimney where burned a small fire.

And now what with the warmth of this room, the security of roof and walls after my so many terrors and wanderings, I became all at once so oppressed by fatigue that I sank into the chair Sir Hector indicated and mighty thankful.

'Boy,' says he, 'I must leave you awhile yet first must we find a name for you something better sorted to your gallantry o' garments, than Adam Thursday, such name might damn the boldest ruffler or the most gallant hero, and thou'rt neither, my poor boy.'

'No, sir,' I answered drowsily.

'No,' says he, stroking his chin thoughtfully. 'Faith there's nothing heroical about you, Adam, so what you lack to the eye we must make up to the ear, yourself being somewhat small and meek, we must fit you with name like a clarion-blast.'

'As you will, sir,' I murmured, blinking sleepily whiles he looked down on me, clicking white teeth with thumb-nail, profoundly musing.

'Bellenger?' said he at last. 'No! Bellcaster? – Hum! Bellcaston-borough? Ha, this should serve. My lord Bell-castonborough – a sonorous mouthful rolling upon the tongue – 'tis very well—'

'But, sir,' says I, struggling against my drowsiness, 'why must I be a lord? I am no fine gentleman.'

'Therefore you should make a right excellent lord.'

'Nay,' says I, uneasily, 'how may I play such part, sir?'

'By being thyself, oaf. Your lord may be meek or arrogant, fool or rogue, the crass world shall fawn upon his title – so be yourself, Adam. And now I'll away, sup meanwhile and bide here until I return.'

'And what then, sir? What will you with me?'

'Save ye from the soldiers, fool – if you obey! And so, for a short while, farewell, my lord Bellcastonborough.' Then downstairs he jingled, and I heard his voice beneath the open casement, the clatter of his horse's hoofs, that broke into a gallop and died rapidly away.

Now, being too weary to trouble for myself, the present or future, I lay back in the chair watching the flickering fire until my eyes closed, and I was upon the brink of slumber when, feeling a touch, I glanced up to see the landlord, Ben, butting at me with his bullet head and touching hoary eyebrow at almost every word.

'Supper, if y'please, m'lord, an' the best we can do, m'lord. If your lordship lacks for aught ha' the kindness to stamp on the floor, m'lord.'

So, having thanked him, I drew to the table and a goodly supper it proved, noble beef and nappy ale, such as had seldom or never come my way, whereof I ate and drank like the famished creature I was, until, finding the pistol irked me, I unbuttoned silken waistcoat and laid the useless weapon by. At length, my bodily needs satisfied, I turned back to the comfort of the fire. Sitting thus, my drowsy glance came upon the battered picture on the opposite wall, the portrait of a grim, fierce-eyed, sharp-nosed lady in ruff and farthingale, and I wondered idly who she might be and, so wondering, slipped gently into slumber.

How long I slept I know not, but this sharp-nosed lady somehow got into my dreams, I thought she was leaning out from canvas and frame to peer at me angrily with her fierce eyes, insomuch that I awoke, and, glancing towards this picture, caught my breath and stared (and no wonder) for, by some magic, the sharp-nosed lady had become marvellously transfigured, glorious with youth and vivid beauty – deep eyes gazing at me beneath low, sweet-curving brows, and set in an oval face whose delicate pallor was off-set by ruddy, full-lipped mouth; a young face, indeed, and yet in these wide eyes and the wistful droop of vivid, generous mouth, I thought to read trouble.

'Sir, is it yourself will help one sore dismayed?'

A voice, soft yet wonderfully clear, such as I had never heard. Mute and unmoving I stared, half fearing she might vanish even while she thus gazed back at me, then I rose, mumbling I know not what.

'I fear I startled you,' said she, and stepping down lightly into the room discovered a narrow opening in the wall over which she slid the picture. 'Sir, you behold one in sorry, woeful pickle!' says she with strange, pretty gravity, and advanced to the hearth; and now (to my further discomfiture) I saw that, despite my high heels, she topped me by fully an inch.

'Sir,' says she again, viewing me with her grave, beautiful eyes, 'myself, I am here to meet wi' one – a gentleman I hae never seen – I am wondering if you are he?'

'No – alas, no, madam!' I stammered.

'My grief!' she sighed. 'Then am I still lost and so far frae my bonny Scotland!' Here she turned to glance down sadly into the fire whiles I stared at her, the proud poise of her head with its glossy hair (for hat she wore none), her close-fitting, travel-stained velvet habit that clung about her shapeliness as though it loved her, the elegant riding-boots, so pitifully mired and worn; from these, my glance stole up to her face, again to see her regarding me sideways and watchful.

'Yourself will tell me you are a fugitive Jacobite, sir?' she questioned.

'Why, madam, I – I – indeed—'

'O, nay, nay,' said she, a little disdainfully, 'Keep your ain counsel then, sir – though ye need nae fear to trust me, I am Barbara MacGregor and my race is royal!' Here she threw back her head and looked at me with air so proud and stately that I stood abashed.

'Indeed I – do trust you' I stammered : 'I would trust you with my life, I think – yes, I am a fugitive also.'

'But an Englishman, I think, sir?'

'Yes, madam.'

'A'weel, whatever o't, sir, God made English as well as Scots, they tell me.' Here she smiled suddenly, and was as suddenly grave again. 'Are ye from Preston fight, sir?'

'No,' I answered, wishing I might have said 'yes'.

'An ill day for "The Cause" sir, yon – a sad, black day for King James, forbye there are many brave gentlemen died there – chiefly MacGregors. Indeed we MacGregors are children o' Misfortune, people o' the mist and mountains, pain and sorrow is our portion, alas for Clan Alpine! Howandever, sir, hae ye chanced o' late to hear word of an English gentleman by name Eustace Ancaster?'

Now at this sudden question I turned and stared into the fire.

'Is he the – the friend, the gentleman you would meet here?' I inquired.

'The same, sir.'

'And you have never seen him?'

'Never, 'tis this makes my situation so—' she stopped and glanced quickly towards the open lattice, for upon the road was sound of hoof-beats coming at wild gallop, and then Sir Hector's voice rang loud and imperious :

'Oho, house – house ho !'

'O God o' Grace !' exclaimed Mistress Barbara, and turned towards the secret panel, but espying my pistol on the table, caught it up and stood with it tight grasped, staring towards the casement with eyes very bright and fierce.

'Lady do not fear—' I began.

'Sir,' she answered proudly, 'a MacGregor never fears ! But there is evil out yon – a very fiend.'

'Indeed,' I nodded, ''tis Sir Hector—'

'MacFarlane !' she whispered. 'And for us he means prison – death belike. Yet I would not have his blood on my hands – I'm sweir to use this pistol on him – open the panel, sir.'

My hand was on it or ever she spoke, but try how I would it refused to budge, whereupon she came to help only to find her efforts equally vain, the panel stood fast.

'Indeed, then it must be the pistol!' said she, and crossing swiftly to the window, crouched there to peer forth, and thither also went I and beheld Sir Hector dismounted, in close talk with the landlord; then, all at once, he glanced up and beholding my companion, swept off his hat with a flourish, whereupon she instantly levelled the pistol at him across the window-sill.

'Away, Hector Keith MacFarlane!' said she, her voice low, yet mighty determined; 'Away, sir, or die for the traitor you are!'

'Nay, sweet Barbara, do not shoot me,' he answered lightly. 'You'd burn powder to your own danger, for yonder come the soldiers! Hark to 'em, child; but for me you are lost and his lordship also!' And sure enough upon the dusk rose a sound distant yet very dreadful to hear, the muffled tramp of oncoming, marching feet. Instinctively I shrank back into the room, and, sinking upon a chair, covered my face, overwhelmed anew with fear of capture and most ghastly death.

I was conscious of excited voices below stairs, a quick, masterful tread, and Sir Hector stood before us.

'So then you've met? You've found each other?' says he glancing from the lady to me and back again. 'Faith 'tis excellent well! And on my life, Barbara, thou'rt grown more beautiful even with this last year. E'gad the world is threatened with another lovely woman!'

'Threatened, sir?'

'Faith, yes, Bab, thou'lt bring bitter strife 'twixt man and man yet, lass. Ye promise marvellous well – I marvel Tearlach could bear to part wi' ye!'

'My father himself couldna' come, sir, as ye ken unco' well, so I marched wi' the clans in his stead.'

'Ay, you were at Solway Moss, I think.'

'And Preston, sir.'

'A braw, wild, bonny maid!' said he. 'But forgive me, Barbara – and yet I presume you will know this young gentleman who honours us with his presence?'

'Not I, sir.'

'Then suffer me to present the justly notorious, or I should rather say, celebrated Lord Bellcastonborough, the hero of divers desperate affrays.'

Hereupon, seeing the lady looking at me, I flushed and rose (feeling myself most shameful fool) and bowed as well as I might, while she favoured me with profound and gracious curtsy.

'My lord Bellcastonborough hath himself endured much for The Cause,' said Sir Hector, seeing I stood before her mumchance, abashed and with head shamefully bowed.

'And himself so young !' sighed she, gently. 'I honour you the more, my lord.'

'Nay, madam,' I began, 'I – I indeed – I—' here, as I thus pitifully floundered, Sir Hector came to my rescue, his strangely beautiful voice seeming, to my ears, full of hateful mockery.

'Indeed, Barbara, his lordship's cruel sufferings should win the kind sympathy of anyone – especially a woman. But now, of yourself, Bab, you were unwise to adventure so far south o' the Border.'

'I gang where I will, sir !'

'Ay, a wilful maid ever, I mind. 'Twas to meet young Ancaster ye came hither, I think ?'

'Enough, sir !' she answered in sudden anger. 'Call up your soldiers, Hector MacFarlane that names yoursel' Keith and Weir to your so vile purposes; you that are Scot that all true Scots cry shame on; you that are traitor to your King, call in your English soldiers and ha' done !'

Sir Hector laughed, and when he spoke his voice was mocking :

'Softly, Bab ! Curb your pretty tongue, sweet shrew, bewitching besom, for my wing is over thee, rebel though thou art, the soldiers shall not harm thee, Barbara.'

'And I tell ye, Hector, I had rather be taken than owe my liberty to the Macfarlane ! So call your soldiers, sir.'

'Nay, they are coming, child, yet are you safe. For though your father is my avowed and most bitter enemy – or one of them, I do not war with maids, Bab. Indeed, you are safe with me. Nay, my lord, keep from the casement, I beg, the soldiers cannot reach here yet awhile! – Barbara, was't not your father's set purpose to wed ye with young Eustace Ancaster? Come, answer me, Bab, for we were unco' loving friends once, thou and I, lang years syne when you were a wee bit lass and I – young and full of hope and faith in my fellows – 'twas Tearlach's will to mate ye with young Ancaster?'

'Ay, 'twas my father's will, Hector.'

'Yet, never having seen this gilded youth, you could not love him, Barbara?'

'Sir 'twas my father's will.'

'Ay!' he nodded, 'Tearlach was aye a tyrant! And the Ancasters, save one, are a thrice-accursed brood, and to mingle thy sweet blood wi' theirs – 'twere desecration! Well, this have I saved ye from, child, for Eustace Ancaster lies dead.'

'Dead?' she repeated in awed tones, and then again: 'Dead? O, are you sure, Hector, sure?'

'Very sure!' he answered with complacent nod. 'I killed him this afternoon!'

'You – killed him!'

'Happily!' answered Sir Hector with his gentle smile. 'But shalt not lack for spouse, sweet Bab, and one far worthier than he – how say you to this noble gentleman, my lord Bellcastonborough?'

At this she stared from him to me, then frowned disdainfully, and I saw her cheek aflame with painful colour; as for me I stood dumb with stark amaze.

'Devil!' cried a voice that, wondering, I knew for mine. 'Devil!' and then, as to the manner born, I clapped hand to sword, but as I drew it my wrist was caught in iron clutch that gripped until my hand unclenched and the sword fell clattering.

'Rash, my lord, most rash!' said he in gentle reproach and, stooping, picked up the weapon and put it into my hand. 'But your lordship is young, full of desperate, high spirit—'

'Devil!' I repeated, staring up into his eyes that now held

a demon of mockery. 'I am no lord as you are well aware, I am—'

'Tush, my lord!' said he serenely. 'Your extremity of caution is needless, here are none to betray you; this is my lady Barbara MacGregor, brave as any man, more discreet than any woman, and with proud father who troubles for no man beneath a lord, so i'faith, my lord, what better escort should my lady have back to her father's hall but your lordship's noble and gallant self?'

'And, MacFarlane, outbye I hear your soldiers!' said she. 'Away to them, sir, and earn your blood money!'

At this, he glanced at her, frowning a little, and from her to me, where I stood listening to the tramp of the soldiers now so dreadfully loud and near.

'My lord' says Sir Hector with mocking bow, 'though the mere thought of wedlock with this lovely termagent, this surpassing shrew, frights you, 'twould seem, yet may you freely trust her. And now, would you stay trouble from her – keep her from yon lattice awhile.'

And so, with another smiling bow, he went from the room.

CHAPTER 11

DESCRIBETH OUR ESCAPE FROM THE SOLDIERS

SILENT and motionless stood I, struck to such panic by the terror of these relentless marching feet that I minded nothing in the world beside, until roused suddenly by my companion's voice.

'And who are you, my lord, who are ye to dare mistrust the honour of a MacGregor?' Glancing up at this, I saw her frowning at me in such anger as put me to great wonder how she should trouble over such small matter with death marching upon us so rapidly.

'Sir,' says she, head aloft, 'I'd hae ye know the honour of a MacGregor brooks nae such suspicion – in especial frae an

Englishman! Look at me, sir – here in my eyes, have I the seeming of one would betray any trust – have I?'

'No – no—' I quavered, still hearkening to that steady, on-coming tramp of feet.

'Then wherefore mistrust me? How dare you cast doubt—'

The words ended suddenly in a gasping sob as, sharp and loud from beneath the open window, rose a hoarse command and the ring and thunderous clatter of grounded muskets; at the which dreadful sounds she shrank back to the wall, staring at me wide-eyed, and trembling like the terri-fied girl she was.

'Death!' she whispered. 'O what must we do? Speak – speak sir, advise me—'

'There is Sir Hector,' I suggested.

'Nay, he is mocking fiend – we must help ourselves but how? What can we do?'

Now, beholding her sudden terror (and surely reason enough) perceiving how, in her loneliness, she reached out to me for counsel and aid, I stood mute, pitying her mightily that she had none better to serve her than this poor, fearful creature that was myself. And as I stood thus abashed, yearning bitterly for a man's strength and wisdom, she spoke again :

'Death is sic an awfu' thing – O, my lord, you'll help me?'

'Never doubt it!' I answered, staring at the sword in my shaking hand.

'Then, sir, be doing it!' said she breathlessly. 'Never stand there so heroic waiting for death – do somewhat – for, O, sir, I'm a woman hath no will to die – yet— Howandever they shall not take—'

But at this moment the door opened so suddenly that I dropped my sword, then in came the landlord swift and fur-tive :

'Quick, my lord and ma'm,' he whispered, 'tread soft an' quick it be!' So saying he crossed to the secret panel, whisked it open and slipped through, beckoning us after him, all in a moment. Swiftly we stepped up and into a small, box-like chamber, which was plunged into sudden darkness as he closed the panel after us, but in the darkness he grasped my arm.

'Mek fast to the lady, sir,' he whispered, whereupon I groped until my hand met and was fast clasped by another, a slim, cool hand, whose smooth touch so wrought upon me that for a moment I even forgot our so pressing danger.

Then, slowly and cautiously, we went forward in the pitchy dark, and I heard the landlord counting his steps in hoarse whisper :

'One – two – three – avast! Starboard it is. One – two – three – four – belay! Steps here, my lord an' ma'm, five on 'em and steady – O!' Carefully we descended these five steps, then halted while our guide struck flint and steel (the sparks leaping vivid upon the dark) until the tinder caught and our eyes were dazzled by the lanthorn he had lighted.

'Bide 'ere, my lord, and don't speak!' quoth he, 'But if you must talk, ma'm, bein' a lady, d'ye see – why do it whispering.'

'You'll leave us the lanthorn?' she whispered.

'Sure-ly ma'm. An' I'll come back s'soon's the coast be clear o' they lobsters.' And away he went.

We stood in small, panelled chamber with table, chair and a rough couch or day-bed, whereupon she sank wearily and with head adroop; thus I was able to remark the dusky splendour of her hair, that yet glowed ruddily where the light caught it.

'Does yourself know Scotland, my lord?' said she suddenly.

'No, madam.'

''Tis a land o' mist and mountain, of windy straths and sobbing burns – 'tis a land o' sorrow and grief for us Mac-Gregor's – and yet the only land whatever – 'tis there I would die an' I must – And here is your lordship's pistol!' And she held it out to me; so I took the thing and dropped it into my pocket.

'There be friends o' mine – brave gentlemen – dead – in London, and now – myself! O, my lord! To die – by the axe—'

'But surely, surely they would not kill you – a woman!'

'And why for no, sir? They have killed other women so, ere now.'

'But, O, not you – not you!' I whispered passionate with terror.

'Maybe not, my lord, maybe not, yet I have my dubieties, and 'tis this troubles me.'

'But Sir Hector promised—'

'Hector!' says she, in hissing, scornful whisper. 'And yet he was honourable once – afore he went abroad, a brave and noble gentleman. I knew him passing well, for I was but a child, my lord, and children know whom they may trust by instinct. But yourself, my lord, have ye no doubts of him, no fears for yoursel'?'

'No!' I answered, and truly enough, for my thoughts just then were all of her, and how I might undeceive her in regard to myself, for each time she named me 'lord' I burned with a guilty shame. And presently she begins again :

'My lord,' says she, but there I stopped her :

'Lady,' says I (and mighty awkward), Lady, I – I would confess – I would have you know that I – I am no lord—'

'How, sir?' she whispered, and contriving somehow to do it very fiercely, 'will yourself dare deny me your name? Do you doubt me yet? Would your lordship affront me? Is it that you—?'

'No, no, madame – no, indeed! Never think it. I – I would but have you know me what I truly am, a poor—'

'Sir, sir, well do I ken a man's name may bring his head 'neath the axe these days, but you may trust myself that is a MacGregor—'

'I do, lady, indeed, indeed I do. I would trust you with – with my life, 'tis all I have! But I would not have you deceived by lies, or wear a rank not my own. Why will you not believe I am no lord?'

' 'Tis yourself contradicts it, sir – your air, voice, speech – my lord, I have eyes and ears and a MacGregor canna be deceived.'

'But, indeed, I am no more than—'

'Enough, sir! Yourself and concerns are naught to me.'

'But think, madam, think! Sir Hector made some mention of – of marriage – 'tis some trick of his, some evil.'

'Marriage, sir – marriage wi' Barbara MacGregor – O and is it this that dreads ye, indeed?' Here she laughed so disdainful and loud that I glanced about apprehensively.

'Hush, madam – no, no, 'tis that I would not have you tricked into belief I am a great gentleman, for truly I have neither name nor—'

'And d'ye think myself would take and wed wi' any man at the bidding o' Hector MacFarlane, sir—'

'But he is so guileful, madam, so full o' ploys and devilish stratagems, and you, madam – and I—'

'Are an unco' poor liar, my lord, I'm thinking. How and ever, my lord Bell – Bellcaston—'

''Tis not my name, lady.'

'Whatever o't, sir, I'll no wed ye, sae dinna fash.'

'But, madam—'

'I repeat, my lord, I will not marry you – no, not even for Hector MacFarlane, so have no fear, sir.'

'Lady, if only you—'

'My lord, be so obliging as to hold your tongue.'

Perforce, at this I sat silent, staring at the lanthorn in a very maze of wondering speculation; and presently comes this thought, viz, could it indeed be true that I had the seeming of a gentleman, to thus easily deceive (and so unwillingly) this poor lady? Here, turning to glance at her, I found her regarding me, white chin in white fist.

'Indeed, my lord, your lordship is no a verra aged lord, I'll be thinking?'

'No, madam.'

'What age might your lordship be, my lord?'

'My age?' I repeated, hesitating, 'I – I am – twenty-two, madam.'

'And yoon's another lee, my lord!' she nodded; whereupon, feeling my cheeks flush, I turned and frowned at the lanthorn.

'The MacGregors would seem hard o' belief!' said I.

'Verra true, sir, as I tell ye, the MacGregors be unco' hard to deceive – And pray, my lord, what hath your lordship done wi' your lordship's sword?'

'Sword?' I repeated, clapping my hand to empty scabbard. 'I must have left it behind.'

'Then 'tis as well I brought your lordship's pistol.'

'I am called Adam!' said I.

'Adam,' she repeated, and methought she spoke it marvellous prettily. 'Indeed, sir, I wadnae take sic liberty to ca' your lordship in fashion sae familiar – forby 'tis no a pretty name.'

'No!' sighed I, 'No, indeed, madam.'

'And yet 'tis no sic an ill name.'

After this we were silent so long that, little by little, I became aware of vague noises all about us, of footsteps that came and went, the creak of boards, voices muffled beyond recognition, and divers other indefinable sounds, and of these (most persistent yet most furtive) a soft noise that was not a scrape nor rustle, and yet something of each, that seemed to creep to and fro on the panelling behind us, so that I turned involuntarily to look thither.

'O, d'ye hear it?' whispered my lady.

'I'm wondering – what it may be.'

'Hands!' says she, rising and clasping my arm suddenly. 'O, my lord – 'tis hands fumbling – fumbling, and for why, think you?'

Wondering and fearful I rose, but in that moment my terrors were whelmed in strange, sweet pleasure, to feel her soft body pressed close to mine, her fragrant breath upon my cheek; thus stood I in ecstasy unknown and all undreamed 'till now.

'Art – afraid?' she breathed.

'No!'

'Yet you – tremble.'

'Not with fear!' I answered, and in that moment swung her behind me, yet one arm about her still, as my eyes were dazzled by sudden line of light that widened, all at once, to a gleaming square blotted out as suddenly by a man's bewigged head and shoulders.

66

'Are you there, my lord – and my lady, too?' said Sir Hector's mocking voice, 'Well, you may come forth, the soldiers are gone.'

CHAPTER 12

GIVETH SOME DESCRIPTION OF A WEDDING

'COLD beef and a sallet,' said Sir Hector, shaking his head, 'is not a very sumptious meal, I fear, but 'tis the best this place affords; be seated, Barbara.' And, having bowed the lady to a chair, he turned to me with very humble obeisance. 'My lord,' says he, 'permit me to return your sword, 'tis blade you have used with deadly effect ere now, and I had rather see in its scabbard than your fist!' And he proffered me the weapon with another elaborate bow; but, stung by his cruel mockery, I folded my arms and stared up at him in anger too deep for any words.

Now, as we thus fronted each other, the sneering smile faded on his lip, his slender brows slowly knit themselves above eyes that widened suddenly and were as swiftly hidden beneath quick-drooping lids, and he passed a hand across his brow with a strangely weary gesture.

'Sirs, sirs,' cried Mistress Barbara, 'I'll hae ye ken I'm unco' hungry! And Hector, if I'm to be your prisoner I'll comport mysel' wi' better grace – after supper.'

'Spoke like a true MacGregor!' smiled Sir Hector. 'Faith, Bab, your spirit matches your face, and that's handsome enough – eh, my lord? 'Twill be thrice happy man woos and wins her – eh, my lord? Be seated, sir, I beg, and, since you have supped, join us in a bottle.'

'Thank you – no!' I answered, and turned to the door.

'Nay, do not deprive us o' your company, my lord' says he, carving the beef. 'Indeed, I fear you cannot, yon door is locked and the key in my pocket. Ha, you frown, my lord, and glance at your sword? Pray use no violence, sir; curb your natural ferocity, I beg. This room is too strait for sword-play, and we might harm Barbara, which would grieve us both, so command your proud spirit, I beg.'

'Sir,' cried I, a little wildly, 'what mockery is this? I am no lord, as you are well aware. I am no fine gentleman but only a very humble, poor person without kith or kin – or even a name – one who, till late, slaved for his livelihood at the desk of – of a—'

But here, glancing from his fleering eyes to Barbara Mac-Gregor's disdainful face, I faltered, stopped and, sinking into a chair, stared gloomily at the floor, while Sir Hector spoke in tones of awed admiration :

'Is he not an actor born, Bab? But for his eagle face, his high and noble air, he might perchance deceive even me! O my lord, my lord!' he smiled, shaking a finger at me, 'why keep up this pretence? I ken you well enough, and if you still doubt this lady—'

'I don't!' said I, hopelessly. 'I would but have her know—'

''Tis true she is a woman,' he continued smoothly, ''tis true she is young, and that women will talk! But Barbara MacGregor would scorn to betray you – and she as great a rebel as yourself! Faith, my lord, your doubt of her discredits both your head and heart, and wounds my lady sensibly, I fear. So come, my lord Bellcastonborough, I beseech you ha' done with all pretence—'

'O enough, Hector!' says the lady, her look more disdainful than ever. 'Never plead with him, sir, 'tis nothing to me that his lordship doubts Barbara MacGregor's faith.'

'I never did – I never shall!' cried I, passionately. ''Tis but that I would not have this man deceive you.'

'And whyfore should he, sir? How shall it advantage him?'

'Ay, how indeed?' murmured Sir Hector.

'As for yourself, my lord,' said she, turning her back upon me, 'who you are and what you are is naught to me!'

'Nay, Barbara, nay,' said Sir Hector, gently, 'his lordship's stubborn reticence is very natural, he is young, his life in deadly peril—'

''Tis no cause for doubting me, sir – and myself a Mac-
Gregor!'

'Furthermore, Bab, 'tis said he hath an iron will, proof
'gainst the blandishments o' beauty! And though my
prisoner – even as you, Barbara, yet is he of a proud, indomitable spirit very instant in quarrel, ready to kiss a
bonny lass as he is to fight. There be many gentle hearts
agrieving, and bright eyes dimmed for him by all accounts –
O youth, youth! And yet to one of such proud lineage and
vast possessions much may be forgiven.'

Mumchance sat I (since it seemed all denials were vain)
filled with an ever-growing wonder at these purposeless lies,
and hot with shame and anger.

''Tis little I thought,' said Mistress Barbara suddenly,
'that I should break bread again with the MacFarlane!'

'And yet thou hast many a time ere now, Bab.'

'True, sir, but the world was younger then, and yourself
a noble gentleman, proud of your honourable name.'

'There is that I hold dearer, child!' says he, with that
same weary gesture of hand across haggard brow. ''Tis this
I have lived for and am content to die for—'

'Prithee what – Hector MacFarlane, tell me!'

'The memory of an angel, –' he answered, his beautiful
voice very sweetly soft and reverent, 'or – the haunting of a
devil!' and he laughed harshly. 'But thou wert a dainty wee
thing in those days, Bab! D'ye mind how I would ride thee
on my shoulder, and thou, for very joy, kicking they bonny
wee legs—'

'Ha' done, sir, ye're forgettin' his lordship o' Bellcastonborough!'

'We were mighty good friends in those days, Bab!'

'Ay, but ye're no the man ye were, Hector. You have
come back from your so long journeyings abroad very sadly
changed, sir. Your very name a bye-word and reproach!
Your traitor foot may no pass the Border—'

'Yet in a month I shall be in Scotland, Barbara – ay, a
month or less.'

'Then 'tis myself thinks you'll no leave it again.'

69

'You mean they'll kill me?'

'And what for no?' she demanded fiercely. 'Are ye no a renegade Hanoverian? O fie for shame on ye! Hae ye no brought divers leal gentlemen tae their deaths?'

'Merely one as yet, Bab – but I have hopes.'

'Why, then, Hector MacFarlane, failing others myself would shoot ye!'

'And upon a time thou wouldst name me "dear Hector" and "bonny cousin"!'

'But now I do name you traitor, sir, and shall do so long as I draw breath!'

'But then—' he sighed, leaning towards her across the table and viewing her with eyes suddenly narrowed, 'alas, you may not live to draw breath very long—'

At this I saw her shrink a little, and her white hands clasp each other, but her eyes never wavered.

'My life is in God's hands, Hector MacFarlane!'

'And mine, Bab!' said he, glancing down at his slim, cruel-looking fingers. 'And mine!' he repeated.

'And what will ye do wi' it?' she questioned a little breathlessly.

'This depends, Mistress Barbara, this all depends.'

'On – what, sir?'

'Yourself, madam.'

Now here, reading some evil in his look, she flushed suddenly, though her eyes met his steadfast ever.

'Well,' says she softly, 'what must I do?'

'Wed his lordship here.'

At this ensued a stillness so absolute that I heard the soft, small murmur of the flickering logs on the hearth.

'Wed—,' said she at last. 'Wed?'

'Become my lady Bellcastonborough – become the proud wife of an English peer who hath risked life, fortune and estates for James. Wed him and you and your noble husband go free.'

And then I was on my feet, had snatched my sword and turned upon him, but in that same moment she laughed, peal on peal, and, knowing myself the poor subject of her merriment, I dropped the sword, and, bowing my head, stood trembling between anger and burning shame until her laughter was done and we silent all three.

'And why?' she demanded. 'Why for would you have me do such wild and woeful thing? Myself that scorns wedlock and would live free – wherefore would ye have me married?'

'Because I am the MacFarlane,' he answered gravely.

'Well, sir, I am Barbara MacGregor, to wed at no man's bidding – in especial yours. So do what you will, sir, do what you will, here's an end o' the matter.'

'Nay, 'tis rather the beginning,' he answered in the same solemn manner. 'An ill beginning for you, madam, but a far worse for his lordship.'

'How – how, sir – how worse?'

'A prison for you, my lady, but for him the noose, the axe, the quartering-block!'

Now here, bethinking me of the ghastly, shameful death all traitors must endure, the hanging, dismemberment and obscene, grisly butchery of it all, I cowered in my chair, sick to faintness. My head above Temple Bar! My body chopped and hewn asunder—!

'Indeed, 'tis not a pretty death, my lord!' sighed Sir Hector, tapping my bowed shoulder gently, 'and you are over young to die in such evil fashion – howbeit your fate is in Mistress Barbara's pretty hands—'

'O, but ye're an evil thing, MacFarlane!' she whispered fiercely.

'You to a dungeon, my poor Bab, and he to the block, unhappy youth! 'Tis for you to choose.'

'No!'she cried wildly. 'No – I winna!'

'I think you will,' he answered gently.

'And how – how if I refuse?'

'This!' he answered and drew from his bosom a small, silver whistle. 'One blast on this, madam, and the soldiers will be upon ye, my poor children.'

'The soldiers?' she gasped. 'So you lied to me? Ye said they were gone!'

'All save five, madam. Must I sound for them?'

'No!' cried I, and whipping the forgotten pistol from my pocket I levelled it full at his smiling mouth – a mouth that smiled yet, though his eyes narrowed to sudden, shining slits. 'Give me that whistle!' said I.

'Indeed t'would seem I must!' said he with rueful laugh. 'Take it, my lord, and – ha, you're too late – see!' and he nodded to the door behind me. Instinctively I glanced thither, and, in that instant the pistol was twisted from my grasp – a jagged flame shot athwart my vision and, clapping hand to wounded head, I staggered and fell, to lie half stunned. Vaguely I was conscious of voices, the shock of cold water and, opening unwilling eyes, saw Mistress Barbara leaning over me, her eyes marvellous compassionate and in the touch of her hands that ineffable comfort of motherly tenderness my sordid life had never known.

'O hath yon devil hurt thee, my lord?'

'My name – is Adam!'

'Art hurt, Adam?' And now the kindness I read in her eyes and felt in the touch of her hands, was in her voice also.

' 'Tis only my head—'

'Then sup this, Adam! Come drink, 'twill hearten you.'

So I drank obediently what she proffered, and immediately fell a-gasping, for the potent spirit well-nigh choked me. And when, at length, I got my breath, she bowed her head above me, lower yet.

'O, sir, sir – O, Adam,' says she in strange voice between laughter and tears, 'I hae said yes – ye're too young to die in sic awfu' fashion – and so I – hae given him "yes"! There is no ilka way, my lord – indeed, I couldna' thole the soldiers, sir, myself to prison, Adam, and you to a death sae ghastly! So we maun obey him, sir! O, Adam, can ye no stand up—?'

And so, with her to aid me, I contrived to get to my feet, and made shift to support myself by a chair back, but the floor swayed dizzily beneath my feet and my sight was dim – and my head throbbed. Presently I was aware of a red-faced man with rich, throaty voice, of Mistress Barbara's cool, slim hand in mine, of uttering such words as the red-

faced man commanded, of fumbling with a ring and thereafter sitting in a chair, my aching head bowed upon breast.
Then gentle hands removed my heavy, stifling peruke, to
cherish me with blessedly cool water so that, after some
while, my spirits thus refreshed, I glanced up to see Mistress
Barbara's handsome face very near my own, and she being
wholly intent on her ministrations, I took occasion to observe her more nearly; the round chin, full, yet determined
mouth, the sensitive nostrils, grave grey eyes with their
lashes so much darker than her hair—

'You—you are better, sir?' she enquired.

'Thank you, yes, madam! But what—what has chanced—?'

'Alas, my lord, they – they have married us.'

'Then, madam – God help you !'

'Amen, my lord – belike He will !'

'And are you my – my – wife, madam?'

'Indeed, my lord, I fear so.'

'Then shall I – may I call you – Barbara?'

' 'Tis as your lordship wills.'

'Well, then,' said I in sudden heat, 'do pray call me
Adam !'

'Vera weel, Adam. And is your head better?'

'Thanks to – to you – Barbara,' said I reaching for my
periwig, and thus, beheld Sir Hector staring down at me,
his haggard face strangely altered, for his wide eyes seemed
vacant and his sneering mouth grim. And then spoke Barbara, bitter and disdainful :

'A'weel, MacFarlane, you've had your wicked way wi' us,
and now what?'

'Red hair !' said he in strange, musing tone. 'Your husband's hair is unco' red, Barbara !'

'And red, sir,' said I, 'they name a fighting colour. Pray
heaven I may prove it so one day – to you, Sir Hector.'

'And now,' says my lady, pointing towards the door, 'if
there be any honour yet in ye, Hector, you'll prove your
words and let us go.'

'This moment, Bab !' he answered, and tugged at the bell
rope.

CHAPTER 13

IN due season was a thud of heavy boots upon the stair, a
loud double knock, whereat Sir Hector opened the door and
there entered a great, swaggering, loose-lipped, bold-eyed
fellow, and yet with a something furtive air about him none
the less, so that a very bloodthirsty, piratical rascal I deemed
him as he stood swaying a little and leering at Barbara's disdainful loveliness.

'Are you Sam Oliver?' enquired Sir Hector, 'Captain of
the *Sussex Lass*?'

'Which I wunt deny,' answered the fellow, still watching
Barbara.

'Are you ready for sea?'

'Which no I ain't!'

'Ah, and pray why not?'

'Which the tide doan't nowise sarve for one thing and for
another—'

Sir Hector picked up a pewter mug (that being nearest)
and threw it at the speaker's head.

'My animal,' said he gently, 'say "sir" when you address
me. Now, are you ready for sea?'

'No, I ain't – sir!' growled the fellow, and rubbing at the
arm wherewith he had fended the missile, 'Ye see, sir, the
tide doan't sarve, your honour, and consequently—'

'My lying rogue,' quoth Sir Hector, frowning, 'the tide
will be at flood in half an hour, and you will sail just so
soon as this lady and gentleman are aboard.'

'Which sail I would, sir, ah, an' willing only—'

Sir Hector reached for a platter, whereat the man flinched
behind up-thrown arm:

'Avast, sir, avast!' he cried. 'Your honour don't give a
pore mariner a chance for no word nor nowt – ye see, sir—'

'And the lady and gentleman are coming aboard at once,

74

reptile, so lead the way!' So saying, Sir Hector took up Barbara's cloak and folded it about her.

For a moment the fellow still hesitated, but, meeting the speaker's wide stare, he turned sullenly and stumped on before us, muttering hoarsely as he went.

At the door of the Mariner's Joy stood the landlord, Master Venus, to bid us a very hearty God speed and fair wind and who, touching me furtively, contrived to whisper.

''Ware, my lord! Watch yon Oliver an' keep your poppers ready!'

The moon was rising and her pale beam made a glory on the sea whereby (despite the blinding pain of my head) I contrived to make out the loom of a fair-sized vessel close in shore and with no blink of light aboard her, alow or aloft.

Now as we came opposite this vessel, there met us five men, rough-looking fellows who, at signal from Oliver, halted within a yard of us, wherefore we halted likewise.

'Well now?' cried Oliver, turning upon Sir Hector in sudden defiance, 'and who might you be as is so free wi' y'r orders?'

'One who'll jail ye for rascally smuggler if you disobey!'

'Smuggler? Wot me?' exclaimed Oliver fiercely. 'D'ye 'ear that, me lads? 'Tis a spy – ay, by the Ten Bones!'

Here went up a growl from his scowling fellows.

'Lads, 'tis a spy I tell ye!'

Here the five surged a little nearer.

'A spy lads, but us knows 'ow to use such vermin – eh? Well then stand by my lads and—'

A roar, a stab of sudden flame, and one of the five, uttering a shrill cry, sank upon the beach, clutching at wounded limb.

'Oliver,' said Sir Hector, gesturing towards the writhing man with smoking pistol, 'yon rogue's hurt should ha' been yours, but I need you to navigate. You have been chartered and paid by this lady to carry her to the coast o' Fife and the sooner you sail, the better for you – now, get aboard!'

'But – but, sir, – you du ha' made me short o' one o' my lads.'

'You'll be short of another if you aren't away in five minutes, rascal!'

'Which I be a-goin', sir, drackly-minute sure-ly, your honour. But wot o' pore Davy?'

'He shall be conveyed to the inn, so away with you, animal!'

Without more ado Oliver led where a boat lay, drawn upon the shingle, into which we clambered and were almost immediately afloat.

And now, as the men began to row, I must needs turn to look back where Sir Hector stood at the edge of the tide watching us (the wounded man behind him moaning and whimpering) and the moon bright upon him. Suddenly he laughed and flourished his pistol in airy salute.

'Ah, my lord,' he cried, 'if hair o' red be truly a fighting colour cut it long, for ye'll be needing it, I'm thinking! Fare thee well, Bab, until we meet again, and may Eros hover o'er thee!'

So came we aboard the lugger *Sussex Lass*, and when from her deck I turned to look back, it was to see Sir Hector MacFarlane still watching us from beyond the tide, the moon bright upon his haggard face, while with much tramping of feet and hauling of ropes, the sails were hoisted, the anchor hove, and we stood out from the land.

And surely no poor youth ever put to sea in greater amaze or more perturbation of mind than I.

CHAPTER 14

TELLS OF DIVERS HAPPENINGS ON BOARD
THE LUGGER *Sussex Lass* AND HOW WE
TOOK UP A MAN FROM THE SEA

HARDLY was the *Sussex Lass* under weigh when cometh the fellow Oliver and bidding us, civilly enough, to follow him, led us across the deck and down a narrow companion way or stair, short but steep-pitched, into a stuffy cabin; and

76

very dismal place I thought it, ill-lit by a reeking lamp that swung above a battered table flanked by lockers which served as seats; on the nearest of which I sank down forthwith, my head miserably athrob with pain.

'Here y'are,' quoth Oliver, 'though 'tis mebbe a bit rough-like for such a dainty piece as y'self, ma'm.'

'Indeed,' says she glancing about with much disfavour, 'it might be cleaner, but 'twill serve. You may go.'

'Eh, go, ma'm?' says he with evil grin.

'You heard me!'

'Oho,' says he, ''tis only Sam Oliver – smart Sam as gives orders aboard this craft, lady!' And now as he lolled upon the table so hatefully at his ease, I knew the fellow was drunk, and felt a sudden qualmish dread.

'Which, ye see, ma'm,' said he edging closer, 'it bean't nowise often as we stows aboard so much loveliness – and when we do, why then, ma'm, we knows—'

'Are you going?' says my lady, and to my wonder she leaned nearer towards that leering, so evil face. 'Are you going?' For a moment he was silent, only he breathed heavily through dilated nostrils – and now something in his eyes and drunk-flushed countenance sickened me and I shivered with abhorrence. Then, or ever I might interpose, he reached towards her a great, clutching hand but, in that moment, out from her cloak flashed a white fist, and he leapt back only just in time to avoid the glittering steel.

'Well – sink me!' he gasped.

'Would you dare touch me!' says my lady, creeping a slow pace nearer him. 'Go, lest you feel the black knife – Go!'

'Well – scuttle me!' he exclaimed, and having stood a moment to gape with dropped jaw, took himself away.

Then dropping that wicked looking knife to the table she sank down thereby, face hidden in her two hands.

'Make fast the door,' she whispered, 'for 'tis an evil beast – and now I – I am afraid!'

So, having bolted and secured the little door that opened above the companion, I sat down and fell to watching this strange wife of mine in silent wonder; and presently she looked up with a shiver :

'O, Adam,' she sighed, 'am I no the craven, for I canna thole the blink o' steel!' here she hid the knife beneath her cloak. 'And to shed a man's bluid—'

'God forbid!' I exclaimed.

'Amen, Adam! And yet 'tis sic an awfu' wicked man, yon Oliver.'

'He shall not harm you while I live, Barbara.'

' 'Tis great comfort for me to ken ye sic a desperate brave young man, Adam!' sighed she, regarding me with eyes very big and wistful.

'God send you be not mistaken in me!' said I fervently. But here, what with the throbbing agony of my head, together with all I had endured of late, both in mind and body, I sank forward across the table in a kind of vertigo and so lay 'twixt sleep and wake; yet in a while, because of her questioning, I opened my eyes and smiled up into her anxious face.

'I – must live up to my red hair!' said I, speaking my thought, 'I must – I will!' Then, pillowing head on arm, I fell asleep.

A troubled slumber haunted by vague terrors – but of a sudden fearful shapes were banished by a shaft of sun, in which glory stood an heroic figure whose lean, eagle features were lit by eyes wherein burned a dauntless fire of courage; at first methought this was Sir Hector marvellously transfigured, and then I cried in passion of joy to know this most heroical shape for none other than myself. Opening my eyes, I found indeed the sunshine all about me, a great, comforting beam, that poured down upon me through the open doorway to show me myself most unheroically outstretched upon the locker, coatless and without wig or boots and covered by Barbara's cloak, but herself nowhere to be seen. Whereupon up started I in sudden panic, when down the narrow companion she came with vision of slim ankles and pretty, light-treading feet for I saw to my wonder that she wore no boots.

78

'O thank Heaven!' she exclaimed at sight of me. 'Are you better, Adam?'

'Save for my hunger, I am very well,' I answered, wondering to see her so pale.

'Why then, Adam – hush! – 'tis my sure belief they do mean to murder us – or worse!'

'Murder us? Who – who – what?' I stammered.

'The ship is anchored, can ye no feel it?' she whispered. ''Tis so I found it when I woke – so I crept on deck wi-out my boots – and, O Adam – they're down in their cabin yonder – at breakfast and – contriving o' their wicked plans – and pistols every man! O Adam what maun we do?'

'Ay, what – what?' said I, desperately.

'Indeed, Adam, there is but one course for ye that I can see.'

'What – what can I do?'

'Why take your pistol to them – force them back to their duty. But, O Adam, dinna kill any mair o' them than ye can help—'

'But,—' says I.

'Disarm them, Adam, fright them wi' your pistol – where is't?'

Scarce knowing what I did, I reached the pocket of my coat and drew thence the broken weapon; then turned I to show her how it was a useless thing for any to trust his life to, but ere I might do so she sped up the steps whispering me to follow.

Out upon the deck there met us a wind sweet and fresh that heartened me somewhat and stirred my hair, for my wig I had left below with coat and boots. Swiftly and silently she led me along the deserted deck and, pausing suddenly, pointed to an open scuttle hard by the foremast.

'Down yon!' she breathed. 'Look!'

With infinite caution I crept forward till, reaching the mast, I leaned there a moment wellnigh overcome with a sick faintness.

'—I say as 'e ought to bring ye fifty guineas – ay, or more!' said Oliver's voice immediately below me.

'Not 'im, Sam, not 'im – theer ain't enough of 'im! No, share an' share be the word.'

'Hows'ever, the lady be mine—'

'No, no, Sam, share an' share!'

'I say she shall be mine! I'll tame 'er, one way or t'other and then—'

My trembling weakness was all forgot in raging horror and fury, a murderous fury unknown till then as, peering over the open scuttle, I beheld Oliver and his foul rogues eating and drinking about a littered table. And now as I leaned above them they talked in hushed voices and with evil, stifled laughter – they spoke of Barbara, and in such beastly fashion that, sickened and shamed, I rose, shrinking from their very vileness – and then, by some sudden trick of wind and wave, the vessel lurched suddenly and I tripped, tottered, clutched wildly to save myself, and pitched through the scuttle to fall crashing upon the table, scattering bowls and platters and all was wild confusion, fearful outcries, roaring shouts, a very pandemonium. But the pistol was yet in my grasp and rising to my knees, I fronted them; and now, my wild fury was tempered by cold anger that cast out all dread, stilled my quivering limbs and left my mind clear.

'Beasts – loathly dogs!' said I, menacing them with the broken pistol. And then seeing how they cowered and shrank I wondered how I could ever have feared such poor wretches, and despised them the more.

'Foul rogues, kneel down!' I commanded. 'Kneel and sue my lady's pardon!' But here she spoke, leaning close above me through the scuttle :

'Their pistols first, Adam! Take their pistols!'

This I did forthwith, the fellows handing me their weapons one by one readily enough, each of which I passed up to Barbara.

'And now,' says I, 'down on your knees, all of you, and—'

'Nay, my lord,' cried Barbara, 'command them rather to haste our breakfast, 'twill do us more good, I'm thinking.

And bid them be quick for O, I'm fair burning tae be shootin' one or two!' Now, glancing up I saw she held two pistols levelled through the scuttle.

'Which of you is cook?' I demanded of the shaking rogues.

'Well, Tom is, my lord,' answered Oliver in wheedling tones. 'Tom's cook, your honour, and a rare bad 'un 'e be! And, sir, if you'll be so kind to ax your lady to take 'er fingers off them triggers—'

'Tom, go and cook,' said I, 'and do your best.'

'Ay, ay, sir!' answered a small, plump man and, touching his forelock, vanished with a marvellous alacrity.

'And now, my lord,' says Oliver, mighty humble, 'if your honour's good lady will only be so obleeging to let them triggers alone—'

'Stand up, rogue!' said I, much emboldened by knowledge of those levelled weapons above me.

'Ay, ay, my lord!' says he, rising obediently.

'Oliver,' quoth I, 'we know you now for a very rogue ingrane!'

'Ay, ay, my lord!' says he, cheerily.

'So take warning – do but try any more villainy and, by heaven, I'll shoot you dead!'

'And sarve me right, my lord, I'm sure!' said he with a leering servility that made me hate him the more, 'But, sir, I ain't as black as—'

'Go up,' said I, 'on deck all of you and set this vessel on her course again.'

'Heartily, heartily, sir!' cried Oliver, making a leg; and away he went with his fellows, and I after them. Now, scarce had we reached the deck than, moved by a sudden suspicion, I thrust the muzzle of my pistol into Oliver's back and bid him stand, the which command he was instant to obey.

'What other arms have you aboard?' I demanded.

'Naught but a brace of cutlashes, your honour, or mebbe three, sir.'

'Bring me to them!' said I. For the moment he hesitated

then, seeing Barbara approach, and feeling my pistol in his ribs again, he led us forthwith to his berth, a noisome hole, and here the first thing my glance lighted on were two muskets in a rack which I, incontinent seized, and three or four cutlasses, which I bade him take up and so, back upon deck. Then having made him throw the swords overboard I watched (and Barbara beside me) while he and his fellows hauled ropes, trimmed sails and set the *Sussex Lass* upon her course again, which done I shouldered the muskets and followed Barbara down to our cabin. Here, having found the muskets primed and loaded, I hid them in one of the lockers convenient to hand. Then, I turned, to find my lady looking at me very strangely, for her eyes were marvellous bright and her red mouth all aquiver.

'O Adam,' said she, in sweet, soft voice; and, setting the pistols upon the table, reached out her two hands towards me. So I clasped these slim hands and, holding them to my breast, stared at her in anxious wonderment.

'Barbara, what is it?' I questioned. For answer she snatched her hands away, and, sinking upon a locker, turned her back upon me.

'Art sick, Barbara?' I said in growing anxiety. Now at this she began to laugh and I, having heard that women are sometimes given to strange, dreadful spasms of laughter with tears, shrieks and the like, was seized of sudden sweating panic and, espying the leathern water-jug, I filled a mug therefrom and proffered it to her :

'Drink this,' said I, kneeling beside her.

'And what for should I ?'

''Twill do you good.' Here she laughed again.

'O, sir,' said she, glancing at me over her shoulder. 'You are none so wise for all your gallantries and fine ladies—'

'What fine ladies?' said I, wondering. 'I have never known any such.'

'And yon's another lie !' she nodded.

'You are the first fine lady I have ever met.'

''Tis not that I reproach you, Adam, for being so fine a gentleman, you—'

'I am not a fine gentleman!' said I. 'MacFarlane lied – deceived you cruelly, I am—'

'O man,' she cried fiercely, 'there's times I hate ye! D'ye dare think I could be so deceived – to wed with any but—'

'Tell me,' said I impatiently, 'tell me, Barbara MacGregor, would you ha' wed me had I been a poor, nameless creature, very humble and desolate – would you?'

'Death should have had me first!' she cried, wildly – and then was a thump of heavy feet above, the light was obscured and down came Tom the cook with our breakfast.

"Tis the best I can do, sir,' said he, knuckling an eyebrow respectfully, ' 'ere be noo bread and eggs fresh aboard, salt pork fried, sir, and prime ale.' So saying he pulled his forelock at us and clattered away.

But, though we ate with right good appetite, it was a gloomy meal since, by her own words, I knew she despised me (such indeed as I truly was) even to death. So we ate in silence, though much was I minded to tell her all my miserable history and yet hesitated, doubting she would believe me and (if she should believe) shrinking from the infliction of such pain it must cause her proud spirit to know herself so cruelly deceived. I was yet debating this within myself when she rose and, without so much as word or look, went forth on deck, which put me to some fears for her safety until I remembered the knife she carried.

And now, because I had a boding fear that Oliver and his rogues would surely essay some villainy against us, soon or late, I began to look to our defences, such as they were.

The cabin was of no great size, but with a smaller cabin opening out of it, wherein were two sleeping berths or bunks, very dingy and uninviting of aspect, a dark, airless place which, like the outer and larger cabin, was unlighted by any window. Yet my comfort was this, viz, whoso ventured against us must come by the door or hatch, the which I found was of stout timbering easily secured by bolts within.

As to our arsenal, beside my sword (which lay within reach) we now had four pistols not counting my broken one, the two muskets and, lastly, Mistress Barbara's knife, which I thought might prove as deadly as any of our weapons.

And this set me to thinking how truly desperate was our case, and what an evil thing that one so young as my lady should run such hazard even to the fouling of her woman's hand with a rogue's blood; and yet better this, hateful thought though it was, than that she fall into the brutal clutches of this black villain, Oliver. And now, sitting thus, chin in hand, I began to cast about in my mind how best I might disappoint these rogues in any attempt they made on us, and looking at my sword and pistols I sickened to think I must use them, for to kill any man, even such notable villains as these, seemed a very dreadful thing. And from this trouble I got me to another, to wit: Mistress Barbara, this wild, proud creature I had married in such strange sort and who (though my wife) was quite above my poor understanding by reason of her sex, and little better than a stranger by association. Now the question was this, viz: did she expect me to make love – to kiss—? The mere possibility filled me with a profound dismay. But here I was struck by a thought that instantly drove all else out of my head – this: since I was not the high-born gentleman Sir Hèctor had named and she believed me, neither was she my wife – hence, need was there none for me to attempt aught in the way of love to this passionate lady who caused me such a wondering uneasiness. Herein I found me some small comfort, and determined henceforth to carry myself towards her with an added respect and all due deference.

I had reached thus far in my excogitations when the light dimmed above me and, glancing up, I saw her peering down at me.

'Come up, Adam,' said she, 'come aloft, for there's a man wafting us from a boat and I jalous he would hae us take him up. Come and see!' Snatching up a pistol, I hurried on deck, and looking whither she pointed, beheld a boat some distance ahead, and one in it who paused, ever and anon, in his rowing to shout and wave an arm.

'How think you, Adam?'

'That you are right,' said I. 'He must be six or seven miles from shore.' And glancing aft, I saw Oliver at the tiller with two of his rogues and all three staring at this solitary boatmen.

'Oliver,' said I, 'yon man signals us.'

'Well, my lord, and what then?'

'We must pick him up.'

'Well, sir, but I think not, your honour.'

'And why not?'

'Well, because us don't want no runaway rogues aboard o'we—'

'Aye,' I nodded frowning, 'we've rogues enough as 'tis.'

'At your service, my lord!' says he smiling, and touching his seaman's bonnet.'

'However,' says I, fingering my pistol, 'if he so desires we must take him up, we cannot leave him so far from land.'

'Well, but can't we, sir?'

'No!' I answered, cocking the pistol, 'Nor will we—' But here at touch from my lady, I turned to see the man and boat so near that I could descry his features, and the very braid and buttons on his coat as, rising, he shouted and flourished an oar.

'Stop!' cried I, turning on Oliver.

'Eh, stop wot, sir?'

'This ship – heave to, or anchor.'

'Why so I would, my lord and willing, only—'

'O Adam – look – look!' Glancing round, I saw the man reel and stagger wildly as his boat pitched on the swell of our bow-wave and then, to my horror, he was gone.

Now I was wearing neither coat, boots, or wig, so, thrusting the pistol into Mistress Barbara's hand, I stripped off my waistcoat and sprang to the bulwark.

'Make Oliver stop!' I cried and (clean forgetting to what perils I left her) plunged overboard. Rising to the surface, and mightily refreshed by the sweet, wholesome tang of the brine, I struck out towards the empty boat and hearing a gurgling cry, beheld the drowning man within a yard of it. Thither swam I, and shouting to the struggling wretch not to cling or hamper me, came within reach, whereupon he instantly seized me, gurgled 'pardon'! and down we went and I helpless; then, his grasp loosening somewhat, up we came to the surface.

'Pardon – m'sieur—!' he gasped again, and again would have dragged me under, but in that moment a merciful Providence sent a drifting oar to smite end on against his skull whereof he suddenly languished – and so aptly that, freed of his clutch, I grasped his collar (his hair being too short and scant to serve me) and thus reaching the boat, contrived to get an arm over the stern and there hung breathless and wellnigh spent.

And now, looking about me for the *Sussex Lass*, my heart sank to see her so far off and I was seized of a sudden awful fear for my lady's safety; but as I stared in growing panic, the vessel came about and bore down upon us, near and nearer, until it seemed she must run us down, then she luffed (as I think they name it), her sails flapped, and a rope splashed within reach, thrown, as I saw, by Tom, the cook. So having made fast the rope about the swooning man he was hove aboard and after him, myself.

'O, Adam,' cries my lady, running to greet me, and with that same wondrous brightness in her eyes, 'O but 'twas a dreadful sight – I thought he would have drowned you—'

Here I snatched the sagging pistol from her lax fingers and levelled it at Oliver who had stolen within a yard of her.

'Back!' I panted. 'Back you – treacherous dog or – I'll be the death – o' you!'

'Easy, my lord!' says he, backing away, 'I don't never mean no harm, sir – no, not a bit your honour—'

'Go!' I cried, 'and send Tom hither with such cordials as you have.'

'Ay, my lord!' says he cheerily, and strode off. And now I saw my lady frowning at me and cherishing the hand my roughness had bruised:

'You near broke my poor finger!' said she, reproachfully.

'Then, madam, pray forgive me,' says I, 'but here is one whose hurt is greater.' And I pointed to the yet unconscious man.

'O, indeed?' cried she, in such bitter anger that I stared amazed. 'And pray what o' me, sir? What o' your wife that you left to the peril of death or worse?'

'You had the pistol, my lady—'

'Pistol!' cries she in a fury.

'And also your little black knife.'

'And is it thus,' quoth she, quick breathing, 'is it thus you would treat your wife?'

'Wife?' says I, shrinking.

'Ay, wife, sir! Are we not wed, heaven aid me!'

'Amen, madam!' says I 'twixt chattering teeth, for I shivered miserably in my wet clothes; at this she flashed her eyes at me and hasted away; then I sank on my knees beside the swooning man. And a strange creature he seemed, what with his close-cropped grey head, shabby sodden garments, great boots and long rapier belted about him; and yet his face was noble, I thought; of a bold and lofty cast of feature, wide of brow, hooked as to nose, square of chin yet with mouth whose shapely lips held a look of kindliness.

And presently cometh Tom, the cook, with a case-bottle and mug, and together we strove to get some of the spirit betwixt the stranger's teeth (very white and fast locked together) and made but sorry work of it. But, doubtless perceiving this, comes Mistress Barbara, takes the mug from me, slips round arm beneath the stranger's neck and, lifting him to her shoulder, does the business all in a moment, and so effectively that after groaning once or twice the man opens his eyes.

'Ah, *bon Dieu*!' he murmured, blinking up into the lovely face above him, 'so then I am a corpse and behold the angels!'

'Nay, sir,' she answered, smiling, 'you are alive and behold only myself.'

87

'But, perfectly, and you are an angel. Yes? No? Then a goddess veritable ! But certainly – the goddess of beauty !'

'Sir,' she answered, smiling down at him very kindly, 'I am merely a woman who pities.'

'And this of all the most divine !' said he in stronger voice. 'But a woman ! Ah ! madam, suffer me !' And speaking, he struggled to his feet and supporting himself by the shrouds, made her a most profound and reverent obeisance, and very stately and dignified I thought him despite his soaked and shabby garments. And now he bowed to me, and, reaching out long arm, proffered his hand :

'Ah 'twas you – I remember all !' said he. 'Young gentleman, dear my sir, though my life these days hath not the sweetness of roses yet I thank you for it, I, Ann Gaston de Vrillac, confess myself your most grateful humble servitor !' And now, as we clasped hands, his keen eyes twinkled. 'The sea, monsieur, she is no friend to me, and myself I am not the fish, so now, but for you, I am the corpse. Sir, my gratitude is yours and such service as I can pay, I pay it but the most surely.'

Now as I stood before him flushed and awkward, somewhat overwhelmed by his flowery speeches, my lady spoke for me in her smooth, soft tones :

'Monsieur de Vrillac, this is my lord Bellcastonborough of whom you may have heard, and I am his wife. And ye're baith shivering wet, sirs, so no more of politeness until you be dry and warm.'

'But we – we have no other clothes !' I stuttered, teeth chattering more furiously than ever.

'Thomas here ahll find ye some.' But at this moment came Oliver, cap in fist and a great bundle of garments beneath his arm.

'Duds, my lord,' says he, 'which, though a bit rough for the like o' your honours, is dry, and which I proffers wi' arl doo respect.'

CHAPTER 15

TELLETH OF RECRIMINATIONS AND ALARMS

THAT night, sitting in the cabin with my lady, our supper done and myself draped in coarse garments many sizes too large, I opened the locker and began to examine our store of arms more carefully and each in turn, particularly as to priming, flints, etc, while Mistress Barbara watched me (having naught better to do) and never so much as a word until at last, becoming somewhat abashed by her so persistent scrutiny, I ventured to question her :

'Pray, Mistress Barbara, why do you stare so?'

'Mistress Barbara!' she murmured, as to herself, and I saw I had angered her again somehow; then :

'My lord,' answered she, very deliberately and in her most precise English, 'I stare at you and stare again because I find 'tis wonderful, 'tis marvellous, 'tis past all belief how fine raiment may advantage some persons – yourself for example!'

'Indeed, yes!' said I, testing the flint screw of one of the muskets.

'In those garments, my lord, that most unlovely guise, your lordship cuts so sorry, so poor, so mean a figure 'tis hard to credit you are so proud, so fine, so great a lord. '

' 'Twere foolish to so mistake me at any time, madam, or in any guise – and your English is mighty pretty!'

'La, indeed, sir, your lordship's kind commendation of my poor accomplishments overwhelms me, I vow!' says she, whereupon I hastened to change the subject.

'The Frenchman, madam, how think you of him?'

'Sir, I dinna, nae lassie wad fash her heid aboot sic an auld carl.'

'I fear I don't understand you,' said I, 'howbeit, I like the man.'

89

'And so you asked him to share this cabin with us!'

'Which offer, madam, he refused for some reason.'

'Because I frowned at him!' she explained, frowning at this moment also.

'And why should you refuse him shelter here?'

'O, my lord, merely because I have no will to sleep so near a strange man.'

'You can bolt fast your door!' said I, nodding towards the inner cabin.

'O, sir, make no doubt of it!' she retorted.

''Tis relief to know this!' said I, stooping to replace musket in locker.

'Ah – and pray, sir, pray what might you mean?'

'That I am as – as much a stranger as this Frenchman, or almost.'

'O – vera true, sir!' said she in hushed whispering voice. 'And gin I should forget to bar my door – whilk is no vera probable, I'll remind ye I hae my skene dhu.'

'And pray what is that?'

'This!' she cried, and whipped forth that glittering knife so suddenly that I came nigh dropping the musket I held.

'You shall have a pistol also,' said I. Now, at this, she stamped her foot and struck the table with her knife in such fury as shocked me beyond words.

'On my soul!' cried she wildly, 'the more I know of you the more do I hate Hector MacFarlane that forced me into wedlock wi' such as yourself!'

'Why, then,' says I, not daring to so much as glance towards her, 'take comfort, madam, for maybe we – we are not married – not truly wed, for—'

'How, sir, how?' cried she, her breath coming stormily. 'Not – not wed, say you? Not – did we no say the fatal words? Did we no stand up hand in hand in the sight of heaven—'

'We did,' says I, turning to lay by the musket, 'but, Mistress Barbara, if I am not the great lord you think me, then neither are you my – my wife, so let this thought comfort you.'

For a moment was a silence, wherein I heard the complaining creak of the ship's timbers as she rose to the surge, and the unceasing hiss and gurgle of the seas; then my lady was on her feet, leaning towards me across the table and I saw her cheeks alternate pale and red, while her eyes, beneath dark-knit brows, flashed immeasurable scorn.

'O!' she gasped. 'O most base – most vile! So, 'tis for this you would deny your name and rank?'

'No!' I cried. 'No—'

'And will ye dare scorn Barbara MacGregor?'

'Not I!'

'Is not a MacGregor fit mate for the proudest—?'

'Yes, indeed!' said I. ''Tis for this reason I would free you of—'

'Haud y'r leein' tongue, sir!'

'But suffer me a word, madam—'

'No more, sir, I winna hear ye! And do not think, my lord, O never fear I will stoop to claim relationship wi' such as yourself – God love me – no! Hereafter you go your way and I mine. Just so soon as we reach land we are strangers – though God and the angels know otherwise, alas!' Which said, she turned away, very stately proud, and, going into the inner cabin, closed the door.

But even as I sat staring after her all bemused, she was back again, a slim, temptuous fury:

'And mind ye this, my lord – O dinna forget this – sleeping or waking I hate ye! Wherever you go my hate shall follow, I scorn ye living and I'll scorn ye dead!'

'Barbara!' cried I, starting to my feet. 'In heaven's name—'

'I did but wed you to – to save your – miserable life – and now—' a great sob choked her.

'Barbara,' said I again. 'O believe me I would not grieve you – I would but strive to be honourable and worthy—'

But, staying for no more, she fled into her cabin, clapped to the door (with sound like pistol shot) ramming home the bolt mighty fierce. And after some while, my examination of our firearms done, and they secure in the locker (save one), I stretched myself above them and with this pistol ready to hand, disposed myself to sleep. But this I might by no means compass, so that at last I arose and, giving up all thought of slumber, reached my sword from the corner and began to polish it, for lack of better employ. And then Barbara's door opened and I wondered to see her still fully dressed.

'I'll thank ye for the pistol!' says she.

'Ay, to be sure!' said I, opening the locker, 'but I thought you asleep.'

'Well, I'm no. And I'll thank ye—'

'Have you been crying, Barbara?'

'Ay, I've been greetin', kind sir, whilk is muckle relief, I'm gey blith an' braw the noo. And I'll thank—'

'Won't you talk the English, Barbara?'

'I'm no juist minded for ony mair cracking the nicht. So I'll thank ye—'

'Then pray be seated, Barbara, and suffer me to explain myself and—'

'Na, na, sir, nae mair o' that, your lordly self is subject I'll no debate wi' ye, here or yon, forbye ye're nae langer ony concern o' mine!'

'Surely we are friends?'

'Ou ay!' she nodded, 'We'll be friends until we part and fu' soon, I hope, if but for the sake o' your leddies.'

'Ladies?'

'Ay, your fine madams that be breakin' their hearts for ye – the shameless besoms!'

'Barbara,' says I, leaning across the table in my earnestness, 'I never made love to a woman, never – kissed any woman in all my life! O won't you believe—'

'A flap-dragon!' says she, and laughed in cruel mockery; but even then I caught her two hands and drew her close, so that she must needs look into my eyes.

'Barbara,' said I slowly, 'I have said but truth, so aid me God!' And then, before she might resist and almost ere I knew it myself, I had kissed her full upon the mouth.

For a moment we remained, mute with surprise and staring, then her lashes drooped suddenly and she shrank away.

'Ah – let me go!' said she in breathless fashion, 'Let me go!'

So I loosed her, amazed at myself, yet strangely glad, the more so, to see her cheeks all rosy, and eyes so sweetly abashed; then she glanced at me sideways, and I saw the corners of her sensitive mouth quiver and lift:

'A'weel, Adam,' said she, her voice very kind. 'I'm thinkin' ye're no sae blate for a beginner!'

'But you believe me, Barbara, you believe that I—'

'O, my lord Adam,' sighed she, turning from me, 'how can it matter what I believe? Howandever, if not over-bold you are nothing backward, so needs must I warn you there can be no more kisses betwixt us since there can never be love.'

'Never?' I questioned, whereat she laughed, yet not very joyously.

'O, sir,' said she gently, 'dinna be sic a fulish Adam.'

'Ah, Barbara,' I sighed, 'would to heaven you were content to have me merely Adam!'

'And now I'll thank ye for the pistol. No, no,' says she, for I had proffered the first to hand. 'I'll take the little, handsome one wi' the silver mountings, 'tis your ain I'm wanting, Adam.'

'This?' said I, showing her old Zachary's present. 'Why, very well, though 'tis not to be depended on.'

'And why for no?'

'Well, look at it!'

'Why,' says she staring up at me with blank surprise, ''tis not primed, Adam, nor charged!'

'And if it were loaded, 'twould never go off, Barbara.'

'Why – why, 'tis – broken!' she whispered.

'So you had better take this other,' I nodded.

'When – when did it break, Adam?'

'I don't know.'

'You mean – 'twas with this broken, useless thing you – leapt upon yon armed villains?'

'Fell upon them!' I corrected.

'Adam,' said she softly, and with that glory in her eyes. 'O Adam, it was – it was – fair hee-roic !'

'No,' I answered, knowing myself all unworthy of such praise, 'small bravery was here, indeed I was miserably afraid and—'

But even as I spoke she caught my hand, clasped it to her bosom and then (O most wonderful) or ever I might stay her she stooped her lovely, so proud head and I felt the sweet, warm pressure of her lips.

'No,' cried I, drawing her to me, 'not my hand, Barbara !'

Now as we stood thus, breast to breast, she with that glory in her eyes, her soft body yielding in my embrace, the night silence was riven by a dreadful cry, a gurgling, inhuman scream that chilled us with very horror of it, and then, as we clung together trembling and mute, a hand began to rap on the door above the companionway.

CHAPTER 16

TELLETH SOMETHING OF THIS FRENCHMAN

FOR a long moment we stood thus clinged together scarce breathing, while the hand rapped softly yet with dreadful persistence; then Barbara drew a sobbing breath and spoke, whispering :

'Adam – Adam, what awful thing is yon ?'

And now, as we listened, the knocking seemed louder, and in it I thought to read a growing desperation.

'I must know what it is !' said I, and loosening Barbara's rigid clasp, took up the pistol and cocked it, while she sank half swooning upon the locker.

'O Adam,' said she in fearful whisper, 'I'm fey – 'tis no canny, yon ! Bide safe here and dinna meddle wi't.'

'I must find out !' said I, setting my chattering teeth, 'I must !'

'Why then, Adam, I thank God he hath made thee so courageous! And I am a MacGregor!' said she, snatching up another pistol, 'so, do as you will, Adam, Barbara Mac-Gregor is at your back.'

Now as I mounted the companion I turned to see her close behind, very pale yet calm and resolute the which greatly heartened me. Reaching the door I rapped upon it in turn and spoke in voice firm as I might:

'Who is there?'

'De Vrillac, m'lord, with ten thousand pardons! I am desolate to trouble you, but, my sir, I can be to you of service better alive than dead, so pray trouble to open ere I become the so useless corpse.'

With trembling fingers I drew back the bolts, the ponderous door was whisked open and in upon me came a pair of long legs so suddenly that I was obliged to cling about them lest I fall, whereupon this courteous Frenchman poured forth a flood of breathless apologies the while he closed the door and bolted it secure.

'Mr de Vrillac,' said I, so soon as we were in the cabin (and he bowing above Barbara's hand), 'sir, we heard a dreadful cry—?'

'Ah, yes,' said he in tone gentle as his smile, 'there was one creep after me with the poignard – the dagger, but myself I see him in good time, my Lord, O yes. And now, if Madam permit, I sit me and show you the so great villainy – if Madam possess the heart indomitable?'

And indeed a vastly different man he looked compared with the half drowned wretch we had hauled on board, for now his close-cropped head was dignified by a handsome peruke (which, it seemed, had been recovered with his boat) and despite weather-worn garments, very grand and stately I thought him. A lean man of haughty carriage, very fierce as to eyebrows, nose and chin, yet marvellous kindly as to eyes and mouth.

'Pray be seated, sir!' said Barbara, 'And my heart is courageous because my husband fears only God.'

'Ah, madam, 'tis for such as yourself so brave, so beautiful

95

and of faith so exquisite that men die with a joy supreme!'
said Mr de Vrillac, while I hung my head, blushing for my
unworthiness.

And now sitting, all three, in this dingy prison, with the
hiss and bubble of great waters all about us, we took counsel
together, on this wise:

BARBARA: Pray tell us, sir, why are you come to us?
And that fearful scream, what was it? O what doth it all
mean?

DE VRILLAC: Yourself, madam! These so evil
mariners-pigs desire your money, your jewels – your so
beautiful self! Wherefore it becomes necessary that your
lord and I we kill some of them. Ah no, dear lady, do not
discompose, it shall be of a simplicity astounding, these
rogues are but seven and we—

MYSELF: (*starting*) Seven, sir? Surely you mistake,
they are but four.

DE VRILLAC: (*bowing*) Pardon, dear my sir, but
seven they number. Three have slept all day – verree drunk.

MYSELF: (*mightily dismayed*) Seven!

Here, even as I spoke, the vessel gave a lurch that nearly
threw me across the table while loud above us we heard the
sails flapping violently, so furiously, indeed, that the whole
fabric of the ship quivered again.

BARBARA: (*clasping my hand*) Think you we shall sink,
Adam? Ah, why doth the ship rock so?

DE VRILLAC: (*bowing*) Pardon, 'tis very simple. This
ship she try to sail herself because I have secured all those so
wicked seamen down below.

MYSELF: But the steersman, sir?

DE VRILLAC: Ah, dear my friend, it was he try so
hard to kill me, and *voilà*! He may not steer now.

BARBARA: (*shrinking against me*) Did you – kill him,
sir?

DE VRILLAC: But no, madam, I think not. With my
sword-pommel I tap him on the head, merely, but for living
or dying, madam, this is in the hands of the good God.

All this time the vessel had been rocking and shivering

with sudden, uneasy motions, so now, full of apprehension, I got upon unsteady feet and, thrusting pistol into pocket, clambered up the companion, the others at my heels, and opening the door, stepped into a sweet fresh wind. The moon rode high above our swaying mast-heads as the lugger came up into the wind only to fall away again and lie wallowing, with sails shivering helplessly; therefore I ran to the helm and had soon steadied her. But now, looking about, I was horrified to see the land within scarce a mile of us and the vessel driving or drifting ever nearer. Desperately I swung the tiller and though she answered in some sort yet, what with the set of the tide and freshening wind, it needed more than my poor seamanship to work her safe out to sea for, do what I would, those ghastly white cliffs loomed ever nearer.

'Sir, sir,' cried I beckoning de Vrillac, 'we are drifting ashore – we shall be wrecked!'

'Dear my sir,' he answered serenely, 'this shall be as the good God wills!'

'But Oliver would know what to do!' cried I. 'The sail should be trimmed – Oliver would know!'

'Then, my friend, I will bring him.'

'But, sir – they may kill you!'

'I think not, sir,' he answered placidly, 'and this is also as God wills! However, I go.' And away he strode forward.

And now, as I leaned to the heavy tiller, I found Barbara beside me.

'So ye ken the manage of a boat, Adam?' says she, standing very close.

'Little enough!' I answered, watching the sails that I might keep them steady and full.

'Yet you have made the ship ride smoothly, Adam. Is there aught you cannot do?'

'An infinite deal!' sighed I. 'But what troubles me is that I cannot make you believe I am no lord but merely—'

But here she turned her back and left me; then she uttered a startled cry:

'What now?' I called.

' 'Tis a man,' she answered.

'Then 'tis a rogue!' said I.

'But—O, he is dead!'

'Then do not touch him.'

'Nay – he is alive, Adam.'

'Then come away!'

'But he is hurt.'

'Then so much the better!'

A hoarse shout, a confusion of voices, the quick tramp of hurrying feet, and Oliver had caught the tiller from me and was bellowing rapid orders which were instantly obeyed.

And thus, after some while, as I stood peering over our lee, to my great joy I saw those ghostly cliffs begin to draw away, farther and farther, until from direful menace they shrank and faded to a vague blur.

And then Oliver spoke:

'Well, my lord, I rackon your honour kept us off and saved the *Lass* and I be grateful, sir, grateful – for, if a bit rough-like, I've got a rare good heart and—'

But at this moment de Vrillac approached us, and I saw moon glint on the pistols he grasped in each hand; and then I started, so sudden, so strangely terrible was his voice:

'Hither, ye pigs of dogs, hither to me!' he cried, and a group of sullen men lurched towards us. 'Now, rogues, *sang dieu* – do as I did command ye!'

A moment's hesitation and then, obedient to the grim face behind these levelled weapons, the men sprang upon Oliver, and, despite his furious struggles, pinioned his arms behind him with cords they had ready.

'So!' cried De Vrillac, 'Now … the rope – at once, *mordieu*!'

'Well, but—' gasped Oliver, writhing in his bonds. 'What would ye? … O merciful God! …'

'Up,' shouted De Vrillac; then Barbara screamed, and I shrank appalled as the miserable wretch was swung aloft – an awful, kicking shape that choked hideously.

'Stop!' I shouted. 'O stop!'

De Vrillac gestured with his pistols, and next moment Oliver lay gasping and groaning on the deck; then Barbara

98

was kneeling beside him and had loosened the strangling noose.

'For shame!' she cried, turning upon the Frenchman. 'O most detestable!'

De Vrillac bowed:

'I implored Madam to carry herself below!' sighed he; then turning upon the shrinking crew, roared at them in his terrible voice:

'Condemned pigs! Ye are all the rogues most black and should hang – most certainly this Oliver would I hang, but this noble lord, this so gracious lady, they say no! Verree well! But now this Oliver, this so black, evil pig, he kneel to Madam and with passion implore her forgiveness – kneel, dog!'

Gasping painfully, Oliver struggled weakly to his knees:

'O lady—' he groaned, 'O ma'm – forgi'e me, a poor soul nigh dead—' and indeed I saw his pallid features all convulsed and streaked with the sweat of his agony.

'So now away with this great rogue-villain!' said De Vrillac. 'Haste him out o' my sight – but quick!'

So they hoisted Oliver among them, and forthwith bore him away below. Then De Vrillac sighed and glanced where Barbara stood frowning.

'Miladi,' he began, but even as he spoke she turned and hurried down into the cabin.

'*Hélas*, my lord,' says he, pocketing his pistols, 'Madam she is a little shocked against me, I fear. But, my sir, I have tamed that beast, O yes! I have broke the spirit of this mutiny, *mordieu*, and changed for you these wolves into the lambs most innocent that skip – *voilà*! And now pray present my duty most humble to milady and so, my friend, goodnight!'

'But, sir, you will surely sleep in the cabin with me?'

'Ah, dear my lord, you honour me, I am grateful! But for this night I lie among my lambs.' With which, he bowed and left me very full of wonder and amaze.

CHAPTER 17

CONCERNING, AMONG OTHER MATTERS, ONE
JAPHET, A MARINER

I WAKED next morning to a sound so altogether unexpected that I started to an elbow, hardly believing my ears, for someone with a great bass voice was carolling away right joyously. Wondering, I arose, and silently as might be, for by the silence beyond the door of Barbara's cabin 'twas evident she still slumbered; so with boots beneath my arm I crept up the companion and out into a radiant morning, where the sun, new-risen, made a glory in the east and had set the ocean everywhere a-sparkle, and with a sweet, soft wind that was a joy to breath. The deck was deserted save for the songster at the tiller, a great, jovial-looking fellow, though very hairy, for his red visage shone forth of a wiry bush of black whisker; at sight of me he instantly ceased his singing (which I was sorry for) and pulling his forelock at me, gave a cheery 'Good morning'.

And now as I returned this hearty greeting and glanced from his good-humoured face to the trim vessel rising easily to the gentle swell, beholding all this glory of sea and sky, and sensing all the joy of it, my late terrors seemed, by contrast, no more than a foolish dream and the pistol, that even then weighed my pocket so heavily, became an absurd and needless encumbrance. As I stood thus, in thought, the steersman's voice aroused me :

'Sir, you'm a'looking at that theer block, eh?'

'Block?' I repeated.

'Ah – that 'un, sir, aloft there at th' end o' the yard ! Pore Sam Oliver come nigh kickin' 'is life out agin that block last night – eh, sir? Lordy-lord, 'ow Sam did kick, sure-ly !'

'How is he this morning?'

'Wonnerful spry, sir, con-sidering as 'ow 'e was 'ung last night!'

'And what were you doing at the time?'

'Me, sir? I were 'elping to 'ang 'im, sure-ly, pore felly! But wot other could a man do, sir, wi' yonder frog-eatin' Frenchman so on-common determinated-like?'

'Where is he – the French gentleman?'

'Why, sir, 'aving washed hisself – ah, and pretty nigh all over too, e's down in the galley larning Tom 'ow to cook.'

'Talking of washing,' said I, glancing about, 'a bucket of water, soap and a towel would be vastly welcome.'

'Wot, sir, be you another as needs washing, constant? You doant nohow look dirty t'me, sir – no! Hows'ever if you feels like sluicing, sluice it is, sir! Oho Roger – Roger ho!' he roared in mighty voice; and presently, in answer to this rousing bellow, appeared a comely young sailor with great rings in his ears.

'Wot's the word, Japhet?' he inquired, knuckling an eyebrow to me.

'Water – in a bucket, Roger! This yere gemman feels like washin' hisself, which doant seem nowise needful to me – hows'ever, water it be, Roger, likewise soap and – the towel!'

'Ay, ay,' answered Roger and dived below, forthwith.

'Fine folks, sir, do ha' mighty strange ways!' mused Japhet, cocking his eye aloft. 'My landlady's darter as works for fine folk, do tell me as they'm for ever a-washin' o' theer-selves – ah, marning, noon an' night!'

'Well, I suppose you wash sometimes?' I questioned.

'Ay, I do, sir!' he confessed. 'I washes myself 'earty and free now and then, which bean't often, seein' as I be a nat'-rally clean man.'

And now, Roger having filled me a great leathern bucket from overside, I stripped to the waist and washed me, finding so great pleasure thereby as put me in mind of my lady's need; wherefore I set Roger questing high and low for something more seemly than a bucket, until he had found a copper bowl and ewer which, though much battered, I thought might serve. With these then I descended to the cabin, and, having filled the bowl to her use, ventured to knock on her door.

'Is it you, Adam?' says she in sleepy voice; hereupon I told her I had brought soap and water but no towel since it seemed there was but one in the ship. At this she laughed merrily, which methought marvellous sweet hearing.

' 'Tis unco' kind in thee, Adam, for O I hae yearned for soap and water!'

Returning on deck I there beheld De Vrillac walking up and down and (to my wonder) in close converse with the rogue Oliver, whereat I chilled with swift suspicion of this Frenchman, and felt mighty glad of the weapon in my pocket; then, even as I stood thus dubious, Oliver pulled off his bonnet, mighty humble, while De Vrillac saluted me with prodigious fine bow.

'My lord,' said he with kindly smile, 'I give you my salutations the most humble. You and miladi have sleep well, I trust?'

'Thank you, very well, sir,' I answered, staring up into his mild blue eyes.

'Master Oliver he tells me you are for Scotland, and offer to put me ashore whereso I will, for Master Oliver – he loves me better at the distance, I think! But I go with you, sir, unless you wish me to make the *adieu*?'

'No, no, sir!' I answered, grasping his hand, much relieved to think my suspicions unfounded. 'Do pray come with us if you please.'

'Then, sir, it is agreed – to Scotland I go! – You, Master Oliver, now tell the cook he come for me when he have clean his great fry-pan. And, my lord, pray tell me – the omelet, does Madam love him – no? Yes?'

'Sir,' said I, glancing after Oliver's retreating figure, 'you have indeed wrought a miracle it seems, changing these rogues into honest men.'

'Ah – ah, sir – but for how long? This Oliver now, I shall not trust him, but no! He smile too often! He love me too much! Some time I suppose he makes it necessary that I kill him, O yes—'

'God forbid, sir!'

'My lord, amen!'

'Mr de Vrillac when you came, we were in desperate plight, today we are safe because these men fear you and so I – I would thank you if I could—'

'Nay, sir, here is but the tit for the tat – you jump into the sea, you do battle with this watery horror, you snatch me from death, *sang dieu*, it is heroic! And therefore my lord—'

'Ah, pray do not call me "lord", my name is Adam – for truly, sir, I should be heartily glad to call you friend.' At this he turned suddenly and caught my hand in both of his:

'But am I not so – here in my heart, Monsieur Adam? Am I not indeed your friend, to serve you as I may? As you save my life so, perchance, I save yours. And now I call thee Adam, and myself, for thee I am always Gaston.'

'Then please, Mr Gaston—'

'Ah, but no, never the "mister" to me, my friend.'

'Then, Gaston, I beg you will share the cabin with me.'

'Perfectly – ah, but Madam?'

'She – she sleeps in the inner berth.'

'So? Then shall I be honoured. Ah, and behold the Tom he beckon yonder, I go – it is the omelet, the last egg in the ship for miladi.' And he hastened away, leaving me to ponder his strange character, and very glad to know him my friend. And from him I got to thinking on myself and the strange posture of affairs in regard to Mistress Barbara, whom I might never honourably claim as wife seeing I was a nameless beggar, a pitiful wretch foisted upon her by a villain to my own bitter shame; and bethinking me of her dismay, her anger and contempt when she should learn all this, I hated Sir Hector the more that he should thus have used me to her humiliation.

And behold ye as I walked, lost in these most bitter reflections, I saw her coming towards me, herself as fresh as the morning.

'Well, Adam, and have ye no greeting for me?' says she,

for I could but stare upon her loveliness. 'Will ye no give your poor wife a good morrow, husband?' But, understanding she mocked me, I flushed and stammered like a mere fool, whereat she laughed. looking me up and down, her handsome head aslant.

'O faith,' says she, her eyes very bright, 'now I see you washed and combed I do protest your face is none so ill, ye have good eyes, sir, your nose is fair and – m-m-yes, your mouth might be worse! To be sure I could wish ye some inches taller, but, having no choice, poor Barbara, alack, must take you for better or worse! So pray oblige your humble spouse with an arm, my lord.'

But, instead of obeying, I stepped back and faced her with as much resolution as I might :

'Mistress Barbara,' said I, shaking my head, 'here is no matter 'twixt us two of "better or worse"!'

'How?' says she, opening her beautiful eyes at me, 'are we not fast wed, sir, are we no?'

'Madam,' I answered miserably, 'I do verily believe here was no true marriage.'

'O!' says she, recoiling a step, her cheeks suddenly aflame. 'O!' says she again, and now I saw her very pale. 'Contemptible boy! Some day – some day shalt know how I can hate! Meantime, my lord and husband, give me your arm, for yonder comes your fantastical Frenchman!'

CHAPTER 18

TOUCHES SOMETHING ON THE ART OF SWORDSMANSHIP

A T this time, my mind relieved of all fears for our immediate safety in regard to Oliver, I must needs begin to plague myself with a thousand dismal speculations anent my own future, seeing myself (as it were) a blown leaf upon the Torrent of Circumstance, to be whirled miserably I knew not whither; moreover, instead of facing my troublous destiny with that careless, lofty indifference the which becometh your true hero, my natural timidity gripped me and, knowing I must soon be an alien, friendless and without money in a strange country, so greatly discouraged me that even Master Bragg and his crab-tree staff seemed infinitely the lesser evils.

Thus, upon a day, leaning to watch the bubbling rush and sparkle of our wake as the ship drave on bearing me ever towards this terror of the unknown, I yearned passionately to be again my humble self perched upon familiar stool in my master's dingy office.

From the which most unheroical thoughts I was roused by a touch, and glanced up into De Vrillac's kindly eyes.

'Art grievous, my friend Adam?' he questioned, and because of his sympathy I felt the smart of hidden tears.

'Yes!' I answered, miserably. 'Yes! It is the future – my utter destitution – my – loneliness!'

'Loneliness?' he repeated. 'But milady, your wife?' I shook my head dismally. 'Ah – so!' he murmured. 'There remains, then, always your sword, friend Adam, with this you may win the fame, the fortune – or the grave so honourable. Ha, it is true, when all other fails, there remains always – the sword!'

'Mayhap,' said I gloomily, 'and for such as know its manage, but as for me, I never handled sword in all life.'

De Vrillac fell back a step greatly surprised and I think a little shocked :

'By my faith,' quoth he staring, 'I am now astonished! *Mordieu*, I am the amazed one! For the sword, she is to the gentleman his first and last resource, his creed, the emblem of his class, the guardian so constant of his honour! And you – you tell me—'

'That I am no gentleman, sir!' said I desperately, and turned to face him, though his haughty eyebrows daunted me somewhat.

'Ha, death of my life!' he exclaimed, his voice fiercer than usual and chin very grim. 'No gentleman? *Sang dieu,* sir – you touch on a matter to me the most sacred for a gentle-man of honour is, I hold, the noblest work of the good God!'

'True, sir,' said I humbly, 'so do I grieve I am no gentle-man, 'tis my shame to be no better than I am! And – and, sir, I would not have you bestow your friendship believing me of high estate and noble birth for, indeed – I – I am no lord but one so humble – so poor that I have not even a name—'

For a long moment De Vrillac was silent, but when at last I ventured to glance up at him I saw that his eyes (despite haughty brows and fierce nose) were marvellous kind, as was his voice also when he spoke :

'Monsieur Adam, if you have the will to speak me more you shall find me a hearer the most patient.'

And so, hanging my head, I told him my whole painful story, whereto he listened, profoundly attentive, until I had done; then what must he do (to my great surprise) but pull off his hat and bow to me in his most stately fashion :

'Sir,' said he, mighty solemn, 'name or no name, I salute you as man of honour the most delicate!' And then, while I stood abashed and naught to say, he caught me in his arms.

'And thus, my Adam,' says he, kissing me on brow and cheek, 'thus doth thy friend Gaston, Ann, de Vrillac take thee to his heart for ever!'

'O, sir,' said I, 'O, friend—' and bowed my head lest he see tears.

'My Adam,' said he presently as we leaned side by side watching this bright and gentle sea, for the wind was fallen light, 'the medal they found about thy neck, might I see it?' For answer I drew forth the medallion and gave it into his hand.

'Hélas!' sighed he, turning it this way and that, 'what fateful story is here, of joy – of sorrow and black despair most tragic! 'Tis strange jewel, Adam, of the most rare, such as no peasant might possess! A lover's gift – see these characters, so close entwined, the A and the H – I think 'twas no beggar fathered thee, Adam.'

'I have hoped as much, Gaston,' said I, thrusting the jewel back out of sight, 'I have prayed I might find my father some day, and that he should deem me a worthy son. 'Tis wonderful to think I may have a father who lives, and perchance thinks on me sometimes.'

'And milady, hast told her this history so strange and piteous – yes? No?'

'No, for she will not hear me. I have told her I am no lord but she will not credit me, she is so cruelly proud and doth but rail at me.'

'Because she is the woman, my Adam, and verree young, and so it is you must endure humbly, O yes!'

'But she is so full o' whims and moods I grow all amazed. If I am humble she flouts me. If I grow angry she laughs. If I am silent she mocks and plagues me beyond enduring.'

'Yet is she a woman, Adam, and therefore to be forgiven.'

'Why so I do, heaven knows, but already she despiseth me in her heart – 'tis beyond doubt.'

'Still is she the woman and therefore to be won. And how? Mark now and suffer my advice because I love thee, my friend. Neither chide nor woo – no, no! Be ever the most gallant and gentle but seek not her company. Let her think of thee how she will, but of thyself tell her no more, and soon shall she hunger to know all, yearn for thy company and grow kind – ah yes, because she is a woman.'

'Tell me, Gaston – think you we are truly wed, seeing I have no name?'

'O, but yes, Adam, and by the Scots law most surely.'

Now at this I was silent, knowing not whether to be glad or sorry, while my companion went on in his gentle voice :

'Howbeit, my Adam, thy first duty to her and thy own honour shall be to kill this so wicked Sir Hector.'

'Kill him?' I exclaimed aghast. 'Nay, heaven forbid! Moreover, he is a great swordsman, as I know.'

'Thou shalt be a better, my Adam – but yes! My first duty as your friend shall be to school you in the sword, and O my faith it shall for me be a joy the most extreme. Come, let us begin now, this moment! Go, fetch thy weapon!' So away I sped forthwith, and was presently back with the sword and found Gaston, without coat or waistcoat, who bid me strip likewise.

'Ah, a colichemarde!' said he taking my sword and, unsheathing it with graceful flourish, glanced along its bright blade and made therewith a supple pass. 'Good,' quoth he, ''tis light, 'tis quick, and of the balance exquisite. See now, you shall grasp him so – not tightly, ah no! The finger round the ricasso – thus! So shall you play the more firm. The body he must poise lightly, ah but lightly – *voilà*! It is now the hand, the eye, the foot, all together, in accord the most perfect – regard, my Adam!'

And speaking, he fell into a posture of fight wonderfully graceful and methought dreadfully grim, for now, as he thrust and parried at the empty air, his whole person seemed transfigured by a terrible joy, his pale cheek flushed, his eyes glowed as if indeed they looked death upon some enemy. And, as the steel flickered and darted, he spoke of prime, tierce and quarte, of seconde and quinte, of feints, thrusts and parades, attacks in the high line and the low, of volts and passes, until my head spun.

Then, giving me the sword, he drew his own (a plain weapon he was never without), saluted, fell to his guard and, then and there, gave me my first lesson in this most deadly yet necessary art that was to so change the whole tenor of my life.

But presently, attracted by the clink of our steel, came divers of the crew to watch (to my no small annoyance) and after them, Barbara, at sight of whom I became so bitterly aware of my ignorant clumsiness and the sorry figure I must cut, that my play grew wild and awkward in the extreme, so that I stepped back at last, filled with mortified shame and venturing to glance at her, saw how she stared on me wide-eyed beneath wrinkling brows, her lips apart; then, as I turned away utterly abashed she spoke in strange, laughing voice:

'Beware, Monsieur de Vrillac, O prithee beware, my husband is very deadly with the sword – they tell me! How think you, sir?'

'That report shall not lie, madam, ah, but no!'

At this she laughed again and I, glancing round, thought to read in her eyes a growing doubt and troubled perplexity ere she turned and left us, her head bent as in profound thought.

'Come, my friend,' said Gaston, saluting me with his sword, 'let us continue.' But, glancing towards the watching sailor men, I shook my head and reached for my coat.

'Aha, is it these good animals, our amiable mariners, do they disturb? Then shall they remove! Begone, my fellows!' says he with imperious gesture, 'you are no longer here!' Whereupon, and meeting his eye, incontinent and without a word they went.

'And now, my Adam, bear your point, I beg, always within the line, let it be for me the constant menace – come!'

So to it we went again with volt and pass and traverse, thrusting and parrying until my arm ached and, seeing me distressed, my companion stepped out of distance and lowered his point.

'Ah, my friend,' said he nodding, 'soon shalt carry death on thy blade, for thou'rt quick, my faith yes! And thou hast the fighting judgement, and 'tis gift of the most rare – soon I make thee swordsman the most dangerous.'

'Will you, Gaston?' cried I eagerly. 'But can you – O can you indeed?'

'But of a surety!' he answered smiling. 'It is beyond doubt.' Now here, because of his faith I pressed his hand but said no word for my gratitude was beyond speech, wherefore he clapped me on the shoulder and smiled down on me in his kindly fashion; says he:

'Some day, my Adam, if God is verree good, I shall watch you kill this so detestable Sir Hector.'

CHAPTER 19

TELLETH OF A WARNING

AND now lest this narrative prove tedious (of which I have some fear) I will pass over such minor incidents as befell us on this most wearisome voyage, for the wind from fair veered often and dropped at last to baffling airs. Nor will I tell how Mistress Barbara capricious and baffling (like the wind) seemed wondrous kind one hour, only to frown and fleer the next, and all for no reason that I could see. But day after day I fenced with Gaston, long and often, for in my passion to learn I forgot myself and all beside; and daily his joy in my progress waxed, for it seemed as some instinct within me seconded his able teaching, thus with every lesson I grew more assured, and therewith was bred in me so vehement a delight, in this dexterous play of glittering steel, as filled me with wonder and vague disquiet.

So will I pass on to a certain calm evening (whereas I sat with Gaston, sword in hand, a little breathless after a long rally) that the man Japhet (the great hairy fellow for whom I had conceived a liking) beckoned me where he stood at the tiller.

'Young master,' says he, as I came beside him, 'I rackon trouble's a-brewing!'

'How so, Japhet?' I questioned anxiously, whereat he cocked his eye aloft at the swaying yard and shook his head. 'What do you mean?' said I, watching his hairy face.

'Well, sir, for one thing, look yonder!' and he jerked thumb towards a certain quarter of the horizon.

'A black cloud!' said I.

'Wind!' he nodded. 'Wind's a-comin' an' plenty on it, I rackon.'

'You mean a storm?'

'I rackon!'

'It – indeed – it looks very threatening,' said I, staring at this ominous cloud.

'It be!' he nodded. 'An' that ain't arl neether!'

'What – what, more?'

'Well – rum's another thing, sir,' said he, sinking his voice, 'and this means more trouble – ah, and plenty o' that too, I rackon. So my word to you gemmen is – keep your weather-eye a-lifting – constant!'

'And this other trouble, Japhet, you mean?'

For answer he jerked his big thumb towards the forecastle.

'Ah – you mean – Oliver?'

'I rackon!'

'What do you know?' says I, whispering now.

'Not nothing, sir! Sam don't trust me nowise, and no more 'e don't trust my mate Roger – but there be summat in the wind, I rackon, whiles you and Monsieur be so busy all day long a-sham fighting each other!'

'Japhet,' says I, laying my hand on his hairy arm, 'should Oliver and the others attack us would you and Roger stand in with us?'

'I rackon!' he nodded, then instantly scowled and shook his head whispering as he did so, 'there be Dick Bettison a-watching of us! A bad 'un be Dick – sheer off, sir, lest 'e suspicion we!' So with a word of thanks I left this honest Japhet and returned where Gaston sat, his back to the mainmast.

'Shall we try another assault?' says he.

'Willingly,' said I, and then, in lower tone: 'I've evil news, Gaston!'

'So?' he questioned, his eyes suddenly keen.

'Oliver is scheming more villainy against us, Japhet says.'

' 'Tis a good soul, the Japhet.'

'Ay, but Oliver?' I whispered, 'what must we do, Gaston?'

'Presently nothing, my Adam. When it becomes necessary I shall kill him with a joy the most sublime! But for the moment we—'

He paused suddenly, and rose as Barbara came towards us, serenely gracious and unhurried, and, seeing the vivid beauty of her, I chilled to think what horrors might yet be in store for her.

'Monsieur Gaston,' said she without so much as glancing in my direction, she chancing today to be at odds with me, though why I knew not, 'Monsieur Gaston I beg you to come below at once and be so good to desire my noble husband to come also.'

Hereupon, picking up our coats, we followed her down into the cabin without more ado.

'What is it, Barbara?' I questioned anxiously, so soon as I had closed the door, for now I beheld her serene no longer, nay, indeed, her looks were greatly troubled, while her hands clasped and wrung each other.

'Look!' says she in weeping tones. 'O look – we are betrayed!'

Then she opened that locker which was our arsenal, and I stared in fearful dismay (as well I might) for our arms were clean gone, muskets and pistols had vanished.

'Oliver!' I gasped; 'Oliver has them!'

'Who else?' she answered with hopeless gesture, as she turned from me to Gaston.

'Now God aid us!' I exclaimed.

'He will!' said Gaston placidly, then going up the companion he bolted the door securely.

CHAPTER 20

TELLETH HOW OUR FRENCHMAN QUELLED MUTINY

'Let us,' says Gaston in his grand manner, 'let us, dear miladi, be seated and—'

'So now do we lie at Oliver's mercy!' said Barbara, shivering.

'Nay, but how,' says I, in staring bewilderment, 'how were they stolen?—'

'Very easily, sir,' cries she, scornfully, ''twas whiles you and Monsieur were above at your play and the cabin unwatched.'

'If Madam will permit me to seat myself,' said Gaston gently.

'Ye know Oliver for murderous rogue,' cried Barbara, glancing disdainfully from one to other of us, 'ye knew this, yet all day and every day you must be at your fencing and the cabin all unguarded – or was it ye meant that I must bide here out o' the sun, mewed up whiles you disported yoursel's to your selfish pleasure?'

'If Madam will have the extreme condescension to permit that I sit—'

'To sit, sir – to sit?' quoth she, turning upon Gaston very furiously, 'And why will ye sit at such time and our lives in jeopardy?'

'Madam, it is that I never stand when I may sit, at any time.'

'Then sit, sir, sit! O fold your hands, both o' ye, and let them murder us!'

'Madam, I thank you!' said Gaston and, having bowed, seated himself in his accustomed corner.

'And you, my lord husband, will you also sit and do nothing?'

'Indeed, dear madam, and wherefore not?' says Gaston, for I stood mute, being at loss for words. 'Since there is naught we may do for this moment, let us all sit and take counsel together, for, madam, we must wait with the grand patience until our rogues yonder afford us chance to strike the blow so needful – or, perchance, madam, yourself hath some strategy the more cunning? Yes? No? Then will you not be seated and honour us,' but without waiting for more she went into her cabin, shutting the door upon us. Saith Gaston, looking after her:

'Some day, my Adam, this so proud lady shall love you with a passion the most intense – my faith, yes!'

'Barbara?' said I, staring, 'Love me? O why, why should you imagine thing so impossible?' But at this he merely smiled, then caught suddenly at the table for the ship had lurched violently while above and around us rose a desolate wailing moan.

'Wind!' I exclaimed. 'The wind is coming – Japhet foretells a storm.'

'A storm?' repeated Gaston in troubled tone, his voice nigh lost in the harsh creaking of the ship's timbers as she began to labour against the rising seas.

'He also mentioned rum – Oliver and his rogues! O Gaston 'twould be awful thing to fight with drunken madmen!'

'A storm!' says he again. 'The good God forbid it!'

'Gaston, how long should they take to be drunk, think you?'

But even as I spoke, and as if in answer to the question, rose a clamour of voices fiercer, wilder than the rising wind; then was a patter of naked running feet and the loud report of a musket, whereupon the running feet checked suddenly, seemed to break into a jig – ending in a heavy fall and dreadful, groaning cry.

'Gaston!' I exclaimed, horror-struck. 'O God—'

'Indeed, but he is verree good, my Adam, for there, I think is now one less for us to kill.'

'Roger!' roared a voice from the deck above, 'O lad crawl – crawl aft if ye can – I dassent leave the tiller – crawl to Japhet!'

'Did you hear?' cried I starting to my feet, 'they have shot Roger – he was our friend! They'll murder Japhet next – we must save him, Gaston, but how – how?'

'Wait!' said he, grasping my arm.

'O, Roger!' cried the voice above, 'are ye hurted so bad, Roger? Can't ye move, lad, can't ye stir? Why then I'll—' The words were lost in a chorus of drunken shouts and loudest of all – Oliver's.

'Avast, Japhet! Stand by now and mind y'r tiller!'

'Ay, and wot o' Roger?'

'Belay y'r jaw tackle my lad, an' keep her free—'

'Well, reef, Sam, reef – the wind's coming—'

'I'll reef when needful! You tend to y'r steerin', Japhet, and I'll tend to this bloody-minded Frenchman as tried to murder me. Below there!' he roared, thundering upon the door with pistol-butt. 'Below there – d'ye hear me? D'ye hear me, ye dogs?'

'Answer!' says Gaston, squeezing my arm, 'answer!'

'Yes, we hear!' I shouted, my voice a little uncertain.

'Well, now,' roared Oliver, 'here be poor fool – Roger layin' dead and all along o' you – and if 'e ain't dead 'e ought to be, and will be! Well, now, we wants the woman – and I wants the blasted Frenchman – we wants all on ye! Well, now, be ye coming aloft or must we try shooting through the hatch-combings. Be ye coming – ay or no?'

'Say "yes", Adam!'

'But – Gaston – in heaven's name—'

'Say "yes"!' he repeated, smiling, 'I think Oliver die quickly – say "yes"!'

'Yes!' I shouted, staring into my companion's grim face in a very agony of doubt. 'Yes – yes, we're coming.' And then Barbara was beside me, shaking my arm in frantic hands.

'No!' she panted, 'no – are ye mad? Death is up yon – ye shall not go!' But as she spoke, Gaston rose and, with word of apology, took off his great periwig, laid it carefully by and instantly covered his head with a close-fitting sailor's bonnet he drew from his pocket.

'The wind he blow and I would not lose my peruke,' says he sighing, 'alas I possess but the one!' Then with courtly bow he turned and began to climb the companion ladder.

'O, Gaston,' I cried, rising to stay him, 'they will murder you!'

'I think not, my Adam,' said he placidly, 'but it is as the good God wills – howbeit, I go – it is the chance we waited with the patience so admirable. Pray keep you and your lady out of their line of fire.' Then he went up the ladder.

Trembling I watched him draw the bolt, swing the door

wide – and in that moment was the stunning report of a shot, a gush of smoke and he was gone; but upon the deck above was a quick, wild trampling of feet. Then, breaking from Barbara's desperate hold, I sprang up the companion, sword in hand, and peering forth, beheld De Vrillac, a grim shape against background of angry sea and sky, bestriding Oliver's prostrate body, and a huddle of men cowering from the pistols he had snatched from the fallen man's belt.

'Ha, dogs-pigs of the vilest!' cried he in his terrible voice. 'Come ye here, come I say and cast me this carcass overboard!' and he stamped upon Oliver with passionate foot. 'Obey or this moment I kill some more of you – obey!'

Whimpering and muttering the men crept forward and stooping, began to drag that awful thing across the deck.

'Wait, Gaston!' cried I, interposing. 'First – in God's name is he dead?'

'My faith, sir,' says De Vrillac with dreadful laugh, 'I do not trouble myself to enquire. Over with him, my rogues!'

'But, Gaston—'

'Enough, sir!'

'But – if he be still alive, Gaston—'

'He will soon be dead which is most desirable, O yes!'

Then, as obedient to De Vrillac's threatening pistols, they hoisted that awful, sprawling thing to the rail, I turned away overcome by a sick nausea; and in this moment came an arm about me steadying my blundering steps, and so presently I found myself back in the cabin, staring into Barbara's pale face.

'He – he deserved it, Adam!' said she in faltering tone. 'He was a most evil man and brought it upon himself – O he deserved it, Adam.'

'But, Gaston,' says I, 'a man I thought so gentle – and so terrible – so merciless.'

Down to us through the open hatchway came the hoarse roar of Japhet :

'Reef down! All hands reef – reef for your lives!'

And, indeed, it seemed the wind piped a shriller angrier note while the hiss of tumbling seas grew ever the fiercer,

the louder and more threatening; but above this growing
tumult, louder, wilder and more despairing, rose Japhet's
hoarse roar :

'Reef – reef !'

CHAPTER 21

TELLETH HOW, IN THE MIDST OF DEATH,
WE TALKED TOGETHER

HOWLING wind, the rageful thunder of buffeting seas
wherein the ship pitched so wildly that often I thought we
were gone, and waited for the choking inrush of cruel waters
that should be our miserable end. A pitchy darkness (for our
swinging lamp, shattered against a roof-beam, had gone out)
and myself bruised, battered and direly sick. Now as I lay
thus in my misery I heard a deep groan, wherefore, my sickness having spent itself, I made shift to crawl thither and thus
presently my fumbling hands came on Gaston where he lay
huddled upon a locker and sinking upon my knees I set my
arms about him, being infinitely thankful for his companionship.

'Can I aid thee, Gaston?' said I, stooping above him.

'Nay!' groans he. 'I pray ... I cry in my soul to the great
God for I am sick with terror the most absolute, my Adam.
To die by the steel, the bullet ... O yes, it is the bagatelle;
But ... to drown! To be choked in that horror of waters,
choked like the so abominable rat ! ... O, my faith, it is for
me the death most terrible !'

'And yet death is ... only death, Gaston. And to drown is
none so hard, 'tis said.'

'Ah but, my friend, it is ... the water! This maketh of
me the *poltron*, the coward most contemptible. I possess for
myself the scorn terrific and yet ... always I tremble like the
little child ... so comfort me, I beg. Until we met I have
been the solitary soul verree lonely ! ... And now ... to die

by the thing I most do fear! ... Speak me comfort, my Adam.'

'Gaston,' says I, much moved, 'O, my friend, I have been lonely too! And now, if we must die indeed, hear me say 'twill come the kinder for thy friendship, death will be the easier for me, as life might have been. All my days I have yearned for such friend as thyself, Gaston, so grand and noble-spirited, indeed I that am so fearful, glory in thy courage ... though as regards thy dealing with the rogue Oliver—'

'O, Adam,' cried Gaston with sound 'twixt laugh and choke, 'brave youth, gentle boy, dost boggle and trouble thyself for such vile dog? Know then he was dead as the meat so salt we devour ... I shot him 'twixt the eyes, so think no more of thing so small. But for thyself, Adam, thy valour is to my cowardice the rebuke ... and thou so young I might be thy father! But, verily, this horror of water makes of me the child ... Hark thee, Adam ... years since I have a friend but we quarrel, we fight, I ... kill him and am the desolate one always ... and so now I am choke in this terrible sea ... it is just. And now, go comfort thy lady, it is, mayhap, that she needs thee more even than I ... go, my Adam!'

And so, fumbling in the dark I came to Barbara's door and knocked, calling her name.

'Yes, Adam?' says she her voice wonderfully clear and untroubled.

'I would but know you are well, or if I may do aught for you?'

'You may open the door and come to me,' says she. So I opened the door, taking care to secure it so, and stood in the darkness holding by her berth against the ship's violent rolling.

'I am here, Barbara, what is it?'

'Only this, Adam ... since death is all about us I would not meet God with a lie in my heart ... I do know you for no lord.'

'Then you believe me, at last?'

'I think I believed you from the first, for your eyes are truthful, Adam. 'Twas pride forbade my belief. Yet you are, I think, at least of gentle birth, and here is some small comfort.'

'No, no,' said I, miserably. 'I am indeed so humble, so very poor and destitute that ... O Barbara ... I have not even a name!'

And there in the pitchy darkness, while the tempest raged about us, I told her how I had been found beneath the hedge, and all my sordid history ... 'And so it is,' I ended, 'because Sir Hector in wedding us hath used me to your humiliation and my own bitter shame that, one day, I will bring him to an account.' Thus said I, clean forgetting, in my paltry pride, the imminent perils that threatened to destroy us; while to think how she must even now be scorning me, cut me to the very soul. Therefore, when at last she spoke I stood all amazed to hear her voice so gentle and sweetly compassionate :

'Poor little baby! Poor little desolate child! O Adam 'tis great wonder ye did na perish wi' the cold!'

After this we were silent some while and the awful thunder of the storm no more to me now than (as it were) a vague background to my thoughts.

'And think you,' I questioned at last, 'seeing I am not the lord you thought me and bare no name ... think you, indeed, that we are ... truly wed?'

'A'weel, Adam, I'm no sae sure o' your English laws, but syne we took each other for man an' wife in the sight o' Heaven, wed are we for ever and aye according to our law Scots. But dinna fash, sir, I'm no juist dyin' for a spouse ye ken, so shall ye be free o' me sae soon as ye will.'

'You,' sighed I, 'you are a great lady . . . very proud and I am but a—'

'Vera true, Adam! I'm Barbara MacGregor and she is ... juist a woman! Now go and leave poor Barbara to her prayers.'

'Wilt pray for me also, Barbara?'

'Are ye afeart o' death, Adam?'

'Very! Are you, Barbara?'

'Whiles I am, whiles I'm no ... And ye'll be vera blithe and glad tae win free o' this marriage, Adam?'

'Yes,' I answered. 'I could never endure your scorn.'

'But if ... if you'd been a lord indeed ... how then, Adam?'

'Why then,' I answered eagerly. 'Ah, Barbara, then truly I ... but no matter!'

''Tis great matter! Tell me!'

'No, madam.'

'And dinna ca' me "madam", my name's Barbara ... as I think ye ken already.'

'No, Mistress Barbara.'

'And dinna "mistress" me, sir!'

'No, Barbara Margaret MacGregor – no!'

'Nay, but won't you tell me, Adam?' sighed she in gentle, wheedling tone.

'No ... no indeed, 'twere folly.'

'Then I'll no pray for ye!'

'Why then—' I began bitterly ... but in this moment, with thunderous shock, the vessel pitched so violently and lay over so dizzily that I was nearly wrenched from my hold ... down and down plunged the ship until it seemed she could never recover; but as I clung there in dreadful expectation of death, out of the darkness came a smooth, round arm to twine about my neck, against my cheek was another cheek wet with tears, and then Barbara spoke, her voice hushed yet wonderfully undismayed:

'If this be death, Adam, let us meet it so! ... And God is beyond! ... And ... O Adam, I will pray for thee ... with my last breath—'

And then from somewhere above us was a splintering crash, a wild, high-pitched, wailing cry, and the vessel righted herself. ... And all this in less than a moment as it seemed.

'What was yon?' questioned Barbara, and her voice still so bravely untroubled that I forgot my own fears in some sort.

'Our masts going, I think.'

'Will this be death, Adam?'

'Mayhap,' I answered miserably.

'Then hold me, Adam, thine arm about me – so ... for death is a fearsome thing!' And in this dreadful moment I set my arms about her and held her close, heedless of storm and peril, and dumb with very happiness. And so thus we waited, our arms about each other, hearkening to the ceaseless clamour of the elements that seemed (as it were) roaring in triumph at our imminent destruction.

'Barbara,' said I at last, 'are you weeping?'

' 'Deed and I'm not!' she answered indignantly.

'Then why are your cheeks wet?'

'This was before you came ... my thoughts were unco' waefu'.'

'Because you were afraid?'

'Sir, a MacGregor canna' be afraid!'

'Then why did you weep?'

'I'll no be tellin' ye. Hark!' says she, suddenly. 'Surely someone is hailing ... O listen!' And presently, sure enough, above blusterous wind and the ceaseless rush and beat of the seas rose Japhet's hoarse bellow:

'Oho, below there! Come aloft ... Oho, come and bear a hand or we'm done! ...' At this I would have left her, but she would by no means suffer me to go.

'For,' says she, mighty determined, 'if we are to die it shall be together.'

'But hark ... there, Barbara, he calls again! There may be a chance for life even yet. I must go.'

'Then will I come with thee.'

So together we crept across the outer cabin and up the companion; but no sooner had I got the door open than I was met by such howling fury of rushing wind and spray as choked and blinded me for the moment.

'Keep back!' I gasped. 'Barbara, stay you below!'

Then, screening myself as best I might against the furious blast, I peered into a haggard dawn whose ghastly beam showed me a whirl of riven, low-driving clouds, a raging sea all about us and the wild, storm-beaten figure of Japhet at the tiller.

Blinded by stinging spray, deafened by buffeting wind, slipping, staggering, clutching desperately at all that offered, I fought my way aft until I was seized, steadied by a powerful arm, and peered up into Japhet's hairy face.

'She'm steadier since the mizzen went!' he roared. 'Can ye keep her afore the wind, sir, whiles I bears a hand along o' mounseer, yonder?'

'Where ... where is he?' I gasped.

'Yonder to looard cuttin' away the wreckage afore we'm stove. ... Can ye keep 'er so? Lookee, I've took this turn to brace the tiller for ye – so ... for she's a-kickin' d'ye see. Ease 'er off to the seas—so! But hold 'er afore the wind! Can ye keep 'er so, young master?'

'I'll do my best, Japhet ... But where are the other men?'

'They ain't, sir! Went overboard, they did, along o' that great sea as swep' us ... there be only pore Japhet left, Lord love me! ... Keep 'er to, my lord ... If we'm took abeam we'm gone, I rackon.'

Then, snatching up an axe, he left me (and mighty concerned) to strive with the tiller that jerked and thrust at me, for all its lashings, like the mighty arm of some malevolent giant ... Forgotten now my fears, my pitiful self, even Barbara, all my thoughts and all my energies bent to the one purpose, viz that I must keep this poor battered ship at all hazards from coming broadside-on to wind and sea ... And I held her, despite blinding spray and raving wind I held her, and knew a fearful joy and wonder at myself therefore, glorying in this brave vessel that she should thus defy this raging fury of tempest ... And then I slipped on the wet deck, my feet flew from under me ... over swung the tiller, bearing me with it, and I helpless as the ship herself. And in this bitter moment of failure I cried aloud :

'O God aid me! O God give me strength!'

And then other hands were beside mine on the tiller, a soft body braced me until I might regain foothold ... a moment's desperate effort and the imminent danger was averted.

'O, Barbara!' I panted, 'O, Barbara!'

'Yes, I am here, Adam,' says she, leaning so near to speak (by reason of the elemental uproar) that her sea-wet, wind-blown hair seemed all about me, 'surely God heard thy prayer! ... And now here must I needs stay ... for I ... dare not go back. And see yonder ... the day is breaking ... is it our last, I wonder?'

But I could not speak just then, being too scant of breath.

And presently, to my great relief, back comes Japhet and after him Gaston, who kept his face turned in-board that he might not look upon the fury of the waves, as I suppose.

'Japhet, whereaway are we?' says I, as he leaned to the thrust of the tiller.

'Yonder in our lee, sir, lays Scotland or should do, I rackon.'

'Scotland!' cried Barbara with a great gladness in her voice, 'O to be there!'

'Sirs, can ye see aught to larboard, yonder?' says Japhet, peering.

'Mist!' I answered.

'Well, sir, yon must be land, I rackon.'

'Yes – yes!' cried Gaston, hoarsely. ' 'Tis the land, indeed, I see him through the mist.'

'Well now, my masters an' lady, 'tis what to do? Shall us bear away afore the gale and chance being pooped ... sinkin' an' drowndin', sirs and ma'm, or shall us try beach-in' of her – which?'

'Beach her!' said Barbara, peering eagerly beneath her hand.

'Which is least dangerous?' said I.

'Neether and both, sir!' answered Japhet shaking his head. ' 'Tis pore chance for we anyway, I rackon.'

'What say you, Gaston?'

'Beach ... the beach, my Adam. O my faith, trust we to anything but this so cruel ... so terrible sea.'

'So be it, then,' said I, though my heart was heavy with misgiving.

'Ay, ay, sirs and ma'm, beach 'er it is, then! But now, if

we might contrive bite an' sup? There be plenty o' food in the galley and in Sam's locker – rum! Rum, my masters, for this be a shiversome wind, and my pore innards arl of a quake-like.'

CHAPTER 22

GIVETH SOME DESCRIPTION OF HOW I CAME ASHORE

BY MIDDAY we had so closed with the land that ever and anon, despite rain and swirling mists, we could descry the vague loom of it, and, once or twice, I fancied I could hear the far-off, sullen roar of breakers. All at once as we gazed thus, mute with fearful expectancy, the rain ceased, the mists were rent asunder and there (to our joy and relief unspeakable) lay a stretch of sandy beach right proper to our so desperate purpose.

'Stand by!' roared Japhet and, shifting the tiller, headed us straight for this kindly beach that seemed to grow rapidly upon us as the *Sussex Lass* drove forward upon the rushing surge until I could see the waves breaking ashore in foaming thunder – nearer until beyond this fury of breakers I could see that sandy level and in the midst thereof a solitary, storm-battered pinnacle of rock – nearer yet ... and then was sudden, grinding crash, a splintering, rending shock that threw me headlong, to lie half-smothered by the great following-sea that broke aboard of us; but in this dreadful moment I heard Barbara's choking cry:

'Adam!'

And, struggling amid this deluge, I found hands that grasped me, arms that clung, and thus, fast locked together, we awaited death. But the ship had ceased her pitching and rolling, only she quivered ever and anon as the mighty waves broke over her.

Therefore, presently looking about us, I saw that we lay, Barbara and I, in corner quite sheltered from wind and wave, amid a mass of fallen rope and cordage, wherewith I contrived to secure us somewhat against the peril of such another sea ... Now as we crouched thus side by side, I heard Japhet's familiar roar and hallooed in return, whereafter he comes clambering towards us, and with him Gaston.

'We'm aground, sirs!' cries Japhet, ''tis the end o' the poor, old *Lass* I rackon. She may stay fast till she goes to pieces or she may slip off into deep water and sink, but – here's goodbye to we, I rackon.'

'And the land, my faith, it is so near!' quoth Gaston, with a hopeless gesture.

'Two hundred paces, about!' says I, measuring the distance with my eye.

'Less, my lord,' says Japhet, 'it aren't above forty fathom. But what matter, 'tis beyond our reach! We'm done, sirs, like the poor, old *Sussex Lass*—'

'Do you mean we ... we must surely drown?' cried I.

'I rackon!' he nodded. At this, Barbara stole her hand in mine, comforting me :

'Never grieve!' she whispered, creeping closer. 'God is with us. ... But ... oh, Adam, if I have said aught to hurt thee ... as indeed I have ... forgive me now, my dear.'

'Freely!' says I, and thereafter sat miserably enough, my face sunk between my hands in a very agony of fear and indecision, staring now at this shore of Scotland that might be our salvation and now at the raging fury of sea that was to murder us, while Barbara, perceiving how I shook, held me the tighter and spoke me comfort, yet I never heeded, staring dreadfully now at the waves and now the shore ... At last, slowly, unwillingly, yet compelled by some power mightier than my fear, I began to loose the ropes that held me, whereat Barbara questioned in swift alarm :

'Ah – what is it? What would you, Adam?'

'To sit here is to perish!' said I, pointing at the ravening flood. 'And I cannot – wait for ... death – cannot watch it creeping on us.'

'Then suffer I shelter thee, Adam, thy poor eyes.'

'Also,' says I, unbuttoning coat and waistcoat, 'I might . . . perchance reach shore . . . with a line about me! Howbeit I must attempt it.'

'No!' cries she, in swift, strange passion. 'I say, you shall not!'

'I must!' said I, and loosing her grasp, I arose, stripped off my sodden coat, grieving to see its bravery so ruined, and laying it by, bade Japhet help me off with my cumbersome boots, whereat he did but gape.

'The current, I think, sets in-shore by the look of it,' says I miserably. 'If I can but pass the breakers . . . God's mercy how they roar!'

'Eh . . . swim, my lord?' exclaimed Japhet, 'swim ashore through that sea?'

'I must needs so endeavour . . . come, my boots! . . . And now I want a line about me, not too heavy, Japhet.'

'Sure-ly, young master. But, my lord, what do your lady say of it?'

'Choose me a line, Japhet!'

'Ay, but,' says he yet hesitating and turning to Gaston, 'you, mounseer, what do ee think now?'

'Friend,' quoth Gaston, grasping my two hands and looking down into my eyes, 'is it that thy heart bids thee to it indeed?'

'Yes!' I answered, and yet clinging to those strong, kindly hands.

'Ah, well,' says he with his gentle smile, 'very soon it is, I think, that we shall all die, my Adam, but love and friendship, these abide.'

So he embraced and kissed me, after which Japhet proceeded to knot a length of stout line about me very dexterously, while Barbara watched great-eyed:

'Adam,' says she, wondering and marvellous troubled, 'why must you seek death alone thus?'

'Because I dare not wait for death to seek . . . us!' says I, stooping to see that Japhet's knots were fast.

'May God be with thee, Adam!'

'And with you also!' I answered and would have turned

126

away but, swift and sudden, she arose and clasped her arms about me and set her lips to mine.

'Oh, Adam,' says she, even as we kissed. 'Oh, dear Adam, there be things greater than nobility of birth ... kiss me again, dear my husband!' So I kissed her and then, in joyous wonder too deep for words, came to the ship's side with Japhet, grasped his big hand, mounted the bulwark and plunged overboard.

Now what pen (least of all mine) should justly describe all the wild fury of this cruel sea that whirled me high on foaming summits and plunged me into sudden deeps, yet bore me dizzily towards the roaring terror of the breakers? ... And then, and almost ere I knew it, I was among them, was sucked down, tossed aloft, beaten, buffeted and cast into shallows where I touched solid earth only to be swept away and back again by the hissing, resistless under-tow – back and back to be plunged anew in darksome, churning depths, whirled up again to light and air, to desperate effort and an ever-growing weakness and despair.

Indeed, I remember little more of this agony till came one mighty billow that caught me up and, rushing shoreward, cast me on the sand, a gasping, sobbing, half-dead creature that clung instinctively with clawing fingers against the hissing backwash that tore and wrenched to drag me back to those awful whirling deeps where destruction waited and death roared for me.

Thus, groaning and sobbing, more dead than alive, crawled I with what of strength was left me, up and away from the ravening monster behind, dragging my battered body on and on until, all power failing me, I sank down at last, my cheek pillowed upon this kindly earth, my crooked fingers deep-sunk within it.

So lay I some while until my strength recovered somewhat, I struggled to my knees and turned. But now, beholding what horror of sea I had come through, I hid my eyes appalled and crouched thus on my knees, gasped forth my thankfulness to that most merciful God that He should have wrought me such miracle.

And truly miracle I found it, for now laying hold upon my line it seemed the great wave had cast me ashore even beyond the rock (which I have before mentioned) and my line, coming about this, had anchored me, as it were, and thus kept me from being dragged back to death by the rushing under-tow.

Presently (though very spent and sore-bruised) I got afoot and waved my arms to them aboard the *Sussex Lass* where she lay, the seas breaking over her very dreadful to behold. And now came Japhet's great voice and yet, mighty though it was, hard to hear above the thundering surf :

'. . . cheerily . . . haul . . . mek fast . . . the rock !'

So I began to haul in my line though slowly for I was very weak and with a strange drowsiness, and oft must pause to rest me a moment for it seemed the line came more heavily so that I sank to my knees yet wrought the more passionately fearing lest I swoon and the rope be washed out to sea. Thus with aching head bowed betwixt weary arms, I hauled until the light line became a stout rope yet still I hauled and strove until I sank down and lay helpless, my face pillowed on the coils of wet rope . . .

'Oho . . . mek fast . . . rock . . . three or four turns. . .'

Japhet was hailing again . . . I must make this rope of salvation secure . . . Sobbing with pain and fatigue I got up upon my feet and reeling weakly, came to the rock that jutted up from the sand excellent to the purpose, and began to stumble about and about it dragging the rope after me and thus winding it many times about the rock until at last I tripped and fell, struggled to rise and knew no more.

CHAPTER 23

HOW MISTRESS BARBARA AND I, BEING ALIVE, AGREED TO PART

I OPENED my eyes to the comfort of a fire that blazed and crackled right cheerily, putting me to such surprise that I would have sat up the better to look about me but found movement so painful that I sank back groaning, and in this moment came Barbara to kneel beside me.

'Oh – thou art safe!' says I, filled with sudden great content.

'Thanks to yourself, Adam,' she answered, smoothing my hair very tenderly.

'Ay, but the others? Gaston?' I questioned eagerly.

'Yourself saved us all, Adam, and now do lie here spent and alas I hae neither bite nor sup to offer you.'

'Thank God that dreadful wind is gone!' says I, fervently.

'Nay, it still rages outside, Adam.'

'Why then where are we?'

'In a cavern. Monsieur found it this morning, and carried thee hither, and here hast lain asleep and moaning ever since, and now 'tis evening.'

'And how cometh the fire?'

'Monsieur set it agoing with the flint of his pistol.'

'And where is he?'

'Out with Japhet seeking village or cot to buy food. Art very hungry, my poor Adam?'

'Why, 'tis no matter,' I answered, frowning because of my bruises.

'Is there aught I may do to thy comfort?'

'No, I thank you ... But here lie I more destitute than ever, Barbara, a very wretch, with scarce enough to cover me and never a penny for more.'

'But your clothes are here, Adam, all of them – even to your sword and wig. Monsieur Gaston brought them ashore on his back and would ha' perished doing it, but for Japhet.'

'Oh, wonderful!' cried I. ''Twas noble in Gaston to run such peril and he so fearful o' the sea!'

''Deed, but he could scarce do less – for you, Adam, for hae you not twice saved his life?'

'And truly this was my own good fortune!' cries I eagerly, 'for he is now become very dear, a friend such as I have yearned for all my days, and is a very noble gentleman besides.'

'Ou ay, he's well enough!' says she, in tone mighty disparaging.

'Moreover,' I went on, 'he is a very wise gentleman, having seen so much of—'

'Oh, la, la!' sighed she and yawned at me behind slim finger.

'Howbeit, I love him,' says I, frowning at her, 'and 'tis my dear hope to prove worthy of his friendship.'

'Ah me – such humility!' cries she, mighty contemptuous. 'And he ye so worship nae mair than middle-aged, bony foreigner, an auld gomeril body, whateffer!' Now at this, what with my aches and pains (and being mighty hungry) I was seized of sudden, hot anger :

'Madam Pertness,' quoth I, 'your irreverent mockery of my friend affronts me—'

'Master Humility,' she retorted, 'I rejoice to know it. Mayhap your so adored monsieur, having permitted you the honour to save his life repeatedly, will suffer ye to kiss the bony knuckles of him an ye so desire.'

'Mistress Barbara,' says I, scowling up at her, 'you have a most bitter tongue!'

'Master Adam,' says she, frowning down on me, 'my certie ye hae yet tae thole the sting o't.'

'No, madam!' cries I, my anger growing, 'I'll not suffer it—' hereupon she began some retort though what I cannot tell, for into my ears I rammed my fingers.

So here were we, within few minutes of my waking and so newly out of the very clutch of Death, quarrelling together, like two heedless children, most bitterly – and all for no reason that I could see.

And when she had talked herself breathless (or nearly so) I unstopped my ears and, finding her silent, began in my turn – calmly as I might :

'Mistress Barbara, I have pledged myself to bring you safe home to your people, and—'

'For the which condescension, noble sir, know me humbly grateful!' says she, bitterly mocking.

'And, madam, whiles we company together, I would beg you so to act that when we part—'

'Oh, part, sir?' says she, her eyes very bright. 'Part, is it?'

'Part, madam,' I repeated very patiently, 'it may be with some small regret to each of us and, I hope, a mutual respect.'

'My regret is that I ever saw you, Adam!'

'It is also mine,' says I, fervently.

''Deed, Adam,' cried she in a fury, 'my misliking of you outgrows my scorn!'

'This I also regret,' says I gloomily, 'though, to be sure, 'twill make our parting the easier—'

And thus we baited and taunted each other, until finally she turned her back upon me, whereat I did the same, and so lay staring at this cavern which appeared very large and with many gloomy recesses, its floor strewn with great boulders of shapes fantastical, one in especial being like a shrouded figure crouched as to leap at me.

Yet presently I must needs turn to steal a look at my silent companion, to find her watching me, sullen-eyed :

'Hast a grievously bitter temper and very hateful, Adam!' says she.

'Why, then . . . pray forgive it,' I answered, sighing.

'And art slavishly humble, and this I hate more.'

'I am what Nature and circumstance made me,' says I bitterly.

'Then do somewhat to aid Nature, be strong to master and force Circumstance tae your ain good, be bold to command Fortune 'stead of meekly suing and pleading—' but here, I, knowing this beyond my powers, turned away and she, mistaking this for anger, cried out on me more angrily than ever :

'Oh 'tis my shame to know 'twas yourself saved my life, I would it had been honest Japhet – ay, or even your adored Monsieur Gaston . . . I think,' says she, rising, 'yes I think I'll out and meet them . . . And yet,' says she in kinder voice, 'mebbe I'll bide with ye . . . if you will but ask me.'

Now the thought of being left in this wild place of gloom and leaping shadows woke in me such dread that words of pleading sprang to my lip, but I checked them for very shame and turned my face to the cavern wall; lying thus, I heard the light tread of her departing feet, yet I never moved until, bethinking me of that evil-looking boulder behind me, I turned about that I might keep it in view. And presently, as I stared on it, this grimly thing, by some trick of the uncertain firelight, seemed to move, whereat I blenched behind my up-flung arm, gasping like veriest craven; and in this moment I saw Barbara's face peeping at me above this same boulder, and then she was beside me, her arm about my shoulders.

'Why, Adam, what is it?' she questioned soothingly.

'Nothing!' says I, hiding my face. 'Naught in the world save that I am like a child – affrighted by shadows.'

'Nay, indeed, I would not truly have left thee,' she murmured and clasped me in her arms.

'I'm naught but a craven coward!' I sobbed, clinging to her, as I had truly been a child. 'Oh, Barbara!'

'A craven – thou?' cries she with a little sobbing laugh. 'Never say so, never think it! Was he a craven that rescued Gaston from the sea? Was he coward that outfaced mutiny with a broken pistol? Was he coward that swam through that horror of raging waters? Here was strange cowardice, my foolish Adam!' And with the word she kissed me ...

And presently was sound of echoing steps and voices and in came our good friends and each with a bundle.

'Gaston!' cried I in joyous welcome, whereat he put down his burden, bowed gaily to Barbara and grasped my outstretched hand in both of his.

'Oh, my faith, Adam,' quoth he, his eyes very bright, 'I joy to see thee so well, thou'rt as one new risen from the grave, the good God be thanked. And thou'rt hungry – yes? Good, for we have food the most excellent.'

'Likewise drink, my lord!' added Japhet, aiding Barbara to open the packages.

'Bannocks!' she exclaimed. 'And – oh, a mutton ham!'

'Also butter, lady, pepper, cheese, salt and – ale!'

Thus presently, seated about the fire, a right joyous meal we made, talking and laughing, clean forgetting our late dangers and distress, yet none of us so merry as Barbara who, seated 'twixt Gaston and Japhet, besets them with a whirling flood of questions, as :

Where had they been? What seen? Had they heard of any fighting and, if so, what clans were out? Was there any talk of Campbells, red-coats or the McFarlanes? Had they learned exactly whereabouts we had been cast ashore?

At the which questionful torrent Gaston looked at Japhet and never a word from either.

'Well,' cries she eagerly, 'can ye no speak? You, monsieur, where in bonnie Scotland are we?'

'Madame,' he began but, at that, she stopped him.

'Good friend,' says she, smiling on him so sweet and gentle as put me to great wonder, minding her late dispraise of him, 'good friend, pray call me Barbara, for we hae lookit into the eyes o' death together and this should breed a loving kindness, so Barbara am I to thee henceforth, Gaston,' and she gave him her hand, the which he held as it had been something vastly precious, as indeed it was.

'Barbara,' says he, 'here indeed is honour, a joy for me the most absolute! You make almost that I forget the empty years – you and my Adam.' Then stooping in his stately fashion, he kissed her hand so reverently that, meeting my eye, she flushed.

'Gaston,' says she, flashing defiant glance at me, 'but a little since I named thee a . . . a middle-aged, bony foreigner.'

For a moment he stared speechless then laughed, such joyous, merry peal as I had never expected from his gravity :

'Bony!' he repeated, staring at his lean hand and wrist. 'My faith but how very much true! But – middle-aged? Hélas!'

'And so, Gaston,' she continued, mighty solemn, 'I do now most humbly entreat your kind forgiveness.'

'Ah, but no no!' cries he, smiling and shaking his head, 'here shall be no cause in the degrees most small—'

'Friend Gaston,' says she, clasping his hand again, 'I beseech thee forgive me – this instant!'

'Then, Barbara, with a joy extraordinaire I—' He stopped for, swift and graceful, she stooped her proud and handsome head and kissed his hand in turn. For a moment he stared down at this sinewy hand (which could be so terrible) and when he spoke his voice was hushed to marvellous tenderness : 'Child,' he murmured, 'but two women ever so honoured me and one was my mother … and both saints in heaven … *Alors*!' says he, after a moment. 'For thy questions, so many. First, we are in the Kingdom of Fife—'

'Why, then,' says she, 'I jalouse we hae some ninety odd miles journeying northwards. And did ye hear aught o' the wicked Campbells?'

'*Hélas*, yes. There is talk of bloodshed, villages afire in the country McLean and among the … I think … Lamonts.'

'Ah, God!' she exclaimed. 'These wicked clan-feuds! Oh, my puir, bonnie Scotland! … And so the clans are up alas! Then must we go by wild ways, and the sooner we start, the better.'

'Tomorrow!' says I. 'And you, Gaston, will you go with us?'

'But surely, my Adam,' he answered, smiling at my eagerness. 'Am not I the creature most desolate except for thee and Barbara?'

'And you, Japhet?'

'Ay, ay, my lord, any p'int o' the compass sarves for poor Japhet Bly, me bein' a lonely, lorn man, like his honour Mounseer, d'ye see.'

'Then,' says I, 'we start tomorrow.'

'Shall you be able – so soon, Adam? For if the clans be out we must gang cannily.'

'What firearms have we, Gaston?'

'Three pistols, Adam.'

'And never no powder nor shot!' added Japhet.

'And what o' money?' inquired Barbara. 'Alas, I hae but few shillings left.'

'I've a guinea – I think,' says I.

'And me, sirs and ma'm,' growled Japhet, 'ain't never

got nowt i' the world save a groat — seven golden guineas o' mine lays down along o' Davy Jones.'

'Money,' says Gaston, finger a-flourish, 'ah — bah, I have it a plenty, oh yes.'

'Why then, to rest,' says Barbara, 'for I'd away early the morn.'

'To sleep on the solid earth again,' quoth Gaston, rising, 'oh, my faith, it will be verree good!' And so, with hearty 'goodnights' he and Japhet withdrew toward the cavern's mouth; and then comes Barbara with her cloak to fold it about me, the which I would by no means suffer, insisting she keep it to her own comfort, which in the end she did, though ungraciously for, crossing to the opposite side of the fire where she had contrived her a bed, she lay down without speaking a word, as, for that matter, neither did I. But after I had lain a while peering very earnestly toward where she lay:

'Adam,' says she, very murmurous and soft.

'Yes?' I whispered eagerly.

'' Tis agreed we part ... for ever ... so soon as I reach my ain folk.'

'Yes, assuredly!' I answered, mighty determined; and then I heard her laughing softly.

'Pray what makes you so merry?' I demanded, wondering and indignant.

'My thoughts!' says she, laughing yet. 'My thoughts, Master Prideful, Innocent, Self-Righteousness! Good nicht t' ye.'

But, instead of answering, I lay frowning up at the dance and flicker of the firelight on the jagged rock above and around me until my eyes closed and I fell asleep. Suddenly I waked, conscious that Barbara was kneeling beside me and then, or ever I might speak, she begins to stroke my hateful red hair very- tenderly, with touch indeed hardly to be felt; and now, having no mind to speak, I lay very still as if fast asleep, until at last she sighed and crept away.

And then I found she had spread her cloak about me, and thus I slept beneath it after all.

CHAPTER 24

I T was with the sun bright about us that we set forth next morning upon that journey destined to work in me a very miracle of change.

A man's body groweth with the years, strong or weak according to his nature, but it is by experience of hardship, of danger and difficulty, loss and gain, sorrow and joy that the latent powers and hidden qualities within him are developed, transforming him out of all knowledge.

And thus did I, by reason of Circumstance (as you shall see) grow out of all semblance to that poor youth, that hopeless drudge had gone his lonely way doubtful of himself as of his future, meekly enduring Fortune's spites and the brutality of Master Bragg.

And so to my narrative :

Now as we went the stiffness of my many bruises wore off somewhat, also there was Gaston or brawny Japhet to aid me in the rougher going, though to be sure we made no great speed. Thus the sun was high when we reached a winding stream which we crossed with small difficulty and, climbing a hill, beheld a lake which Barbara said was called Loch Leven. And here, insisting we rest a while (to my great comfort), she points us a small island in the lake and upon it a castle wherein Queen Mary of Scots (that most unhappy, luckless lady) had been pent, but whence she escaped only to fall into greater evils, and finally bow her lovely head to the cruel axe. All this Barbara told us in that sweet husky voice of hers, so different from her ordinary clear tones.

And so on again, keeping the lake to our left until we reached a wooded country, with great hills rising beyond and higher than I had ever seen, and thus into a little, quiet hamlet where was a tavern or, as she said, a change-house, a poor place after our great English inns, and here we entered, to be greeted by a quick, black-haired man who stared us up and down, hailing us in outlandish tongue, yet methought pleasant to hear, in the which strange speech Barbara answered him.

'But yourself has the English, gudeman,' says she, 'let us speak it. I am a MacGregor o' that ilk, and these my friends.' Here the man saluted us again and with prodigious respect.

' 'Tis food's our want,' says she.

'And drink, ma'm!' added Japhet.

'Ay, and four plaidies,' says Barbara.

'Likewise powder and shot and — ale, ma'm!' quoth Japhet.

'Can ye find us a' these, gudeman?' questions Barbara, whereupon the man blinked, and shouted: 'Elspeth!'

At this appeared a buxom woman to whom Barbara spake in the Gaelic, and with whom she retired whiles the landlord, having drawn us tankards of ale (very excellent strong), began to set forth an appetizing repast, talking the while in his queer, clipped English:

'Waefu' times, sirs, wha' wi' the bluidy Campbells, burning and slaying honest bodies, an' the wild MacFarlanes raidin' an' rievin', black be their fa'! There'll be mony a braw laddie stark an' bluidy i' the heather 'twixt here an' Pairth, I jalouse.'

'We heard the clans are fighting,' says I.

'Fechtin' d'ye ca' it, sir? Herself she wad name it murder ... MacFarlane an' murder gang together, like Campbell an' corbie, ye ken. 'Tis no juist a canny time tae be awa' north, I'm thinkin' – an' a noble leddy wi' ye forbye – whisht!' and he turned away as Barbara entered.

'Master Gow,' says she to the landlord, 'your gudewife tells me the McLeod is hame.'

'Ay, my leddy, an' wi' twa-three hunner claymores at his back!'

And presently we ate and drank with good appetite yet

silently, for Barbara spake little, and her look was troubled. Gaston seemed too busied with his thoughts, Japhet too hungry, whiles I must needs be picturing those braw lads stark and bloody on the heather, and wonder uneasily what perils might be waiting us in the north. At last Barbara sighed and spoke:

'Friends,' says she, looking on us, her beautiful eyes very sad, 'I hear evil tales of fighting ... of death in lonely places ... Alas for this poor country, my dear, bonny Scotland!' Here her eyes brimmed with quick tears, 'Alas that Scot should slay Scot, but thus hath it ever been! Now God forbid I should bring you into needless dangers and so – nay, hear me, Gaston – and so, because I ... I must needs to my father, I would bid you all farewell, here and now ... I pray God speed you all safe back to England—'

'And how of me?' says I.

'Adam is yet weak of his hurts,' quoth she, not looking at me, 'and also ... though he is my husband, 'tis my desire that we ... that we should part—'

'Part?' I repeated, hot with sudden anger.

'And no time,' she went on, and still unheeding me, 'dear my friends, no time better than now—' here she rose, sighing, 'so fare ye well, Barbara MacGregor's prayers shall go with you.'

'Mighty fine!' says I, bitterly, 'but why not suffer me to finish eating?'

'Adam,' says she a little breathlessly and very heedful of me at last. 'O, Adam, what do you mean?'

'That I'll not suffer you to go a-tramping this evil country alone, for one thing.'

'You'll not suffer me – you?' cries she and laughed, whereat the anger within me leapt to sudden, cold fury.

'Be silent, madam,' says I, staring into her widening eyes, 'if I am your husband you go south with me into England or I go north with you, so ha' done with your fleering folly and choose, madam, choose!' Now here ensued a silence wherein she stared on me, her eyes very wide, her vivid lips apart, for all the world as if she now beheld me for the first time in her life, while Gaston looked up at the rafters and Japhet hid his hairy visage behind his ale-mug.

'Choose!' I repeated fiercely; 'North or South?'

'North,' she answered with look and tone marvellous, humble and meek, 'I . . . I must go North . . . and I thought . . . yourself said—'

'So be it!' said I and, reaching hat and sword, pointed to the open door. 'Come, madam, let us be gone!'

'But . . . Adam, I . . . we—' she faltered, shrinking from my outstretched hand; now here, chancing to meet Gaston's bright eyes, I stood somewhat abashed, whereupon says he, gently:

'We are forgetting, as I think, our powder and shot, my Adam.'

'And ale!' quoth Japhet. 'Can't us tak' some along, my lord?'

'And . . . our plaids!' said Barbara. 'We shall need them a-nights amid the heather . . . And, alas, all to be paid for with thy money, Gaston!'

''Tis my joy *véritable*!' says he smiling at her wistful look.

Anon the landlord brings us all that we had ordered, and now, with sundry wags of head and winks of eye, shows us a musket.

'A noble piece, sirs!' quoth he. 'A braw, bonnie piece whateffer, and vera comfortin' tae a traveller in sic dowie, unchancy times!'

'Aha!' said Gaston, running his eye over it. 'An English musket I think, yes?'

'Wheesht, sir, 'tis juist a bit gun I happed on y'ken, and yours for twa pun English!'

'Then, my friend, I give for it one guinea – no, yes?'

'Mak' it ten shilling mair, sir, an' I'll gie' ye powder an' ball wi' it. And mind ye the country 'twixt here an' Pairth is fair switherin' wi' wild caterans, MacFarlanes and sic-like feckless bodies, and och 'tis a braw piece yon – tak' it for five an' twenty shillin' English and say nae mair.'

So in the end Gaston bought the weapon which Japhet insisted on carrying. Next Barbara showed us how we must fold our plaids and twist them over our left shoulders, then, having bought as much food as she thought proper, together with a flask of spirits and another of ale, we bade farewell to our host and his wife and set out on our perilous journey northwards.

CHAPTER 25

THE WHICH IS CHAPTER OF WEARINESS

I WILL not set down all that befell us from day to day, since this narrative already groweth apace, and much yet to tell; so will I hurry on to come at him that seemed my evil genius and whose solitary heart and grief-stricken, cankered soul drave him ever on to that relentless and bloody vengeance which in the end led inevitably to his own dismay and undoing.

It was, then, the third evening of our wanderings (for we followed devious tracks) when, spent and footsore (or I at least) we entered a wild country of jagged heights, foaming torrents and gloomy, desolate glens where bush-girt summit and rocky slope seemed to scowl upon us as we plodded over toilsome way. Indeed as, trudging wearily thus, I lifted my awed gaze to beetling cliff and rugged mountain grim and monstrous against the gloomy heaven, I shivered, for this forbidding country woke in me a sense of evil omen and deadly menace.

At last, having reached a sheltered place where stunted trees rustled fitfully in the stealthy nightwind and a brook ran sadly murmurous, Barbara stopped.

'Let us camp here the night beside this burn,' says she. 'How think you, Adam?'

'Yes,' I answered, 'anywhere,' and, unwinding heavy plaid I laid by sword and belt; then whiles Japhet did off the pack that held our supplies and with Barbara began to set forth supper, Gaston made a fire and I began to gather store of wood therefor. Thus presently I found myself among trees, and had collected a great armful of sticks when I recoiled suddenly and stood, sick and weak with horror, staring down into eyes that glared up at me, awful and sightless, out of a pallid, dead face ... A great, red-headed fellow in ragged tartans; and looking upon his terribly marred face I shivered to see what a Scottish claymore may do.

Slowly I backed away from this ghastly thing, back and back until something tripped me and glancing thereby, I saw a pair of brawny legs rigidly out-sprawled from a whin-bush. So stood I betwixt these two dead men whiles into my mind rushed the landlord's prophecy: 'There'll be many a braw lad stark and bloody in the heather.' ... And then I heard Barbara's sweet, clear voice:

'Adam, oh Adam!' And she was coming to seek me! Therefore I turned and sped towards her, stumbling in my haste.

'Why, Adam,' says she, eyeing me anxiously, 'thou'rt unco' pale, thou'rt all fordone, I doubt.'

'Yes,' I answered, 'yes I ... I'm very weary.'

'Then come you and eat!' said she, and brought me to the fire, the which was crackling merrily, whereby she had spread my plaid; so down sat I though taking care to face that darkling stretch of woodland. Supper ready, we ate and drank in an unwonted silence, our spirits being oppressed (as I judge) by the forbidding aspect of our surroundings. At length Barbara, seated beside me, leaned to peer into my face.

'Thou'rt still very pale,' said she, 'is it the fatigue?'

'Yes,' I answered, moving that I might still watch that gloomy wood.

''Deed you are still too weak for such hard travel. But in two days or less we should reach ... our journey's end.'

'Good!' I nodded. 'But what then, Barbara?'

At this she gave me a troubled look, then, sighing, gazed into the fire very wistfully.

'I have never told you of ... of my father, have I, Adam?'

'Yet I know him for very proud gentleman, troubling

for none beneath a lord in rank. 'Twas so Sir Hector Keith, or MacFarlane described him.'

'Also he is blind, Adam. It is this, I think, hath so embittered him, for, being so kin to the McGregor he was once captain of the clan.'

'I grieve for his blindness,' says I, 'but I fear he shall grieve more bitterly to know his daughter wed to nameless beggar.' At this, she shrank nearer the fire as if suddenly chill, and presently spoke, whispering:

'Need he know this, Adam?'

'Yes!' I answered. 'Oh, be sure Sir Hector will tell him soon or late! 'Twas but for this he wed us ... to humble your father's pride ... Yet will I make Keith's triumph an empty one – in the end.'

'How, Adam, prithee how?'

'Soon as you come safe home I shall ... disappear ... leave you to wed one more suited to your rank than nameless I.'

'Ay, but what o' yourself, Adam dear?'

'I shall still have Gaston, I pray God!'

'Gaston!' she repeated in hissing whisper; and then, leaning so near that her hair brushed my cheek. 'Ah, shall ye no grieve a wee while for your puir Barbara?'

To the which I was dumb lest I say too much, but turned away and rolling myself in my plaid, lay down (miserably enough) and composed myself to slumber. But even then she must needs bend over me to whisper close in my ear:

'Is it naught to thee to think o' thy wedded wife in another man's arms?' With which, she left me.

CHAPTER 26

WHICH TELLETH OF AN ALARM BY NIGHT

THIS night, sick with weariness as I was, sleep refused its comfort (and small wonder), for Barbara's last words grieved and angered me, and I lay a great while full of uneasy speculation concerning the future and wondering miserably what must become of me ... Suddenly up started I to an elbow, peering towards that dark and dreadful woodland whence had come a vague, furtive movement, a leafy whispering; and now I saw that Gaston sat up listening also.

'Gaston,' I whispered, 'what is it?' Dumbly he signed me to silence. And then my flesh crept with horror to hear the wood full of dreadful sound, the fierce rustle of leaves, snapping of twigs and most dolorous outcries – as if, indeed, those dead men were up and fighting together; then Gaston was afoot and I saw the glitter of his sword as into the firelight rushed the wild figure of a woman who beckoned and called on us in despairing voice, though what she said I knew not. Then Barbara was questioning this distracted creature in the Gaelic, whose breathless answers she translated for us:

'She says they are beset by caterans, broken men, robbers! She says they are murdering her husband ... Oh, what can we do?'

'But, dear my child,' says Gaston gently, 'it is of the simplest, we must instantly kill some of these robbers, is it not? *Mordieu*, it is!'

'Ay, ay, sir!' growled Japhet, taking up the musket. 'I'm wi' you, mounseer, let's lay them robbers aboard!' and I heard the click of his long musket as he cocked it.

'Come, then, if it must be,' sighed Barbara.

'But – not through the wood!' cries I, snatching sword and plaid.

'Oh what matter the way?' she retorted querulously.

'It matters greatly,' says I. 'So bid the woman carry us another way.'

And now, having hurriedly collected our gear, we set off with the terrified woman speeding on before.

Soon we were forth of that frowning glen, upon a heathery slope tending steeply down to where, afar, stood a large homestead, its small windows aglow, whence came a confused hubbub, pierced, ever and anon, by a fierce, high-pitched rallying cry.

Breathless and trembling I stumbled on between Japhet and Gaston whiles ever those hateful sounds of conflict grew louder and more dreadful. Twice I stumbled and nearly fell, but on I sped careless of all but the scene before us ... An open doorway where two men fronted many and one of these two a very giant in kilt and tartan armed with a great sword called claymore, his comrade, short by comparison and very slight yet marvellous nimble, his narrow blade darting and glittering as thus, with ponderous swing of claymore and lightning thrust of smallsword, these two withstood the many. But now Gaston halted to wind plaid about his left arm, bidding me do the like.

'For,' says he cheerily, 'you shall find it very proper for such close melée.' And in this moment I admired to see him so assured and serene and, striving to be the same, prayed inwardly that I might prove worthy such friend.

'Be us ready, sir?' says Japhet, spitting into the palm of his big right hand. Here, meeting Gaston's questioning, anxious look, I nodded since speech was beyond me just then.

'*Bien!*' smiled Gaston, 'let us now advance, but tenderly – so! And remember it is always the point, my Adam!'

I heard Barbara cry out to me, but never heeded since all my attention was for the solitary two who yet made head very gallantly against their many assailants; suddenly the smaller man staggered and fell but was instantly bestridden by his gigantic comrade who, whirling his mighty weapon still kept their foes at bay.

'*Voilà!*' exclaimed Gaston. 'It is now I think necessaire that we run – *en avant, mes amis!*'

And indeed run we did, side by side, a-down that heather-slope ... then Japhet's mighty voice bellowed fiercely as we burst into that reeling fray ... And now steel flickered all about me ... I heard shouts, groans, dreadful outcries, took a numbing blow upon my plaid-arm, lunged desperately in reply and remember little else save a wildly joyous delirium, a time of raving, tumultuous uproar and ceaseless effort, a confusion of smiting arms and trampling feet ...

and then I was on my back panting, and Japhet bending over me.

'Bean't hurted, my lord?' he panted.

'No ... but you ...' I gasped, 'you ... blood.'

'Bean't none o' mine, sir!'

'But where is Gaston?'

'Pursooin'! Lord, my lord, but Mounseer do love a fight!'

'What then, have they run – already, Japhet?'

'Ay, my lord, run it is, and wi' Mounseer and the big Scot a-stern of 'em!' And then, even as Japhet helped me to my feet, came Gaston running to clasp an arm about me.

'Art not wounded, my Adam? Yes? No?'

'Nay,' says I, sighing, 'only I would I had supported you better, for oh, Gaston, I—' and then I stopped for, as we stood thus in the light of the doorway, I saw my sword all stained and dim and came near dropping it from surprise and disgust, and yet felt something of jubilation also. I was yet staring at this tell-tale stain when I heard voices, and, turning, saw the great Highlander looming gigantic 'gainst the lighted hall beyond and beside him the slim man who now saluted us with courtly bow:

'Gentlemen,' says he in strangely pleasant voice, 'I salute my deliverers with the profoundest gratitude and beg they will honour me by—'

But now I cried out (as indeed well I might) for this man whom we had so surely snatched from death was none other than Sir Hector Keith MacFarlane himself.

CHAPTER 27

TELLETH HOW I HAD WORD WITH SIR HECTOR

AND now, staring into this pale, so hated face, I took a sudden step forward:

'Sir Hector Keith—' I began, but with movement incredibly quick the gigantic Highlander twitched the sword from me, and as I stood thus discomfited, Keith looked down at me with his slow, mocking smile.

'Now, on my soul,' he murmured, wiping a trickle of blood from his brow, 'here is truly joyous reunion! Well met, my lord, well met. Dugald Dhu restore his lordship's sword instantly!' Forthwith his companion thrust back the weapon into my lax grasp; but now I hung my head, and then Barbara was between us.

'And is it yourself, Keith?' says she bitterly. 'Is it liars and murderers we are the salvation of?'

'Indeed no, Bab, no!' he answered lightly. ''Tis juist Dugald and myself, by the mercy o' heaven—'

'Had I but known,' she cried passionately, 'you had been left for yon Lamonts to make an end o' – ha, they've hurt ye, I'm thinking!'

'A thwack o' the pate, Bab, no more – thanks to the fiery valour of my lord Bellcastonborough and his gallant friends, to whom again my humble thanks ... And, faith, Barbara, I joy to see thee so bonnie and blooming, 'tis sure matrimony agrees wi' you fine.'

'Be silent, sir!' she cried, stamping her foot and clenching white hands in such fury that Gaston stepped to her side :

'Pardon,' says he, bowing, 'but is it that the gentleman offends? No? Yes?'

'And pray how then, sir?' inquired Sir Hector with engaging smile and graceful bow.

'Then,' says Gaston, bowing also, hat flourishing, 'I shall have the honour very distinguished to beg monsieur to step aside with me and—'

- 'No, no, Gaston!' cried Barbara, clasping his arm, 'here hath been enough strife and bloodshed for one night!' and she pointed to the trampled grass that showed ugly stains where the light fell. 'Gaston, I present to you Sir Hector Keith, once The MacFarlane, my father's honoured friend and my own ... loved companion! Keith – Monsieur Gaston de Vrillac!' Hereupon they saluted each other very ceremoniously, murmuring the usual politenesses :

'Your most humble servant, sir!'

'Yours ever to command, monsieur!'

'And now,' says Keith, beckoning us to enter the yawning doorway, 'since we are all such very kind and loving friends, pray step within – the door is down you'll have noticed, this was the work of our other kind friends, the Lamonts, but no matter. Dugald shall be our door, so enter, I beg – you shall find supper, a bottle, and comfortable beds.'

'And – soap?' sighed Barbara.

'Even that, Bab, so – will ye no step in-by?'

'No!' says she, mighty determined, 'better the open brae than the hospitality o' the Keith!'

'So be it, child!' he answered, passing hand across haggard brow with that weary gesture I remembered. 'A'weel,' he sighed in that quaint speech that he (like Barbara) adopted at times, 'then 'tis myself will be bidding ye fair gude-nicht for there's ain ben sair needing me.'

'First, pray tell me whereaway we are, Hector Keith?'

'Yonder lieth Ladenoch Glen, and this is Willy Drummond's house of Auchterlochie.'

'And whaur is himself, Hector?'

'Lying sore wounded along with Alan MacAlan, and none to tend them but Drummond's wife – the servants are all fled. So ye see, Bab, the sooner I—'

'Bring me to them!' cried she. 'Why will ye keep me here yammering? Bring me to them!' So saying, she entered Auchterlochie House, and we after her, across a wide, stone-paved hall to a panelled chamber hung with arras and warm with the comfort of fire and candles which showed a supper table brave with silver, glass and fair napery, whereto Keith invited us with a gesture, bidding us sup forthwith whiles he aided Barbara with the wounded gentleman above stairs.

'Pardon, monsieur,' says Gaston bowing, 'but if I might also assist, I profess some small art surgical for wounds of the steel, the bullet?'

'*Grand merci!*' cried Keith joyously, and falls to the French like any native; so away they went all of them, leaving me alone with Japhet.

'Sir,' quoth he, after some while, jerking big thumb

tablewards, 'he give us the word to eat, I think? So, my lord, what of it?'

'I'm not hungry, Japhet.'

'Well, I be, sir – famishin' be Japhet!'

'Then eat!' said I, drawing a chair to the fire and sitting down. 'Eat your fill, Japhet.'

'Ay, ay, my lord, but – not here, I rackon. This bean't no place for I, d'ye see. Somekkin' bold wi' the leg o' this yer bird, likewise a cut or so o' ham, not forgettin' a slice o' beef and bread, I'll go eat outside, my lord, where I can keep my weather-eye on that theer big Scotsman – which, my lord, I don't nowise like the cut of his jib nor yet his spars nor hull.'

'Why not, Japhet?'

'First, because there be too much of him, sir.'

'He's not much bigger than yourself, Japhet.'

'Ay, but then he be a Scot, my lord, and I naturally don't trust no Scot – wi' their naked legs an' arl! So, wi' your permission, sir, I'll out an' see as 'e don't come no manner o' tricks.'

'Very well, Japhet – only see you don't start any more fighting!'

'Which, sir, there aren't no manner o' man nowheres more peaceable nor Japhet – 'specially when eating.'

Being alone, I sat staring into the fire and marvelling at this most strange turn of Fate that should bring us such weary way, through country so wild and desolate, in time to save from death this man for whom (and with such reason) I bore such deep animosity; had we but chanced to journey another way, or encamp but few moments later, then doubtless Keith would now be lying dead at the hands of the Lamonts instead of playing host to us in this desolate House of Auchterlochie. I now began to consider how best to carry myself towards him so long as I must company with him; but presently, what with the warmth of the fire, the comfort of this great, cushioned chair, and my vast bodily fatigue, I fell asleep; but only to dream horribly that I was fleeing from the dead men in the wood, who pursued me, nodding their bloody heads and flapping their limp arms, until I awoke gasping – to see Sir Hector Keith lolling in the opposite chair and watching me beneath drawn brows.

'You were dreaming, I think,' says he.

Now to wake thus and find myself so suddenly a mark for his hated scrutiny wrought in me such burning humiliation that I sat tongue-tied and abashed, shifting in my chair, the very picture of youthful awkwardness.

'An evil dream, I think?' he questioned; and now I answered him despite myself, as it were :

'Yes, sir !' said I, in tone I thought contemptibly humble.

'Drink this,' says he, and, filling a glass with wine, he thrust it upon me. Obediently I took the wine, raised it to my lips, then setting it down untasted, rose and bowed (as much after Gaston's grand manner as possible) :

'Sir Hector Keith,' says I, speaking impressively as I might, 'permit me to say I drink only with my friends !'

He stared at me a moment betwixt narrowed eyelids, then laughed softly.

'And I vow,' quoth he, nodding, 'no proud gentleman, north or south o' the Border, could have done it better ! Indeed, such haughty coldness, such lofty pride might fash even myself, ay it might so, did I not call to recollection a certain poor, wretched lad naming himself Adam Thursday—'

' 'Tis all the name I have, sir,' says I, fronting him boldly as I could.

'Faith, Adam,' he nodded, 'marriage hath improved thee out o' knowledge, the timorous, chirping fledgling croweth like valiant cockerel ! And pray why wilt refuse to drink with me?'

'Because I . . . I don't drink with . . . my enemies !'

'Ah? And when was I your enemy?'

'From our first meeting.'

'Nay, on that memorable occasion I mistook you for one I had the happiness to—'

'Murder !' says I.

'Tush, boy.'

'He was but a boy also, it seems, sir.'

149

'True, Adam, and thus, having had less time for sinning the surer of Heaven. 'Twas a fair day, yon – you'll mind how I showed you that ancient devil, his father? Well, the paper you gave him smote him down, ay – blasted him like the lightning o' God, – he hath never walked since, I hear.'

''Tis you,' cried I, blenching from Keith's evil triumph, 'oh, 'tis you are the devil!'

'Ay, belike I am,' says he pensively, 'this or angel o' vengeance—'

'Vengeance?' I repeated scornfully. ''Tis oft-times a cloak to murder, a screen to base and selfish purpose!'

'And here,' smiled Keith, 'egad, here we have a Daniel come to judgement – and so young! Faith 'tis a very sucking Daniel! ... Ha, boy!' cried he with sudden terrible change, 'child – think on your own mother! How, d'ye blench, boy? Conceive of her homeless, destitute, with none to aid or pity ... wandering ... mile on weary mile ... a helpless prey to all and any brutality ... calling on Death in her misery, until she sank at last and, dying in her piteous wretchedness, fled soaring to be a joyous saint in heaven. ... Aha, d'ye weep, boy, d'ye weep? But what avail your futility o' tears? Act! Act!'

Stirred greatly by his wildly passionate vehemence, I glanced up and saw him frightfully transfigured, his haggard face convulsed as by some dreadful spasm, his eyes glared, sweat glistened on brow and cheek, his griping hands clutched as at some invisible foe ... 'Act!' cried he again between snapping, white teeth, 'somewhere, belike, lives the devil that wrought her bitter misery ... act! As she suffered, so make him suffer, – act, boy, act!'

'Sir ... oh sir,' cried I, moved by his anguished look, 'there is only God may truly avenge such cruel wrong, for He is just and will repay to the uttermost—' And there I stopped for Sir Hector was laughing at me, dabbing lightly at his glistening brow with dainty handkerchief.

'Ay, but,' says he, fetching out his snuff-box, 'this same God gave ye arms and legs, boy – fingers to grip sword or pistol, how then, Master Adam?'

'God can smite deeper and truer than I, or you, Sir Hector Keith!'

'So – you'd fold your hands, leaving your just vengeance to God, would you, Adam? A'weel, a'weel and why not?' sighed he, viewing me over with such disparagement that I felt shame for my lack of size and brawn, and knew again all the old, bitter contempt for my puny self. 'Ay, why not?' he repeated, 'for 'tis very plainly manifest Nature hath not formed you to be the avenger of any, no – not even your own dead mother!'

Then I was afoot, had kicked back my chair and whipped out my sword.

'Liar!' I parted, 'Devil!' And all so suddenly that Sir Hector, in the act of tapping his snuff-box, dropped it and let it lie unheeded.

'Upon ... my ... soul!' he murmured, staring.

'Draw, sir!' I cried. 'Defend yourself!'

'Such fire! Such bloodthirsty boy!'

'Fight!' cries I, stamping in my fury.

'And why for would ye fight me, Adam?'

'Because I hate and mistrust you.'

'So yourself is in the fashion, eh, Adam? For there's many do hate, and none that trust me save my foster-brother, Black Dugald yonder ... But how am I your enemy – did I not find you a braw, handsome young wife?'

'Ay, and one I'd be free of!' I retorted wildly. 'For you tricked her into wedding me and now—'

'Ah, can it be you do not love her, Adam?'

'No more than she loves me.'

'Alack, but ye sound a doleful pair! But have you not wooed her?'

'Nor ever shall! And here was no true marriage, as well you know, and as I've told her! And 'tis for this—'

'You told her, Adam – ha?'

'Indeed, she knows me for the nameless, destitute creature I am ... and needs must scorn me in her secret heart.'

'Why, then, 'tis for you to win such name she shall learn to love and honour thee despite herself, Adam.'

'Ay, despite herself!' quoth I, bitterly. 'I want no such reasoned love – in especial hers ... and ... and now, sir – draw and let's ha' done!'

'Nay, put up thy sword, boy.'

'No!' I gasped, 'you . . . you tricked her into this cruel, hateful marriage that you might use my shame to hurt her father's pride.'

'The boy hath perception!' he nodded.

'But you shall not use me to your vile purposes, sir.'

'Indeed, yes!' says he, with another gentle nod, 'you are a means to an end, and thus shall I use you – though with the best will in the world towards yourself, Adam. For I vow there is that about you at times, a look, an expression, *a je ne sais quoi* that touches me sensibly, a something in your eyes, your voice that finds an echo—' He stopped suddenly, as from somewhere overhead came a sharp cry followed by a dismal groaning.

'Yon will be poor Alan beneath the probe!' he muttered, 'I must to him!' And, catching up his snuff-box, he hurried from the room, leaving me to stare after him, sword in hand, very fool-like; and as I stood thus, listening to his hasty feet go up the stair, Barbara entered, and, closing the door, leaned against it. Brighteyed and pale she was and breathed as she had been running.

'Put up your foolish sword!' said she softly, yet the look and tone of her cut me like a whip.

'Why, truly—' I began, but her gesture silenced me.

'And must ye be so eager to show off your new-learned tricks o' fence!' says she, fixing me with her burning glance, 'you should be asleep in bed, you were safer there.'

'Bed!' cried I. 'Am I a child to be ordered—'

'What other?' she retorted. 'Better your bed than be ... talking so ... with yon Keith!'

'I talk with whoso I will, madam.'

'Ay, and *of* whoso ye will, sir! You tattle, sir, you and your silly sword ... and you tattle o' me that is your wife, you make mockery o' me to the Keith – ah, you tattle like any peevish spey-wife.'

'And your tongue is a torment!' cried I in fury. 'Oh truly I shall be happy to bid you "goodbye"!'

'Ay, 'twas so ye told Keith.'

'Ha, then you were listening – eavesdropping!'

'To every word, sir! And for your goodbye – when you will sir ... tonight ... now! Keith shall squire me on my road, doubtless I shall be safer with him.'

'Keith?' cried I. 'The man you so hate?'

'He is, at the least, a man o' birth and breeding, sir.'

'And one you name "liar" and "murderer"!' says I, scornfully—

'So I am wife you'd fain be rid of?' she demanded, dimpled chin out-thrust.

'For your own happiness,' cried I.

'Oh hateful to say thus to Keith ... to humble me so bitterly.'

'But—' I began.

'So you want no woman's love, Mr Adam? Well, I pray God no woman may ever stoop to love you.'

'But, Barbara—'

'Ah – go to bed!' she cried and opening the door, showed me a passage with a room at the far end, where burned a light. 'Yon is your chamber, sir, 'tis all prepared – go you to bed!'

'You are cruelly unjust as you know. What I said to Keith—'

'I heard, sir! And good night t'you!'

'Ah, why must you pry and listen?' says I angrily.

'Because I heard you crying on him to fight, and would not have you killed, so I came and – heard!'

'I spoke no ill, no disrespect of you ... 'twas but the pain of knowing you tricked into wedlock with such as I ... of ... of knowing myself so poor that you must—'

'Oh, get you to bed!' said she again, turning from me wearily. But now, seeing her so pale and all adroop with fatigue (even as myself) I went to her very humbly, and thus saw her weeping silently.

'Why, Barbara,' says I, venturing to take her nerveless hand, 'believe me I never meant to hurt you – ah never –

never! Oh pray believe me!' and, forgetting all else, I clasped her in my arms.

'I do believe thee!' she sobbed, and for one happy moment her tear-wet cheek touched mine, then I felt her stiffen in my hold. 'Ay I do believe,' she gasped, 'every word you told Keith, and so ... I hate you, Adam, I hate you!' Then, breaking from me, she fled out of the room. For a moment I was minded to follow her, but instead sought the chamber she had prepared for me and so, very miserably, got me to bed – a luxury I had yearned for mightily but found it now a very nest of thorns. For, feeling myself indeed so poor a creature, so solitary and cruelly misjudged, I covered my abased head, and there, in the merciful darkness, wept long and dismally, until finally I sobbed myself to sleep, like the over-wearied, desolate soul I was.

CHAPTER 28

SHOWETH HOW WE LEFT AUCHTERLOCHIE

A HEAVY hand upon my shoulder waked me to a grey dawn, by whose dim light I saw a great, hairy visage above me, and I started up in blinking alarm:

'Oh, Japhet is ... is it you?' I stammered. 'Is aught amiss?'

'Dunno, my lord, but she'm off, your leddy's away, slipped 'er cable, d'ye see, and here be I a-rousin' o' you according to mounseer's orders – so up wi' you, my lord, quick and quiet.'

'Eh? Gone? D'you mean – Barbara?' cried I, and, leaping from bed, began to dress myself with shivering haste.

'Ay, ay, my lord!' answered Japhet in hoarse whisper. 'Slipped 'er moorings an' stood out and away, she 'ave. And speak soft, sir!'

'Gone?' I repeated, struggling into my boots. 'But how ... when? How'd you know?'

' 'Twas mounseer give me the word, sir.'

'And where is he?' I questioned, huddling on my coat.

'Pur-sooin', sir, an' you an' me to follow, quiet, sir, im-mediate, my lord, and – no breakfast! And you'm forget-tin' your wig, sir!'

'Come!' I whispered, clapping it on anyhow, 'we must haste.'

'Ay, my lord, and wi'out bite nor sup!'

'No matter, let us go!'

'You'm forgetting your plaid, sir.'

'Is it long since she went?' I inquired, rolling the plaid about me and turning to the door.

'Dunno, sir. And you'd best bring your sword, sir.'

'Ay, give it to me, Japhet ... and now let us go.'

'And empty as drums, my lord, never a crumb to com-fort our innards withal!'

Treading softly I stepped into the gallery, and was in-stantly arrested by a terrifying, whistling roar at no great distance.

'Japhet, what is it?' I whispered, groping for my sword-hilt.

'Only the big Scot a-snoring, sir – wi' his naked legs an' arl!'

On I went again, more cautiously than ever, to the stone-flagged hall; and here, though the place struck chill and damp by reason of the shattered door, I beheld Dugald Dhu outstretched upon the floor muffled in his plaid and very blissfully asleep, past whose great bulk crept we – out into a cold and misty day-spring.

Thus we left that desolate house of Auchterlochie, nor did I pause for backward glance, but hasted whither I des-cried Gaston waiting, on the brow of a long ascent, his tall form stark against the dawn and who, wafting to us with his hat, vanished down the further slope.

Reaching this eminence I checked in some alarm for all about us was a billowing mist, very clammy and wet, that chilled me as I stood endeavouring to pierce its blinding folds.

'They are before us somewhere, Japhet,' says I, peering, 'come, let us hasten!' Our way being down hill we went at speed, but having run some distance and still no sign, I halted and bade Japhet to shout.

'Ay, ay, sir,' he sighed dismally, 'though no man can't be nowise expected to hail hearty and free wi' his innards so empty as mine, my lord, hows'ever I'll do my best!' Hereupon he lifted his mighty voice in such roar as might have rivalled Stentor himself; and almost immediately came an answering call and, to my wonder, behind us. So round turned we, and hasting thither presently made out a vague blur that resolved itself into our companions, my lady seated upon a small rock mighty composedly with Gaston standing beside her hat in hand.

Now I was miserably cold and hungry and to find her thus seated so demurely placid (and myself all distraught on her account) angered me beyond measure, wherefore I greeted her frowning, but ere I might utter one word of reproach, she began on me with her haughtiest air and in her broadest Scots-English:

'Fie an' shame on ye, sir! Can ye no let a puir body be – will ye no see I canna thole your company, and wad fain gang my lane?'

'How, madam, how,' cries I, 'you run off, you steal away and now—'

'Master Adam, sir,' says she, disdainful, 'pray why this persecution?'

'Persecution?' I exclaimed in angry amazement, 'do you call it persecution—'

'I do, sir! An a poor soul hath a mind for her own company and to travel alone, must she be followed, sir – dogged and pursued like a pickpocket? Oh, wretched me! Oh, hateful you! For shame, sir.'

'Nay, rather think shame o' yourself, madam, to run off at such ungodly hour, to steal away so sly and furtive, ah, how dare you?'

'Because I am Barbara Margaret MacGregor, and—'

'No!' says I. 'By Scots law, at the least, you are my

wife and shall obey me until I ... I choose to release you.'

'Obey? ... You?' says she, dwelling on the words; then she laughed until, stung by her cruel scorn, I turned away, and thus beheld Gaston seated afar off with Japhet beside him and each with his back to us.

'Barbara,' says I, patiently, 'when you are ready we will have our breakfast.'

'I am wondering,' said she, surveying me, chin in hand, 'if there be any woman in the world would ever obey – such as yourself.'

'Indeed yes,' I nodded, 'you will.'

'My grief!' she exclaimed, opening her beautiful eyes very wide in mock amazement, 'ye'll no mean that?'

'Ay, but I do, Barbara.'

'Then ye'll no think I would?'

'I know it! And now enough o' this folly, madam – remember you are a woman, and do not carry yourself like silly, peevish child. Come, let us join our friends yonder.'

'Oh,' cried she in flare of sudden temper, 'don't put on your airs o' mastery wi' me, sir! I vow 'tis pitiful to see you ape the man thus – yourself that is no more than a poor, wee-bit laddie, a miserable, small creature that shall never—'

But ere she might say more I sprang at her as if to strike, yet in that moment checked the blow for very shame, and then I recoiled as swiftly, for she was up, a raging fury and out flashed her knife; but, catching her wrist, I wrenched and twisted until she dropped the steel and I set my foot upon it.

'Murderous creature!' I gasped. Then snatching up the knife, I forced it back into her unwilling grasp.

'Take it!' said I fiercely. 'Take it, woman, and strike if you dare – stab me an you will!' But she stood motionless, staring on me very strangely.

'You ... would have struck me!' says she at last in plaintive tone, as to explain the weapon in her grasp, 'you meant to – strike me, Adam!'

'Ay, but did not,' I answered.

Here she let fall the knife, and stood looking down where

it lay between us and, lifting her hand, began to cherish her soft smooth cheek for all the world as I had indeed smitten it.

'Wouldst ... strike me ... now?' she questioned.

'I had rather kiss you!' says I to my own amazement.

At this she glanced up quickly, viewing me with look gravely calculating:

'If ... you ... did—' says she slowly.

'Well?' I demanded, and for answer she stooped and took up the knife.

'Ah – your hand is bleeding!' she exclaimed.

'Your knife is very sharp.'

'Will I bind it up for ye?'

'Nay, 'tis no matter. Let us join the others.' But now, having put away the knife, she sat down again.

'I did vera wrong to miscall you,' says she, drawing cloak and plaid about her shapeliness, for the mist seemed thickening, 'I confess 'twas wrong, sir.'

'Indeed,' says I, bitterly, 'I am at all times sufficiently aware of my so many imperfections and weaknesses, I have prayed against them.'

'Oh – prayed, Adam?'

'Ay, constantly! That God would work a miracle on my behalf, transforming this puny self into the man I fain would be. But the days of miracles are past, it seems, and I must remain ... what I am. And now, pray, let us be going – wherever you will.'

'Adam,' says she, her voice all sudden kind, 'this Scotland is dangerous travelling these days, but myself am a Scot and may go safe where strangers cannot – so 'tis that I stole away, for I am determined to journey on alone.'

'So will we go together till you be come safe to your own people,' says I.

'Might I bind up your poor hand, Adam?'

'No, I thank you.'

'Will ye no suffer me, Adam ... dear?'

'I ... I have my handkerchief.'

'Why, then, gi'e a ca' on yon ithers and we'll hae break fast.'

'Not here,' says I, shivering.

'And why for no?'

''Tis desolate place and no wood for a fire.'

'Then we maun dae wi'oot. Are ye no hungry?'

'Famished! But I would eat in more comfort, and yonder is a wood to shelter us, so come, pray get up!'

'I winna! Gang whaur ye will, sir, but here bides Barbara!'

'Then I must carry you.'

'Ye shall na' and ye couldna! Forby I'm no saw heavy as some!'

'Indeed you are beyond my poor strength, I fear!' says I, miserably, 'howbeit, if I cannot bear you so far, Japhet shall!' And I hailed him forthwith whereat he hasted towards us, looming gigantic in the mist.

'Japhet,' said I, and in that moment Barbara arose, frowning on me, 'Japhet, madam desires breakfast.'

'Why so do I, sir, ah an' so does mounseer, being empty as so many drums. And over theer t'starboard lays a bit of a wood where us can build a fire for, my lord and me'm, this do be a perishin' cold country, I rackon, which mak' me to wonder at these yere Scottishers wi' their naked legs an' arl!' Now at this, Barbara laughs blithe as any bird on bough, talking to Japhet so merrily that he (though solemn by nature) falls a-laughing too.

And so, having joined Gaston, we went on together until we reached the wood, where we found a place of rocks, and here, in sheltered cleft, we made our fire and thus breakfasted in some comfort and kindly good-fellowship despite the chilly mists of the inclement morning.

CHAPTER 29

GIVETH SOME DESCRIPTION OF
VISCOUNT SCARSDALE, A FUGITIVE

TOWARDS noon the mists cleared and a kind sun beamed, so that my heart was greatly uplift and I went, as it were, on tiptoe, finding in these sun-dappled glens and rugged heights a wild beauty all undreamed; moreover, my aches and pains were gone and I, inured to hard travel, went full of a joyous vigour and such high spirits that I fell a whistling softly to myself until, seeing Barbara regard me with look something wistful and troubled, I checked; whereupon she questioned me, sighing:

'Where did ye learn yon tune, Adam?'

'Tune?' I repeated, wondering.

'Ay, 'tis the pibroch o' the McLeods,' and she whistled it over to me sweet as piping finch, that same lilting air I had heard by moonlight in a wood, as I would have told her, but:

'Adam,' says she, with look more wistful than ever, 'my thoughts are dooms sad, for 'tis of you and my father I'm thinking ... ere sunset we should reach his castle o' Drumlossie.'

'So soon, Barbara?'

'How will you meet him, Adam, how carry yourself I'm wondering?'

'Honourably, I hope.'

'Meaning you'll tell him you're no the great lord?'

'Just that!' I nodded.

'Oh, then, I would you'd forget your honour – a wee while – for my poor father's sake ... and mine.'

'Nay, Barbara, I'm determined to speak truth with my first words, for all our sakes.'

'Hear me, Adam!' says she, very earnestly. 'My father

160

is today a poor gentleman, but desperate proud and ambitious ... Years syne himself and the great Earl of Ancaster were friends and comrades in the French wars and it was agreed I must wed the earl's son, Lord Edmund—'

'Did you love him?' I demanded.

'Adam, 'twas my father's heart-wish. But Lord Edmund was killed three – four years agone, so 'twas settled I must wed Lord Robert, the earl's second son, but he ... disappeared, and now ... Eustace ...'

'They would seem an unfortunate family, these Ancasters.'

'True, Adam, and I think their curse is named – Keith, Hector Keith, that today is man so smiling and terrible yet one I mind lang syne very gallant and gentle and was called MacFarlane.'

'You think Sir Hector is destroying them, Barbara?'

'I know his hate is unco' fearsome and deadly, and yourself knoweth he killed Eustace ... And at Drumlossie we are like to meet the Earl's eldest son, Lord Scarsdale, that hath fled there for refuge, for my father, though he lives very hermit-like, is still the Earl of Ancaster's trusted friend.'

'So here's the reason Keith married you to sorry me, Barbara?'

'Yes, Adam ... and also, I think, for despite of the McLeod o' McLeod that is another friend to the Ancasters and rode to Preston fight for love of King James and me, the poor Ian!'

'McLeod?' says I, halting suddenly. 'A tall, splendid, handsome gentleman?'

'Why he's tall, Adam, and no' uncomely.'

'Ah – so 'tis him you love!' cried I so bitterly that she opened her beautiful eyes at me for wonder.

'Why, no,' says she, a little troubled. 'I ... I loved no man ... But my father, Adam, my father – himself that was once so rich and powerful, is now blind and ailing ... very forlorn, of fortune none and powers less, and I, oh, Adam, I am all is left him the day ... and he hath set his heart and all his hopes on my wedding power and riches!'

'Then, alas for him when he shall know the truth of it,' quoth I, bitterly.

'But, Adam,' says she in wheedling tone, 'I was wed to ... Lord Bellcastonborough!'

'There is none such alive!' says I, trudging on again.

'But my poor father so believes, for, oh alas, Adam, Keith hath sent word to my father telling him I am wed to a great English lord ... very rich ... very powerful ... And my father is eager to welcome your lordship, hath made preparations in your honour ... such as he may – so Keith told me last night at Auchterlochie.'

'The man is a devil!' cried I, fiercely.

'Ay, doubtless, Adam ... But you ... if ... when you meet my father will ye no' be my Lord Bellcastonborough a wee while, Adam – play the part of a great gentleman for sake of himself that is blind and ailing – ah, will ye no'?'

'Never!' quoth I. 'And see you not that such imposture were to no purpose, for Keith shall but triumph more and wound your father the deeper when he shall denounce me for what I am – as he surely will.'

'Howandever,' sighed she, 'I may contrive if ye'll but suffer my poor father to think o' you as he will, Adam ... dear?' Now it was in my mind to tell her the folly of such duplicity when I saw Gaston (who with Japhet went before us) halt suddenly, and clap hand to sword as forth of adjacent thicket stepped a small, chubby gentleman who flourished his hat and bowed, and bowed.

'Madame and gentlemen,' cries he, posturing elegantly, 'with excuses none and advocacy passionate I crave your aid to unhappy, distressed gentleman of high degree yet fortunes for the nonce abased – famishing, foredone, lost in this most cruel, despiteful country—'

'Whisht sir!' cried Barbara, dimpled chin a-jut, 'there's some do love this bonny land.'

'Certainly, certainly, madame!' says the little gentleman bowing instantly. ''Tis all in the point of view, but—'

'Who is he, sir, this gentleman ye speak o'?'

'Ah, madame,' sighed the small gentleman eyeing us

something dubiously, 'is't not enough to know him for noble gentleman sore distressed?'

'Where bides he?'

'This way, dear lady, but a mere stone's cast!' With which, the speaker turned and brought us to small, bush-girt ravine, and here, 'gainst a rock, beneath a pent of boughs very ill-contrived, lay one all swathed about in cloaks and plaids; at our approach he sat up but, espying Barbara, he rose, and very nimbly I thought for starving man.

'Madame,' cries the little gentleman wafting gracefully with bedraggled hat, 'behold my very noble friend!'

A tall, shapely man, his finery of velvets and laces sadly weather-stained who bowed profoundly to Barbara and saluted us, but gazing the while large-eyed upon her loveliness.

'Pray, madame,' says he, 'can you direct two distressed travellers to Drumlossie Castle?'

'Indeed I can, sir,' she answered, flushing I thought beneath his fixed gaze, 'but what would ye at Drumlossie?'

'Lie sheltered, madame, until I can win south into England.'

'Are ye a Jacobite, sir?'

'Hem! Hem!' cries the little gentleman before his companion might answer. 'We are, madame, as you will perceive, but poor wayfarers, this and no other, simple souls, dear madame, bemused, bewildered, lost and something dismayed being as 'twere woeful castaways yearning homewards.'

'Havers!' exclaimed Barbara, 'here's a many words yet nothing said, indeed, sirs, you're unco' cautious and pernickity I'm thinking, and if ye canna trust the honour of us 'tis us bid ye find your way as ye may.'

''Sheart, madame,' said the tall, handsome gentleman smiling into her eyes, 'I crave pardon for my friend's so excessive caution, for 'tis certain you are a Highland lady, and therefore loyal Jacobite as we. John, you may speak!' Hereupon off came the little gentleman's hat again:

'Why then, madame and sirs,' said he, a little pompously, 'hem! hem! I have the honour to name to you my lord Viscount Scarsdale—'

163

'Scarsdale?' repeated Barbara, falling back a step, 'Oh, then, sir, you are—?'

'Richard Ancaster, Viscount Scarsdale,' says he, hand on heart, 'yours most devotedly.'

'Oh!' cried she, viewing him with troubled eyes, 'And I am Barbara MacGregor.'

'Marvellous!' he exclaimed. 'Then you are to be my sister-in-law, you are to wed Eustace!' And, catching her hands, he smiled down on her as he would have kissed her.

'Well met, Barbara, well met!' he cried gaily, 'I protest brother Eustace is an infinite lucky fellow.'

'Ah no – no!' she gasped, recoiling, 'Oh, my lord, d'ye not know – have ye not heard the direful news?'

'Not a word!' says my lord, wondering. 'How should a poor fugitive hear aught? I've been on the wing since Preston rout, hiding from the red-coats and the accursed Campbells.'

'Alas,' sighs she, wondrous gentle, 'word is that Eustace ... your brother ... is dead.'

Now at this I blenched, remembering I stood at that moment in this poor, dead gentleman's very garments.

'Dead?' says the viscount, in whispering tone, yet clasping hands but the tighter (or so I thought). 'Great God! And so young! How came this, was it chance of battle or headman's axe?'

'Neither, my lord. I've heard tell it was a duel—'

'Ah – so?' he whispered, 'who ... who killed him?'

'Sir Hector Keith.'

The viscount uttered an inarticulate, choking cry and, dropping Barbara's hands, recoiled until the rock stayed him, and here he leaned like one smitten faint, his head bowed, his open palms flat against the rock behind him.

'Keith!' he whispered, and his handsome face showed pale and drawn between the long, dark curls of his periwig, while his hands began to pat the rock in strange, futile sort. 'John,' he murmured, his wide eyes staring on vacancy. 'Oh, John Rapton – d'you hear? MacFarlane is alive! He hath struck again! There is now only my father and ... me ...'

164

'God forbid it, my lord!' cried the little gentleman, wringing his hands. 'This may be but idle tale ... Ah, madame, is this indeed fact veritable?'

'Sir,' answered Barbara, glancing from the speaker to my lord's rigid form, ' 'twas Sir Hector Keith told me but yestreen.'

'How?' cried the viscount, starting violently, 'is he in Scotland ... Hector Keith ... hereabouts?'

'Indeed and he is that, my lord, verra proper to your purpose!'

'Purpose?' he questioned. 'What, pray?'

'Vengeance for your dead brother, sir.'

'Yes, by God!' cried the viscount, rolling his fine eyes very ferociously. 'But, alack, Fate decrees my vengeance must sleep a while, for I must to England with all speed ... Come, John, let us for Drumlossie with Madame Barbara and these good gentlemen.'

'You'll be well acquaint with Sir Hector, my lord?'

'Acquainted?' cried the viscount with a kind of gasp. 'John, tell my lady, explain!'

'Madame,' quoth Mr Repton, bowing, 'pray know then that Edmund, Earl of Ancaster, was blessed with offspring five – four sons and a – four sons, madame, gallant gentleman all, but ah woe, – three do now lie dead, cut off in their youthful bloom by the bloody hand of Sir Hector calling himself Keith, for he goeth under names amany, reft out o' being, lady, snatched from joyous life, madame, plunged to the dismal shades o' death by dastard steel and bullet—'

'Enough, my good John,' sighed his lordship, 'no more ... But,' cries he, suddenly fierce, 'vengeance sleepeth, to wake anon, his hand shall smite home, ay by heavens! But for the present – patience! Come, Barbara, let us to Drumlossie Castle!' So saying, he reached her his hand in fashion very gracious and stately, walking thus beside her with little Mr Repton, heavily burdened yet seemingly mighty content, trudging behind, whiles I followed after, betwixt Gaston and Japhet.

And now, though the sun still shone bravely, my late joy

was clean gone and I full of gloomy foreboding; and as I went thus deject, I could hear Barbara's clear voice in question and answer, and wondered sourly what they could find to talk on so mighty friendly, envying my lord his handsome and stately person, his ready tongue and polished manners; and, watching them, I saw how oft she turned to look up into his comely face, and how ready he was to take her hand on the least excuse, and once I saw him stoop and kiss it unrebuked (the which sorely grieved and angered me); and once she suffered him to lift and carry her over the merest rill, though I had oft seen her cross more difficult places nimbly enough on her own pretty feet. Now all this bred in me such hopeless, despairful misery that Gaston laid his large, kindly hand upon my shoulder and falling back with me behind Japhet's huge stolidity :

'Never grieve you so, my Adam,' says he softly, 'yet if grieve you must, strive to show it not a whit – no! The Gentleman Complete must wear the mask. To suffer with the smile engaging, to break the heart with an aplomb superb, to die, *par exemple*, with the dignity of a fortitude unshakeable, this is as I think, worthy the Gentleman Complete.'

'But, Gaston,' says I, miserably, 'I am no gentleman, and—'

'*Sacré:*' he exclaimed, 'Wilt affront me – yes? For, though so young, thou art my friend – and shall a De Vrillac so honour one that is no gentleman? By the Holy Name – no! Thus, Adam, being Gaston, Ann, De Vrillac's friend proveth thee gentleman beyond all doubt. As for thy so adorable Barbara, she is the woman, ah perfectly! She talks to my lord but she thinks of you, Adam – oh yes! It is the wile feminine. I judge it is, mayhap, that she desires you shall also bear her in your arms, some day.'

'Ah, Gaston – if I only dared! But I lack the strength and—'

'*Sang d'Dieu!*' quoth he, fiercely. 'Have you ever made the trial? *Mordieu* – no! Then how shall you be sure? She is of a spirit high and, I think, desires in you some small ferocities – the masterful – heroical. Be humble to God, Adam, but to a woman you love, this maid you so worship – ah bah!'

'How know you I so love her, Gaston?' At this he laughed, and clapping long arms about me, held me so a dozen strides or more, then :

'Behold, my Adam,' says he, 'the good God gave me eyes, also ears ... thus I do prophesy that one day this lady, so proud and lovely shall lie close in thine arms, with a content the most sublime, oh yes!' Here, reading in his kind, wise eyes, the grave assurance of his words, I caught my breath for very wonder he should believe such miracle might ever be.

'But, Gaston,' says I, 'oh friend, I am a nameless beggar!'

'Nay, Adam,' quoth he with his grand air of serene finality, 'thou shalt be what God, thyself and Gaston Ann de Vrillac are a-fashioning, to wit : a gentleman of the spirit high yet nobly humble.'

At this, I could but grasp his hand, for speech was beyond me.

'Come now,' says he, halting suddenly, 'heed them not yonder nor grieve, 'twere folly. The grass here is level, let us see if thou hast the stroke I taught thee, my thrust infallible, the which, if played at the moment just, may never be parried.'

And so, being here screened from view of our companions, we drew our swords and faced each other.

'See, Adam, you play your point in the high line, your wrist – ah, but supple! We are in quarte – good! I now make the attack – so! Now instantly you cut over, make your thrust and – *voilà*, I am the corpse! Perfectly! 'Tis stroke no man may stop if delivered at the moment unique. Aha, my Adam, thou art the asp, as quick, as deadly, you become the swordsman veritable, oh but superb. I have the pride for you intense – embrace thy Gaston! The good God bless thee, my Adam!'

And so, when he had kissed me joyously, and I thanked him from my heart for his care and praise of me, we went on after the others.

CHAPTER 30

TELLETH VERY LITTLE

THE sun was westering when we reached a little village, a poor, pretty place, its one street ending at a loch whose wide, dark waters were enclosed by tree-clad slopes and soaring crags, a prospect methought very sadly beautiful.

Now as we entered this village, faces peered at us, from doorways and windows, sullen and aloof. But suddenly a woman cried aloud in the Gaelic very joyously, and came running and others with her, women and children mostly, for the men were few and old. So came these villagers flocking about Barbara in happy welcome and she greeting them as gladly.

'Oh, Adam,' cries she, all flushed and bright-eyed, 'these are my MacGregors, all that is left of them hereabouts alas – these are my ain hame folk!'

Presently they brought us to a small inn or changehouse hard beside the loch, and here there met us a tall, old man, a very patriarch, who, baring silvery head, welcomed us with a grave courtesy, but to Barbara he sank on one knee to kiss her hand, very proud and dignified in his homage; whereafter she vanished with his daughter, they chattering like any magpies.

Now when we had washed and eaten, Barbara beckoned me to follow her and, standing beside the loch, she pointed across the waters aflame with sunset.

'Adam,' says she, looking at me very wistfully, 'yonder, ayont the loch, is Castle Drumlossie, and there my poor father waits to do honour to my lordly husband.'

'Why, then,' I began, but she checked me with upraised finger:

'Wait, Adam, first how think you of my lord Viscount Scarsdale?'

'A very great gentleman,' I answered, my gaze on the shining water.

'He is that, Adam. And what more's in your mind?'

''Tis strange we must meet him so far from England, he is out of place hereabouts and—'

''Tis no in the littlest bit strange or wonderful whateffer!' says she. 'For he is fugitive from the English, and, like us, bound for Drumlossie, also he is son o' my father's friend, the Earl of Ancaster ... Why d'you no like him, Adam, and him so great a gentleman, forby?'

'Indeed, I've scarce spoke with him, Barbara.'

'But you would never shame me to this gentleman, Adam?'

'God knows it!' I exclaimed. 'But what—?'

'You would not make o' me a liar, Adam?'

'You know I would not, Barbara. But pray—'

'For, d'ye see, dear Adam, I was telling him you are the great lord and earl of Bellcastonborough!' So saying, and, or ever I might find words adequate, she turned to leave me; but in this moment comes my lord viscount himself, his stateliness something marred by haste, and with bow to me, leads Barbara aside, speaking very earnestly. So I left them, and went wandering on, staring down into the placid water and hearkening to its mournful lapping.

But after some while, back comes Barbara, frowning:

'A'weel, Adam,' says she petulantly, 'I might hae saved mysel' yon lee aboot ye, for my lord hath changed his mind and will push on tae the hoose o' a friend twixt here and Edinboro'.'

'Doth this grieve you, Barbara?'

''Deed no 'tis just as well, considering Castle Drumlossie is no exactly sae commodious as aforetime. We'll be crossing the water in a wee while, I'll go tell old Angus to prepare his boat.' And away she went, but scarce had she gone than cometh Gaston and stands awhile also staring down at the waters and never a word.

'My Adam,' says he at last, 'seeing it is that you desire not my lord his company, it is now that I rid you of him

– see yonder!' Looking whither he directed, I beheld my lord (sure enough) striding back through the village with little Mr Repton, heavily burdened with cloaks, plaids and bundles as usual, trotting sturdily at his heels.

'Why, Gaston,' says I wondering, 'how is this?'

'Ah, but it is of the simplest,' he nodded. 'I tell my lord that Monsieur 'Ector shall doubtless pursue and follow us to Drumlossie and – ah well, behold my lord is – away!'

CHAPTER 31

TELLETH WHAT BEFELL AT DRUMLOSSIE TOWER

BONNET in fist, old Angus helped us into his roomy boat watched (as I guess) by all the villagers, who waved us smiling farewells as the stately patriarch, shipping a pair of very long and clumsy oars, began to row us across the loch, and doing it with that austere dignity that seemed natural to him in all things.

And now I saw this loch much longer than I had deemed, with many craggy headlands thrusting out into the dark waters, notably one that soared up clothed with small trees and dense brush.

'Yon is Drumlossie Crag!' says Barbara. 'And there, in its shadow, is Castle Drumlossie!' Now, looking whither she pointed me, I caught my breath – for there, in place of the stately pile my mind had pictured, I saw a gaunt and desolate tower that lifted battle-scarred walls above a ruin of tumbled masonry, charred beams and unsightly heaps that once had been clustering cottages; but upon that grim and battered tower a pennon fluttered bravely.

'Yes,' said Barbara, a note of defiance in her voice, her lovely head proudly erect, 'yon is Drumlossie Tower, my father's castle ... what is left of it, and ... my home.' And here, though her glance never wavered, she looked at me through sparkle of slow-gathering, painful tears, and I, turning to stare again on this woeful ruin, saw no more than a misty blur.

'See, my father is expecting you,' says she, 'yon flag waves to honour my noble husband, my lord Bellcastonborough!'

At this, trying to laugh, she sobbed and turned her back on me. The boat glided up to a small jetty with flight of worn, stone steps, and here old Angus, bonnet in hand, bowed us ashore, refusing Gaston's proffer of payment with lofty magnificence of gesture.

Up hill we went through the desolate ruin of this little hamlet, up past tumbled wall and battlement, across a weedy courtyard to the great tower itself where, in the mighty wall, was a small, scowling door clamped with massive iron bands. Now as we approached, from behind this door rose a sudden, howling scream so fierce and wild that I recoiled, and Japhet also who stood agape and fumbling with his long musket; then the door opened and there appeared a figure methought very strange and pitiful – viz, an aged, limping man in faded tartans, upon his head a rusty helmet, by his side a ponderous sword, beneath one arm a great bagpipe the which he was blowing right lustily, filling the air with its deafening music.

Playing thus, he swung upon his heel and limped on before us into a little hall or antechamber scant of furnishings, up a narrow, stone stair, through a second bare chamber and so into a great and lofty hall dim lit by narrow openings high in the walls; its cracked pavement was strewn with rush, with deer and goat-skins much the worse for wear. Against the panelling, which showed split as by random blows, hung sorry remnants of tapestry, with broken antlers, two or three Highland targets and rusty weapons. But amid all this ruin and decay, athwart the frayed skins upon the floor ran a broad strip of rich carpeting from the great, arched doorway at one end, to a small, raised platform or dais at the other; and here, seated in massive chair, his slim elegance supported by velvet cushions sat a man, a splendid figure in kilt and plaid, where silver gleamed and jewels sparkled, a slender, shapely gentleman of no great age, yet whose lean face wore an eager, peevish look and whose white fingers tapped and fluttered on his chair-arms as he peered towards us with wide, blank stare.

Up this strip of carpet limped the piper in full blast, and, reaching the dais, halted behind his master's chair and instantly his wailing pipes were mute. And after a moment's impressive silence, the gentleman arose and spoke in English sweetly clear and precise as Barbara's speech :

'Gentlemen all,' said he, bowing towards us, 'Tearlach MacGregor gives ye greeting and fair welcome. Drumlossie is not what it was ere the wars harried us, they tell me, and our people are something scattered, I hear. Yet our walls still stand and Drumlossie himself can still do honour to his guests, God be thankit. Be welcome, sirs ! And thou, Barbara, dear my daughter, art wed, I'm hearing.'

'Indeed, my father.'

'And to a right valiant and noble gentleman, high in favour with the King's Majesty. Heaven bless thee, child ! Come, make your husband known to me. For my lord I am, as you may see, cursed with the sorrow of blindness. Pray draw near that I may touch and be acquaint.' And now Barbara was beside me, speechless and with head averted, but her hand found mine and, clasping it fast, she brought me where her father waited.

And as I stood mute before him, his blind eyes staring into mine, he reached out his arms and I felt the touch of those light-hovering, sensitive fingers upon my face like the caress of fairy hands.

'Thou'rt young, my lord,' he murmured. 'A'weel, so much the better ! ... And thou'rt worlds differ to our great Hielan' bodies ... But 'tis a hawk-face ... a dreamer's brow ... a resolute mouth ... a fighter's chin. 'Tis face speaketh thy pride o' birth. 'Tis face with power to achieve and strength to hold. Glad am I, my lord, to know my daughter in care of one so capable to her weal and safety in these troublous times. My dear young lord accept a father's blessing.'

Thus and much more spake he, and I for the most part

dumb or murmuring I scarce knew what. At last, when Gaston had been duly presented, Sir Tearlach drew me aside with an air of some mystery and no little concern :

'My lord,' says he with a sort of gentle, pouncing eagerness, 'I will not as yet trouble you with business, but since you are, as I'm assured, so high in the King's favour, there is matter of much import to yourself as my son-in-law, and to myself, I would have you bring to His Majesty's ken and notice, right speedily. To the which end I would beg the favour of your company after we have supped.'

I was about to plead some stammering excuse when a bell tinkled and Barbara joined us (to my great relief), to tell us supper was ready. Sir Tearlach frowned, sighed, then, setting his hand upon my shoulder :

'Come, gentlemen,' says he, 'let us to table. Pipe Roderick!' And so, with Barbara's fingers fast clasping mine and her father's sensitive hand upon my shoulder we went forth of that noble, ruinous hall, old Roderick limping and piping bravely before us.

Now, seeing how Sir Tearlach seemed to cleave to me in his blindness; beholding his woeful, haggard face; noting how frail he was for all his stately pride and valiant showing, I knew that, come what might, I could never undeceive him in regard to myself.

Thus surely was never more distressful meal (for me, at least) than this supper; for, at Sir Tearlach's right hand, I must needs come in for the greater part of his attention, and he so full of gentle, eager questioning ! To all of which I answered as best I could, or as I thought would most please him, though I kept my eyes abased for very shame. Yet more than once when I was at loss for a reply Barbara spoke for me, interposing very deftly; and once when Sir Tearlach was asking me of the King and his court, Gaston made answer for me, and having thus captured our host's interest, held it.

Supper was nearly done, and I yearning with all my heart to be away, when Sir Tearlach suddenly raised his hand and seemed to listen profoundly.

'Did you hear aught unusual, my lord?' he questioned softly.

'No, sir,' I answered, wondering.

'Ay, but I do!' says he. 'Being blind my hearing is the more acute ... I heard a creeping footstep ... 'tis there again – hearken!' And now, sure enough, as we sat silent all, the old tower seemed full of a vague stir that grew upon the quiet, a strange hushed clamour, the tread of stealthy feet, a clink of steel ... And then I knew the door behind me was opening, yet I sat stricken motionless by the wild and terrible transformation in Sir Tearlach – his delicate nostrils flared, his lips, back-drawn, showed gnashing teeth, his blind eyes stood round between widened lids, his whole body seemed shaken by a dreadful palsy, while from his writhen lips leapt a torrent of soft, hissing speech :

'Treachery ... treachery, 'tis in the air, I smell it! A thrice damned traitor pollutes my hearth! ... What, Keith ... Hector Keith ... are ye there, black MacFarlane?'

'Even so, Drumlossie!' answered that strangely sweet voice and, whirling in my chair, I espied Sir Hector in the open doorway, with his mighty henchman Dugald at his shoulder and divers wild-looking fellows beyond.

'Pah!' exclaimed Sir Tearlach, with gesture of fierce loathing, 'you poison the air!'

'Then hold your breath, Tearlach, and hearken—'

'Dog!' cried Sir Tearlach, lifting clenched hand, 'vile renegade, had I my sight death should choose betwixt us. As 'tis – speak and be done! What would villainy with Tearlach MacGregor of Drumlossie?'

'Hard words, Drumlossie!' quoth Sir Hector with his slow, bitter smile. 'Were I all you say I might hang you from your ain flag-pole up aloft.'

'Ha, is it murder? Is it flame and ravishment, MacFarlane?'

Sir Hector merely laughed.

'Speak,' cried Sir Tearlach, 'speak and be done!'

'Sit then and hearken!' answered Sir Hector. 'Faith

thou'rt a poor creature, Drumlossie, a selfish soul, making o' thy blindness a black tyranny.'

'Liar!' gasped Sir Tearlach.

'Black tyranny!' repeated Sir Hector. 'For your own base purposes you would have wed Barbara to each or any of the accursed Ancaster brood, but I have saved her from this abomination, Tearlach, and set her beyond reach of your vile scheming. I have given her spouse of my own choosing—'

'Liar! Liar!' panted the blind man.

'I have wed her, Tearlach, very securely to a poor foundling, one Adam Thursday – there he sits yonder, a good lad and a promising but with naught in the world of his own – not even a name!'

For a long, dreadful moment was utter silence wherein I (for one), sat mute and still, not daring to lift my eyes, yet I was aware that Sir Tearlach had risen and now stood, his shaking hands reaching out to me like one in passionate supplication. At last:

'My lord,' said he, in choking voice, 'oh dear my lord, vindicate yourself! ... Say Keith lies! ... Tell me it is not true! Speak my lord, speak!'

A moment longer sat I, shamed and mumchance, then I was afoot and facing Sir Tearlach's daunting figure and wide, sightless glare, answered him as well as I might:

'Sir,' said I, very conscious of Sir Hector's sinister, mocking presence, '"Tis true I am no more than nameless foundling, 'tis true that I ... that we were tricked into this unhappy wedding by Sir Hector, but, God aiding me, I will yet prove myself worthy of Barbara's love and get me a name shall be her pride to bear—'

'You ... you confess ... you are no lord ... an imposter?'

'Though despite myself, Sir Tearlach. But, sir, 'tis my dear hope I may come of such gentle stock as your touch indeed proclaimed me, and—'

'You confess yourself a ... nameless foundling ... a beggar ... a child of shame—'

'No!' cried I. 'Never say so! Never dare so think for whatever—' But turning from me, Sir Tearlach fronted Keith like a madman.

'A dog's death on ye, Hector!' he gasped. 'May you rot for this, bone and flesh! May your foul heart crack with a grief keener than mine! May you writhe in hell's torment! May God refuse—' He choked, smote wildly at the air and, reeling, would have fallen but that old Roderick caught him and Barbara leapt to clasp him in sheltering arms; and so they between them got him from the room.

And now, turning upon Sir Hector, I saw he mocked no longer, but stood regarding me in such sort that the bitter reproaches on my lip were never uttered.

'Why, Adam!' says he gently. 'Why, Adam, lad!' And taking off his hat very gravely he bowed to me. 'Get you an honourable name will you, Adam? Faith, now you shape well, boy, so well that here's myself wishing you all success. Indeed I'm thinking your Barbara shall be pouring benedictions on my head one day. And therefore here's myself would speak ye word of warning, to wit – beware o' yon blind tyrant, yon purblind hypocrite that seeth more than you think – especially by night! And so, Adam, fare you well! ... Monsieur de Vrillac, your servant.' Thus saluting us, hat a-flourish, he was gone.

'Oh, Gaston,' says I, miserably, 'how think you of it all?'

'*Mordieu*, I think you rob Monsieur 'Ector of his triumph! He is a *rara avis*, my Adam, a bird of the strangeness is Monsieur 'Ector, yes!'

'He is a devil!' said I, bitterly.

'Hum!' quoth Gaston, fingering his chin, 'it is the saying that the devil he is a gentleman! But attention, Adam, reflect and ponder you, for Monsieur Keet he make us the warning, aha, and against this blind, so grievous gentleman with the name so *difficile*—'

'But I do know Keith for rogue and liar, Gaston.'

'Yet now of this blind personage, Adam, this gentleman that seeth more than we think – especially in the dark, ha?'

'But he is indeed blind, Gaston, 'tis evident, 'tis beyond all doubt, besides – Barbara hath said so.'

'Ay,' he nodded thoughtfully, 'but there is a blindness by day that seeth by night and I—' he paused suddenly as came a knock, and the door, opening, disclosed old Roderick and a squat, red-headed fellow with Japhet behind them musket under arm.

'Sirs,' said Roderick in his high, complaining voice, 'himsel' begs ye'll forgi'e his 'tendance on your honours selfs, himsel' being sair stricken, y'ken sirs. Here's wine, sirs, and yon's the bell, forby your beds be ready when ye will.'

'Sink me, gentlemen,' says Japhet so soon as door had closed, 'you can burn, scuttle and sink me if ever I see such a land as this here, no nor never such folk as these Scottishers wi' their bare legs an' arl! Wot I says is, let's skip our moorings and stand away dracklyminute! I'd rayther sleep under bush than this here ruinated old hulk, full o' ghostes, it be!'

'Ghosts?' says I. 'Man, what d'you mean?'

'Well, my lord, leastways if they ain't ghostesses they'm Scottishers, which be worse, wi' their bare legs an'—'

'How many, Japhet?'

'Why, sir, I can't 'ardly say. They pops an' peeps from darksome corners ... this old place be full o' corners. And they was five as ate supper wi' me and most on 'em doddlish exceptin' carrotty-poll as they calls Colin. So wot I says is—'

'Bed,' quoth Gaston, rising. 'Let us to bed and see what tomorrow shall show us, for this poor *château* is more than ruin, and its blind *seigneur* is gentleman of a quaintness – but yes!' And he rang the bell.

'Why then, wi' your permission, sirs,' says Japhet setting musket to hand in the chimney corner, 'I'll berth here this night, I rackon.' Then the door opened to show old Roderick and Colin, each with flickering taper.

'Sirs,' piped the old man, 'an ye'll bed-wards – follow us!'

CHAPTER 32

TELLS HOW I FOUND HAPPINESS, AND A
WARNING CAME TRUE

THEY led us across the dim, echoing hall and along
crooked passages until we reached a narrow stair in the
thickness of the wall the which Roderick turned to mount,
beckoning me to follow. So, bidding Gaston goodnight, I
climbed after the old man who limped before me, muttering
to himself and pausing now and then to turn and light me
up this steep ascent. Up we went and up, turning ever to
the right until he paused at last, a door creaked open and he
ushered me into a dismal chamber where stood a battered
press, a chair and a great bed draped with dingy curtains.
Still muttering to himself the old man turned to set down
the candle but in that moment started so violently that he
nigh dropped it and stood peering, the taper flickering in
his palsied grasp and all because of light, quick footsteps on
the stair. And then as old Roderick stood thus strangely
terrorized, Gaston's bewigged head appeared round the
sharp spiral and next moment he was in the room.

'It is but, my Adam,' says he, glancing keenly about this
somewhat forbidding chamber, 'that I would know where
thou'rt lodged. It is, I perceive, an *appartement* charming,
but so airy, *ma foi* – yes! 'Tis, I think, chamber better
suited to myself – go thou below, Adam, for I shall sleep
here with a contentment the most *extraordinaire*.'

But at this, old Roderick protested so vehemently that
Gaston was for bundling him out until I ended the matter
by vowing the place would suit me well enough since I had
small mind to sleep, whereupon Gaston, having viewed the
door and its fastenings very particularly, nodded:

'Ah, well, the bolts are strong,' says he.

'What's in your mind, Gaston?' I questioned.

'Monsieur Keet, his warning, Adam. Should aught chance to part us, you shall seek me in Edinburgh at the Lion of Gold and so Goodnight.' And away he went with old Roderick muttering behind.

Being alone, I crossed to the window and opened the lattice on a night of argent splendour for the moon, high in glory, touched all things to glamorous beauty; she waked small glitterings in the water that rippled against the base of the tower immediately below me; she softened the harsh outline of rugged crag and mountain peak; she woke in me vague longings, fears, hopes ... that were banished all and suddenly by a soft rapping on my chamber door. Wondering, I crossed the room and, drawing the latch, beheld Barbara.

'What is it?' I questioned anxiously. 'How is your father?'

'No sae well but he might be better,' she answered. 'But I'm wondering why they have put you here, 'tis chamber never used.' And, stepping into the room, she crossed to the bed, drew back the dim hangings, folded back the covers, and smoothed the pillow and all with such pretty care as was a joy to see, for no one had ever done so much for me ere now.

'I see old Meg hath tended to your comfort,' quoth she, 'but – why here?' And she knit her slender brows in frowning perplexity.

' 'Tis well enough!' I answered. 'But ... Barbara ... what of tomorrow ... you and I ... the future?'

'Ay ... the future?' she murmured and seating herself on the bed (to my joy) slim ankles crossed, hands demurely folded in her lap, she stared pensively at the glory of moonlight that poured in a great beam through the open lattice; and I noticed she had changed her travel-worn clothes for a dainty gown I thought vastly becoming. 'The future,' she repeated, 'what doth it hold for us ... what?'

'This depends on myself, Barbara!'

'Oh, pray how?'

'Are you ... my wife?' At this she glanced up at me with troubled eyes.

'Himself – my father sayeth "no," Adam.'

'What say you, Barbara? 'Tis no matter for any other.' Here, clasping shapely arm about the bedpost she leaned her head thereto, seeming to ponder the question; then sighing, she pats down the bed at her side thus inviting me to be seated. So there sat we very silent, she gazing wistfully at the radiant moonbeam and I at her. And after thus deliberating, she spoke, her gaze still abstracted:

'How say you of it, Adam?'

'This!' I answered, endeavouring to seem as offhand as possible. 'That since I was wed to you under false name, since you vowed yourself to no more than an empty name and title that is but a sham, under these circumstances, no matter what the law may hold, be it Scots or English, yet in the light of reason, of common-sense and justice to you and your father, I think you are free of me, Barbara.'

'Oh!' says she, softly; and then frowning at the moonbeam, 'Yon was unco' eloquent, sir! Do you want me to be free o' you, Adam?' Here, finding me silent, she leaned so near that her shoulder touched mine and her sweet breathing fanned my cheek. 'Art so eager to be ... away from me, Adam?'

'Never!' I muttered, my every sense yearning to her warm and tender loveliness. 'Never, God knoweth!' And then, forcing my hungry gaze otherwhere, 'yes,' says I bitterly, 'tomorrow I will be gone.'

'Oh?' she murmured again, drawing away the better to survey me. 'And what will you be meaning with your no – yes, Adam?'

'This is Goodbye, Barbara. Tomorrow I shall be away ... very early.'

'And for why, Adam, if you please?'

Choking back the eager words upon my lips, I turned and would have risen, but upon my shoulders came her two hands to keep me sweetly prisoned, and leaning near she questioned me again:

'Why will you be leaving me, Adam?'

And now, forgetting all but the tender lure of her and

my own helpless longing, I answered in breathless whisper :

'Ah, because I love you, Barbara ... have loved you from the beginning ... shall love you to the end ... living and dying ... always and for ever !'

'Oh, Adam !' she murmured; and then again : 'Oh, Adam ! Yet ... you would leave me !'

'Yes,' says I, 'yes, I shall leave you, Barbara ... But ... only because I would have you happier than I might ever make you ... Wed to one more worthy ! A man ... strong ... handsome, tall and bold ... like, like—'

'Like Ian McLeod, Adam ?'

'Ay, him or – anyone that is the perfect opposite of my-self.'

'Because you so love me ?'

'Because I love you better than my life or aught else in the world, Barbara.'

Her hands dropped from me and leaning back 'gainst the bed-post she viewed me very strangely.

And thus side by side upon that unlovely bed in this dis-mal chamber, 'twixt light of moon and candle, we sat very silent awhile. At last, venturing to glance at her, I saw she was looking at me through a sparkle of tears, though her lips were curved to smile ineffably tender and, when she spoke, her voice seemed marvellous glad :

'Why, then I think the future need na trouble us, Adam, for you'll be leaving Drumlossie tonight, but ... oh my dear, you'll be taking ... your wife wi' you.'

'Barbara !' I stammered. 'Barbara ... what ... oh what do you mean ?'

'That if, Adam, if you're willing to front the world and dare fortune with your ain wife and your sword ... and the little, broken pistol, Adam, that I've cherished for love o' you, then I'm bold to follow my husband ... over the hills and far away ... to the world's end and beyond ... for, oh my dearest dear, 'tis in my heart that I just canna do wi-out you.' And then we were in each other's arms and, oh wonder of joy, her sweet mouth had sought mine. And in this death-less, ageless moment, my old self-distrust was gone, my doubts and hesitations all forgot, and I leapt, as it were, from timid youth to resolute manhood, and all (as I am verily persuaded) by the pure, sweet magic of Barbara's kiss.

But presently, holding her fast against my riotous heart, I must needs question my happiness :

'Art sure ... art certain there will be no regrets? Art very sure canst love such as I?'

'Such as thou?' she repeated softly, nestling within my arm. 'Oh foolish Adam to doubt! For, dear my heart, when you quelled the mutiny on the ship I began to love and marvelled at you. When you swam the terrors of that raging sea I loved and gloried in you. But ... tonight, when you would have sacrificed your love for love of me ah ... tonight I love you infinitely more than I dreamed I ever could, for now, my Adam, now do I know thee for such noble, valiant gentleman I must needs pray God make worthy such husband.'

Thus sat we whiles the broad moonbeam crept across the floor forgetful of all save our two happy selves and the wonder of joy that lay before us.

'At midnight!' says she, a little breathlessly. 'At midnight we steal away ... thou and I, my Adam. We'll to Edinburgh ... to Andrew MacAndrew, that is my lawyer body, for I have money, a very little, dear, some hundred pounds Scots, by the year. This shall keep us until—' she paused suddenly, and lay in my arms staring up at me, scarce breathing. 'Did you hear it, Adam, yonder by the door – a wee, rustling sound?'

'A mouse!' I whispered.

'Nay,' she breathed, trembling a little, ''twas like a hand upon the latch!' Then all in a moment she was afoot, and together we crept to the door and flung it wide. But though we sought and peered into every angle, we found nothing.

' 'Twas but a mouse!' says I, and kissed her.

'And it draws to midnight and I must make ready,' says she, and kissed me, and so sped away down the winding stair, leaving me in such rapture of happiness that I trembled, for mingled with my joy was a great awe, a very reverence, but of fears for the future or doubts of myself never a one, as I did on my sword, and, laying hat and cloak ready to hand, came back to the window. And now as I leaned forth into the radiant moonlight, this world, the night, the universe itself seemed more glorious and all athrill with the magic of what was to be, and I prayed fervently within myself that God would make me worthy.

Suddenly, fancying I heard a light step behind me, I turned in eager expectation, and then stared in some surprise to see the candle out. Wondering at this, I stepped from the window and now saw the door stood wide, a dim square of yawning upon the blackness of the turret stair, and in this blackness something that crept, a vague shape stealing on soundless feet ... flitting beside the wall ...I espied a crouching form ... a glimmer of steel. And now I saw this furtive, stealing thing was Sir Tearlach MacGregor grasping a sword, and my flesh chilled, for this blind man could see ... was creeping towards the bed. Now on his way he crossed that bright moonbeam and instantly clapped hand to eyes and shrinking away, went shambling by the wall till, being in shadow again, he straightened, and, stepping lightly to the bed, made such murderous play with his sword that I gasped in horrified amazement; in which moment he turned, and, seeing me in the shadow, came at me with silent leap. Avoiding his out-thrust steel, I whipped forth my own sword, and as our blades met, backed away, parrying his deadly attacks as best I might, beseeching him to forbear :

'Hold sir!' I cried, 'Sir Tearlach ... in God's name—'

But silent ever, and utterly regardless of my weapon, he rushed upon me, stabbing desperately ... and then I felt him upon my point, writhing upon my blade. I heard a dreadful, choking scream and, leaping back, saw him sink to his knees, to his face, and lie there in the dimness horridly mute and still and with a ghastly, ever-widening stain upon his white linen.

With that death cry ringing in my ears, I shrank to the wall and crouched there utterly dismayed and half-swooning with horror ... And then I saw Barbara on her knees beside that awful thing ... heard her speak in gasping, broken whisper :

'Blood ! ... Oh, Adam ... was it you? Ah, what have you done? God forgive you ... there is a father's blood betwixt us ... always and for ever ... Oh God, pity !' And as she looked up at me I read in her wide eyes bitter reproach and horror of me. Then was clamour on the stair, clattering feet, shouts and uproar ... Sword advanced, I turned to meet what might be, but she barred my way arms out-flung against me, in her eyes that same stark horror. And so, scarce knowing what I did, I leapt to the open casement and, forcing my way through, plunged out and down.

CHAPTER 33

GIVETH SOME DESCRIPTION OF MY
WANDERING BY NIGHT AND BLACK DESPAIR

N o w though, in this bitter moment, death would have been right welcome, yet no sooner was I amid those dark and stifling waters than I struck out instinctively, swimming deep. Presently, coming to the surface, I found myself in the shadow of a great, overhanging rock; here my foot touched bottom, and wading ashore through the oozy shallows I turned my back on that grim Tower of Drumlossie and began running wildly at my topmost speed, nor did I check until I was among the trees that clothed the foot of Drumlossie Crag. There paused I, in shivering misery, to fetch my breath and take off my draggled peruke that clung blinding and half-stifling me; and now (to my wonder) I found that I still grasped my sword, and was minded to hurl it away, since the accursed thing had (though all inadvertently) blasted all my hope of future happiness with Barbara and my peace of mind beyond redemption. But in the end I sheathed it, and, having wrung the water from my sodden wig and clinging coat-skirts, ran on again, fast as ever; yet with every yard my yearning for Barbara, the touch of her, the sound of her sweet voice, grew to such agony that I paused, at last, half-minded to go back, but, bethinking me how she had said her father's blood was forever betwixt us, I hasted on again, caring not whither.

Thus tramped I, despairing, until the moon failed me, and I reeling with weariness; but on trudged I blindly in a dim world, slipping oft and stumbling, falling only to rise and struggle on through a nightmare wilderness, and nothing heedful. For what are bodily harms and darkness to one that goeth in such hopeless, black despond as mine?

And all my thoughts were of Barbara, the radiant wonder of her, and she forever lost to me! ... Sometimes, as I stumbled on through the gloom, her loved voice seemed crying to me out of this horror of darkness, remote and desolate:

'Adam, oh, Adam ... there is blood betwixt us!'

And ever as I went her dear name whispered in my footsteps, my labouring heart beat and throbbed to it: Barbara ... Barbara.

It was as I descended a steepy slope that I fell heavily, and, lying face down amid dewy heather, spent and all foredone, I cried upon the Almighty to give back my love to me or take to Himself my unhappy soul. But as I lay thus in torment of anguish too deep for tears, in place of the death I supplicated, this most wise and merciful God blessed me instead with the gentle solace of a deep and dreamless sleep. Since rather than dying thus cowardly, a poor, futile creature, 'twas His Divine purpose that I must, by anguish of mind humbly endured, by hardships and perils outfaced, work out my own salvation, and in the end find something of manhood – as you shall see.

CHAPTER 34

TELLETH HOW SIR HECTOR WAS BALKED
OF HIS VENGEANCE

I AWOKE to find the young sun bright about me, very warm and comforting, therefore I lay awhile upon my heathery bed, gazing up at the sky, its blue immensity cloudless and serene. Birds were piping in pretty chorus near and far, dew sparkled, and I, heartened and refreshed by dreamless slumber, sat up eagerly to look about me; but remembering suddenly why I was here thus solitary, I sank back again, heartily wishing myself whelmed in that deep slumber whence is no awaking.

And now, with my despairing gaze lifted upturned to that so distant heaven, I yearned bitterly for her who, but for my cruel fate, would have been beside me even now, and in my passionate grief I reached forth desolate arms and whispered :

'Barbara !'

From this useless repining I was roused by sounds the most unexpected in such wild desolation and at such hour, viz – the oncoming murmur of voices. Sitting up, therefore, I glanced about, and thus saw that I lay in a small hollow or basin, thick girt with bushes save for that long, grassy slope down which I had tumbled in the dark.

And now glad was I of my sword, since I was determined that rather than be taken by English red-coats or Highland clansmen I would die fighting and so end my hopeless yearning and cure my heartbreak once and for all.

And now these unseen talkers had drawn so near that I could catch their every word; quoth one voice :

'Sir, by your leave, hereabouts we may break our fast and rest awhile, remote from chance espial.'

'Ay, 'twill do, 'twill do !' answered a second voice

peevishly, 'anywhere, only hasten man, for God knoweth I'm famished and spent. Oh, an accursed country, this, like the cause I was betrayed into fighting for ... my father was too wise to be lured for all their promises ... ha promises! I was the fool! Damn the Stuarts, says I!'

'Check, check, my lord! Have a care, I—'

'Tush, man, who shall hear us in this vile wilderness? Let me but win safe to England and I'll shout for fat George, for Hanover, or any save these Stuarts.'

'Why, 'twere notably politic, my lord. Also your noble sire—'

'My father – ay verily. He is my hope, for what with this new-proclaimed Whiggism, his passion for the Protestant Succession, his power and interest, he shall prove me loyalest o' the loyal – can I but get me clear of this detestable Scotland. But breakfast, man – what have ye for me?'

'Alas, but three poor oatcakes that just suffice your lordship.'

'Nay, nay in Heaven's name; what of the trout you bought of yon cottager?'

'My lord, the trout must be cooked.'

'Then cook it, man – what the devil, cook! I'll snatch a wink of sleep meanwhile.'

'But, my lord, to cook I must have fire and a fire means smoke and smoke, my lord, maybe—'

'Hell and furies! Must I starve by reason of your doting fears? A fire, John, this instant!'

'Why very well, my lord. Yet, having regard to our plight so desperate and how narrowly we 'scaped capture last night ... and that the MacFarlane, 'tis bruited, lurketh in our vicinity, your lordship were better advised to—'

'MacFarlane be cursed! Light the fire man, and let me eat!'

And presently I saw a thin, blue smoke go up beyond the bushes, an ever-thickening column that ascended high, for the morning was very still.

Now although pretty certain who these speakers were, I crept forward, and, peering through my screening bushes,

looked down into a little, pretty glen that, narrowing in the
one direction, opened out in the other to a broad slope thick
with underbrush and stunted trees, while almost immediately below me, cuddled and swathed in cloak and plaids,
lay my lord Viscount Scarsdale wooing sleep, what time
little Mr Repton, something haggard and wayworn, busied
himself at the small fire he had kindled though ever and
anon as the smoke thickened he glanced round about with
a very evident and timorous anxiety. As for me, the sight
of their food, the rich savour of the roasting fish bred in me
such rage of hunger that I lay snuffing its delectable fra-
grance, scarce conscious of aught else until aroused in
manner sudden and terrible. For upon the brooding stillness
rose a fury of fierce shouting, and glancing fearfully thither-
ward, I saw a flicker of steel amid the thickets, and thence
leapt four men in ragged tartans, wild fellows armed with
round shields and long swords ... My lord sprang up and
had snatched forth a pistol, but, doubtless perceiving resist-
ance vain, he hid the weapon in a crevice of the rock whereon
I lay and turned to these oncoming assailants with open
hands reached out to them.

'A friend, my good fellows,' cried he very earnestly, 'I am
your friend!' Nevertheless these men advanced brandishing
their weapons in horrid fashion and one of them pricked little
Mr Repton so shrewdly that he dropped the half-roasted
fish into the fire and leapt up with a piteous, bleating cry.
Now, shivering lest these poor fugitives be butchered before
my eyes, I drew my sword; but as I looked where and how
I must leap down to their aid, rose a loud, tuneful whistling, and forth of the trees, astride a shaggy, ambling, little
horse, rode Sir Hector Keith, with his gigantic henchman
Black Dougal striding at his stirrup.

Little Mr Repton was instantly on his knees again and
seemed to be praying, my lord the viscount stood dumb and
rigid, his fine eyes staring very wildly on Keith who, advancing at the same leisured pace, dismounted and took off
his hat.

'Well met, my noble brother-in-law, well met!' says he in

bitter mockery. 'Knowing yourself was in these parts and concerned in this fool's rebellion, I ha' sought you right diligently, and egad my zealous loyalty is notably rewarded!'

Motionless as one dreadfully spellbound, and utterly abashed stood my lord. Gone now his stately grandeur, for verily as I watched, his easy arrogance and air of high nobility seemed to vanish before Keith's pale, fleering smile, his very stature seemed to shrink, his shapely mouth showed all a-twitch and when at last he spoke it was slowly and with visible effort:

'What . . . what now . . . Hector MacFarlane?'

'First, Charles, news from the South. I have to acquaint you that, save for your lordly self and noble, hoary sire – the Ancasters are defunct. Eustace hath paid the price, ay – Eustace died and went to his account scarce a month since, whereof the earl your father languisheth. And this day, Charles, I rejoice to know that you will follow your brother Eustace very presently.'

'No . . . no!' cried Mr Repton wildly. 'Sir Hector . . . in God's name—'

'Nay, sir,' retorted Sir Hector, not deigning glance at the pleading wretch, 'nay, my good Mr Repton, say in Angela's name rather – she that these same Ancasters shamed for my sake and drove to misery and death.'

'Nay, sir . . . indeed, 'twas never for certain known she died. Verily she may live yet, Sir Hector, waiting to be found, she may be.'

'She is dead, sir, dead – murdered by these Ancasters, father and brethren, twenty years ago . . . She lieth in some nameless pauper's grave . . . that sweet, tender body! But the tears she shed live in my heart . . . they choke me now! The moans of her bitter agony ring in my ears . . . they deafen me now to all but – vengeance! Her innocent blood crieth to me unceasing, and I have ears! Ha – vengeance!' he choked, and I saw in him again that terrible transformation I had beheld ere now – his eyes glared, his body shook, his haggard features were convulsed as by some sharp spasm, he lifted clenched hands towards Heaven. 'Ha – death!'

cried he, then the dreadful paroxysm seemed to pass, he drew hand across gleaming brow wearily and spoke in his customary sweet-toned voice :

'Now for yourself, John Repton, good worthy sir, 'bate your apprehensions, these wild MacFarlanes, these wolves o' mine, shall prove very lambs to thee, shall bring thee safely to the neighbourhood of Edinburgh, or whereso you will. Myself is wishing you a safe and speedy journey, sir.'

'Ah, but ... but ... Sir Hector,' quavered the little gentleman, voice and look imploring, 'what of my dear lord?'

'Aha, our noble Charles? Hearken, my good Repton, should you come home safe to his lordly sire, to the noble earl, you shall tell that ailing gentleman that his Charles, his last surviving son – remains and abides in my bonny Scotland – till the last trump! And so, worthy John, farewell!'

'Sir – ah, sir,' wailed Mr Repton, still upon his knees, 'as you hope for mercy at the Judgement, show mercy now—'

'John Repton, for that sweet flower untimely nipped, for my young wife reft from the heart o' me, for this so young and innocent blood I'll exact just requital here and now, or, at the last great Judgement, may Almighty God refuse me. And so, sir, once more – farewell!' Then turning, Sir Hector spoke to his wild followers, whereupon these scowling clansmen seized upon poor, little Mr Repton, and despite his tearful outcries, his prayers and futile struggling, dragged him away.

'And now, Charles, dear brother-in-law and murderer of my young wife – to settle our final account.'

'Wait ... wait! ...' Trembling hands outstretched, a pallid, sweat-streaked face, tongue that stammered miserably : 'Hector ... Hector, I swear ... I had no hand ... no part in it ... I swear—'

'Charles, all Ancasters, save one, were and are perjured liars! Dougal, ye have the rope?'

'Inteety, Hector,' answered the big man, unwinding a stout cord from his great person, 'she hath carriet it this week and mair.'

'Hector,' gasped my lord sinking feebly to his knees, and so shamefully abject I could not bear to look on him. 'Hector I ... swear ... before God—'

'Charles, you'll be, I guess, before God in very few minutes, so – pray, man, pray!'

'Mercy!' screamed my lord, but even then Black Dougal was bending over him, great hands dreadfully busy with the strangling cord ... I heard a choking wail of despair ... And then, with this ghastly sound in my ears, I slipped and stumbled somehow, anyhow, down the rocky descent, and, crying out I know not what, ran at Keith with levelled sword.

My appearance was so sudden, my aspect so wild and purpose so evident that Sir Hector, backing away, instinctively drew to defend himself and our blades crossed. And in that moment he knew me.

'What, Adam,' says he, 'is't you, lad? Ha – away, boy, take heed lest I hurt ye!' and he parried my attack with such disdainful carelessness that I all but ran him through.

'Kill me if you can ... kill me!' cried I, pressing him ever closer, for, having naught to live for, death held no terrors. Moreover, I saw in this man the first cause of all my present griefs and, hating him accordingly, found myself (God forgive me) yearning passionately to end him. And now as our steel whirled and darted, I felt that same sense of power and joyous elation that I had known hitherto only when I swam; also though Keith was very quick, I found his method vastly different to Gaston's deadly timing and accuracy – his parades were more open and his point thus the less threatening, whiles I, mindful of my master's teaching, parried with the forte of my weapon, keeping my point ever in the line. Thus, presently spying an opening, I lunged over the wide sweep of his blade, felt my point go home, heard him gasp, and had him transfixed just above the elbow. Freeing my sword as Sir Hector reeled back, I would have followed ... but a mighty arm was about me, my sword was wrenched from my grasp, and Black Dougal's knife glittered before my eyes ... Then Keith cried out to him in the Gaelic. Dougal answered fiercely but, crushing me to earth, sheathed his weapon.

Now as I lay thus, my glance happened upon Viscount Scarsdale, where he crouched against the rock, fumbling for the hidden pistol. I saw him snatch and level it at Sir Hector and (moved by impulse sudden as strange), I rolled myself at his lordship and grasped his leg, deflecting his aim as he fired; uttering a shrill oath, the Viscount kicked me sprawling, and when I sat up he was gone, only Sir Hector knelt beside Black Dougal's huge, outstretched bulk, spattering the wounded man with his own blood in his endeavours to come at his hurt; but now, seeing me stir :

'Come you, Adam,' says he, 'come and help, for, and no thanks to you, my right hand is nigh useless, and Dougal lieth sore hurt.' And now, as I knelt to aid him, what was my wonder to see that Sir Hector's tears ran fast as his blood !

'Ay,' he nodded, catching my eye, 'Dougal is my foster-brother, and a coward's bullet hath snuffed his faithful life I fear me.' So between us, having found the big man's hurt, we staunched and bound it up as well as we might, which done, Sir Hector stood looking down on the unconscious man and mightily troubled.

'Here's death,' he sighed. 'Ay, Dougal's a dead man un-less I can bring him to the comfort of a bed and skilled nursing. Go fetch me the pony.' But, smitten and dismayed by the speaker's ghastly pallor, I hesitated :

'Nay, sir,' says I, 'first what of your own wound?' and I pointed to his hand that seemed no more than dripping smear.

'Egad,' quoth he with wry smile, 'you pinked me like a master, boy. But here's no great matter as wounds go, for all the blood. Find me a stone, a round pebble – the one yonder shall serve.' And now, having unbuttoned and rolled up coat and shirt sleeves, at his direction I bound this smooth pebble tight upon his wound with his kerchief and a strip from my plaid, and, the bleeding thus checked, brought the little horse whereon we set ourselves to hoist the sore-stricken giant; together we hove, we panted and strained and thus at last, with great labour, contrived to get him upon the animal, whereto we secured him as firmly as possible. I now brought Sir Hector his sword and hat. the which he accepted with murmur of thanks; then, turning to be gone, paused to look me up and down in strange sort, and yet when he spoke, instead of angry reproaches for his hurt (as I had expected) this strange man smiled on me, eyebrow whimsically cocked, clapping me on shoulder with his sound hand as a friend might have done.

'Faith,' says he, 'thou'rt more man than I judged thee, young Adam, wherefore, should we ever cross steel again, I'll play more cannily. And so, till we meet again, adieu, boy!' Then, grasping the horse's bridle, he set off with long strides and I, of a sudden desperate lonely, stood to watch him out of sight. But he had gone thus no great distance when Dougal's inert great body began to sway perilously, and as Sir Hector clutched at and strove desperately to steady him I saw his wound had broken out anew, for his finger-ends were spouting blood. So came I running. And when I had stayed his bleeding, we went on together, the little horse with his swaying, senseless burden, plodding between us.

CHAPTER 35

IN WHICH I STRIVE TO COMFORT MY ENEMY

I T W A S as we stood to recover breath after climbing a sharp ascent that Sir Hector questioned me suddenly :

'Adam,' says he in that quaint Scots-English that I loved for Barbara's dear sake, 'Adam, wherefore did ye no suffer yon villain to shoot and murder me?'

'Because it would ha' been murder,' I answered.

'And yet yourself seemed unco' determined to finish me when ye had me disarmed, wounded and defenceless, but for poor Dougal here, ye wad hae killed me, Adam, 'twas in your eye – and wherefore?'

'Because you are my enemy,' cried I, 'my curse, the reason for all my bitter griefs.'

'Aha? Then why are ye with me now, Adam?'

'God knoweth!' I answered. 'Except it be that you are hurt, a weak, helpless creature that I pity.'

'A vastly magnanimous youth!' says he, mocking. 'But pray why are ye no wi' your bonnie young wife, my lord Bellcastonborough?' Now at this I was dumb, for what with my rage against him and sick yearning for Barbara, I could have sobbed outright. So we trudged on again some while and never a word.

'And you cheated me o' my vengeance, Adam!' says he pensively at last.

'For the which I am heartily glad!' I retorted.

'Yet do I nothing grieve,' quoth he, 'for what is not is yet to be, and an enemy ever dieth too speedily. And here's, moreover, my lord viscount will die an hundred deaths 'twixt here and the Border – seeing me in every shadow, hearing me in every furtive sound, for he knows my vengeance is sure, to the which worthy end you this day saved my life, and are yourself thus the means to his destruction hereafter, a joyous thought for you, Adam.'

'A damnable!' I muttered.

'And now, my sweet and most virtuous lad, having outfought me by some unchancy trick or juggle, you bind up my hurt, aid me with my poor Dougal and tramp the heather with me – why?'

'For lack of better company, mayhap,' I replied.

'Spoken like graceless oaf!' he nodded. 'And lookee, my poor fool, who travels with Keith walks i' the shadow of death – be warned!'

'Boast not, sir,' I retorted, 'for I have no more dread of death than of you, indeed, should it come 'twill be very welcome.' Here he checked his long stride to view me askance 'neath cocked eyebrow.

'Death?' he repeated, 'Ha – hum!' And so fell to a fleering silence that angered me not a little; and thus we travelled some distance 'ere he spoke again; then:

'And so Drumlossie made the attempt?' says he. 'Our creeping Tearlach would ha' removed Barbara's so youthful spouse, ha?'

'How ... how should you know this?' I gasped in stammering amaze.

'Master Adam, sir, I do know many things.'

'What ... what more?' I questioned, breathlessly. But, seeing me so eager, he did but wag his head at me, leaving my question unanswered; but after a little:

'Sir,' says he. 'I mind how upon a time thou wert a timid lamb, today thou art a hell-fire roarer, spitting in the very eye of danger, how cometh such notable change, prithee?' Here I, in my turn, not deigning answer, he seemed to meditate, and presently questions me again.

'So – art not afeard o' dying, boy?' says he so wistfully, that I answered on the impulse:

'No!' cried I, bitterly. 'Death is a happiness I have prayed for!'

'And yourself married scarce a month!' he exclaimed, and I saw he did not mock me. 'Alack for wedlock!' quoth he. 'Alas for our poor Bab—'

'Stop!' cried I, and, stung beyond endurance, I whipped out my sword and faced him.

'How, my noble lord,' says he, grim lips curving to sudden smile, 'would you draw on and finish your wounded man?'

Now was I instantly ashamed, and, sheathing my hateful weapon with clumsy fingers, turned and went on again, feeling myself the merest fool. But in a little while he comes beside me and laying hand on my drooping shoulder speaks me very kindly in that strange, sweet voice of his:

'Lookee, Adam, I did but rally thee, for that it irks a body to have his life spared and saved to him both on a day – not to mention this arm of mine ... and yourself but a feckless boy, d'ye see?'

'Why then, sir,' I answered, and awkwardly enough, 'I crave your kind forgiveness that I ... drew on you ... 'tis my regret, sir, it was all unworthy the Complete Gentleman.'

'Hum!' says Keith, rubbing his chin and eyeing me like one something at a loss. 'Howandever, Adam, I'd hae ye ken I meant no manner o' disrespect tae your bonnie leddy wife.'

This he said with such transfiguring smile as warmed the heart of me, insomuch that I wondered.

It was something past noon, as I judge, and we plodding around the base of a hill whereby flowed a pleasant, noisy stream, when a voice hailed us from above, and, glancing up, I espied a tall and stately woman beckoning to us from the hillside.

'Why, Margaret,' cried Sir Hector, sweeping off his hat to her, 'God bless thee, Meg, what do ye out-by on the brae? 'Tis as ye'd expected us.'

'Whyfore else should I be here, MacFarlane? Whyfore else should I hae prepared cherishings for my Dougal's hurt?' she answered hastening to examine the wounded giant with knowledgeful eye and quick, deft hand, while Keith watched anxiously.

'How is he, think you, Meg?'

'The sooner he's abed the sooner he'll be abroad. 'Tis no siccan great matter tae son o' mine and a MacFarlane forby. And what o' your ain scaithe, my jo?'

'Naught to boggle o'er, Meg.'

And now, despite her stately bearing and upright figure, I saw she was much older than I had deemed.

'Adam,' said Keith when he had kissed her heartily, 'salute Dame Margaret MacFarlane, my honoured foster-mother.' And when we had bowed and curtseyed to each other, Dame Margaret brought us to a track that wound gently up the brae.

'Hector,' says she, as we climbed the hill, 'my sister Kirsty is back oot o' England, ye'll mind Kirsty, I'm thinking?'

'Kirsty?' he repeated with a kind of gasp.

'Hersel', Hector, that was maid to my leddy Angela afoer ye wed – twenty weary years syne.'

'Is she here, is she with you, Meg?' he questioned eagerly

'Nay, she's awa' tae Dunfermline.'

'How comes it she's back in Scotland? She was house-keeper and much esteemed—'

'Ay, but the auld earl, being sick, hath shut his muckle hoose in Sussex and turned Kirsty oot – and after all these years! Forby she's no' awa' empty-handed, ye ken ... there's papers ... letters, my jo! Ay, there's letters frae the deid ... a cry frae the grave ... your ain bonnie lady Angela.'

'Letters?' cried Keith and, with the word, was away running up the hill very nimbly for all his wound, whiles I, catching the horse's bridle, followed with the old dame, who trudged sturdily beside me, muttering in the Gaelic.

Topping the ascent, we came on a goodly farmstead pleasantly situate amid ricks and byres whence, at Dame Margaret's call, issued three brawny fellows to aid her indoors with the wounded man. As for me, being weary and famished, I sank down upon a great settle beside the house-door, and bowing head in hands, fell a-grieving for my lost Barbara. Now suddenly I was startled out of these woeful thoughts by a hoarse, moaning cry within the house, very terrible to hear; and then I saw Keith leaning in the door-way and on his features such look of anguish as no words of mine may ever justly describe. Into the yard came he a faltering pace or so, then stood, his agonized face upturned to heaven while from his quivering lips broke a dry and awful sobbing. Then, tossing his arms aloft in wild, des-paring fashion:

'A child!' he groaned. 'She bore me a child ... and I never knew! God pity me ... I never knew ... Twenty weary years!' Now, presently catching sight of me, he came and, sinking beside me on the settle, sat dumb awhile, shaking as in an ague fit.

'Adam,' says he at last, brokenly and with voice and look pitifully humbled, 'oh, Adam ... oh, lad – better you had killed me, ay would to God I were dead, boy ... I ha' known pain and suffering ere now, Adam, but never ... never the like o' this. See here, boy, read – read!' And into my hand he thrust a piece of paper, yellowed by time, whereon, traced in faded characters, I saw these words:

DEAR MY LORD AND FATHER,

'I am very near my time and destitute. Dear sir, I have known the misery of hunger. I am all alone and something fearful. Therefore, my father, because of the innocent child I am soon to bear, have pity. Send help lest we perish. The kind person that beareth this is faithful friend and trustworthy. So in Jesu's name, and for sake of the little life now springing, aid now your despairing woeful daughter,

'ANGELA.'

Folding this most piteous letter very reverently I placed it in Keith's nerveless hand and both of us dumb awhile.

'Well, Adam,' says he at last, staring up at me 'twixt his spread fingers, 'thus my young wife supplicated twenty years agone – and all in vain! "The little life now springing!" This should have touched the vile heart of blackest tyrant, but – not my lord of Ancaster's ... Twenty years! Our child will be man or woman ... flesh of her sweet flesh, bone of my bone ... born and bred in misery ... a hardened rogue ripe for the gallows, mayhap ... a poor waif o' the streets – our child! Oh shame! Oh death! Ah, why do I live? God be merciful and strike me dead!'

Now, seeing him in his agony, the masterful soul of him thus abased, I clean forgot my bitter hate, and, moved by sudden impulse, set my arm about his bowed and stricken form, striving thus to comfort him, dumbly to be sure, since I was choked and blinded with sorrow for this poor, distressful lady. At my touch, Keith glanced up at me keen-eyed and askance:

'What, d'ye weep, Adam?' says he, harshly. 'Can ye weep? Would I might, for such tears are precious to God, I guess, and may ease a breaking heart. But tears are no' for me, boy – this heart cracked years syne ... And today our child, her daughter is, likely, thing o' shame creeping the highways, our child my son may be rotting on some gibbet—'

'Nay, sir,' cried I, 'Oh, Sir Hector, why so plague yourself? Why dream such evil of thy poor young wife's child?

She was, I judge, a lady very pure and sweet and gentle and ... and yourself, sir, in those days, a gentleman of honour. Thus then, an God be just, a child o' such begetting should prove worthy of his blood.'

'Ha, boy!' cries Sir Hector with fierce gesture, 'you talk like feckless fool! You would cozen me with talk o' God's mercy – ah, but ... if a man hunger he will steal, if a woman lack she will sell herself! ... So do I walk the floor of Hell.' And, starting up violently, he falls a-striding to and fro with the look and motions of a madman. Yet presently back he comes and snatching my hand between his two, grasps it fast, looking down on me with such wistful, pleading eyes as wrung my very heart.

'Tell me – tell me, Adam,' says he breathlessly, 'you – you that I found a timid boy and now prove a man – on your soul – think you this lost child o' mine that I so hunger for, this child ... born in misery ... bred in want ... with no fostering care to guide ... may yet live today worthy its sweet mother ... 'scaping the thousand pitfalls of blind Youth and trusting Innocence ... ah, think you so, Adam?'

'Yes!' cried I passionately. 'Yes! For since God is truly all mercy and love and justice, sure am I the son of such parentage lives, and shall live, worthily – come what may.'

Now at this he loosed my hand, laughing wildly.

'Ah, lad ... lad!' cried he, 'would to God I were young enough to so believe!' Then, with the same fierce, despairing up-flung gesture of his arms, he turned and strode back into the house, spattering blood from his wounded arm as he went.

And presently, as I sat lost in gloomy abstraction, to me cometh Mistress Margaret and her voice, like her look, wondrous kind:

'Young sir,' quoth she, laying her two hands upon my shoulders, 'may the Guid Being bless thee in all thy ways, and love be thy comfort abiding – amen! And now, my bonny jo, I'll be thankin' ye for tellin' sic wise cracks tae himself, the MacFarlane, my ain Hector, eh, but the puir body's nigh daft wi' grief and lack o' sleep – and the skelp in's arm, forby. I'm joyful tae ken himself hath siccan friend as yoursel' – ay, I heard a' ye spoke him, sir, anent God and His mercies, though ye're ower young to ken the ways o' the Almighty sae muckle well, I jalous. Howandever, Hector's awa' tae bed wi' a heartening dram in's wame and 'tis time ye were sleeping, too, by the looks o' ye. But first, my bonnie lad, come ben and eat!'

'And pray how is Dougal?' I enquired, rising.

'He'll be his ain man again sune, praise be!'

So saying, she brought me indoors and, seating me at well-laden table, took joy to keep my platter filled and mug brimming. Thereafter she led me to small, cosy chamber sweet with lavender. And here stood a bed, plumply inviting. So, when I had washed me, I slipped betwixt smooth, fragrant sheets, and sank forthwith into the blessedness of sleep.

CHAPTER 36

TELLETH OF A MAN'S AGONY AND THE
REASONS WHEREOF

A RAPPING on my chamber-door waked me to a glory of sunshine and, sitting up in bed, I lay blinking in this kindly radiance right blissfully; but, the knocking being repeated, I called in answer and into the room stalked Dame Margaret, herself cheery as the morn, and shows me, over her arm, my garments (this woefully ill-used finery) all very carefully pressed and brushed and folded.

'Eh, my young gentleman,' says she, shaking her head at me, ''tis sinfu' shame tae treat your bonnie claes sae wanton! A coat o' fine velvet fit for prince! And a sark o' lawn and, oh my heart – wi' ruffles o' French point! Howandever, I've done what a body may wi' 'em, ye shall be mair kenspeckle the noo, I'm thinkin'! And himself is waitin' breakfast for ye.' And away she goes before I have half done thanking her.

So, having washed and dressed, I found my hard-used clothes so much the better for Dame Margaret's care that I took pains to comb out the long, tangled curls of my great periwig to look my poor best, and thus down to breakfast.

I found Sir Hector busied with a great pile of documents, but now he leaned back in his chair and nodded.

'Lookee, Adam,' says he, directing my attention to these papers with disdainful flirt of his fingers, 'I am learning how noble and just is the passion of hate. For here is indictment of such soulless villainy, such black treachery, such shameless hypocrisy as should cast from tenderest heart all sense o' pity, and nerve the weakest arm to smite wi' stength o' giant. These be the secret papers of that very noble nobleman the Earl of Ancaster ... Here now is small item of personal interest – hearkee!

> 'To Captain Treeby of the *Albatross* pink for transport of special cargo to the Spanish Settlements – Two Hundred Guineas.'

I was that "special cargo", Adam. Ay, boy, I was beset in a London street, stricken unconscious, carried away on that hellish ship and sold into slavery—'

'A slave?' I gasped.

'Here be the shackle-marks, boy!' and speaking, he drew up his long lace ruffles and showed me the ugly print of old scars upon his wrists. 'So I slaved 'neath a pitiless sun, in pain o' body and agony of mind, while my young wife starved in England. But I broke free at last ... They hunted me with dogs – but I got away. I was lost in the wilds, I languished with famine and sickness and lay down to die. But I was succoured and healed by savages, kinder folk than their Christian brethren, for I was not to die, being preserved for a righteous vengeance. So back came I to England and this mockery of civilization, where the rich and highly-placed may sin and sin and walk immune. I sought my wife ... they told me she was dead and, faith, boy, Death became my servant to smite her slayers whenso Chance offered ... And now to breakfast.'

Here he clapped his hands, whereat entered Dame Margaret and a comely maid bearing sundry dishes very delectable; and when I, yearning to hear more of Keith's adventures, ventured to question him, he merely scowled, bidding me eat, and eat I did! There was (as I well remember) a noble salmon – such dainty fare as I had never tasted ere now. Our meal over at last, Keith leaned back, cocking an eyebrow at me.

'Master Adam, sir,' says he, mocking, 'you make no politely insincere inquiries as to your sword thrust – this arm o' mine, so am I fain to remark, 'tis so well that I shall be blithe to try you again at least occasion. Indeed, you are become a very hell-fire, roaring blade by accounts, for what's this I'm hearing of your brawling and blood-letting at Drumlossie? Nay, gape not, lad. There's little I don't ken hereabouts; this is the MacFarlane country and I am The MacFarlane.'

'And yet, sir, but small while since you called yourself Keith.'

'Ay, my mother was a Keith.'

'In England I heard you named Weir or Weaver.'

'Ay, this was for purposes political.'

'You are a man of many names, sir.'

'Yet but one purpose, Adam. Ay, one, hitherto, for now I've another, to wit – to seek out my unknown child ... But how came you to cross steel with Tearlach, laird o' Drumlossie?'

'Ah, sir ... sir,' quoth I, miserably, 'I ... killed him!'

'Faith now, did ye so, Adam?' says he, cocking his eyebrow at me in the same sly, whimsical fashion. 'And was it for this you soused yourself in the loch?'

'Yes,' I muttered. 'He lay dead . . . by my hand . . . Barbara's father!'

'Neither one nor other, lad,' answered Sir Hector, 'you did but scratch the rascal. Tearlach is alive and well, devil take him! And Barbara is not his daughter.'

'Alive?' cried I, jumping to my feet. 'Alive? Thank God, oh, thank God! I'll back ... I'll back to Drumlossie and her ... my loved Barbara.'

'Then you'll lose your labour, Adam, for she's away seeking you, she and your French gentleman and the big sailorman. They left for Edinburgh last night.'

'Then I'm for Edinburgh this instant!'

''Tis long and weary march, boy.'

'No matter. I bid you farewell, sir.'

'The country 'twixt here and yon is full o' thievery and murder, Adam.'

'Sir, I've naught to lose save life, and that I'll adventure gladly.'

'For – Barbara's sake, boy?'

'Indeed and indeed, sir.'

'At a guess, Adam, I'd say you love this wife of my providing, eh, lad?'

'With all my heart!' cried I, fervently. 'So much, Sir Hector, that when I mind how and why you tricked her to marriage with beggarly me, I'm vastly glad to know my steel hath bit and marked you! So often as you see this scar, sir, think shame of yourself to so dupe a lady so sweet and nobly innocent. Sir, it is now my joy to take leave of you.'

'Zounds!' murmured Sir Hector, drawing out snuff-box and tapping it gently. 'Spoke like a true cock o' the game and honourable young sprig o' gallantry! Faith, you grow on me, Adam, on my soul you do. I'll suffer your company so far as Edinburgh. We start in half an hour.'

'Sir, I start this moment!' quoth I. Sir Hector, having snuffed with much relish, dusted himself and shook his head at me.

'As you will, fool boy!' he murmured. 'But so sure as you travel alone, so surely will you perish by the way and your lovely Barbara be widowed. So, an you truly love her, Adam, and what's more, if she love you, school your hot impatience and bide for the MacFarlane.' Which said, he rose and went from the room, leaving me in state of such miserable indecision that twice I crossed to the door, minded to be gone; but in the end I sank upon the settle in the ingle and sat staring on the fragrant, smouldering fire of peat, my senses in very tumult of joy that my hands were clean of Sir Tearlach's blood, and fierce impatience to be away for Edinburgh and Barbara. From these reflections I was roused by Sir Hector, cloaked for travel and bearing a plaid and Highland bonnet the which he tendered to me.

'You'll find these comforting 'twixt here and Edinburgh,' he nodded. 'Have you any weapon beside your sword?'

'No, sir,' I answered, rolling the plaid about me as I had learned from Barbara.

'Why then, take these!' and he laid two silver-mounted pistols on the table. 'Have you money?'

'Little enough, I fear.'

''Tis no matter, only attempt no bestowal o' money on Dame Meg unless you'd take a clout o' the ear. And now, if you're ready, we'll be wending.'

So out we went into the trim farmyard where stood Dame Margaret with her three brawny fellows and the little horse saddled and bridled. Sir Hector reached his hand to these men, who, all three, touched knees to earth, then he turned to kiss and be kissed by the dame who, when I tried to thank her, kissed me right heartily, bidding Sir Hector take care of me, whereat he smiled very grimly as he got to saddle.

And thus we set forth, I walking at his stirrup; yet must he often turn to waft farewell and now, I saw that Mistress Margaret (this masterful dame) was weeping.

'Ay, faith,' says Sir Hector, noting my wonder, 'Meg is persuaded she will never see me again ... and she is blessed with the second sight, 'tis said. Ah, well, Death however he come, shall be my friend and have cheery welcome ... To rest awhile, and, waking, find again those loved and lost so long – here's a fair thought, Adam lad, and a comforting.'

CHAPTER 37

GIVETH PARTICULARS OF A MOMENTOUS CONVERSATION

SURELY never did sun shine brighter or the world seem more joyous (to me at least), for Hope danced beside me since my thoughts were all of Barbara and the rapturous gladness of reunion; thus, forgetful of the lurking perils of the long, weary miles before us, I strode right blithely and, looking from earth to heaven and heaven to earth, thanked God within my soul, that I was alive.

Presently, feeling a light rap on my Scots bonnet, I glanced up, to see Sir Hector looking down on me sombre-eyed.

'Young dreamer – awake!' quoth he. 'We're desperate far frae Edinburgh and your Barbara, my wee man!'

'When should we reach there, think you, sir?'

'Faith, it all depends. Ay, 'twill depend on our two selves if we reach there at all, Adam. 'Twill be a case of wit or weapon all the way. For whereas you would certainly ha' perished in some bog, or drowned, or been massacred by wild caterans for an accursed Englishman or by red-coats for tory Jacobite, or by tories for a whig, I have enemies everywhere, and a both sides very blithe and eager to dim their steel in blood o' the MacFarlane—'

'Why, I've heard they call you traitor,' says I, staring up at his haggard face, and I saw him flush painfully.

'True enough, Adam,' he nodded, ' 'tis but to be expected.'

'Sir, which cause do you favour, which side are you on?'

'Whichever serves me against the cursed Ancasters.'

'But are you Jacobite at heart?'

'Not I!' quoth he with such quick fury that I started; then clapping hand on my shoulder, 'Hearkee, Adam,' says he, 'though I hate the Stuarts, 'tis all one to me who snatches the throne. My politics, my creed is no more than the final extermination of this brood of high-bred villainy calling itself Ancaster. But for the present this very proper ambition must wait, I am speeding south on hopeless quest ... my child ... the child I learned of but yesterday ... My wife in her misery wrote four several letters to her thrice damned sire and brethren ... I have them here!' and he touched his breast with a finger. 'These letters were writ from four divers places in and about London – there shall I seek news of her and the child ... Twenty years! Dooms me, 'tis a long time, Adam! And yet there may still live some do remember her.'

'Sir,' says I fervently, 'I pray God there may.'

'Amen!' quoth he, taking off his hat. And so we went in silence some while, he drooping in the saddle like man utterly deject. Rousing at last, he looked down on me, smiling:

'Adam,' said he, 'd'ye mind how we went thus before, in England, you at my stirrup? 'Twas not so long since, and yet you were but sorry, timid lad then, a poor creeping, spiritless thing – faith thou'rt vastly changed!'

'God send 'tis for the better,' says I.

'Hum!' quoth he, cocking his eye at me again, 'some folk may esteem a quick-tempered, hoity-toity, froward youth whose sense of honour is so preciously delicate he's apt to be whipping forth steel with a – one, two and into your vitals on the least occasion, a young fire-eater that yet can flush like timid maid, sulk like gross hobbledehoy – there may be some folk to tolerate or even love such – Mistress Bab, for instance!' Here, meeting his quizzical glance, I flushed instantly, and striving for retort, was dumb.

'And d'ye love her, boy – so very well?' Now this he said so wistfully that I answered from my very heart:

'Oh, Sir Hector, there are no words for it ... She is become my very life, the only reason for my existence – losing her I am glad to die.'

'Ay!' he nodded. 'Ay, lad, so loved I once. She was even younger than your Barbara, I guess ... a sweet, shy maid of such tender beauty and loveliness, such radiant purity . . . innocent as a flower, and – they destined her for the satyr-arms of his merry and glorious Majesty, Charles by the Grace of God etcetera. The noble earl her father had ambitions, you'll perceive she was his stepping stone to favour and preferment. But I, though poor gentleman and fugitive even then, I won her love. We wed in secret, but scarce had we known our joy than we were betrayed by yon fawning hound Tearlach MacGregor. Well, my lord's lofty plans thus nipped, she was driven to her death, and I . . . I am extremely alive and well these Ancasters know it. And egad, Adam, thou and I betwixt us, have cheated them of Barbara's beauty and what they value more, the sordid dogs !'

'Sir, what mean you by "more"?'

'Base lucre, Adam – gold, money.'

'But, sir, Barbara hath so little – some poor hundred pounds Scots, by the year,' says I, repeating her own words.

'Howbeit, boy, she would have been an Ancaster, but for you and me – yet, mark me, these huckstering, fine gentlemen never wed for mere beauty alone – never do aught except with eye to their own profit.'

'What riddle is this?' cried I, all bemused. 'And you said, a while since, that she – Barbara – was not Sir Tearlach's daughter.'

'True enough, Adam. She is of better stock, far nobler lineage—'

'But,' says I, in stark amaze, 'she believes him her father.'

'So do many others, lad. Howbeit she hath little o' Tearlach's thin blood in her veins, for the which you and she should be duly grateful.'

'Then who – what is she?'

'All true MacGregor, Adam. Only child of Donald MacGregor, chief o' that ancient, misfortunate clan. For poor Donald was attainted of treason, his estates and possessions all forfeit to the King's Majesty. So Donald carried his sword to France and there, having married and begot your Barbara, died in battle very gallantly. Tearlach married his widow, and, carrying her and the child to Drumlossie, contrived to break her heart, within the year, howbeit she died, poor lady. Thus, d'ye see, Adam, Barbara would be a great heiress should this attainder ever be revoked.'

'Then I hope to God it never will be!'

'Why so, my fool lad?'

'Because I am no more than a beggar.'

'Hum!' quoth he. 'Yet a mighty proud one. Ay, and one Mistress Barbara is very passionately a-seeking at this moment.'

'Tell me, Sir Hector,' says I, after we had gone a while in silence, 'are we indeed truly married, Barbara and I!'

'Faith yes, no fetters matrimonial were ever truer welded. Why d'ye ask?'

'Because I was wed under false name, a foolish, preposterous title.'

'Well, Adam, I gave the worthy parson such poor names as you possessed, to wit – Adam Thursday, a name so passing ridiculous that I tacked thereto Bellcastonborough for sake of euphony, faith, it sounds like a charge of cavalry, a very notable effort of imagination.'

'Then you ... gave also my right name?'

'Ay, if such be your right name – thus: Barbara, Margaret MacGregor, spinster, to Adam Thursday, Earl of Bellcastonborough, bachelor? Thus it runs in your fair wife's marriage lines and register of Holy Church.'

'And why, ah why did you trick her into this sorry marriage?'

'To save her from a worse, and, in especial, for the confounding of two rogues.'

'Whom do you mean?'

'Observe now, Adam! Scarce was Barbara of age marriageable than the Earl of Ancaster, being then high in court favour and with his hucksterly eye on profit, bargains with Tearlach that if, by Majesty's favour, he can procure dead Sir Donald's attainder of outlawry rescinded, Barbara, his heiress, shall wed one, or any, of his sons, and they, the noble earl and Tearlach aforesaid, shall cut up her inheritance betwixt 'em. So all's explained, boy! And yonder is a

pleasant burn, rill, brook or freshet, its pretty babble whereby we will sit and discuss our dinners.'

CHAPTER 38

TELLS OF A SUDDEN ONFALL

As we ate thus side by side, the little horse cropping con-
tentedly hard by, we talked together on this wise :

MYSELF : Sir, you knew that Sir Tearlach's blindness
was a lie?

SIR HECTOR : No such thing, Adam; the man is blind
enough by day, being one of those strange creatures can see
only in the dark – a nyctalops is the word, I think. His
sight was always feeble, I mind, and the malady hath grown
on him. Howandever, my warning was not unreasonable,
eh, lad – he found you awake and ready, 'twould seem?

MYSELF : Is he a little mad?

SIR HECTOR : 'Twere charity to say so, but then, Adam,
you stand 'twixt him and his dearest ambitions, ay egad –
and the insatiable greed of the Ancasters likewise, so beware
o' them also. Pass me the loaf, boy.

Now as we ate thus (and with rare appetite) I noticed how
my companion's keen glance was for ever aroving from me
to the solitude about us, questioning (as it were) every
thicket, every rock and bush, near and far; the which,
minding me how perilous was travel in this unhappy Scotland, I instantly voiced my apprehension :

MYSELF : (*impulsively*). And yet if she be travelling ...
if Barbara is with Gaston ... with Mr de Vrillac, she should
be safe?

SIR HECTOR : Indeed, Adam. A very capable person
your Frenchman, of experience varied, faith a gentleman
par excellence, and with a pretty turn for arts surgical. He
spoke much of you at Auchterlochie and protests himself
much your debtor, boy.

MYSELF : (*and my heart leaping*). My debtor?

SIR HECTOR : He told how you snatched him from the sea, – *le monstre horrific*. He waxed lyrical on your dash through the breakers ... Hum ! At a guess, 'twas he taught you that devilish trick o' fence caught me napping, ha ?

MYSELF : (*eagerly*). Yes. But he learned me more, Sir Hector, ah, so very much more that I pray to be worthy his noble friendship.

SIR HECTOR : (*mocking*). 'S life ! And a very youthful, pretty spirit o' humility ! Thus should dutiful son meekly revere honoured sire !

MYSELF : (*passionately*). Would God I were indeed his son ! With such blood in me what matter for my lack of size and ... hateful red hair !

SIR HECTOR : Go to, boy ! Pish, fie and tut – tut ! Speak me no disparagement o' red locks.

And off came the small riding-wig he wore and showed a crop of auburn hair, short, thick, yet plentifully streaked with silver; but in this moment his roving glance became fixed, and, setting the wig back on his head, he smoothed it in leisurely fashion, nodded, smiled and spoke :

'Go on wi' your dinner, Adam, but watch me and be ready wi' your pistols?'

'Pistols?' said I, staring into his impassive face.

'Indeed !' says he, cutting himself another crust from the loaf betwixt his knees. 'Observe, Adam, that when a twig moveth and no wind it behoveth the traveller to be wary. We are watched, boy, I spied a blink o' steel behind yon thicket.'

'But what ... who would molest us?' I stammered.

'Well, Adam, to name a few – there's the McLeans, the McLeods, the Lamonts, the McKenzies, the Stewarts of Appin, the Gunns, the Grants, and others a-plenty, all fair yearning for this head o' mine. But as for yon spies – here's to learn !' and lifting his rich, sweet voice he cried out in the Gaelic. Ensued a time of breathless suspense (for me, at least), and then from behind a boskage, at no great distance.

stepped two men, the first a small fellow armed with a long musket, the other big and burly who bore a great sword and brazen-studded shield or targe.

'Yon is the McLeod tartan!' said Sir Hector and rising, crust in fist, he threw up his arms, calling on them (as I supposed) in friendly greeting, for the men began to approach, viewing us narrowly. Meanwhile Sir Hector, having eaten what remained of his crust, flicked the crumbs from him with laced handkerchief, folded his arms and watched the men's slow advance with eyes serene, but between lips up-curved in gracious smile, murmured to me:

'In your pockets ... hands on pistols, but stir not unless I bid ye ... be easy, lad!'

The two men halted within a few yards, muttered together, eyeing us the while with looks of dark suspicion. But, smiling yet, Sir Hector spoke them in his pleasing voice and to such good effect that their doubts seemed to pass; the big man made to sheath his great weapon, but suddenly his small comrade, pointing at Sir Hector's scarred wrist, plain to sight beneath his ruffle, called out and levelled his musket; even then, Sir Hector unfolded his arms ... I saw darting fire, a puff of smoke, heard a sharp report and the little man, dropping musket to clutch leg, spun round and fell as Sir Hector leapt upon the big fellow ... I saw his smoking pistol rise and fall, a whirl of coat-skirts and fluttering tartans, a shimmer of aimless steel and the big man went down beneath the unerring stroke of that smoking pistol-barrel – and all this in as many moments. Standing between his fallen assailants, him that lay stunned and him that cherished bloody leg and snarled, Sir Hector drew forth his second pistol, cocked it, seemed to hesitate and finally put it away again.

'Now, Adam,' says he, shaking his head, 'I'll have you note and remember the crass humanity o' the MacFarlane, for here lie two would ha' murdered me, yet am I content to spare these rogues that shall perchance attempt my life another day, wae's me!' So saying (and to my shocked amazement) he instantly smote the groaning fellow's pate so shrewdly that he suddenly languished and sank down silent and inert as his fellow.

'Sir ... sir,' gasped I, 'the man was wounded and helpless!'

'Adam,' says he, sighing, 'a Scot is seldom helpless until he's completely dead. So will I have you truss me these fellows securely, my wound hath opened and bleeds somewhat – nay I can do till you tie me these McLeods, their belts wi' strips from their plaids shall serve ye fine.'

So, while he watched and directed, I bound the two men fast as I could and thereafter tended his wound, anointing it with a salve Dame Margaret had given him. This done, he bade me heave the fellows' musket into the stream, the which I did.

'And now,' says he, carefully recharging his pistol, while into the saddle-bag I tumbled what remained of our viands, 'now, Adam, the sooner we march, the better, for where are two McLeods shall be others and—' his eyes opened suddenly wide and what was my alarm to hear thudding feet, to see a third assailant close upon us, then even as I cried a warning, Sir Hector leapt to action incredibly rapid. I glimpsed the narrow glitter of his blade as he leapt ... steel rasped but, hampered by his wound, Sir Hector missed his thrust and was tumbled headlong ... yet somehow my blade was out in time to meet and parry the steel that would have transfixed him as he lay. For a breathless, dreadful moment we stood, this new assailant and I, our blades so close engaged we dared neither strike or stab; then, rising to an elbow, Sir Hector shot him through the body, and, crying out, the man sank at my feet, his convulsed face staring up at me very horridly for, even as I looked, he was dead, and he a comely man in prime of manhood. Then Sir Hector rose, and glancing down at his ghastly doing, nodded complacently.

'A McLean!' quoth he. 'Dour and dowie are the McLeans! A'weel, here's one the less o' them, which is some comfort. Go, Adam lad, and catch me the pony whiles I prepare 'gainst further eventualities.' And seated cross-legged beside this dead man, he set about re-loading his pistols whiles I, sickened to the very soul by my companion's utter callousness, went after the little horse.

And after a while we left that place of death and both of us very silent. On we trudged, taciturn and gloomy, until turning aside from the rough track we had followed (for in this wild country roads there seemed none) Sir Hector began to urge his sturdy mount up a heathery, boulder-strewn ascent crowned by scowling crags.

'It must be the high lands for us, Adam,' says he clapping me on shoulder, 'paths o' the deer and the like shy creatures.' But, shrinking from his touch, I neither looked at him nor spoke.

'Eh?' he demanded angrily. 'What'll be sticking in your gizzard now?'

I merely looked at him.

'Ha, the devil!' cries he, pettishly. 'Why must ye glower on me, boy? Answer me, sirrah jackanapes!'

'You ... murdered that man!' said I, breathlessly.

'Now, as I remember it, fool Adam, that man would ha' murdered me, ay and yourself, like as not.'

'He was but one 'gainst us two and ... and ... however, no need was there to kill him.'

'Child, when hast seen as much o' this sorry world, of blood and violent death as I, you'll be less squeamish, mayhap.'

'God forbid!' cried I very fervently.

'Pah!' he exclaimed contemptuously. And so was silence while we climbed the steep until the ground became more level and we reached a place of rocks, huge rugged masses, betwixt which the way ran narrow, trending down to a deep gorge or valley where a stream foamed along its rocky bed. And here, pausing to survey the country behind us and before, Sir Hector began to mock at me :

'Sweet master Adam, delicate sir,' says he, flourishing at me with his hat, 'thou art, beyond all possibility o' doubt, a very tender, ladylike young gentleman, too infinite nice for this poor, rugged, battle-torn country of Scotland.' Here, pausing for answer, he cocks scornful eye at me but, finding me silent, falls to it again.

'Zounds and i' faith, Adam, you are truly more maid than

man. I doubt me our poor Barbara shall have but a sorry bargain of 't—'

Stung at last beyond all restraint, I turned on him in black and savage fury:

'Murderer!' I cried, 'ha' done with my wife's name or by death and hell, I'll cut me another mark on your carcass, wounded though you be!'

In one motion, as it seemed, he was out of the saddle and fronting me, sword bared and hat a-flourish.

'At your service, Sir Nameless Foundling!' quoth he. So then and there, upon that bleak eminence, we fell-to with ring and clash of purposeful steel, I with such impetuous fury that twice he all but transfixed me in the first rally. But, bethinking me of Gaston, his wise dictum that he who fights in anger fights like fool, I curbed my passion, and presently was all a-thrill with that joyous exaltation the which at such times uplifts me above all thought of peril or defeat. Gradually the fleering smile faded from my opponent's grim mouth as, despite all his skill and caution, I forced him often to break ground and twice, beating his point, I made to lunge and as oft restrained myself until, seeing a chance for that most deadly thrust of all, I cut over, had him at my mercy, and in that instant (moved by some impulse) stepped back out of distance and saw him wipe great drops from his furrowed brow, staring on me with eyes dismayed and unbelieving.

'I grow old!' quoth he, hard breathing, 'and egad, you fight as you loved it. And you ha' profited by your Frenchman's schooling, boy.'

'So much so, sir,' I answered, 'that thrice I might have killed you.'

'True enough, braggart boy. And yet I stand untouched and there's the wonder! Why, Adam, why – since hate o' me jumps in you?'

'Because I am no murderer,' says I, making to sheath my sword, but moved by sudden fury at my disdainful words, he rapped me smartly on my Scots bonnet with the flat of his blade.

'Damned arrogant younker!' cried he. 'Come again, murder me an you can!' And then, even as I stood hesitant, something hummed fiercely between us and next moment Sir Hector gripping me by the collar, had rolled with me behind a jag of rock.

'A bullet!' says he. 'And there'll be others aplenty – keep down!' But seeing him lift head to peer cautiously down the ascent, I did the like, and thus glimpsed men that crawled and crept amid the brush and mossy boulders below.

'My grief!' muttered Sir Hector, his haggard face much grimmer than usual. 'Yon are accursed Lamonts, my ain maist particular haters.'

'Why, then, let's run whiles we may,' says I very urgently.

'Ay – off with ye, lad! But as for me I maun bide and meet what shall be, for yon ban-dogs would follow and pull me down ran I never so hard. So our fellowship ends, Adam – fare thee well, a prosperous journey and my humble service to your lady Bab . . . Wilt shake hands, Adam?'

'But, sir . . . what do you mean?'

'That, except for a miracle, my journeying ends hereabouts. And my quest just beginning! Ah, well, 'tis the luck o't.'

'Sir, you tell me these Lamonts will . . . kill you?'

'No, lad, I'm meaning they and we shall most heartily endeavour to kill each other, for 'twixt the Lamont and the MacFarlane is blood feud highly cherished being hoary with tradition. Therefore, Adam, this being no chance attack by the way but my own private quarrel, I'm bidding ye away. Take you the pony and ride, Edinburgh's afore you . . . Barbara. I'll see to it that none o' yon cursed Lamonts shall follow you – for some while, at least. I'll hold 'em in play, this place is good for defence.'

'Yonder, sir, is a better, I think,' says I, and pointed him where, by the mercy of Providence, was a small cave or rather, deep cleft beneath this great crag where one might lie fairly sheltered from flying shot.

Hardly had Sir Hector glimpsed it than, with joyous chirrup, he crawls thither (and I after him), and begins making a rampire or breastwork with large stones and such movable boulders as served (and I aiding him), for, says he, and sweating with the labour :

'Even a pebble may turn a bullet—' almost as he spoke was the loud report of a musket and a shot smote the rock above us.

'Ah,' quoth Sir Hector, ramming a small stone into his breastwork, 'the game begins. Up with you, Adam, yonder's the pony, quick's the word ... run lad and good luck t'ye !'

I peered down the heathery slope where it seemed every bush and boulder screened lurking death; I glanced down the steep pass into that sheltered glen where foamed the torrent – beyond which lay safety and – Barbara; I looked at my solitary companion and went on building our rampart though my hands shook somewhat. Perceiving which, Sir Hector paused in his labours to eye me askance, and when he spoke his voice was harsh and his look sinister and mocking :

'What, my hero,' he jibed, 'will ye flout death? Are ye so eager to die and yourself so lately wed? Go fool – get you to Barbara's arms !' Here I looked down into the glen once more and, yearning to be gone, wedged another stone into place.

'Art shivering, boy, is it fear o' death?'

'Yes,' I muttered.

'What then o' your brag that death was joy, or some such vaunt?'

'This was when ... I thought Barbara for ever beyond my reach.'

'So? Then 'tis love for her hath turned thee to such frighted, trembling creature?'

'But creature that will fight !' says I, laying sword and pistols to hand, even as he had placed his own.

'Nay, begone, lad,' says he, stripping off his braided coat and folding it neatly by. 'There's yet time – on to the pony and away. I'll have no blood o' yours on my head. Off with you, Adam !' Heeding him not at all, I began folding my plaid about my left arm for shield as Gaston had taught me.

'Ha, d'ye defy me, then?' cried Sir Hector, fiercely, whiles I ordered my plaid very carefully, still heeding him no whit.

'Will you dare so disobey me, ye pallid, shivering fool?' cries he.

'No!' says I. 'For, remark, sir, I take no orders from you – now or ever.'

'Why then – will ye risk your paltry life for me?'

'No, for Barbara.'

'How so, my youthful ass?'

'Because, sir, by staying with you despite my craven fears I may feel a little more worthy of her love.'

'Ay, but,' says he, taking up one of his pistols to peer at the flint, 'how if you be slain in my quarrel?'

'I shall die for – Barbara.'

'Nay, boy,' says he, speaking slowly and still fumbling at his pistol-flint, 'here is … just … arrant … folly! Faith, Adam, I'm minded … to … clout you o' the ear for … pig-headed, sawney—'

But even as he spoke, I felt his hand on my bowed shoulder, a very comradely hand that, somehow, stayed my trembling; and looking up into his grim face I saw there look comforting as his touch.

'Egad, Adam, thou'rt a numps,' said he with a short odd laugh, 'ay, thou'rt a very addle-pated jobbernowl … and yet … I guess … thy Barbara might think otherwise could she spy thee now! And so, away to her, Adam lad, and leave me to settle the accounts of as many o' these accursed Lamonts as kind heaven shall permit.'

But, seeing I made no move, he frowns on me, rubbing his chin as one at a loss.

'And but a little since – we were at swords-point!' says he softly; then with sudden ferocity: 'God knoweth you no friend o' mine. I – despise ye, boy!'

'Nor you friend to me,' I retorted, 'I hate you!'

'Hate me, is it, Adam?' quoth he, suddenly mild again and turning to watch the menace below. 'Hate me? Why, very well – begone!'

217

'No!' says I, angrily.

'Wherefore no, ye small, pallid fool?'

'Sir,' says I, bowing to him as much after Gaston's high manner as my cramped position would allow, 'for two reasons, — first that I am afraid, and second, because I believe the "Complete Gentleman" could never run leaving his worst enemy to face such deadly odds alone.'

'Why now, what wild rant is this, Adam?'

'Sir, being destitute and nameless, I must needs live, or die, as near a very noble gentleman's concept of the "Complete Gentleman" as possible. And so, here I bide with you, Sir Hector, to meet whatsoever God wills as boldly as—' here I flinched and cowered as another musket-ball whined close above us; whereat Sir Hector cursed softly and dragged me down beside him.

So there I lay, my heart jumping as I peered very fearfully through a chink in our rocky breast-work, my every nerve strung to dreadful expectancy which, as slow minutes dragged, grew the more unbearable until at last, viewing my companion's face so grimly intent yet serene as ever, I questioned him, whispering:

'How many are they, think you?'

'Fifteen, I make 'em, Adam.'

'Then why do they bide so still? What stays them?'

'Myself, boy. I've earned me some small repute with the pistol, Adam. Thus, and kenning the MacFarlane by sharp experience, they'll wait till the sun's down and light uncertain, then 'twill be the steel, they'll come with a roar and rush! Now when they do, and mark me, Adam — up to your knees, level pistol across the rock afore you but don't pull trigger till you can see their eyes — wait for my word and — be steady! Is't understood?'

'Yes, sir, yes!'

'Then, so soon as your pistols be empty, afoot with your sword, 'twill be point against edge, and point is ever the quicker ... And ... whatever o't, God send you safe out o' it for your Barbara's sake ...'

We lay thus till sunset, our watchful foes trying a shot a

us ever and anon, but showing no more of themselves than glint of musket-barrel or flicker of sword. But as the sun went down they grew more venturesome, first one and then another creeping nearer, stealing up towards us from bush to rock, from rock to bush – an ever-oncoming menace.

''S death, boy!' exclaimed Sir Hector suddenly grasping me by the arm. 'Over yonder.... did ye see him?'

'No, sir, no ... what ... who?' I quavered.

'The greatest, dourest fighter of 'em all, Alastair Mohr ... a giant, Adam, Lamont's kinsman and champion o' the clan. His fame rings loud in Scotland, a great, swashing fellow keepeth a tally of his killed and hath sworn to have this head o' mine to hang in his ingle, so if you find chance for shot at him – aim well.'

And now ensued another period of waiting – a hush so tense, so ominous and (for me) fraught with all imaginable horrors, ghastly wounds and death in fearsome shapes – that I could have screamed to break this dreadful stillness; instead, I spoke:

'Why don't we try a shot at them?'

'I'm sweir to waste our powder, Adam, however, I'll try what may be done to break this monotony.' Taking off his hat and holding it by one corner, he edged it gently above our rampart ... then, as I scanned that line of hidden foes, a bush stirred, forth of its leaves stole a musket-barrel. Sir Hector fired, the musket, jerking heavenwards, exploded, the bush seemed violently agitated and voices cried as in question and answer.

'One!' quoth Sir Hector, and began to re-load his weapon, but I cried to him in shrill warning as – up from rock and bush leapt fierce, shouting men that came bounding up towards us, steel flashing, shields aloft ... And then I saw him and nearly dropped my pistols ... a giant indeed, a very monster of a man that, for all his huge bulk, ran leaping like a deer, and flourished a great two-hand sword high in air terrible to see. Above their clash and roar and high-pitched battlecries I heard Sir Hector's pleasant voice close in my ear:

'Be ready, Adam! Steady, comrade! Level across the rampart and wait ... wait till I give word.' And the sound of this calm voice checked my panic, the sight of him kneeling beside me serenely undismayed and, moreover, to hear him name me comrade, so heartened me that for the moment I came very near loving him. With my pistol steadied across the rock before me and teeth clenched, I watched our fierce adversaries rush to our destruction, overleaping all obstacles, tartans fluttering, swords glittering ... nearer ... nearer yet, until I might see the brazen studs upon their targes ... glaring eyes ... mouths agape ... gnashing teeth.

'Give fire!' cried Sir Hector.

Aiming at our nearest assailant I pulled trigger, felt the weapon leap in my grasp and then, clean forgetting my second pistol and half blinded by smoke, was thrusting desperately at all that offered, for now the narrow front of our cave seemed full of the whirling flash of smiting steel, and all about us deafening clamour, the confused uproar of shouts, hateful screams and cries. But our cave being so straight and our foes so many they hampered each other in their fury to come at us.

Close beside mine, Sir Hector's sword whirled and darted, horribly dimmed ... time and again I felt my point bite deep amid that swaying press of bodies. And now, once again I knew that thrilling, joyous exaltation uplifting me 'bove fear, pain of wounds, even death itself ... I heard myself shouting.

Then was fierce, commanding roar, the press unwillingly drew back and in place of the many were but two, and one of these this gigantic fellow, Alastair.

'Ha, Alastair Mohr to me ... to me, Alastair!' cried Sir Hector, but in that moment was borne back, and then the giant, bestriding the breast-work, came at me. Roaring derision, he whirled up ponderous sword but, even as it turned flashing in air, I leapt aside and ran him into the leg. Down whizzed the terrible blade, burying its point in the sod and, as he wrenched it free, I was in again and twice felt

220

my sword bite deep. Reeling and gasping he swung once more, but I, watching that dreadful blade with eyes of terror, bowed myself beneath its ponderous sweep and, as the giant swung with it, I leapt, stabbing him again and yet again; then espying him falter, hurled myself upon his unprotected flank and drave in a thrust with all my strength ... I saw his sword fall ... I heard him bellow, felt blood spatter me, was seized by a mighty hand, shaken, whirled aloft and tossed aside, crashing down into blackness and oblivion.

CHAPTER 39

HOW WE WERE TAKEN BY THE MCLEODS

I HEARD a babbling voice; someone was stooping over me, a face peered down at me through a mist, hands were shaking me, and the voice calling me so insistently that I would have answered, yet could not. But, the mist clearing somewhat, I knew that someone was telling me, over and over again, that I was not to die, the which assurance comforted me mightily as I struggled up through the whirling mist. Thus, as my brain cleared, I found myself lying in Sir Hector's arms, and all about us armed figures muttering together and every eye on me ... and Sir Hector's trim wig all askew with blood trickling beneath it and he all unheeding; therefore I spoke, finding it strange effort :

'Sir ... you ... bleed !'

'God love thee, Adam,' says he, with choking laugh, 'I'm well enough, how is it with yourself now ?' I told him I was better.

'But pray, sir,' says I, greatly troubled, 'who are these men, and why do they stare on me ?'

'These are McLeods, lad, and they stare with very excellent good reason, for here's you hath outfought and slain Alastair Mohr Lamont, the greatest and dourest fighting-man 'twixt here and the sea—'

'What,' I gasped, 'is he dead ... the big man?'

'He is that, Adam – see yonder.' Now, looking whither he directed, I beheld a monstrous, sprawling leg upreared helplessly above our tumbled rampart and also a great arm that, rigid and motionless, seemed yet to threaten me with knotted fist and shrinking, I covered my face, sickened with horror; whereat Sir Hector clapped his arm about me again.

'Eh – what now, lad?' he questioned anxiously.

'Sir, I did not think to kill – God forgive me!'

'Did ye no', Adam? Well now, from your actions, comrade, I judged you a little earnest to have him comfortably dead – the which is well, for Alastair would ha' killed you, ay and myself, too, and joyed to do it, so let your qualmish soul be comforted. Also to die in battle is none so ill, better clean thrust or speedy bullet – ay, any swift death rather than lingering disease.' Thus he cherished and strove to comfort me, what time our new captors went to and fro collecting the gear and weapons of the slain, which done, they came thronging about us again, one shewing me the dead giant's great sword and all of them vastly cheerful.

'Canst walk, Adam?' says Sir Hector aiding me to stand; but, though I made the attempt, my legs so shook and head athrob with such blinding pain that but for the sinewy arm about me I should have fallen.

So, at Sir Hector's imperious behest, strong hands lifted me upon the little horse and we set off, Sir Hector walking beside me and all about us glittering steel, flutter of kilt and plaid and bonneted heads that turned, ever and anon, with eyes to stare on me.

'Sir,' says I, struggling against the painful drowsiness that gripped me, 'Sir Hector, what of the Lamonts?'

'All happily dead, comrade, or run off. These McLeods crept and took 'em in flank and rear, and well for us they did. And yet, egad, our case is little bettered, mine at least, for, being proclaimed traitor by the Jacobite lords, my life is forfeit to any that take me.'

'What, sir ... God forbid they should kill you.'

'This may depend on the McLeod, lad. For you a week or so of prison, for me, if McLeod wills, the axe or rope, unless my wit can save me, the which I'm bold to think it may, since death shall not touch me, I guess, until my vengeance be accomplished.'

'Do you know the McLeod, sir?'

'Very well, faith – he was my friend and would be now but for politics, Tearlach and the Ancasters.'

'Is his name Ian?'

'It is that, and what then, lad?'

'I saw him once in England.'

After this I remember little more of our journey, for the drowsiness thickening on me I rode, as it were, in a dream that grew to a sick nightmare, for whensoever I closed my pain-racked eyes, needs I see again the giant Alastair's sprawling leg and huge dead fist upflung in dreadful fashion to smite me down.

CHAPTER 40

HOW I MET A FRIEND AND PLEADED FOR AN ENEMY

A THROBBING glow was all about me, an angry light that showed great carven rafter beams and walls richly panelled but all charred and blackened as by recent fire.

Sitting up, I saw I lay upon a bed of heather, a worn cloak spread over me to my comfort, a cloak I knew for Sir Hector's, but of himself I saw no other sign.

Therefore (and despite bruised body and painracked head) I scrambled afoot and coming to a window, its stone mullions chipped and blackened by flame, I beheld a wide courtyard where burned several watchfires and armed men all about them. Now as I gazed I espied one who stood solitary beside a fire, sinewy hands crossed upon the pommel of sheathed broadsword, a tall, comely man in splendour of kilt, sporran and plaid, and in his bonnet the eagle-feather of chieftain-ship: then my heart leapt, for, despite his changed habit, I knew him on the instant. Very still he stood, frowning down on the fire like one in some perplexity.

Now presently, and almost unconsciously, I began whistling that same haunting tune I had first heard in a moonlit wood, that magic tune never to be forgotten, whereby my whole life had been so marvellously changed; and, remembering how that, but for this, I had never known my beloved Barbara, my eyes grew dim, my whistling faltered and died. But it seemed he had caught it, for his head had gone up like a winding stag's and as I began to whistle again, he came striding towards me whiles I leaned forth of the shattered window; so thus we confronted one another and, for a moment, neither spoke; then:

'Sir,' says he with stately bow and speaking in his careful English, 'myself is happy to see you recovered of your hurts and vera deeply honoured to meet gentleman of such well-proven gallantry and prowess! Sir, to have conquered Alastair Mohr Lamont in single combat ... inteet words fail me ... the country rings with it already! Sir, the McLeod begs you will pray consider yourself his very honoured guest, and welcomes you to his house – or what fire and fury have left of it—'

'Nay,' I cried, reaching out my hands to him, 'Oh, Mr McLeod, ... Sir Ian, don't you know me?'

'Eh, eh?' says he in greatly altered tone, stooping to peer into my face. 'Why ... save's a'! Can it be ... will it be .. young Adam?'

Now, seeing him thus doubtful, I snatched off my great periwig and leaned yet farther towards him through the window.

'Son o' the world! Oh, God o' Grace!' he exclaimed and clipping his great arms about me, had me out of the window altogether. 'And 'twas you,' says he, swaying me gently in his powerful grasp, ''twas yourself slew Alastair Mohr ... there's gillies o' mine saw it done! 'Twas you Adam, wi' your bit sword! Aha – red hair for ever! Oh

224

my bonnie wee man, by the books 'tis myself is proud to ca'
ye friend!' Then, with his arm about my shoulders, he
brings me to the firelight, there to view me up and down
with great particularity. 'Ay but you're changed, Adam,'
he nodded, 'you're grown a wee, you're taller—'

'These boots,' says I.

'No, no,' he answered, ''tis yoursel' – there's an air about
ye, – a cock o' your heid, – ye're a man, Adam!'

And now, seated side by side on a couch of plaids by the
fire, he so plied me with questions one upon another that
I scarce knew how to answer. Howbeit, when I had said as
little of the fight as I could, I recounted all that had befallen
me since our parting in England, and he listening wide-eyed
and with such quick interest and kindly sympathy that I
loved him more than ever.

'Losh man!' he exclaimed when I had done, ''tis nae
wonder ye're sae marvellous changed, here's experience for
a lifetime! ... And so she ... Barbara, married ye, did
she, Adam, whilk I'll confess t'ye, being my friend, grieves
me sair ... for I had hopes. A'weel, she never showed me
any great encouragements ... and I maun confess this
matter of Alastair Mohr Lamont makes ye in some sense
worthy. For there falls one observation – David slew Goliath
at safe and canny distance wi' a pebble and they made him a
king for 't! But yourself, my bonny wee Adam, met
Alastair point and point, foot to foot, and ended him in
vera douce, genteel and gentlemanly fashion, and so 'tis
thy friendship honours me, and I'm thinking Barbara
couldna' hae chosen better gentleman, no – not even in Scotland! And here's my hand on't, friend Adam.' So I grasped
that strong and generous hand, but when I would have
spoken, came nigh to sobbing instead.

'Oh, Sir Ian,' I began, but there he checked me.

'Hoot awa', friend Adam. Ian's my name t'ye and here's
myself blithe tae serve ye when and how I may.'

'Then, Ian, I would to God I might show you how very
precious your friendship has been and is to me ... how it
has helped me ... how proud it makes me ... And now

there is one service I dare ask of you, one gift I would have of your friendship.'

'Speak and 'tis yours, Adam. What may I bestow on ye?'

'Sir Hector MacFarlane's life ... his freedom.'

Now at this the McLeod looked at me very much askance, then turned to scowl again at the fire, while I watched him in no little trepidation.

'Eh, but,' says he at last, and frowning still, ''tis yoursel' is the canny chiel, Adam, 'tis the wily body y'are, the sly, sly person! For weel y' ken MacFarlane is traitor, so proclaimed and put to the horn by the confederate clans.'

'Nay, indeed, Ian, rather is he gentleman loyal to King George and the Protestant Succession, as you to James and the Jacobite Cause.'

''Tis no a bad obsairve, yon, Adam. Howandever, you ask o' me the one thing impossible. Man, I'd jeopard life for ye, but dinna ask me this for I am pledged, as are other loyal gentlemen, to yield him up, if taken, to the mercy o' the confederation—'

'The which will be no mercy as you may guess, Ian.'

'Indeedy, Adam, I'm thinking the man will hang.'

'But he was your friend, Ian, once on a time.'

'Vera true, therefore I'm no' precisely joco in the matter. But I am McLeod o' McLeod, Adam, and juist canna free you MacFarlane wi'out forswearing mysel'.'

Now at this I broke into such passion of pleading, such arguments and eager protestations that he stayed me at last with upraised hands:

'My certie, Adam,' says he, frowning at the fire again ''tis plain tae see ye love the man—'

'Love him?' cries I, all amaze, 'no indeed, no – he is my enemy!'

'Then God send me sic enemies as yoursel', Adam. However, I winna set the man free, no – not even for you, Adam what way on earth of the world could I? ... But, whist Who's tae hinder ye from freeing him yoursel' – not I.'

'Oh, Ian,' I stammered, 'do you mean that you ... tha I—'

'Well, but ye're sae notably accomplished in freeing o' puir prisoners, Adam – eh? There was one in England, I mind, a puir, hunted fugitive that ate your supper and learned ye the McLeod pibroch – ye saved him frae the English soldiers ... a'weel, here's for ye to save yon enemy o' yours frae the McLeod! Up wi' ye, my bonnie wee man, I'll point ye where he lieth prisoned.'

Up I scrambled and, when I had grasped his hand, thanking him as well as I might, he led me round a wing of this great house (its cruel devastation plain to see by light of the fires and a rising moon) and so, by way of a flame-blackened arch, into a second courtyard surrounded by buildings more or less ruined, before one of which a man paced to and fro, who, at word from Sir Ian, fetched a lighted lanthorn and, unlocking the door, motioned me to enter.

It was a small, barren chamber, with pile of heather in one corner, and thither I went in some eagerness, then paused wondering since, save for myself, the place was empty; but feeling an air blowing I glanced thither and saw a small opening that had been a grated window, for the bars, torn from the weathered mortar, lay now beneath this window through which, it seemed, Sir Hector had made his escape. Somewhat troubled and disappointed I hasted back where Sir Ian waited me in shadow of the blackened arch.

'He is gone!' cried I. 'He wrenched away the window bars—'

'A'weel, Adam, I'm no altogether breathless wi' astonishment. 'Tis hard to cage an eagle, y'ken. But here's all your eloquence on his behalf clean thrown away, your pleading wasted labour.'

'No,' said I, slipping my hand within Sir Ian's arm, 'it taught me the McLeod is generous as I dreamed him.'

'Eh, man,' says he, giving my arm a friendly squeeze, 'tis yourself is the courtier.' Seated again at the fire he asks if I'm hungry.

'Not very,' I answered, whereat he shakes comely head at me:

'Here's no the way tae answer,' sighed he reprovingly, 'and a sheep's head singed tae sup on, man, 'tis sinfu' tae waste sic an opportunity. However, Adam, eat your best.'

Here he clapped his hands, whereat came two great fellows, sworded and dirked, bearing a pot whence issued a right delectable savour ... And there, beside the fire in the courtyard of his ravaged house, Sir Ian played host to me with as much stately courtesy as we had been seated in his great hall itself.

And now as we ate I ventured to ask why he and his men went in such warlike trim.

'Well, Adam,' says he, glancing up at the ruin, 'ye may hae noticed this house, that was my mother's birthplace, herself was a Drummond o' that ilk – I say that this house is something the worse by reason o' fire and flame? My ain people hae suffered also and myself fugitive in England. But I'm back to lead them in small matter o' retaliation, and maybe the acquiring o' flocks and herds, wha kens? We march north in the hour.'

'Then, by your leave, Ian, in the hour I'll be travelling south.'

'Ay, to Edinburgh, Adam – 'tis a weary way, a hundred miles and better! Man, I'm wishing ye safe there, for these be ill times, perilous travelling, especially for Englishmen by reason o' this accursed Act o' Union. And so I'm asking ye to take this in memory o' me.' And drawing the signet ring from his finger, and despite my remonstrances, he slipped it on mine. 'Nay keep it and wear it, Adam, 'tis well kent by a' leal gentlemen and folk o' condition 'twixt here and the Border. Yon ring, shown to the right people, y'ken, shall be meat and drink t'ye, shelter and a' manner o' kindness, but – shown to the wrang 'twill mayhap win ye six inches o' steel, a bullet or prison, so, friend Adam, look that you use it with a' due discretion!' After this, we finished our supper in a somewhat gloomy silence by reason of our so imminent separation, for already was stir and clash of arms where his clansmen were marshalling.

By his orders the little horse was brought to me, the

saddle-bags crammed with provision of all kinds, as also store of powder and shot for my pistols. Scarcely was I mounted than he brings me Sir Hector's weapons also, for says he :

'MacFarlane will be glad o' them, I'm thinking.'

'Nay, but,' I demured, 'he will be miles away ere this!' Sir Ian shook his head :

'Not he, Adam, I've kenned the man frae my youth up, and 'tis no like Hector tae leave friend i' the lurch, whatever o't. He'll be watching the blink of our fires at this moment ... And so farewell t'ye, friend Adam !'

He walked with me to the gate of the courtyard, pausing there to grasp my hand.

'Blessings on y'r bonnie red pow !' says he, laying his big hand upon my head. 'Happiness and good fortune, Adam, and my service and devotion to your bonnie lady Barbara.'

'Goodbye, Ian !' said I, my voice very hard of control. 'You are such noble friend, I ... pray God we meet again soon ... Goodbye !' And so I rode away, but turning for a last look, saw him stand gazing after me, his stately form dark against the fire-glow, his hands crossed upon sheathed sword, and thus I looked and looked until the hot tears blinded me.

CHAPTER 41

TELLETH HOW I FOUND AGAIN SIR HECTOR AND HIM QUARRELSOME

THE moon, rising very large and bright, showed me the way I must go, a rough track that dipped and wound amid trees and bushes, across a little heath, down to a narrow gorge abrim with shadow where a riotous stream babbled. Scarce had I reached this place of gloom than, sudden and loud, an owl hooted very dismally and so near that I started, and at once became filled with all manner of uneasiness; the brooding stillness, the awful solitude, the wild desolation bred in me such yearning for companionship that I was glad of the sturdy animal betwixt my knees and took comfort in his windy snorts, the familiar creak of saddle, and ring of his iron-shod hoofs, as we traversed this rocky place ... The owl hooted again and so much louder that instinctively I drew rein and sat peering, my apprehension tempered by a dawning hope ... Then a voice spoke:

'Is it yourself, Adam?' Answering I know not what, I was out of the saddle and, stumbling in my eager haste, ran towards this voice, espied a shape amid the shadows and clipped my arms about it while other arms clasped me, and so for a moment we stood.

'Why, Adam!' says he, and then stooped to pick up my bonnet that had tumbled off, 'faith, lad,' says he setting it back on my head, 'no one in this wide world ever gave me such greeting since— Howbeit never was such meeting of enemies, boy.'

'I brought your plaid and cloak, sir.'

'And there was a thoughtful Adam!'

'And Sir Ian sends back your sword and pistols.'

'Egad, and 'twas like him! 'Tis a lovely gentleman, Ian; I mind him lad at school ... I gave him his first rod and learned him how to cast ... *eheu fugaces*!'

Then came we to the little horse where Sir Hector girt on sword, pistols and cloak, but when I held the stirrup for him to mount he hove me into the saddle instead, and on we went together.

'Did I startle ye back there, Adam?'

'Why yes, sir,' I answered, 'but then, indeed, I am so easily affrighted.'

'Hum!' quoth he. 'There was Alastair Mohr! He tossed ye into a bush, Adam, or you'd be lying dead as he. And your sickness is by with?'

'Yes, sir, I can go afoot quite well if—'

'Tomorrow, lad, for by this light you show devilish frail and ghost-like.'

'Yes, sir,' I answered miserably, 'my weakness ever shame

me, but I think – had they suffered me to eat more in my boyhood I might ha' proved stronger and taller now.'

'Ha – did they starve ye, Adam?'

'Well, I was always somewhat hungry, sir. But Ian – the McLeod said I had grown.'

'So you have, lad, and pretty well out o' my knowledge o' thee.'

After this we went in silence and at such pace that I wondered at the vigour and endurance of him; and great comfort was it to see with what unerring instinct he chose our course, over-leaping brooks, plunging into dark ravines, striding assured through glooming woods and mazy boskages. And when I ventured to remark on this:

'Faith, Adam,' he answered grim-smiling, 'I know this country like my hand, I had been dead man else. Scotland is a kindly country to the lorn fugitive, she hath caves and thickets to shelter him, dens and hidie-holes, 'tis to one of 'em we go.'

The brooding night seemed full of vague sounds, stealthy creepings, furtive rustlings that should have troubled me had I been alone; an animal wailed despairingly from the lonely heights above us, bats wheeled and hovered, a bird piped shrill alarm and the moon, high risen now, showed the more plainly the awesome glamour of this wild and rugged countryside; but now my late unease and fearful apprehension were transformed to a kind of romantical rapture in the beauty of it all, and this merely by reason of my companion, his quick vitality and serene confidence, his walk, his grimly resolute air, the very shape of him.

'Adam,' says he suddenly, 'I'm thinking my life's work will be done right soon.'

'To find your child, sir?'

'No!' he answered, faltering somewhat in his tireless stride to frown up at me. 'No! I've word from the south that the Earl of Ancaster comes to Scotland armed with powers from King George's new Council, to inquire into the matter o' this foolish and mismanaged rebellion. My noble lord hath turned cat-in-pan, he hath forsworn cause, politics, and religion to howl for George and the Protestant Succession. A papistical tory for Rome-ridden James, a Protestant whig for George ... a rat, boy, a snake, wriggling back to power and favour, turning his coat to clap it about his Jacobite son and proclaim him zealous loyalist and hater of all Jacobites ! ... Well ... so much the better !'

'But, sir, how shall this be better?' I questioned, but he never heeded, walking like one lost in profound meditation. Climbing a slope he seized the bridle, turned in between great rocks, steadied the pony down a narrow steep and we were in a small dingle, where a little rill gushed between ferny rocks, with pretty ripple, all sparkling beneath the moon, a right pleasant place to see, as I said.

'Pleasant enough !' he answered, gloomy and thoughtful. 'Here have I lain many's the night.'

Scarce had I dismounted than he comes to this little cascade and drawing aside a bush, shows a narrow opening in the rock through which he vanished. I heard the flicker of his tinder-box, saw a glow, the flicker of a candle and, entering at his word, found myself in a roomy cave methought very marvellous, as I told him.

'It hath served me well in the past,' says he, beginning to fumble along a ledge of rock above his head. 'Ay, lad, here have I crouched and heard them talk would ha' slain me ... and here, upon juist such night as this, a man died. I buried him out yonder—'

'Died sir ... you mean—?'

' 'Twas him or myself.'

'You ... killed him?' With hand yet groping, he glared round on me, mouth curled in its mocking, sinister smile.

'Ay, I did so ... dead as mutton – ha, damme !' he exclaimed with sudden petulence. 'D'ye blench from me, Sir Niceness, d'ye condemn me for 't, – you that kills and weeps therefore? Lookee, when I twitch trigger or lug steel I do it to kill, and having killed I do not whine o'er the corpse, Master Virtuous Hypocrisy. They call me Black MacFarlane, Bloody Hector, and the like pretty names and with some reason, d'ye see ! Moreover I'm a lone man and sufficient unto myself – so, be off – I grow sick o' you and your maid-like squeamishness.'

'Also I think you are over-hungry, sir,' says I, bowing; 'permit that I set forth your supper.' At this he scowled at me, but his fumbling hand lighting on that he sought (the which proved to be a small, sealed packet) he scowled at this instead. So forth I went and loosing the pony's girths, did off the saddle-bags and seating myself in the moonlight, set out in tempting array the goodly fare Sir Ian's bounty had provided and called Sir Hector. And presently forth he comes, an open letter in his hand but pauses to rub his chin and scowl from our supper to me very sourly.

' 'S death, boy,' says he nodding grimly, 'there's times I fair yearn to lay strap about that puny body o' thine !'

'Sir,' I retorted, staring up at him, 'no man may ever attempt such indignity but shall smart for it !'

'Would ye slay him then, my giant-killing pigmy ?'

'No, sir. I should choose my spot and blood him merely.'

'Faith now here's braggart boy, here's empty vaunt and boasting !'

'Not empty, sir. For thanks to my so loved friend Gaston I hope to be such master of fence that this my puny body shall prove terrible in action – though I pray God I may never again take life ... And here, sir, is a kippered ham, with fish, oat-bread, cheese and usquebaugh.' Sir Hector sat down, and thus we supped together, the moon very bright above us. Now whiles we ate, Sir Hector stared on me and I on him and each of us very silent.

'Adam,' says he at last, 'd'you mind the first time I met you?'

'Very well, sir,' I nodded, 'you would ha' murdered me.'

'And small wonder, fool, you wore young Ancaster's clothes. But I said then that some day you might be worth a man's powder and shot. Well, I'm thinking you are.'

'Sir,' says I, bowing as well as I might, 'you honour me, I think.'

'So much so,' he went on, 'that I'm minded to try you again at the "sharps".' And he tapped his sword.

'And pray why, sir?'

'Because in all my experience, and it hath been long and varied, no man ever so bested me, and yourself, being no man but mere boy, it follows that you outfought me by merest accident. The light is fair enough so, after supper, we'll to 't again.'

'Never in this world, sir!' I answered.

'How then, must I strike thee, fool?'

'Strike or kick me, as you will, but I'll neither fight or fence with you again.'

'Why so, Adam?'

'Because, despite my skill and all my care, I might kill you.'

'Well, Master Braggart, and am I not your hated enemy?'

' 'Tis you says so,' I answered.

'Liar!' cries he. 'You ha' named me so repeatedly.'

Scowling he arose and went into the cave whence I heard him striking flint and steel to light his candle. After some while he calls me and so, when I had packed our viands into the saddle-bag, to him I went and found him seated on pile of dried heather that was his bed.

'Adam,' says he, gesturing me to sit beside him, 'I'm thinking you were wiser to leave me here and travel on alone.'

'Why so, sir?'

'For very good reason, he answered, showing me a close-written sheet of paper. 'I find here ill news o' myself. The nearer to Edinburgh the safer I should be – but I am here warned of five rascals, men especially chosen and hired to waylay me and see to it that I never reach Edinburgh – or any other where this side the grave.'

'Why then, sir, 'tis plain you must be very watchful.'

' 'Tis so my nature, boy.'

'But four eyes shall see more than two, even eyes so quick as yours.'

'Hum! Wilt risk thy life again for me, Adam?'

'With you, sir.'

'Ay, to be sure!' says he with a laugh and eyeing me ask-ance. 'We are enemies, 'tis fact is apt to escape me.'

'None the less, sir, I will aid you all I can should danger threaten.'

'Tush!' he exclaimed scornfully. 'I shall suffice myself, as I have ever done!'

'Though you are not gracious, sir.'

'Oho!' he jeered. 'How an I ride off and leave ye?'

' 'Twould be impossible, sir.'

'How so, my young ass?'

'I learn from the McLeod that it is not your nature to leave any one in the lurch.'

'Hum!' says he again and sets himself to burn his letter very carefully in the candle bidding me, and none too kindly, to bring in our plaids, for the night air struck chill. This done, he commands me beside him on his heather bed and to sleep, for says he :

'Ne'er heard I younker with such clattering tongue!' And out he puffed the candle.

So, with my cloak and plaid about me, and never so much as a good night, I closed my eyes and sure enough (and despite the dead man buried so near me) I presently sank to deep and dreamless slumber.

TO MY PATIENT READER

It is with no little misgiving that I find how very many pages I have filled, and bethinking me how much is yet to write I grow fearful lest I try your kind patience beyond bearing. Yet would I crave your sufferance a little longer. And if I seem over-particular in this part of my narrative, if indeed I dwell too much on the various chances and small happenings that befell Sir Hector and myself, I can but sue pardon. For indeed, it is the recall-ing of this strange companionship that is for me (and ever must be) a memory sadly wistful yet never-fading and for very good reason, as those may learn who shall trouble themselves to read all that I have here so painfully set down.

And so will I again to my narrative.

CHAPTER 42

OF HOW WE WRANGLED BY THE WAY

NEXT morning, having washed at the little spring very well and breakfasted right heartily, we set off in the early sunshine, Sir Hector astride the pony, since I vowed myself very well able to walk. But finding him in a fleering mood, observing him cock his eyebrow at me, I started on him ere he might begin jibing at me :

'Sir,' says I looking very steadfastly on him, 'is it on business of God or the Devil, you are bent?'

'Eh, boy – eh?' quoth he, clean forgetting to mock.

'Are you intent on errand of mercy or blood?'

'Be plain, lad, be plain !'

'Would you redeem a life or take one, sir?'

'Sink your parables and talk to the point, boy !'

'Sir, do you dream of slaughtering your foes or seeking your lost child?'

'Tush ! No more o' that – let be !'

'Nay, Sir Hector, I fain would know your mind touching this poor lost creature.'

'Ha, lost indeed, boy? It may be dead ... or worse ! Ay and must plump to hell or soar to heaven without such fatherly aid as mine – enough o' this !'

'And yet, sir, I think there may be tears in your heart for your child, living or dead. I begin to wonder if you are evil as you would seem, for, looking back, saving your detestable proneness to bloodshed, all you have done seems to some good end—'

'Aha, in especial wedding you to an heiress, eh, lad?'

'This was damnable !' I cried in sudden fury, and halted that he might ride on before but, checking the pony, he beckoned and called :

'Forgive that,' says he contritely, ''twas speech unjust, and said but to hurt thee, Adam. Come, go beside me and I'll answer thee fairly. Know then that I am very intent upon the final extermination of these Ancasters, lad.'

'And what then of your child?'

''Tis grown, like enough, into creature I should shrink from appalled.'

'And also one you might lift to better things, sir. If you but seek diligently, eager to cherish this poor creature, fair or foul, God, being just and merciful, may teach your solitary soul a joy unknown, a happiness beyond your dreams.'

'Oh, Beelzebub !' he exclaimed pettishly, 'you talk like a sucking parson ! And damme, what know you o' the Almighty to talk with such assurance, noddy?'

'Sir, He was the only friend I ever had until He gave me Gaston ... and my Barbara.'

'Indeed and what o' me, Adam? Since all is from God, they say, He gave you myself – for enemy, ha? And, moreover, 'tis God's will bringeth Ancaster to Scotland ay, into my very claws at last, and by God's good aid I'll see this noble, ancient rogue never wins back to England – no, nor his lordly son either – except it be in their coffins. And what d'ye say to this Sir Piety?'

'Not a word, sir.'

'Ha, damme and why not?'

'Because it seems no word o' mine can touch you.'

'Then save your breath.'

'Indeed, sir.'

So thus went we, he riding before and I trudging behind, forgetful of weariness, dreaming ever of Barbara, her loveliness and radiant beauty, the ineffable joy of our reunion; then, too, the happiness of clasping Gaston's hand, of reading the welcome in his kind eyes, hearing it in his gentle voice and quaint speech. Thus no desire had I for word with my morose fellow-traveller since I went in world of mine own wherein he had no part. Thus tramped I in a dumb content, very happy with my thoughts until Sir Hector reined up suddenly, and, tugging watch from fob, scowled from it to me.

'An hour and ten minutes, as I live!' quoth he, fiercely, 'seventy minutes and never so much as chirp or bleat out o' you! Art a bitterly stubborn lad, very quarrelsome, very peevish and sullen!'

'Not sullen, sir, thoughtful.'

'Ha, and what d'ye think on?'

'Barbara, sir, and of my dear friend Gaston who—'

'Great Heavens! And why must ye dream o' yon fellow, this scrawny Frenchman?'

'Sir, he is a very noble gentleman and my loved friend!'

'Ay, lad, you share your friendship these days 'twixt God Almighty and this lank foreigner – eh?' And with this he looked on me in such sort that I came near striking him.

'Be ashamed, sir!' I cried, wildly, 'you affront an absent gentleman and blaspheme your God!'

'Wilt fight me on your Frenchman's behalf?'

'No!'

'For your friend God?'

'No! Ah, why must you so torment and plague me? You do but dishonour yourself and teach me scorn of you, Sir Hector.'

'How old are ye?' he demanded.

'So far as I know, sir, twenty or thereabouts.'

'And rant like grey-bearded pedagogue, a very pedantical, pragmatical oaf!'

Now at this and his hateful jeering look I was blinded by rush of sudden tears, and bowing head upon my crossed arms, fell to strange, wild passion of grief, and went thus stumbling on, anywhere to be away from him. But, even then, as I blundered forward wiping my tears and choking back my sobs, he rode up beside me and clapped hand on my shoulder.

'Tush, Adam!' says he. 'Never break your heart for such small—'

But I threw off that would-be comforting hand, fiercely ashamed of my unmanly outburst, and stared up at him through my tears.

'Sir Hector,' says I, desperately, 'we part here, 'tis enough! You joy to shame me that am ashamed of my poor seeming. I have tried, sir, to make the best o' this sorry creature that is me ... I have striven to show valiant when very fearful ... I would be a person of honour ... to live worthily. But you ... ah, you make all my endeavours seem of none avail ... Sir, you shall not so humiliate me again!' And I turned to be gone: And then he reached out his two arms towards me in quick, impulsive fashion, and :

'Adam,' says he, gently, 'forgive me, boy!'

'Never!' I cried passionately. 'Never!' And in that moment saw the stealthy, murderous thing that menaced his life and, leaping, clasped him in my arms, drawing him down close in my embrace ... A ringing shot that echoed afar, a searing, rending agony and I was on the ground, and Sir Hector out of the saddle, bounding towards that betraying powder-smoke ... Dimly I was aware of other shots ... a fury of clashing steel, and then he was bending over me and I gazing stupidly at the blood that came oozing through my coat-sleeve.

Speaking no word, he proceeded to come at my hurt, and I striving not to flinch the while; but no sooner did I behold how the bullet had torn my flesh than a sick faintness mastered me and I swooned away.

CHAPTER 43

TELLETH HOW IN THE DARK WE JOINED HANDS

I CAME to myself with the tang of fiery spirit on my lips, to find Sir Hector seated beside me cross-legged and my wound very deftly bandaged and, though it throbbed and smarted, much less painful than I could have hoped – as I told him.

'But you fainted!' says he, eyebrow cocked.

'I am not yet used to blood, sir,' I answered, 'or being shot. I hope to do better next time.'

'Eh? Next time, boy?'

'Indeed, sir. This country seems full of bloodshed and shooting.'

'And d'ye count it so little to ha' saved the MacFarlane's life, then?'

'I count it a privilege, sir.'

'Hum!' says he, and proceeds to collect the various instruments of his surgery, viz, a probe, scissors, the salve, lint, bandages, etcetera, all furnished us, as it seemed, by the kindly forethought of Dame Margaret.

'Privilege!' he repeated, eyeing me very much askance. 'Ha! Howandever you are fortunate 'tis no worse, and your left arm!'

'Yes, sir.'

'A mere flesh-wound, boy, no bones broke and no bullet to be cut out. Wilt take another sup o' the cordial?'

'No thank you, sir.'

'Why then we'll go on. Can ye ride?'

'I could walk, sir.'

'Tush! Let me help ye to saddle.' So up I got, and presently we started, my bandaged arm slung before me.

'You look all the wounded hero!' says he, after some while.

'I'm sorry I fainted, sir,' I retorted, bitterly, for it seemed he but mocked me again.

'So now, Adam, now it seems I, too, owe ye my life, egad like your transcendent Frenchman.'

'He, at the least, sir, did not jibe at me therefore.'

'Nay but, Master Adam, a lad that goeth up and down slaying giants and saving lives is apt to grow above himself, ha?' To this I made no answer, but kept my head averted, and when he spoke, heeded him no more; and thus we went in silence for a great while until the mountains gave place to gentle hills with prospect of broad and noble dales and valleys.

Towards evening, we struck a track the which we followed, and thus, as the shadows began to creep, I espied that filled me with awe and great pity; for this track now brought us to what had once been a large village but today – no more than a dismal waste hideous with flame-blackened ruins.

'Here is Jacobite work, Adam!' says my companion, pausing to view this mournful spectacle. 'This was my lord of Mar's pretty method to check pursuit of his so ill-commanded and oft-defeated army. I'faith there's scarce a village left 'twixt here and the Ockhills yonder, and all for a runaway prince who—' He paused suddenly as from amid this blackened waste rose the voice of a man singing very dismally, and the words (the which I came to know very well) these:

> 'I like ane owl in desert am
>   That nightly there doth roam.
> I like unto ane sparrow am
>   On the house-top alone.'

The unseen chorister pausing for breath, Sir Hector whistled softly, whereat, from the ruin of what it seemed had once been a small church, came one methought very unlike either owl or sparrow, being a great, shambling fellow, very neat as to person and sober of dress, who, beholding Sir Hector, pulls off his hat and hastes forward, his square, freckled face so bright with glad welcome that my heart instantly warmed to him.

'Well met, Archie-man!' said Sir Hector as they clasped hands. 'And will you yet be haunting the old place?'

'Ay, inteet and inteet, Hector! I maun gaze upon the warks o' the ungodly, and in this howling desolation I sing frae heart unco' waefu' ye ken. I sat me in the ruins o' my puir, wee kirk dreamin' o' the bonnie faces I'll never see there ony mair. And, oh man, the weddings! The christenings! The braw hame folk wha' harkened tae me in prayer and discourse! Whaur are they the noo, ma puir, scattered flock? A'weel Guid's will be done!'

'Woeful times indeed, Archie! But here shall spring another village mayhap, in better days. Meanwhile, have ye ever a message for me – a sealed packet, Archie?'

'Na, na sir, it went by Kenneth McGill, he'll be waiting ye tomorrow's morn at—' Here, and with little bow to me, he fell a-whispering and in the Gaelic.

Presently Sir Hector brings this gentleman where I sat in the saddle gazing upon the mournful scene.

'Adam,' says he, 'this is Mr Archibald Forbes of Kirribardie.'

'O' that ilk, sir!' says Mr Forbes, bowing.

'Besides being minister o' the kirk, Mr Forbes is also laird o' Kirribardie and the Shaws, where 'tis like he'll play host to us on our way South, Archie – my young friend, Mr Adam Thursday!' And when this gentleman and I had shaken hands and smiled on each other, Sir Hector spake him awhile in the Gaelic, then beckoning me, strode off again at that long, tireless stride of his.

This night we camped amid woods in secluded spot beside a rippling burn and very well sheltered from the wind that blew chill. And here his first care was for my hurt, the which I thought he eyed a little anxiously, what time he bathed, anointed and bound it up again as deftly methought as any surgeon in the world.

In the same assured fashion he kindled a fire with sticks, carefully chosen, that he told me were of the candle-fir and, seated in its cheering warmth, we supped, though my arm troubled me not a little, the which he was very quick to perceive, whereat I made so light of it (for very shame) that he from anxiety swings to the other extreme and questions me in his most sharp and pettish manner:

'Why, then, must ye sit there and glower so mumchance?'

'Sir,' I answered, growing peevish as he, 'I fear lest I reawake your so bitter animosity.'

'Ha, the Devil!' he exclaimed, and thereafter we ate in silence, and my arm nagging very spitefully. At last, our supper done:

242

'Adam,' says he, 'you may ha' remarked I have not thanked you for ... for taking that hurt on my behalf.'

'I have sir – but then I expect no thanks.'

'Why must you do it, Adam? Why come 'twixt me and death?'

'Sir, I cannot say. 'Twas an impulse.'

''Twas not for love of me, lad, I guess?'

'It was ... an instinct, sir.'

'I'm just wondering whence sprung this instinct?'

'This only God knoweth, sir.'

'Well, how doth your hate for me? Grows it any?'

'Nay, sir, 'tis rather changed to a sad pity.'

'How?' cries he, angrily. 'Pity, egad!'

'Yes, sir, pity!' I repeated, giving him scowl for scowl. 'I must needs pity any that is such very solitary, unhappy creature.'

'Pity, damme!'

'But, sir, you are thus lonely, thus miserably forlorn merely, I dare to say, because you have devoted your life to hate.'

'Is not my hate justified?'

'Truly, sir, very fully, I'll never deny it. But could you only have loved someone a little you had not been man so desolate now.'

'So – ye'll dare pity me – me, the MacFarlane?'

'Ay, with all my heart, sir.'

'Then – by Heavens, thou'rt presumptous young jack-anapes and – ah, get ye to bed!' And he gestured fiercely towards the pile of fern and heather he had gathered. So there, very obediently, I laid me lapped in cloak and plaid and presently (despite the irk of my wound) fell asleep.

But at dark and dead of night I awoke in much pain, and heard a great wind abroad that sighed and wailed like the voice of Desolation, and therewith the dismal whisper of falling rain. And now, in this pitchy gloom and no eyes to see, I wept for very misery and loneliness, smothering my bitter grief within my plaid ... And yet – he heard! Nay, by some strange sense, he seemed to divine the true reason

243

of my sorrow (ah, surely this should have taught us!) for, in the darkness, his arm came about me folding me in its comfort, and, stooping near, he spake in such voice as I had never heard from his lips ere now :

'So, art lonely, too, Adam? Is't pain o' soul as well as body, lad? And wert right, Adam, for truly ... lonely man am I indeed, and 'tis you this night ... ay, 'twas yourself taught me the pain of it ... And now, Adam, now – here's myself hankering for friendship at last! How say ye, boy?'

'Oh, sir,' I gasped, checking my sobs for wonder, 'is it ... can it be my poor friendship you'd have?'

'None other, lad, none other! Hearkee, Adam, the life you saved this day I'd toss aside, ay, and glad to do it – for thee, Adam. So – pity me an' ye must, lad, but ... hate me no more! Here's my hand to thee.'

So there in darkness, wind and rain our hands met to clasp and cling, and in this moment I forgot my pain and felt within me such great content, such quick, strange pulse of happiness and therewith, too, such yearning, wistful sadness as should have told me all, or warned me of what was soon to be.

'Sir Hector,' I whispered, 'oh – dear my friend!'

And presently, my grief and pain thus wonderfully eased, I fell asleep, my hand fast locked in his.

CHAPTER 44

OF MY GOOD COMRADE

MIST, and a cold wind that chilled me to the very marrow, an evil, swirling mist, that held an icy rain, through which we moved like ghosts within a dream. Yet Sir Hector's voice was cheering, and his so vital hand warm on mine as he strode, close at my stirrup.

Thus, when he asked me how I did (which was often) I contrived, because of his own indomitable spirit, to smile down into his anxious eyes and answer him heartily as might be.

So went we in a marvellous good-fellowship at last, though indeed his voice, now so altogether kind, seemed often strangely remote, while the lean, hawk-face upturned to mine (and grimly scornful no longer) showed at times no more than pale blur that grew alternate very large and very small upon my fevered vision.

And now, as he tramped beside me, he talked (in despite of wind and rain) telling me, what I had oft yearned to hear, of his wild adventures and perils in those strange lands across the world, tales of the slave-gangs, of savages, of the bloody doings of pirates – and all, as I guess, to take my thoughts from the pain of my wound that with every mile increased upon me. For now, though I shivered with the cold, my arm seemed on fire and all fiercely athrob. But the pain that I endured, this misery of rain and wind, the wild solitudes about me, these served only to draw us nearer, knitting our friendship the faster. And seeing him so miraculously changed – so tender of me, so anxious and quick of sympathy – all this, I say, waked in me such passion of love for him as hath endured and shall endure whiles life be mine, ay and beyond it too.

Much (and yet all too little) do I remember of this our last day's journey together, and this but in snatches ... I recollect his arm about me, my head on his bosom and a cup at my lips ... I mind how my dreadful shivering turned to a burning heat and we moving on again through the wet mist that swirled about me, writhing into shapes fantastical and dread, with, chief amongst them and ever recurring, the stark and never to be forgotten form of Alastair Mohr, his dead fist awfully upraised to smite me down ...

Hours of plodding hoofs and creaking saddle, of pain and cold and heat, of ghastly, writhing phantoms – but ever and always my dear companion's arm to steady me, his firm, strong hand to clasp and comfort mine, his voice in my failing ears speaking me brave encouragement.

The rain passed, the mists vanished, forth beamed the

blessed sun though his kindly rays had no power to warm me ... and the dreadful phantoms all about me still – Alastair leaping to furious battle ... Alastair reeling and bloody ... Alastair dead yet forever menacing – until, in my terror and agony of soul, I cried aloud :

'Oh, Sir Hector, God knoweth I had no thought to kill him !' And my good comrade understanding, spake me in his strange, sweet voice :

'No, boy, no – God knoweth this and hath, perchance, healed Alastair's wounds, and so, dear lad, be comforted.'

Creak of leather and plod of hoof, rain once more and a blusterous, cruel wind that caught my breath, that choked and smothered me ... Little else do I recall of this terrible day save unending pain and fevered, wild imaginings. And yet in despite of all the misery and anguish of these last hours fain would I live them yet again.

I was reeling through a world of raving darkness when, through the wet murk, I espied a beam of light that winked and was gone, that, twinkling forth again, grew larger, brighter, to the dazzling glare of a wide-opened door. And then, instead of ceaseless rain and cold, buffeting wind was heavenly warmth and quiet, a soothing and most blessed peace, an ever-deepening sense of comfort that lulled me to forgetfulness of all things.

CHAPTER 45

GIVETH SOME DESCRIPTION OF A MAN OF PEACE AND HIS METHODS

I like ane owl in desert am
   That nightly there doth roam
I like unto ane sparrow am
   On the house-top alone.'

VOICE, like tune, was familiar and yet waked me to a troublous wonderment of the great bed wherein I lay so luxuriously disposed, a vast bed very artificially carved and hung with rich curtains, such bed indeed as I had never seen, much the less lain in, ere now.

Staring up beyond the canopy I saw a heavily beamed ceiling, and my gaze, roving thence, came to an open lattice beyond which green leaves bright with sunshine stirred in lazy wind. My glance, wandering yet, showed me a stately, pleasant-faced woman very busily a-knitting, the while her shapely lips worked soundlessly though quick as her needles.

Having watched this lady some great while I was minded to question her, and so :

'Madame, if you please!' says I, but she never so much as raised eyelid, or faltered in her soundless whispering. Therefore I tried her again :

'Pray, madame ...' And now I found that I was whispering also, and, moreover, gasping with the effort, the which troubled me greatly. I now essayed to sit up and felt it such vain labour that I fell a-trembling; but in my surprise and dismay, I spoke again and this time she heard me, for laying by her knitting she was beside me in a moment.

'Ma' puir bairn !' says she, laying cool hand to my brow and wrist. 'The Lord is vera kind !'

'If you please,' says I in feeble croak, 'where is my dear friend?'

'Wull ye be meaning the MacFarlane?'

'Yes ... yes !'

'Himsel' was awa' eight days syne.'

'Eight ! Days !' says I utterly dismayed.

'There, there – dinna fash, ye'll be seeing him again sune.'

'Where am I, please?'

'At Kirribardie, whilk is no' a bad place tae be at any time.'

'Mr Archibald Forbes' house?'

'Ay, that same. Himsel' is in the garden noo, and I'm his sister Alison, and a' he's got in the warld being wifeless, puir man ! And yoursel' is named Adam, and 'tis vera near death ye've been, Mr Adam, and but for Erchie's prayers and my nursing 'tis in your grave ye'd be. I maun juist acquaint ma brither Erchie wi' this grand and mercifu' dispensation o' God.' And crossing to the window she leaned forth, calling with her soft, pleasant voice in the Gaelic; and presently Mr Forbes was beaming upon us cheery as old Sol himself. He wore no coat, and his shirt-sleeves, rolled high, showed a pair of mighty arms, with vast spread of shoulder, his neat wig, donned in my honour with evident haste, was waggishly askew, but his comely, freckled face held that same look of frank good-nature I had found so winning before.

'Mr Forbes,' I said and, despite my weakness, contrived to reach him my hand, 'pray, sir, did my friend Sir Hector leave any message ... for me? Though first, sir, I would thank you and Mistress Alison for all—'

'Na, na, Mr Adam,' says he, 'rather let us a' gie thanks tae the Guid Being for this miracle o' your preservation.'

'With all my heart, sir,' I answered, folding my hands. So down to knees plumped this great, pious gentleman, and so heartily that the vast bed shook, and forthwith gave thanks to God for my recovery.

'And noo, sir,' says he, yet kneeling and smiling at me above his clasped hands, 'I'll try it o'er again in Gaelic, 'tis tongue mair familiar tae me, sir.' The which he did, and with such passion and fervour of gesture as shook me again where I lay. Then he sat by me on the bed, and diving into pocket of his threadbare waistcoat drew thence, amid divers other articles, a crumpled letter which he clucked over, smoothed and passed to me: so, breaking the seal, I read this (a letter that I treasure yet and ever shall):

'At Kirribardie in haste
'August 12th, 1716.

'My dear Adam, the most heroic man may swound with pain but very few may endure the day through and no complaint nor even a single curse. God bless thee! Fain would I stay beside you in your sickness, but here is news of such moment I must away this hour. But I leave you in good hands and this comforts me. Archie is gentleman

248

of honour and minister of God right potent in prayer, they tell me and (which is more) Mistress Alison is notably skilled in curing hurts of the body. So let these brother and sister, father and mother you until I return – now and henceforth your true and loving friend

'HECTOR MACFARLANE.

'I pray a speedy cure on thee. And thou hast youth, Adam, and a spirit very determined. So be quickly well for thy Barbara's sake, whom I shall seek on thine account in Edinburgh.

'Farewell.'

And when I had folded this letter :

'Mr Forbes,' says I, 'have you had word or news of Sir Hector since this writing?'

'Inteety, sir, twice – there wass a deid man picked up in Dounie Glen scarce five miles hence and anither beyond the Whustle Crag.'

'But, sir, how shall this be news of him?'

'Because these were baith deid by his ain hand, sir.'

'How is this known?'

'Sir, he left on each his sign manual, I hae ane o' them here in my pouch, 'twas man o' mine found the body y'ken, and this paper on the same,' and diving into another pocket, Mr Forbes drew thence a handful of objects, amongst which I noticed a knife, yarn, an onion, a battered tobacco-box and a paper, crumpled and weather-stained whereon I read these words writ large :

'A warning from Keith

'HECTOR MACFARLANE.'

'Och-aye!' sighed Mr Forbes as he restored this with his ther goods to their vasty abiding-place. 'War is the scourge ' God, sir, a black, black business ! Myself am man o' peace era meek and long-suffering, abhorring a' violence frae me era soul, and yet ... eh, sirs ... yon Hector is a bonnie, onnie fechter ! And yon is Alison wi' your physic, I'll ack tae ma delving.'

And now followed long hours of deep slumber and drowsy wakefulness until, thanks to Mistress Alison's skilful nursing and my own eager will to be up and away, my health so improved that upon a day I sat beside the open lattice looking down into the sunny garden where Mr Forbes laboured cheerily with his four burly men, while Mistress Alison, knitting as usual, talked to me in her soft and pleasant voice. And because the Scots-English she used is hard for me to write I will simplify it (as indeed I have done throughout this my narrative).

'Indeed, I thought you deid when Hector carried ye in, Master Adam.'

'Carried me ... did he?'

'Ay, like shepherd doth a lamb, o'er his shoulders. And baith o' ye spouting rain!'

'And now I grow well again, ma'm, thanks to you. And pray call me Adam.'

'And God's mercy, Adam! Ay, and your Barbara! Is she so vera beautiful, Adam?'

'Yes, yes, indeed. But who ... how knew you of her?'

'You cried upon her in your fever ... you talked wi' her ... you called her "wife". Verily I think 'twas love for her brought you out o' the Shadow.'

'I know it was!' I answered. 'And did I rave much?'

'You did that – o' battles and wind and rain, ay, and giants, and weep you would, then I'd make believe I was Barbara and you'd be comforted awhile. Ah truly, love is a wondrous thing and very gift o' God...'

'Yes,' I answered, yearning again for Barbara, 'surely love is the greatest blessing of all.'

'Adam, I'm wondering o' yon strange jewel about your neck, 'tis a bonny thing.'

'Yes, it was my mother's, as I think, but—' I paused suddenly to listen, for on the air was a sound of rapid hoofs, a matter to wonder at in this secluded place; therefore we both peeped from the lattice and espied two horsemen, hatted and booted like dragoons, who rode into the yard and forthwith began to shout and halloo very peremptorily:

'House! House – ho! Hi, you there, you fellow wi' the mattock, hither – d'ye hear!' Mr Archie slowly straightened his broad back, as did his four sturdy fellows, and surveyed these vociferous strangers with his mildly jovial look.

'Wha' would ye, sirs?' he enquired, advancing, mattock in hand.

'Are ye the Reverend Forbes of Kirriebardie?'

'I am that.'

'Why then you've a gentleman here by name Mr Adam Thursday,' said one horseman.

'Ay, ye have so!' nodded the second, pulling out a paper. 'A person calling himself Lord Bell – hum! – castonborough. Well, we want him ...'

Now at this, I shrank from the window in no little consternation.

'On the bed wi' ye, Adam, I like not yon men!' said Alison, and half-carrying me thither she covered me up and stood, cool hand on my brow, hearkening to the rumble of voices below. Then was clatter in the yard, a great trampling on the broad stair, a jingle and rattle, and the door was thrust open and in upon us strode a squat man, his long cloak and great, spurred boots very dusty, a black-avised man who stared on me narrow-eyed from the tilt of his dusty hat.

'You, sir,' says he, making prodigious rattle with sword-hilt and spurs, 'are ye one, Adam Thursday, calls himself Lord Bellcastonborough?'

'No, sir,' I answered, 'my name is Adam Thursday.'

'Why, then, 'tis you I'm wanting, so – up wi' you.'

'On what count, sir?' I enquired, never stirring.

'No matter!' he answered fiercely. 'My orders are to apprehend you.'

'Whose orders, sir?'

''Tis no matter for that either!' he retorted insolently. 'So up wi' you – up, I say!' and he came stamping and jingling to the bed, but, ere he might touch me, Alison's large, capable hand checked him, and her large and gentle eyes surveyed him, nothing daunted by his scowling ferocity.

'Sir,' says she, pointing him away with steady finger, 'this is a sick-room y'ken, and I'm asking you to step back downstairs and do your business there, if ye please.'

'Woman,' he cried, 'out o' my road lest you be hurt!'

'Nay then ye maun hurt me,' says she, fronting him gently resolute; and then Mr Forbes stood in the doorway, his mighty shoulders nigh filling it.

'Oh, man,' said he, good-humouredly, 'when ma suster Alison bids any man gang doonstairs – 'tis doonstairs yon man maun gang. Come awa' friend and crack wi' me.'

'Silence!' roared the intruder, with stamp of heavy boot. 'I'm Barry, of Ogleby's Horse, Captain Barry, and I'm taking my prisoner with me!'

Archie Forbes advanced smiling, his two great hands upraised as if in benediction:

'The Guid Being – bless ye!' said he fervently, and then – those mighty hands swept suddenly down and clutched fast ... I saw two great military boots kicking vainly aloft, a dusty-hatted head that bumped the floor as Mr Forbes strode from the room ... I heard a fury of gasping oaths, a shout, a heavy, jingling crash, a dull thumping and, thereafter, wailing outcries ... Then Mr Forbes was beaming on us from the threshold.

'Erchie,' enquired Alison, her gentle hand smoothing my hair, 'wha' was yon?'

'Yon was the Captain body ganging doonstairs, Alison,' answered the reverend Archibald, glancing on me with flicker of an eyelid.

'Whaur is the ither man, Erchie?'

'Tammas and Torquil are sitting on him, Alison, till these men o' war and violence be ready tae leave us in peace y'ken.'

'A'weel, Erchie, tak' heed tae their pistols, lest blood be spilt.

'Their pistols be in the water-butt, Alison.'

'Oh, Mr Forbes,' cried I, reaching out my hands to him ''twas wonderful to see how you quelled him! To be so mightily strong, so calm and sure! I would God had made me more like you.'

'Whisht!' exclaimed Mr Forbes, taking my hands and smiling down on me, 'the Great Being formed ye in his ain image, Adam, ay – and tae be Alison's friend and mine and Hector's comrade! Man, what mair wad ye ha'e? And ca' me Erchie!' And off he strode.

'And, what a man!' cried I, clasping my hands.

Now at this Alison stopped stroking my brow to kiss it.

'Erchie is the strongest man north o' Tweed, Adam!' says she. 'He beats a' at the wrestling and tossing the caber – forby the glory is to God!'

CHAPTER 46

TELLETH OF JOYFUL REUNION

VERY much could I write of the peaceful hours I spent with these so kindly gentlefolk, hours wherein our friendship, one for another, grew to a love that hath endured these many years, thank God. But I will haste on to that day when, being able to totter from bed to window, I was to come downstairs for the first time, borne in Archie's mighty arms; but I (in my foolish eagerness) must essay this alone, with the result that I fell, breaking open my wound afresh, so back to bed went I.

For it was now, in this hour of Alison's tender ministrations, gentle reproaches, and mine own bitter disappointment, there came to me that ineffable joy, that deathless moment so long dreamed and so passionately yearned for ...

I heard sudden clatter in the court below and then – a voice, so sweetly clear there was no mistaking, and, reeling to the window (despite Alison's protests), I leaned forth:

'Barbara!' I cried. She wheeled her horse, I saw her lovely eyes widen at sight of me, and then she was out of the saddle .. I heard her light, quick feet upon the stair, the door swung open and we were in each other's arms.

'Oh, Adam,' she murmured, 'my dear ... my love! How

pale you are! And so thin and frail!' And she was kissing me, smoothing my hair, clasping me to the sweet haven of her bosom, and both of us weeping for very joy.

'Lie you down again, dear heart,' she sighed, 'back upon the pillow ... nay then I'll lie beside thee! Now, my own dear, tell me of yourself. Hast missed me, Adam? Dost love me as I thee?'

'You are my very life!' says I, nigh dazzled by her mere loveliness. 'Without you I had died! 'Twas your dear memory made me able to endure! 'Twas our love brought me back from death ... oh, Barbara!'

And presently she nestling beside me, full of eager questioning, I told her of all that had befallen me since fleeing from Drumlossie, yet, most of all, I spoke of Sir Hector and my new, great love for him.

'But,' says she, kissing me on each eye, 'you say no word o' your fighting, Adam; your battles and Alastair Mohr Lamont.'

'No,' said I, 'no – he haunts me yet.'

' 'Tis small wonder,' cries she, with little shiver. 'I saw Alastair once! ... Oh, my very own Adam,' says she, lifting her dear head the better to look at me, 'Oh 'tis very wonderful ... 'tis dreadful to think you can be so – very terrible!' And here she nestles to me again, closer than ever.

And now, in her turn, she tells me of her despair to see me vanish into the dark waters at Drumlossie, and how Gaston comforted her by vowing no water might drown me. She told how Sir Tearlach, his wound proving of small account, had shut himself away and no word of explanation. And then – how oft we kissed while she described how painfully they had sought me, and her ceaseless anxieties on my account; and how, reaching Edinburgh, they had been sumptuously entertained by the Earl of Ancaster.

'And didst tell him of our marriage, Barbara?' I asked her

'Indeed, and to be sure I did, my Adam, and, though my lord showed something disappointed, he vowed himself my very good friend for her sake, and was very pressing in his offers to serve me.'

'And yet,' says I, 'Sir Hector bade me beware – warns us of these Ancasters.'

'Ay, but then, he hates them so bitterly. And this reminds me, dear love, but for Hector we had not known this present happiness. See you, Adam!' And she shows me this letter, (the which I do also keep) viz:

'Edinburgh
'August 23rd, 1716.

'Dear Bab. My lady Barbara. Right respected madame, these.

'He hath in single combat slain a giant, Alastair Mohr Lamont, no less! He hath so played the man for thy sake, I must needs love him for his own, and herewith do pronounce him the MacFarlane's honoured friend and only comrade-in-arms – and thus altogether worthy even of thy so lovely, peerless self. You shall find him with Archie Forbes at Kirriebardie. I beg you kiss him to forgetfulness of all past pains and hardships (for ever by with I pray). Say to him I come anon to bless ye both, and am ever his and your own friend and humble servant in all things to command,

'HECTOR MACFARLANE.

'*Nota Bene*. Beware of the Ancasters that being nigh to ruin and death (God be thanked) are desperate. So take heed, Adam shall tell thee wherefore. My duty and service to Monsieur the Duc de Vrillac.'

'Now look on the back, Adam.' So I turned the letter and saw this:

'Tearlach of Drumlossie is not your father, Bab, 'tis truth I learned some while since. You are only child of Donald, the MacGregor himself, of the which I can shew you all needful proofs.'

'Do you believe this, Adam?' says she very wistfully.

'Ay, truly!' I answered.

'Why, so doth Gaston,' she nodded. 'And I never loved – him as daughter should – and yet ... But, ah, what matter since now I am thine for ever. And now I've marvellous surprise for thee, Gaston is below stairs! Nay, impatient boy, bide you still, there's more ... for, Adam, when you saved a poor drowning Frenchman from the sea you also saved one of the noblest (here she kissed me) proudest (here again) richest and highest gentlemen in all France! And now I'll call him to thee!' The which she did sweet as any piping merle.

And presently Gaston stood in the doorway smiling on me with that look of his, so piercing, so wise and yet so very kind; but even so, as I gazed up at him and he so strangely magnificent from vast, glossy peruke to gilded spurs, all this, together with his customary air of command and high nobility, so wrought on me that my words of eager welcome died within me, and:

'Sir ...' I faltered.

'Monsieur?' he retorted and swept me one of his grand bows. 'I am indeed the honoured one to meet gentleman of a renown so stupendous, my faith, yes!' And then he was beside the bed, had caught my hands and kissed me on either cheek. And now, he sitting beside me, we talked like the old and loving friends we were, he plying me with questions and especially relating to Barbara's true parentage.

'Ah but of a certainty,' says he, nodding stately head, 'this Monsieur Tearlack, this blind, creeping gentleman of Drumlossie (ah, *sapristi*, what names)! he could never beget lady of the spirit so noble, ah, *mordieu*, such flower of womanhood as thy Barbara, no! For many the asticot, the so wrigglesome worm, father a skylark? But it is the absurdity! I have dispatched agents of mine to London, to Paris, enquiring of this matter of her heritage. I shall myself see your King George, also ... Now for these gentlemen of Ancaster, hum! You say your so loved enemy, your 'Ector Keet, he warns you – but perfectly! It is the plot and counter-plot. We now perceive the pot of roses.'

'You think Sir Hector is right, Gaston?'

'I think he is the gentleman of a perspicacity, ah, but certainly! He loveth not these gentlemen – no?'

'He hath suffered very bitterly by them, Gaston. And yet I would he had not wasted himself on mere hate ... or shed his enemies' blood so wantonly.'

'But, my Adam, I beg you reflect and ponder you this – the gentleman complete can do but two things by his enemy, he must kill him with a speed the most gracious or love him with a passion sublime, forgiving all. Am I right? Name of a name, I am!'

'Pray, Gaston, would you consider Sir Hector a gentleman complete?'

'Thy story so proveth him. He shall perhaps honour me with his friendship one day. But, my Adam, is it that he hath ever seen this talisman of thine (pardon!) this so strange jewel?' And from the folds at my bosom Gaston very gently drew forth that quaint locket I have ever worn about my neck, with its two letters entwined. 'Didst ever show it him, Adam?'

'No,' I answered, 'I rarely think of it—'

'And yet, my Adam, herein perchance is thy fortune, and this a charm warding thee from all evil.'

'That were a pretty thought, Gaston, for this jewel belonged, as I suppose, to my dead and unknown mother.'

'And hast 'scaped perils verree many, Adam.'

'Think you it strange, Gaston, that I should so love him – Sir Hector?'

'Aha, and whence cometh this so deep and quick affection?' he questioned, yet studying the jewel.

'I think 'twas bred of hardships and dangers, Gaston ... And – ah, Gaston, I wounded him! I might have killed him thrice, ay and was so minded.'

'But certainly, my Adam, this is understood.'

'And he was so serenely undismayed in battle ... so wondrous patient with me ... on our last journey.'

'Perfectly, Adam. He is the gentleman.'

'And he is ... and hath ever been ... so terribly alone.'

'Didst ever speak him of thine own solitary child life, my Adam, thy so piteous tale?'

'Indeed, no, I could think but of him ... And, Gaston, I have heard him cry on God in his agony of soul ... I have seen him weep – ah, bitterest tears for his lost child.'

'Eh – child?' exclaimed Gaston, his stateliness for the moment quite gone. 'Such tears do but honour any man. But of this child, *mordieu* – this lost child, was it a son?'

'This he knoweth not, 'twas born in want and misery whiles he languished in slavery overseas.'

'And you showed him not this jewel – no?'

''Twas never in my thoughts, Gaston.'

'*Sang dieu!* A pity! For I have a thought, Adam, and my thought tells me he shall perchance know it, ah, but verree well.'

'Know it?' says I. 'Know my locket – Sir Hector?'

And now, reading somewhat of Gaston's meaning, my breath caught and a great, yearning hope sprang within me.

'See thou – these two letters!' says Gaston, tracing them with his finger, 'A and H – this last might stand for – Hector.'

'Yes ... yes ... for Hector!' said I, and began to tremble. 'And the other letter ... oh, Gaston ... the other for – Angela. She was his young wife driven forth to die ... lost homeless and desolate! And my own mother wandered so ... an outcast ... she died 'neath a hedge and with—' my voice choked; and so was silence whiles Gaston stared on me and I on him through my burning tears. And now, to us came Alison and Archie (these good friends) and with my Barbara betwixt them; but she, espying my distress, ran and had her loving arms about me in a moment.

So there, Gaston in elbow-chair and the others seated upon the great bed, we talked of this, very earnestly and yet could get nowhere.

'Howandever,' says Barbara, at last, 'should this indeed prove so, then I am Barbara MacFarlane, and this, my noble husband, is grandson to my lord the Earl of Ancaster.'

'No.' says I, shaking my head, 'dear heart I shall be – Sir Hector's son!'

'*Fort bien!*' said Gaston, with his air of grand finality. 'It is now of the simplest – I go. I find Monsieur 'Ector. I show him the jewel. He shall say "No" or "Yes" and – behold all things are settled! Is it not? My faith, it is!'

'Would you go?' cried I, eagerly. 'Will you? Is Edinburgh far? Would it take long?'

'Not with my horses, Adam!'

'Then ... will you take him my jewel ... soon, Gaston?'

'But, my Adam, this moment!'

And so, in the hour, with his four armed gentlemen behind him, Gaston spurred away south on this mission for me, like the kind and loving friend I have ever proved him.

But he had been gone only a short time when was wild gallop of hoofs and clatter in the yard below, with a frantic shouting in Gaelic.

'Why – 'tis Torquil!' said Alison, rising.

'Ay, I sent him tae Edinburgh last nicht,' answered Archie and, closing the lattice, went softly from the room. But now, seeing my Barbara's troubled look and how anxiously she questioned Alison in the Gaelic:

'Pray,' says I, pushing back my pillows, 'what is Torquil's news?'

'Why, Adam,' says Barbara, slipping her arm about me, 'he tells there are soldiers on the road – and dragoon forby!'

'Nay, my dear,' says Alison, gently, 'let us no' trouble our invalid—'

'Dragoons?' cried I, beginning to shake. 'For me? Are they coming here? Speak, Alison, I must know! Tell me, Barbara!'

'Why, yes, dear heart,' says she, her lovely eyes very troubled. 'It is but right I should tell thee, my own dear. The man saith there are troopers drinking at a change-house scarce a mile hence ... that they are coming ... for thee, my Adam! And that they mean to burn this house.'

'Why, then ... my clothes!' says I, looking about for them. 'Pray bring me my clothes.'

'Na, na, now, Adam!' cried Alison, her sweet calmness shaken at last.

'Yes!' cried I, clenching my chattering teeth. 'My clothes! At once! Ah, for God's sake never delay! I must go to them before they reach here ... meet and stay them on the road. Bring me my clothes ... obey me this instant! I must go to them—'

'But oh, Adam ... dear Heart, what will they do to you?'

'My clothes!' I cried. 'Bring them, I say, or by God I'll go in my shirt!'

Thus, seeing me so passionately determined, they brought my garments and I did them on with Archie to assist me, the while he alternately pleaded, protested and blamed himself very bitterly.

'Bide whaur y'are, man Adam ... We're six men wi' yoursel', and can haud the hoose fine! And, oh, man, 'tis a' my ain doing y'ken! ... I shouldna ha' droppit yon captain body doun the stair. Ah, bide wi' your bonny wife, Adam!'

'No, no, Archie!' cries I, as we struggled with my long boots. 'I cannot screen myself behind your friendship at such time – I will not, she – my Barbara would scorn me if I did, ay – and so should I. Only please, Archie, lend me a mild horse, for I'm not used to the saddle ... And now my hat and I'm ready.'

Down the broad stair went I, Archie's long arm to aid me, and there met Barbara and Alison and both of them very pale. Clasping Alison's hand, I thanked her hurriedly as well as I might for all her goodness, but she silenced me with a kiss and sped away, leaving tears on my cheek. Then Barbara's loving arms were close about me, her dear head bowed upon my shoulder, but never a sob or tear.

'And wilt make thyself go through the terrible breaker again, my Adam?' says she, her voice muffled in my embrace. 'A'weel, 'tis the same merciful God above us and .. thou'rt mine own wonderful Adam. Thy way o' danger i ... the way of honour and ... but ... oh God send thee back to me for ... without thee now I ... just canna live.

Out in the yard stood Archie and his four men, all ver

silent and grim, and with a horse whereupon he lifted me.

'Adam,' says he, with mighty hug, 'Guid's wi' ye friend o' my heart ... and here's mysel' tae pray for ye, forby my lads and me shall hae oor clay-mohrs handy y'ken ay, wi' a musket or twa and sic-like – ah, the Great Being bless thee!' With which, he turned swiftly away.

And so, while Fear clutched me and my craven flesh shook and sweated, I rode forth to meet – what was to be.

CHAPTER 47

WHICH IS CHAPTER OF FAREWELL

THE road stretched before me very straight and dusty, though little I heeded as my nag ambled gently along, for my mind was groping blindly to know who should send troop of soldiers for such as I. Yet, having regard to the troublous times, I began to image and picture to myself all those obscene horrors of the traitor's doom, viz, rope or axe, the embowelling and dismembering block, until, with every yard, my apprehensions so grew that long ere I espied the inn or change-house, I was sweating anew in panic. And now, moreover, I must needs recall Gaston's words anent my jewel, how it had been a charm for me against all evil, and the knowledge that I had it no longer in my keeping, troubled me very greatly.

Suddenly, topping a rise, I saw the inn and heard it, too, for before it stood horses stamping impatiently and from within it came a riotous hubbub of shouts and unlovely singing, the which of itself so appalled me that, but for my Barbara, I must have galloped back; yet now the pure, sweet memory of her, the knowledge of her faith and pride in me (however undeserved) gave me faith in myself and destiny, nerving me with a courage so miraculous that, riding up to the inn, I found myself hallooing so lustily as surprised none so much as myself.

Thus sat I shouting until out jingled a buff-coated fellow to learn the reason, to whom I tossed my reins and dismounting, strode into the tap.

At my sudden entrance the clamour subsided somewhat, whereupon I demanded an officer, and was pointed to a door, whereon I knocked, and instantly opening this door, beheld three men seated at a table and one a little drunk, in whom, to my dismay, I recognized that same Captain Barry, of Ogleby's Horse.

'Pray,' says I, looking from one to other, 'who commands here?'

'I do, sir,' says a something languid gentleman, a pinch of snuff at his high, thin nose. 'Who asks?'

'Sir,' I answered, removing my hat and bowing, 'I am Adam Thursday, here to yield myself to your custody.'

'Are you, b'gad!' says he, forgetting to snuff.

'I am, sir, though I cannot understand—'

'Ha, damme!' cried Captain Barry, rising very unsteadily, 'I mind his peaky phiz. I'd know the rat anywhere—'

'Sit down, Barry,' says the other, dusting snuff from himself, languidly. 'Sir, I am Major Charteris and—'

'Let's to horse, Charteris!' cried the Captain, thickly. 'Let's to our quarry ... burn the house, trounce the men and kiss the women, ay and—'

'Be silent, sir!' said the Major, his nose seeming a little more hooked.

'Silent, Charteris, silent? But ... good Ged, don't we—'

'Silence, Captain Barry!' The Major's voice was gentle, but then his nose reminded me of an eagle's beak, also his sleepy eyes glittered evilly. 'You offend me, sir!' he murmured, 'You disparage the Service with your cursed, scoundrelly tongue! Pray, ha' the kindness to convey your drunken carcass out o' my viewing, and keep hidden, sir, if you've sense enough! Manvers, get the men to horse, we return to Ballashiel at once!'

So, to horse we got, and away we went at an easy pace, I upon Archie's ambling steed surrounded by jingling troopers and glittering steel; and thus with tramp and clatter until, about noon, we reached a hill whence I looked down upon a very large house, something betwixt a turreted castle and fortified manor, and set within a wide, embattled courtyard, where soldiers marched, bayonets a-twinkle.

Chancing beside the Major as we descended this steep hill, I ventured to question him:

'Pray, sir, whither do you take me?'

'Yonder, sir,' he answered, very civilly, 'to Ballashiel.'

'And why, if you please?'

'Faith, sir,' says he, shaking his head, '"tis past me, unless you are one o' these unfortunate rebels, poor devils!'

'Nay, sir,' cries I, very earnestly, 'I am no rebel.'

'So much the better!' he nodded. 'However, here we are, sir, and the wherefore of it you shall know very presently, I nothing doubt.'

And in a little while we clattered into the court-yard and halted. Here to us came two or three officers and one in a plain dress, a sombre, sad-faced man who beckoned me and no word. So I dismounted and, betwixt two soldiers with fixed bayonets, followed this sombre man into a guard room, where they searched me for hidden weapons, feeling in my every pocket, etc. This done and nothing found (as I had told them) they brought me into a great, echoing hall with a raised platform at one end. And here, in great elbow-chair and propped by many cushions, sat an aged, very stately gentleman, nobly wigged and clad; upon the red-covered table before him were books and papers, and on these papers his two hands rested, lean, pale, shrivelled hands, that twitched ever and anon, like one corner of his shapely mouth; and, looking on these twitching hands, I noticed that when they moved (which was seldom) it was with a strange, unnatural heaviness. Now looking from these hands to his face it seemed as I had seen it before – an old face yet all unwrinkled, and very still save for that odd, one-cornered twitching of the mouth, but the eyes were bright and strangely alert in that smooth, still face. So I stared on this stately gentleman, striving vainly to remember where

I had seen him before; and then I became aware of a droning, weary voice uttering my name :

'... he is known, my lord, as Adam Thursday, calling himself Lord Bellcastonborough. He is also known to have been consorter with proscribed rebels themselves in frequent communication with the accursed Pretender Stuart himself, a go-between, my lord, a bearer of letters treasonable, a complotter against the King's most excellent Majesty and the weal of the realm.' Here the aged, magnificent gentleman closed his vital eyes so that his face seemed instantly dead, and spoke with soft and furry indistinctness :

'Le' him b'searched !'

Hands grasped and held me while other hands quested all about me again until, from one of my pockets quick fingers drew a thin sheaf of papers.

'My lord – these letters !'

The vivid eyes opened with sudden glare :

'Le' me see them ! Come you hither also and summon Mr Jus'ice Yarrow.'

'Sir,' cried I, struggling against the hands that still grasped me. 'Those letters are none of mine. I swear to God ... I never saw them till now—'

'Silence !' roared a voice that waked the echoes ...

And now came other gentlemen to that red table of judgment; heads were bent over these rustling papers, voices muttered; fingers pointed, and I in a daze.

'Evidence most damning !' said one voice.

'And taken i' the act !' said another.

'Guilty !' spake a third.

'No !' cried I, 'No ! Those papers were never mine. I swear before God I—' But my words were shouted down, a hand was clapped upon my mouth ... And then I saw those twitching lips move, heard their uncertain utterance :

'This evening a' sunset !'

Then I was compelled away. They hurried me along stone-flagged passages and up winding stairs, to an airy chamber, nothing like the cell I had imagined, for it was well furnished, and with a lesser chamber opening out of it wherein was a bed. Now here, when my conductors would have left me, I clutched the sombre man by the arm, shaking it and supplicating him in wild panic :

'Oh sir ... sir,' cries I in my desperation, 'oh pray what ... what will they do to me ... at sunset?'

'Shoot you!' said he, and sighed and shook his head. 'There are few executions here, thank God! But ... alas for you, young sir!'

'Shoot me?' I gasped. 'But they can't ... they cannot! 'Twill be murder!'

'Alas, sir!' sighed he, 'is not every political execution – murder?' So saying, he shook his head again, stole his arm from my nerveless clutch and was gone with slam of door and rattle of key in lock. At the which fateful sound I sank to the floor and lay there a great while, more dead than alive. Nor can I bear, even now, to think or dwell on this dreadful time of wild horror and black despair. So will I pass to that moment when I started up at sound of brisk footsteps without. Trembling, I stood there while key turned in lock and then, the door opening, I caught my breath, for, bowing to me on the threshold stood Viscount Scarsdale. And very noble and warlike he seemed in his new King's uniform.

'Oh, sir,' I stammered, 'oh, my lord, thank God you've come to me ... You ... you at the least know me ... know the truth ... can speak for me—'

'Alas, Mr Adam!' he answered gently. 'I grieve to disappoint you. I come but to offer such solace as I may, sir, wine, pens and ink, in fine, sir, to do aught a gentleman may for one in such deplorable situation.'

'You mean they ... will shoot me ... out yonder?'

'Indeed, sir! Out yonder! You may see the wall, the very fatal spot itself from the window here.'

'But I am no rebel, no spy or traitor, as you know – you, my lord ... you saw me when yourself was Jacobite fugitive – you saw me with Sir Hector and—'

'With Barbara, my poor soul!' he murmured, lolling beside the window.

'Ah ... you mean ... she is the reason for my murder? You – you lust after her beauty, her fortune ... ah, villainy! Murderer!'

'Hush, sir, hush! Endeavour to compose yourself to more manly fortitude. Your case is hard, I do confess, but you had the supreme misfortune to cross the Ancasters, and, sir, this is ever fatal. Sir, I shall do myself the joy to send you a bottle of very excellent wine—'

'No – no!' I said. 'Instead I pray let me have pen and paper ... I beg! Sir, I would write to my Barbara ... my wife! Sir—'

'Nay, nay,' says he, backing to the door, that I saw stood ajar, 'why trouble yourself? I shall see her anon. I shall tell her how you died like a valiant gentleman, her name on your lips. Ah, Mr Adam, she will be lovely widow! 'Tis my ardent hope to comfort and console her ere long, for—'

'Villain! Murderous beast!' cried I, and leapt at him; but he threw me off, easily enough, and drew his sword.

'Be wise, sir!' said he, blade levelled. 'Pray compose yourself! Why suffer before you must? Once more I repeat, sir, I am here—'

'Zounds and so am I!' said a cheery voice, and Sir Hector stepped lightly into the room and his eyes were joyous. 'Aha, right noble brother-in-law,' says he, flourishing out his steel in airy fashion, 'this falls pat! Here's yourself and myself and plenty o' space for this our final conversation. Dougal!'

'She's here, ma Hector!' And instantly Dougal loomed gigantic in the doorway.

'Thy dirk in his throat, Dougal, should he attempt to shout! So, my lord – be silent! And now – come to it – with a will!'

Their swords met, shell to shell, and so were motionless for a long, breathless moment; and I heard Sir Hector speaking softly 'twixt curling lips:

'D'ye see it, Richard – d'ye feel it, Dick – stealing in the vitals o' thee – death, y'dog!'

The viscount never spoke, only he glanced towards the

narrow casement ... then at the knife glittering in Dougal's eager hand, then with sudden flash of movement they began to fight. It was desperately fierce yet very brief – a flurry of whirling steel, the stamp of a foot and my lord stood transfixed from back to breast, glaring wide-eyed upon his mocking slayer, then he was down, his eyes still fixed in that horrified glare while with one hand he fumbled awkwardly among the reddening laces at his bosom.

'So,' says Sir Hector, bending to stare down into these awful, fast-glazing eyes, 'there's for ye, dog! Traitorous rogue, murderous villain, and damned merciless brother, may thy sins drag thee down to everlasting fire, to deepest ... faith, he's gone! And so soon! A'weel, the tale is told – this should strike his doating father dead as he! And so, thank God, my work is done!' Thus speaking, Sir Hector wiped his sword upon the dead man's fine, new coat, and, sheathing it, beckoned to Dougal :

'Throw it in yonder, Dougal Dhu!' he commanded.

So Dougal dragged this ghastly, sprawling thing into that smaller, inner room, and, closing the door on it, went forth into the passage outside. Then Sir Hector turned to me, viewing me up and down, eyebrow cocked :

'Well, Adam,' says he, 'hast no greeting for thy father, boy?'

'Father?' I repeated, questioning. 'Then ... sir ... 'tis true?'

'Can ye doubt it, Adam? Could any crass fool doubt it any more – even such as I? Did we not love despite ourselves, lad? Come to thy father, son o' mine !'

So I ran to clasp him and be clasped, clinging to him in a sort of ecstasy whiles he, taking off my great periwig, falls to stroking my hair, very tenderly.

'Red locks !' says he, with his quick, odd laugh that now somehow, was pain to hear. 'Red hair ... and I never guessed; Egad, and ye hated it, rogue-lad !' And, stooping suddenly, he kissed the curls at my temple. Then as we stood thus, heart to heart, he laughs again.

'So ... they starved ye in your boyhood, did they, Adam?

And you son o' the MacFarlane! Ha, well – that father's curse on 'em wheresoever they be – let them rot! Howandever, son o' mine, here we stand at last for a little while, properly placed, dear lad. We've fought each other, and for each other, we've scorned and hated and yet, dear God! with this same love hid from each other all the while ... and this love is stronger than death, I guess ... But come, my Adam, our time is short, sit you here wi' me and let us talk whiles we may. And first for your jewel, that you never thought to show me, ay me – would to God you had!' So I drew forth the medallion the which he took as it had been holy relic, viewing it some while in silence. At last he spake, murmuring:

'This, Adam boy, was my betrothal gift to your mother, see now – here's the trick of't – look!' And, speaking, he gives a twist and the locket flies open, showing the miniature of a smiling, young face and graven round it the words:

Hector to Angela. For ever.

'Ay, here's your father as he was, Adam – none so bad a youth, I'm thinking!'

And truly this face that smiled radiant with youth, showed very comely, and yet had in it also something of that eagle look I knew so well.

'You've the same cock o' the head, boy, the same tilt o' the chin, but your mother's eyes and mouth. See here again!' From his breast he drew a second locket fashioned the same though larger and, opening this, he showed me a face of such gentle beauty that I caught my breath and, mindful of her bitter sufferings, tears blinded me, yet I must dash them away to look and look and to read the words:

Angela to Hector. Beyond death.

'She'll be nothing changed, Adam, I shall know her again on the instant – but, as for me zounds, the years have altered me vastly and for the worse, egad! And yet mayhap I'll be young again and she shall see me at my best – for death is kind that way, I've heard.'

'Death?' says I, yet gazing on this lovely face.

'Why, we all must die, Adam. See now, I'll show ye one more trick – behold!' Now opening the back of his locket he placed mine therein, closed it and – the two were but one.

'So – there's for ye, son o' mine,' says he thrusting this most precious thing into my hand, 'take and keep them for your father's sake, there's little else he hath to leave ye, and – s'death, look at the sun – leaping to bed! Off wi' your coat, Adam!'

'My coat?' says I, starting. 'Nay, sir, what—'

'Am I no' your father, boy?' he demanded, though in voice marvellous gentle then, with swift gesture, reached his arms to me. And now, when I would have said so much, I choked for very love of him.

'Adam,' says he, holding me fast, 'since our time grows so short I'd fain hear thee name me "father", ... once or twice. Talk, lad, talk – for the minutes speed away! See, old Sol yonder standing tip-toe on the hills. Come – give me your coat!' And, speaking, he stripped off his own.

'Father,' I cried wildly, 'oh, dear my father – what would you do?'

'Do, son o' mine? Take a leap through the dark into light, no more.'

'Oh, sir ... sir—' I gasped.

'Call me "father", boy and, knowing me thy father – obey! Give me thy coat and clap on this o' mine.'

'No!' I cried, clipping it fast about me, 'you shall not die for me.'

'Tush!' says he, angrily. 'What matter now or later? And 'tis journey I take blithely since 'tis for thee, Adam lad and thy Barbara ... and then, mind ye, boy – your sweet mother waits to give me welcome, ay – the lost shall be found, son Adam, and my weary journeyings all past and by with ... give me your coat! Ha, Dougal – hither man!' So, between them, they did off my coat, that so weatherworn garment of blue velvet, with its torn and stained left sleeve ... And now, what with my late sickness, my present anguish of grief and horror to know that this father, found but now, must be so soon forever lost to me – what with all this, I say, I came very near swooning. Yet I remember seeing him, serene as ever, smoothing the long curls of my periwig about his face and buttoning my coat about him.

'Ancaster's coat!' says he, staring down at it. 'To die in young Ancaster's coat – egad, there's humour in't! And now – ha, look at the sun, almost gone – with a curse! A'weel, a'weel, I'll be above all cares very soon. Nay, never weep, Adam, shed no tears for me, boy – I go to my rest and ... your dear mother's arms ... an God prove kind. And remember, Adam, better swift death than lingering disease ... clean steel or bullet, 'tis so I've ever hankered for't. And lookee, boy, fearing I might ha' small chance o' speech wi' thee, I writ a letter, 'tis in this pocket. And now, Adam, you must away. I would not ha' ye here when they come for me. Off with him, Dougal – nay, first ... kiss thy father, son o' mine! My love to thy Bab. Awa' wi' him, Dougal Dhu – choke him to obedience an need be!'

I heard Dougal groan, saw my father smile, very pale and serenely resolute ... Then the door had closed on him, and the turnkey, whispering Dougal in the Gaelic, pointed us away.

Little else do I recall until I found myself stumbling up a steep roadway, Dougal's mighty arm gripped fast above me, and both of us weeping at every step. We reached the hill-top at last and from this eminence might look down upon the place of my suffering, but I kept my eyes averted, and pressed on until upon the evening stillness rose a sound of dread, the roll of muffled drums. Dougal stopped and, whimpering in awful fashion, wiped sweat from his haggard face and I, looking westwards, saw the sun was set.

'See ... yon!' groaned Dougal, pointing with shaking finger and, shivering, I looked.

Twinkling bayonets, soldiers marching and one in their midst who wore a travel-stained coat of blue velvet, the left sleeve torn – my coat.

And he went to his death with that selfsame serene assurance, that stately defiant carriage of the head I knew and loved so well ... I saw him stand, erect in his bonds, against the mossy wall . . . all alone as he had ever been, his eagle face towards his slayers. I heard a rattle of musketry, saw that solitary figure sway, totter, and sink to earth a crumpled heap ... and then, gasping wild prayers and vain lamentations, I would have run back to him. But Dougal's arm was fast about me, his harsh voice, broken by sobs, rang loud in my ear :

' 'Tis for ye'sel' he died! 'Tis for ye'sel' he lies yonder! 'Tis ye'sel' is the MacFarlane! Come awa', sir, come awa'.'

'He is ... my father still ...' I gasped. 'Kneel, Dougal ... kneel we while he ... passes up to God!' But now, when I would have knelt, this same God, in His mercy, lent me blessed forgetfulness awhile ...

It was long past midnight when we reached Kirribardie, and I nearly dead with grief.

But, as I crouched with my gentle Barbara kneeling beside me, in this so dark hour it was my father himself gave me some respite and surcease from my bitter woe for, as she clasped me, was rustle of paper, and remembering his letter I took it out. Then my Barbara (since I was blind with my tears), read out to us this, his last message, to wit :

'Hail to thee, MacFarlane, greeting to thee Adam, son of mine. Believe and know that I am but where I would be, and that she I loved and lost is with me evermore. I thank God to have known thee, son Adam, and do even now report well of thee to her that gave thee being. And our crowning happiness shall be this – to know thee worthy, son Adam, and that, with thy Barbara to love thee, thine aid and comfort, thou shalt live to far better purpose and taste more of earthly joy than ever did thy loving and now right joyful father

'HECTOR MACFARLANE.

'*Nota Bene*. Should Barbara give thee a son, let one of

his names be Hector, so, peradventure, I may live and joy in his joys and triumphs. For, son of mine, I am not dead, only risen above it. And so, a while farewell.'

Now here, as I do think, this my narrative ends – this tale of those hills of adversity, of trial and peril, so hard to climb, yet over and beyond which I have found so much of good, and a joy of sweet companionship beyond the telling. The years have rolled since then, yet never a day but I think on this lonely man, my father that twice gave me life. And it is my Barbara's joy to think that in our little Hector's quick, fearless glance, in the serenely-assured cock of his small head is something of that other Hector, that right noble gentleman – The MacFarlane.